Ruby

Books by Lauraine Snelling

A Secret Refuge

Daughter of Twin Oaks   *Sisters of the Confederacy*
The Long Way Home

Dakotah Treasures

Ruby   *Pearl*

Red River of the North

An Untamed Land   *The Reapers' Song*
A New Day Rising   *Tender Mercies*
A Land to Call Home   *Blessing in Disguise*

Return to Red River

A Dream to Follow   *Believing the Dream*
More Than a Dream

High Hurdles

Olympic Dreams   *Close Quarters*
DJ's Challenge   *Moving Up*
Setting the Pace   *Letting Go*
Out of the Blue   *Raising the Bar*
Storm Clouds   *Class Act*

Golden Filly Series

The Race   *Shadow Over San Mateo*
Eagle's Wings   *Out of the Mist*
Go for the Glory   *Second Wind*
Kentucky Dreamer   *Close Call*
Call for Courage   *The Winner's Circle*

Ruby

LAURAINE SNELLING

BETHANYHOUSE
MINNEAPOLIS, MINNESOTA

Ruby
Copyright © 2003
Lauraine Snelling

Cover design by Dan Thornberg
Cover building photo: Nebraska State Historical Society Photograph Collections

Published by Bethany House Publishers
11400 Hampshire Avenue South
Bloomington, Minnesota 55438
www.bethanyhouse.com

Bethany House Publishers is a Division of
Baker Book House Company, Grand Rapids, Michigan.

Printed in the United States of America

Library of Congress Cataloging-in-Publication Data

Snelling, Lauraine.
  Ruby / by Lauraine Snelling.
    p.   cm. — (Dakotah treasures ; 1)
  ISBN 0-7642-2222-8
  1. Inheritance and succession—Fiction. 2. Fathers and daughters—Fiction.
3. Women pioneers—Fiction. 4. Medora (N.D.)—Fiction. 5. Sisters—Fiction.
I. Title. II. Series: Snelling, Lauraine. Dakotah treasures ; v 1.
  PS3569.N39R83   2003
  813'.54—dc21   2003002571

Dedication

Friends can make a life richer, push one to higher accomplishments, keep one from making mistakes, and pick up the pieces when one does make errors in judgment. Friends can also trigger books. Ruby is dedicated to my writer-friends, the Round Robins, Chelley, Kathleen and Kitty.

Thanks in bunches.

LAURAINE SNELLING is an award-winning author of over forty books, fiction and nonfiction, for adults and young adults. Besides writing books and articles, she teaches at writers' conferences across the country. She and her husband, Wayne, have two grown sons and four granddogs, and make their home in California.

Acknowledgments

Historical societies are great research places for historical writers, and for this new series I thank the North Dakota Historical Society at Bismarck and Diane Rogness, the curator at the Chateau de Mores in Medora, for information and early pictures, of which there are few, of Little Missouri. Doug and Mary at the Western Edge Bookstore in Medora added bits and pieces to this series and directed me to the most helpful books and maps.

I am blessed with the most able and helpful assistant in Cecile, who has learned she is part brainstormer, part editor, part encourager, and part researcher. When she came to work for me, she didn't realize she would lose sleep over the characters in these books.

Thanks to husband Wayne for becoming more expert in the care and feeding of a writer under deadline and for all the research, reading, and remembering he contributed. It sure helps to be married to a man who can pull historical dates out of his mind without looking them up and who enjoys being a partner of this writing life of ours.

My editor, Sharon Asmus, and all the staff at Bethany House Publishers did their usual fine work, for which I am extremely grateful. I waited a long time for an agent, and Deidre Knight has helped make my writing life both simpler and more diverse. Thanks all of you.

CHAPTER ONE

New York, April 1882

Scolding never did any good.

Ruby Torvald, hands on her hips, glared at her nine-year-old sister. No, of course Opal had not meant to break the Dresden shepherdess. Of course she had only been looking at it.

But how often had she been told to look, not touch?

"Opal, you knew better."

Strawberry curls flying rampant about her freckled cheeks in spite of the French braids Ruby had plaited so carefully that morning, Opal refused to meet her sister's frowning gaze.

"Uff da! What am I going to do with you?" *What am I going to tell Mrs. Brandon, and more importantly, how am I going to pay for that?* Ruby picked up the pieces, halfheartedly fitting the full skirt onto the upper body, along with the head. As if any shepherdess would really wear a flouncy skirt like that and full petticoats too. Only the lamb at her side and the shepherd's crook gave an inkling of the purpose of the figurine.

"I . . . I'm sorry."

Ruby tried but failed to trap the sigh that seemed a continuation of many others.

"I really am." With the toe of her shoe, Opal traced the rose blossom woven into the Aubusson rug on which she stood.

"I know you are. But you need to think of how sorry you might be before . . ." Ruby laid the broken pieces in the trash basket at her feet. Perhaps if she rearranged the bric-a-brac on the whatnot table, Mrs. Brandon would never notice the shepherdess was missing. "Go back to the schoolroom and write fifty times on the board, 'I will not touch other people's things.'"

"But, Ruby, I already did all my lessons, and you said we would go to the park after Bernie's nap."

Ruby closed her eyes to steel herself against the beseeching looks from the young girl in front of her. She'd had to be more mother than sister in the five years since Bestemor died. How much easier life had been when they had lived with their grandmother.

You mustn't go around feeling sorry for yourself, she scolded. *No one wants to attend a pity party, even though you'd be the guest of honor.* She pointed in the direction of the stairs, ignoring the last pleading look thrown over Opal's sturdy shoulder.

Ruby took the basket back to the kitchen and dropped the pieces in the garbage.

"Not another one." Mrs. Fleish, the head housekeeper of the Brandon mansion, gave Ruby a pitying glance.

"Ja, and now I have to tell the missus."

"That shepherdess was one of her favorites."

"I know." Ruby exchanged a look with the woman who had taken her under her wing those five years ago when Ruby and her small sister, Opal, had joined the staff at the Brandon house. Ruby had started out as a maid but, because of her love for children, had moved up to nanny's helper and had often filled in when one of the many governesses parading through had left—or been dismissed.

She was the only one who could handle twelve-year-old Miss Alicia, the eldest of the Brandon children, who was far too bright for her age. Penelope, at ten, was a willing pupil, until she and Opal got their heads together, a sure sign that mischief would soon show a face. Jason had spent much of his eight years with his nose in a book but had little regard for the demands of a teacher, unless she was presenting a topic of interest to him. Ruby knew how to charm him into being interested in anything he needed to learn, so Mr. and Mrs. Brandon had finally given up looking for a new governess.

"Don't worry, miss, she won't fire you, not even for that bit of fancy clay." Mrs. Klaus, the cook, looked up from peeling potatoes, the skins curling into the bucket kept for compost in the garden. "She knows you are the only one who can manage her children."

"She won't think I'm managing very well today. She caught Jason sliding down the banister. He said he was studying the properties of friction between wood and cloth at high rates of speed."

Cook coughed to cover a chuckle. Her favoritism of the eldest son was a well-documented fact. Ask any of the children who it was that always got the biggest cookie or the choice of puddings.

Might as well get this over with so it isn't hanging over my head like the scimitar in the story we read this morning. Ruby dusted her hands off on her apron, raising a slight cloud of chalk dust since this was her schoolroom apron, then hung it on the hook. "Is she in her sitting room or the sunroom?"

Mrs. Klaus glanced at the carved walnut clock on the wall. "Most likely the sunroom now. She'll be calling for tea any minute. If you want to wait and take the tray with you, might be a good time for you to talk with her."

"I promised to take the children to the park, so I need to get this over with."

A bell chimed three times as they spoke.

"The sunroom." Cook set a plate of lemon bars on the silver tray already waiting on the table, along with bone china cups, a pitcher of milk, a sugar bowl with tongs for the sugar cubes, and slices of lemon on another plate. Napkins lay folded on the side and teaspoons gleamed on the white damask. Three golden daffodils made a splash of color in a crystal bud vase.

"Here 'tis." Cook set the cream-toned teapot on the tray. With hands across her ample front, she studied the tray to make sure all was in perfect order. Mrs. Brandon loved to have her afternoon tea just so. But then Mrs. Brandon liked to have most things just so. She would have liked 'just so' to have included her children, but they constantly disabused her of that notion.

Ruby picked up the tray and, turning, backed out the swinging door that led from the kitchen to the butler's pantry and thence to the walnut-paneled hall leading to the living quarters.

"Is it teatime?" Alicia, the eldest Brandon daughter, leaned over the regal carved banister and stage-whispered down to Ruby.

"Yes. But isn't it Penelope's turn today?"

Alicia shook her head and, with shoulders back, paraded down the stairs. "I traded with her."

"And who might you be this time?"

"Queen Victoria." The girl held out a limp hand. "You may kiss my ring if you like."

Ruby rolled her eyes. "Nay, and I shan't curtsy either. Sorry, Your Highness. Please follow me or lead the way, as you prefer." She took a few steps and paused. "Why did Penelope agree to exchange tea days with you?"

"She was indisposed." Again the regal tone.

"Oh." *I have a feeling I should ask what she means by that, but . . .*

They entered the sunroom, its rich gold tones burnished by the westering sun. Pots of palms, schefflera plants, and ivy topiaries brought in touches of green, and a pudgy pot covered with waxy gardenia blossoms leant a fragrance all its own. Ruby set the tray on the low glass table in front of the rattan sofa where Mrs. Brandon leaned against the gold-and-orange-flowered cushions.

"Thank you, my dear, that looks lovely. Alicia, you may pour today. Ruby, you will join us, will you not?"

Now I won't be able to make my announcement and a hasty retreat. Dutifully she responded in the affirmative and took the chair indicated.

"Milk or lemon, Mother?" Alicia looked up from pouring steaming tea into one of the cups.

"Milk today, please, and one lump."

Alicia added the milk and a cube of sugar before passing the cup and saucer to her mother.

"Thank you, well done." Lydia Brandon, her hair the same rich sealskin brown as her daughter's, only knotted loosely on top of her head instead of flowing in ringlets down her back, smiled at her daughter.

"So, tell me, what has gone on behind my back today?"

Ruby swallowed a gulp.

"Milk or lemon?" Alicia asked with a smile for Ruby.

"Lemon, please, and two lumps." *I need to be extra sweet, or I shall banish my recalcitrant sister to the attic to dine on bread and water.* How she hated having to apologize for her sister's antics. Ruby accepted her cup of tea with thanks and lifted it to her lips.

Perhaps tea and cookies would sweeten Mrs. Brandon too. Or leave a mellow glow that would be dashed to smithereens like the mortally wounded shepherdess.

"Lemon bar?" Alicia waited in front of her offering the cookie plate.

"Thank you."

"Now, my dears, back to my question, which you have both so assiduously avoided."

Ruby started to confess but stopped when Alicia began.

"Penelope had an accident."

"Is she injured?" The calm tone said this was nothing new.

"N-o-o, but . . ."

"But?" Mrs. Brandon watched her daughter over the rim of her cup.

"But Benson, her favorite bear, is."

"And. . . ?" The pause lengthened.

"And Jason was conducting an experiment."

"With the bear, I take it?"

"Yes, Benson was captain of the raft that Jason built and floated on the goldfish pond. He was adding rocks for ballast and . . . well . . ."

Her mother took another sip of tea. "And . . ."

"And Benson fell into the pond, and Penelope jumped in after it, and she came up all muddy with a lily pad hanging from her hair, so Nanny put her and the bear in the bath, and they had to run the water out twice." Alicia grimaced in disgust. "She was filthy."

"I see." Mrs. Brandon put her cup down and took a bite of the powdered-sugar-covered bar.

"And Jason?"

"Mr. Klaus said he could help clean out the goldfish pond since his experiment got Penelope in trouble."

"Very good of Mr. Klaus."

"You won't tell Father, will you?"

"No, Jason shall."

"Oh, he won't like that."

"No, but confessing one's sins builds character."

"But building a raft wasn't a sin, was it?"

"No, but putting Penelope's favorite bear on the raft when he knew it would upset her was not an act of love, was it?"

"N-o-o. But . . ."

Ruby could tell that Alicia was feeling a bit confused. She nibbled her lemon bar. Was this a good time to tell Mrs. Brandon about the shepherdess? Wasn't Opal in the same fix as Jason?

"The wise man thinks ahead about the consequences of his actions. Will what he does injure someone or cause someone grief?" Mrs. Brandon carefully watched her daughter and smiled at Ruby to include her in the conversation. "We must all consider our actions. The Bible says we should do to others as we would have them do to us, does it not?"

"Yes."

"An excellent precept to live by."

Ruby sucked in a lungful of air and sighed it out. "I have something to confess."

"Oh?" Mrs. Brandon turned so she faced toward Ruby. "And what has Opal been up to now?"

Ruby knew how Jason would be feeling when he spoke to his father. "The Dresden shepherdess is no longer."

"Aah." Mrs. Brandon closed her eyes for a moment. "My mother gave me that."

"I am so sorry. I . . . I will pay for it. Can it be replaced?"

"It could be, but that is not what will help Opal to be more careful." Lydia brought a hand up to her throat. "I think she must come tell me this herself, and I will decide what must be done." She looked to Alicia. "When we have finished our tea, you will go tell Opal to join me in the library."

She held out her hand to forestall Ruby both in speech and action. "Enjoy your tea, and then you may take the children to the park as you had planned. I heard Bernie laugh, so I know he is up from his nap. Jason will wait on the bench in the foyer for his father to come home. Waiting, like confession, is good for the soul."

"Yes, ma'am."

— ✥ —

Opal cast a worried glance over her shoulder as Ruby ushered the others to the front door.

"But, Ruby, aren't you going to wait for me?"

"No. We will be back soon." She steeled her heart against the imploring look from her young sister. Perhaps if she had been more stern Opal would not be in this position now. Surely she could better learn how to discipline her charges in ways to make them think before acting.

Once out the door Penelope walked close beside Ruby. "You want me to push the pram?"

"No, I'll do that. I thought you were going to bring your hoop."

"No fun without Jason. I wish he didn't get in trouble." Her lower lip quivered.

Alicia took her sister by the hand. "Come, I'll push you on the swings."

They crossed the street to the park, where spring had splashed bright greens, yellows, pinks, and reds of tulips, daffodils, and primroses around the grounds. Robins dug for worms in the grass, and squirrels chattered from newly leafing branches.

Ruby followed behind the two girls with the pram, then lifted Bernie out to sit on the swing with her. At two and a half he longed to run after his older brother and sisters and frequently ended up with bruises for his efforts.

"More," he squealed as she walked back as far as she could go before lifting her feet to swoop forward. She kept both arms around the ropes and her hands locked around his chubby belly to keep him from flying away from her.

Penelope's laughter reminded her how infectious was Opal's. If Opal were here, she would be pumping as high as the sky, challenging Jason to go higher than she.

Ruby leaned back and pumped enough to make Bernie squeal again in delight.

"More. More."

When they finally left the swings, lights were beginning to show in the windows of houses bordering the park.

"You think Papa is home now?"

"Papa home," Bernie echoed, clapping his hands.

"That might be his carriage now." Ruby nodded toward the equipage trotting toward them as they crossed the street.

"Perhaps we better go round to the back then." Alicia took her sister's hand. "Come, I'll race you."

Ruby bit back her admonition that young ladies shouldn't be running foot races and followed the two girls, the pram wheels bumping over the crushed gravel.

"A letter came for you," Mrs. Fleish said when Ruby set Bernie down inside the kitchen door. "It's on the hall table." She bent down to swoop up the small child. "How's my Bernie today?"

"Swing. Ruby, swing me high."

"Have you seen Opal?" Ruby asked.

"She's up in the schoolroom." Mrs. Fleish handed Bernie back to her. "Supper will be ready whenever Mr. Brandon is finished with Master Jason. I sent the girls to wash up."

"They're not eating in the nursery tonight?"

"No. Mistress said since this was a family-only night, the three eldest would eat with them in the dining room."

"So it's you and me, young man." Ruby kissed Bernie's round cheek. "And Opal."

"Nanny?"

"Her too." She started toward the hall to retrieve her letter, remembered that she might be disturbing the discussion between Jason and his father, and climbed the back stairs to the second floor instead. She peeked in the schoolroom to find Opal still writing on the blackboard, then went on to the nursery to hand Bernie off to Nanny.

"He'd swing as high as the others if I could figure a way to keep him safe in my lap. He's slippery as an eel at times."

"Now, that I know for sure." Nanny, who'd been with the family since Alicia was born, took her charge off to clean him up, nuzzling his cheeks to make him laugh. Everyone loved to make Bernie laugh.

Ruby unpinned her hat and set it on the dresser in the room she and Opal shared. After hanging her shawl in the chifforobe, she tucked a few stubborn strands of hair back in the golden coil at the base of her head. Only with braiding could she keep any kind of order to hair that owned far too much curl for a proper woman of her twenty years and station. Inhaling a modicum of courage, she returned to the schoolroom.

"We missed you."

"I know." Opal dropped the chalk in the tray at the base of the board. "She . . . Mrs. Brandon . . . said I make life more difficult for you." Opal left off staring at the chalk on her fingers and gazed at her sister. "D-do you hate me?"

"Oh no." Ruby flew across the room and gathered her sister into her arms. "I could never hate you. I get angry and impatient, but no matter what you do, I shall never hate you. I will always love you."

"I don't want to have to tell her something like that again." Opal hid her face on Ruby's shoulder.

"Good. Then you will be careful what you touch, right? Only your own things or with permission, right?" Ruby could feel her sister nodding.

"I finished my fifty times writing."

"I saw that."

"I'm hungry."

"Ja, supper will be ready soon. You go wash now." She kissed her sister's cheek.

Hearing heavy footsteps on the stairs, Ruby peeked outside the schoolroom door. Jason lifted each foot as if it were granite.

"Are you all right?"

"I have to help Mr. Klaus clean out the fishpond, like he said, and buy my sister a new bear if she wants one."

"I see."

"And I have to eat supper in the dining room."

Ruby kept a straight face with some difficulty. She knew he preferred eating in the nursery because then he could read while he ate.

"You better hurry and get cleaned up." That was another thing. In the nursery one did not have to change clothes, and Jason did not like dressing for supper.

"Oh." Jason pulled a letter out of his pocket. "I found this on the table for you."

Ruby took the proffered envelope. "Thank you." What could it be? She never received letters from anyone. She glanced at the return address. *P. Torvald.* Her father. A letter from her father. Her hand shook as she hastened back to her room to read in private. *Lord, he is still alive. All these years I've been praying to see him again. Perhaps he is coming back for us after all. Perhaps . . .*

CHAPTER TWO

My dearest daughters,

I must beg your forgiveness for the long time between letters. I am sure you must have thought I passed on from this world, but life here in the West has been a myriad of experiences—and not all of them good. I attempted gold mining, with some small success, and finally parlayed that into a legacy that I can pass on to my two treasures. While I had hoped to be able to send for you before now, the sad news is that I am dying. We have train service here, so I have enclosed tickets for the two of you to come and claim your inheritance. God willing, if you come quickly, I will have a chance to see your sweet faces before I pass on into the next life, where I know your mother is waiting for me, I can only hope with open arms. I know I have no right to ask this, but please come soon to Dove House in Little Missouri, which is near the military cantonment on the west bank of the Little Missouri River in Dakota Territory.

Your far,
who has always loved you.
Per Torvald

Ruby read the letter again, fighting the tears that blurred the spidery script. Why did he wait so long? *God of all, what am I going to do?* She closed her eyes, waiting for an answer to scream down from the ceiling or burst through the panes of the mullioned windows. She strained to hear, willing sound to ring in her ears. Even a whisper would do.

Nothing.

She could hear Bernie jabbering to Nanny as she bathed him. Water was running in the girls' bathroom. A giggle came from Alicia's room. Most likely Opal was helping them dress. But she heard no sound that could in any way be construed as an answer to her plea.

She opened her eyes to see the two train tickets in her hand. *Lord, all I ask is that you get us there to see him before he dies.*

Now, how to tell Mrs. Brandon and the family? *But first I must tell Opal.* Which she did as soon as the others paraded down the stairs, Jason trailing ten steps behind.

"But I don't want to leave here." Opal stared at her older sister, her mouth an O that matched her eyes.

"You have always said you wanted to meet our father, and now you will have your chance."

"But I wanted him to come here."

"Remember your dream that we were going to live with our very own far? You said it made you so happy." Ruby handed her the plates to set on the table. "Now is our opportunity." The longer word sounded more important than chance and one that couldn't be argued against.

"Why did he leave us with Bestemor after Mor died?"

Opal, I've told you this enough times to . . .

"I know you told me that Far was so sad and wanted to make lots of money."

"He thought he could do better out West in the gold fields. Many men went west."

"He could have taken us with him."

Ruby shook her head. "We were much better off at Bestemor's. She loved us very much. There weren't houses or milk or good food out West, especially for a young girl and a baby." She'd read, too, of terrible blizzards and such heat in the summer that it shriveled and dried out folks, since in some places water was scarce. Silence fell as they both disappeared into their own thoughts.

"Far could have stayed."

"Perhaps." Ruby had often thought that too. At least at first, when she had sobbed into her pillow at night with missing both her dear mor and far. He could have come back or written more often and kept them apprised as to where he was.

"But what about the Brandons?"

"I will talk with them after supper. Let's eat quickly. I'll tuck you into bed so that I . . ." The thought of leaving this place that had been their home for more than five years and these people who treated them more like relatives than employees made Ruby want to double over and weep into her apron. They were the only real family Opal had known since Bestemor died when she was too small to remember, and Mrs. Brandon was the only mother since theirs had died bringing Opal into this world.

"We'll be going on the train, as we did last summer when we went to the seashore."

Opal took her chair and propped her elbows on the table. "Do you think I will have a horse?"

"What made you think of something like that?"

"Well, everyone in the West rides on horses, and we have to be brave and not be afraid of the Indians."

Ruby just shook her head, and they ate in silence for several minutes. Ruby's thoughts wandered around cowboys and cavalry and Indians and covered wagons. She'd read newspaper accounts of the building of the transcontinental railroad, of the Indian wars, and the gold rush. The more she thought, the more she wondered whatever in the world possessed their father to request their travel to such a Godforsaken place.

"I'm finished." Opal pushed her plate toward the center of the table.

"What do you say?"

"May I please be excused?"

Ruby looked from Opal to the napkin ring beside her place and back to meet her sister's gaze. Opal followed where her sister's glance had gone and rolled her eyes. She folded her napkin in precise fourths, smoothing the creases with her thumb and inserted the center point into the silver ring. Laying it exactly two inches from her plate, she looked up. "Now may I be excused?"

"You may."

The sigh and the eyes that rolled so far up as to appear to be painful conveyed her extreme impatience with such trying and unnecessary strictures.

Ruby felt like doing the same. If only there was someone else to be in charge. Someone who could take over the responsibility for their welfare, a responsibility she felt so keenly.

— ❧ —

With Opal in bed and the three Brandons, who had come upstairs when their parents dismissed them, now getting ready for bed, Ruby followed their usual routine. She reminded them to be about their business, granted permission for books to be read in bed, promised Penelope she would come back and read to her, and checked one last time on Bernie, who was fast asleep, before finally slipping down the stairs, letter in her pocket.

Following the sound of adult conversation coming from the library, she tapped on the door before entering.

"Yes, Ruby, what is it?" Mrs. Brandon looked up from the needlepoint canvas she was stitching in the light of the gas lamp.

"Do you have a minute?"

"Of course, dear." She glanced at her husband, and he looked up from the account book at his desk and nodded.

Ruby crossed the room. "I received a letter today from my father, and I believe I should read it to you."

"All right. Would you like to sit down?"

"Er, yes . . . no . . . ah . . ." Ruby shook her head and removed the letter from the envelope. She unfolded the page, began, then cleared her throat and began again. When she finished, she looked up to see the husband and wife exchanging glances.

"I've always feared something like this might happen one day." The sorrow in Mrs. Brandon's voice made Ruby want to weep. "I don't suppose there is an alternative." Mrs. Brandon gave Ruby a hopeful glance, but at Mr. Brandon's clearing his throat, she shook her head again. "Oh, I know you must go, but what shall we do without you?"

Since Ruby had no answer to that question, she kept silent, all the while wishing she had not been the bearer of bad tidings to people who had been so good to her.

"You will leave in the morning, then?" Mr. Brandon stated more than asked.

"If that is convenient." No sooner were the words out of her mouth than she wanted to haul them back. Of course this was not convenient for them. It wasn't convenient for her either, but if she wanted to see her father before he died, if he hadn't already, they must be off as soon as possible.

"Then we must get to your packing." Mrs. Brandon set her needlework aside and stood. "I'll tell Mr. Klaus to bring a trunk down from the attic."

"But, I have no trunk there." Ruby thought of the two carpetbags and three boxes she had brought from Bestemor's house.

"You will need one, and I have several garments that I've been meaning to give to you. One, especially, will do as a traveling suit. Mr. Brandon, dear, will you see to paying Ruby what we owe her?"

"Of course, my dear." He looked toward Ruby. "Your wages will be in an envelope for you by morning. I will have Klaus ride down to the station tonight to see what time the first train leaves tomorrow."

Feeling a bit like a brittle leaf tossed before a brisk wind, Ruby nodded, thanked them both, and took herself back upstairs to begin her packing.

A short time later, Mr. Klaus, man of all chores for the Brandon household, lugged a steamer trunk into her room. "I am so sorry to hear you are leaving, miss. We shall miss you both dreadfully."

"Thank you. And I all of you."

"How they will find someone to replace you, I'll never know. Will take two, maybe three."

Ruby bit her lip. Her heart felt as though a gigantic hand was squeezing the blood from it. "Perhaps we will be back. Who knows what will happen?"

"If your father is dying, why did he not just send your inheritance on?"

"I don't know. But I do want to see him again if at all possible, so the trip is inevitable."

"You could leave the little one here. Mrs. Klaus and I would take good care of her."

"Again, thank you." *Oh, please don't make this so difficult.* "But someday down the road, she would hate me for not letting her meet the father she has dreamed of for so many years."

"Ach, I know, but there was no harm in offering." He glanced toward the closed door to the sleeping quarters. "She is asleep?"

"Ja, she had a hard day."

A smile tugged at one corner of his mouth. "Finding a hard day for her is not hard." He touched his forehead with one finger. "I'm off to the station. I'll take care of your baggage in the morning. You just leave it right there."

"Thank you, Mr. Klaus." Never, since the day they moved in, had she heard him speak so many words at a time.

A few minutes later Mrs. Fleish followed Mrs. Brandon into the room, their arms buried beneath both girls' and ladies' garments.

"What is this?"

"Just some things for your new life. I thought this one would be good for traveling." Mrs. Brandon held up a brick-red traveling dress with sheer long sleeves and high neck. The fitted bodice and multigored skirt of heavy silk were finer than anything Ruby had ever owned.

"There are gloves and this hat to match." She held up a brimmed felt with a low veil that swooped slightly down in the front, all in the same color as the dress. "I know my shoes are too small for you. Had we time, I should have ordered you some."

"Mine will be fine. How can I ever thank you?"

"No need. These were destined for someone's closet other than mine. I just had not done anything about that yet."

Mrs. Fleish laid dresses, petticoats, a navy coat, and a hat on one of the chairs. "Here are some things for Opal. You might have to take them up a bit, but they should be serviceable. Let me pack for you. I am an expert at getting a lot into a small space."

Ruby stepped back from the maw of a trunk that looked big enough to hold a horse, a small one perhaps, but a horse nonetheless. "As you wish."

"Do you think there will be school books in Dakota Territory?" Mrs. Brandon pulled several books off the schoolroom shelves. "If you need more, all you need do is write and ask." She handed them to Ruby. "And remember, dear, if things aren't what they seem in that rough land, you are always welcome back here."

"Thank you."

— ❧ —

In the morning the family gathered in the parlor to say good-bye. The girls were crying, and that set Bernie to howling. Jason maintained the sober mien of his father, his eyes shimmering with tears he refused to shed.

Mr. Klaus hauled the girls' trunk and boxes out to the carriage while everyone hugged Ruby or shook her hand. Mrs. Fleish handed her a sealed envelope, along with a wrapped box.

"One is your pay, and the other something to remember us by." She dabbed at her nose with her handkerchief, at the same time patting Ruby's shoulder with her other hand. Cook handed her a basket and gave Opal a small box.

"For on the train. I hear food is terribly costly."

"Ah, we better be going, Miss Ruby." Mr. Klaus, hat in hand, stood in the doorway.

"Thank you, all. We'll write and send you our address." Ruby put a hand on Opal's shoulder and nudged her toward the door before the tears she was fighting could burst forth.

Mrs. Brandon, her hands on her daughters' shoulders, called one last time. "God bless."

"Ja, God bless," Mr. Brandon echoed.

Ruby let Mr. Klaus help her into the carriage to settle next to her sobbing sister. "Hush now, all will be well." She said the words as much for herself as for Opal. *Please, God, all will be well.*

Ruby fought the tears once more. How could they, who were so blessed to be with this family, possibly leave for such an uncertain future? But then again, how could they not?

CHAPTER THREE

Searching for your father. Searching for your father. The train wheels clacked out the rhythm, driving the words ever deeper into Ruby's mind. No matter how hard she concentrated on the needlepoint piece in her lap, the clacking reverberated clear from the soles of her feet to the top of her head, setting the gossamer veil that draped from the brim of her hat to quivering. Here they were, only on their second day heading westward, and she was already counting the hours—even the minutes—until their arrival.

"Tell me about Papá." Opal flopped back down in the seat across from her sister. So far, the train was not full enough that they were confined to only two seats.

Ruby hid a smile behind her hand as she dabbed at her dripping nose with a handkerchief. The draft from the frequently opened door seemed to be bringing on a cold, the last thing she needed to distract her. Their father had never been called Papá, with the accent on the second syllable, as far as she knew. He was Father, Far, or, as their mother had called him, "Per, dear," as if the two words were inexorably linked together. But for some reason Opal had taken to calling the father she had never known Papá, in the French manner.

"What to tell you this time?" *"Tell me about Papá"* had become Opal's incessant request just as the train clacked out its own beat. "I remember how fine he and Mor looked when they dressed up to attend a soiree or a concert. Mother loved music, and while Father only tolerated the 'highfalutin' classical music, he went along for her sake."

"What kind of music did Papá like?"

"Oh, fiddle music and dance music of all kinds. Far loved to dance. Give him a good polka or reel or pols any day. He liked to be moving not just sitting." And he loved to dance with all the beautiful women, Ruby had learned when she'd asked her mother why she was crying one day. But this was not the stuff to be told to a starry-eyed young daughter who needed a father that could hold his own to the likes of Mr. Brandon. She had once heard Opal wistfully wish for a father like the head of the home they had just left. Ruby doubted Christopher Brandon would have abandoned his two young daughters to the care of his aging mother-in-law as Per had, whether he had just lost his beloved wife or no. Sometimes when she allowed herself to think of how and why he'd left, she used words like deserted or abandoned, and those words alternately stabbed her heart or ignited her fury. Some things were better not thought about. If only he had written more.

"So what did Mor and Far wear when they went out?"

"Mor always wore shades of blue because Far said blue made her eyes sparkle like the fjords of Norway on a summer's day. She could have passed for royalty anytime, she held herself so beautifully. I believe the word grace was created to describe our mor. Even when she was growing big with you, she moved like water flowing over stones in a creek bed. She tried to teach me to move and bend as she did, but grace like hers is either born into one or not. And it definitely skipped over me."

"I think you move beautifully." Opal cocked her head to study her sister. "Only you are quick like the birds that hop around searching for seeds."

"Why, thank you." Even as she said the English words, Ruby could hear her mother saying *mange takk* and *tusen takk*, speaking still the language learned at her mother's knee. Though Ruby's mother had been born in America shortly after her family arrived and settled in Brooklyn, New York, where so many others from Norway had already taken up residence, she had passed on the language to her daughter, unlike many of the other immigrants.

Strange how so many memories had surfaced since she'd boarded the train. Perhaps they came because she sat still long enough for them to catch up with her. That thought provoked another memory.

"I remember one birthday, it must have been my tenth. Mor decided I must have a party. She loved to give parties, you know, and this one was no exception. I always wanted a pony—"

"Like me."

"Ja, just like you, and—"

"Do you think I will have a pony when we get to Dakota? I want to ride astride like Rupert down the street from the Brandons. He is learning to jump."

The envy in her voice told Ruby that Opal had dreamed of a horse far more than she'd admitted.

"But he never let any of the rest of us ride his pony. Said we might ruin its mouth. How can you ruin a horse's mouth?"

"I have absolutely no idea."

"I sure would like to have a pony"—Opal's eyes, more sapphire than blue gray like her sister's, lit up like crystal reflecting candle flame—"or a real horse." The words were said with the awe of one talking about a dream beyond expectation. As if a pony had possibilities but a horse would be a miracle.

Ruby dabbed her nose again. Along with the runny nose, her head was beginning to feel like someone had stuffed it with wool batting.

"Please, Opal, don't go getting your hopes up."

"But we could buy a horse with our inheritance."

"We will only have an inheritance if our father dies. Wouldn't we do better to pray for him to get well from whatever is making him ill?"

Opal nodded. "I s'pose. Do you think maybe he was wounded by a gunshot when he was saving the bank from the robbers or protecting the town from the Indians?" She stared at her sister, willing her to join in the fanciful.

"Opal Torvald, where do you hear such things?"

"Ah . . ." Opal looked out the window, suddenly assuming a look of such innocence that she could make an angel look like a street urchin.

"Opal?"

The young girl's shoulders rose and settled on a sigh. Her voice dropped so that the wheel song overrode it.

"What did you say?"

"I said in the men's car where I hid behind a seat."

The words came fast and nearly inaudible, but Ruby needed only to decipher about every other word to realize what her sister had been up to. She attempted to assume the calm that Mrs. Brandon had tried to instill in her. Taking two deep breaths, she sat straighter, needing the rigidity of being tied to a steel post to keep her from taking Opal by the shoulders and shaking her until her teeth rattled. Ruby deliberately loosened her clenched fingers, modulated her voice, and put the aforementioned steel into her words.

"And when did you trespass into the men's car?"

"When you were sleeping." Opal studied the crease she was forming in the skirt of her dress by repeated pinching between thumb and forefinger.

"During the night?" *Calm, keep your voice calm. Do not let her see that you are upset. You must keep the upper hand here or you will fail in your duties of older sister.* Ruby watched as Opal shook her head. "I trusted you to sit right there in your seat and read your book."

"I know, but I got tired of reading and you weren't awake to tell me stories, and that boy who is sitting two seats behind you asked me if I wanted to come and so I did and . . ." Opal peeked out from under impossibly long eyelashes. "I'm sorry, Ruby, I won't do it again."

"I wonder how many times I have heard those words?" Ruby kept her tone conversational. It was true that Opal seldom had to be scolded for the same infraction twice.

"And you didn't say I couldn't go to the necessary and the place we were hiding was just on the other side of the door and I thought you wouldn't mean I couldn't go anywhere. I mean—"

Ruby held up a hand, then blew her nose, dabbing no longer sufficient to do the mop-up job. "Enough. Right now I am having a hard time just thinking. There's no way I can unravel one of your storied excuses."

"Oh, do you not feel well?"

Ruby caught herself in a shiver. How much more thankful she was becoming that Mrs. Fleish had included two quilts in the box that now rested under her feet. Something to remember them by, indeed. A second shiver made her reach down and pluck one of the quilts free to wrap around herself.

"Are you sick?" Opal's eyes darkened.

Was it fear that Ruby saw there?

She blew her nose again, wishing she had a steaming kettle to bend over and inhale the heat and vapor. Steam always made a cold feel less severe. She mentally looked around the car again, wishing for a seat out of the draft, but the other four seats facing were all full, and she didn't want to cram their belongings into two seats until they were forced to. They would be changing trains in Chicago in the morning.

"Would you please bring me a cup of water?" She held out one of the cups Mrs. Klaus had packed for them. How a good cup of hot broth or lemonade would relieve her head right now. She thought to the packet of headache powder in the basket. She would mix that in the water, and perhaps that would be all she needed. She huddled into the quilt. What an unfortunate time to feel so ineffectual.

Opal held out the full cup. "Here, I didn't spill any."

"Good." Ruby tapped some of the powder into the cup and stirred, then drank it down, making a face at the bitterness.

"Icky, huh? I don't like medicine either." Opal looked out the window. "It sure is taking us a long time to get to Dakota Territory."

Ruby would have laughed at both the comment and the doleful look on Opal's face if she had felt up to it. "We are moving very fast. It wasn't that long ago that the only way west was by horse-drawn wagons. And it took months then, not days. Take out your history book and read the next chapter so we can talk about it. Write down the words you don't understand. Perhaps if I sleep for a time, I will wake up feeling better." She stared sternly at her sister. "And don't you get out of that seat except to use the necessary, and then come straight back. You hear me?"

Opal nodded, her arms locked across her chest and lower lip thrust out enough to attract the coal dust that floated so freely through the air.

"Opal?"

"I heard you."

"And you will mind?"

A nod.

"Good. I am trusting you." Ruby stood and wrapped the blanket all around her, then using her arm as a pillow, folded herself into the two seats and closed her eyes. She heard the door open and felt the cool draught on her face, but opening her eyes took more effort than she could summon.

"How is your sister?" The conductor's voice echoed through her fog.

"Not so good."

"You'd best be taking good care of her, eh?"

"I know."

"You need to heat something up, you can do so on the stove."

"I will tell her."

"And the coffeepot is always on."

And like mud, totally undrinkable. Ruby fell asleep on that thought.

— ❧ —

The conductor's voice announcing another stop woke her. She had no idea how much later. Seeing her reflection in the window told her that night had fallen. Several people were lined up with their baggage, ready to disembark.

She glanced at the other seat to see it empty, the quilt rumpled as though Opal had been there and left in a hurry.

Surely she is in the necessary. The thought made Ruby realize she needed to go there also, so she sat up carefully, grateful that the pounding in her head had ceased.

Opal was not in the necessary.

Ruby stared into the wavy mirror. She looked bad enough to scare small children. Huge purple swaths circled under her eyes, her hair hung in disarray with tendrils hanging and pointing every which way, and her cheeks held sufficient pallor to indicate incipient death throes. She rinsed her mouth out with water, dampened her fingers to tuck and smooth the errant strands of hair, and patted her cheeks to force back some semblance of color into her face, other than that of her red nose.

Now to locate her missing sister.

She thrust open the door and exited, missing a fatal crash

with a cigar-smoking gentleman by a mere hairsbreadth.

"Excuse me, miss." He stepped back and pressed himself against the train wall to allow her passage.

"I . . . I'm sorry. Pardon me." She knew her face now bore sufficient color. The heat of it fairly radiated in front of her.

She swayed her way back to her seat to find Opal huddled under the opposite quilt.

"Are you all right, Opal, dear?"

A nod moved the part of the quilt nearest the armrest at the wall. At least she thought it to be a nod. "Has something happened I should know about?"

"Indeed, it has," said a voice just to the right and behind her.

Ruby turned to find a red-faced man whose midsection stuck out far beyond the foot-long cigar clamped between fleshy lips. The man's eyebrows formed a straight line above a bulbous nose, slightly flattened at the end, that reminded her more of a pig's snout than a human feature.

Ruby felt the first real laugh since they had left the Brandons' begin in her midsection and work its way upward. She covered it with the closest thing to a ladylike cough that she could muster.

"I see." She covered her lower face with her handkerchief.

"No, you don't see at all, for I have not begun to apprise you of the actions of that . . . that . . ." A shaking finger pointed at the quilt-covered child. Only her shoes peeked out from under the blanket. "That hoyden," he snarled from between teeth clamped on the stupendous cigar. His checkered vest wore the dusting of ashes from more than one of the smelly smokes.

Ruby rose to her full five feet five inches, squared her shoulders under the shawl she'd donned to keep off the chill, and faced her attacker. She glared at the bowler hat still perched on his head, fanned the smoke that he'd expelled in her face and now billowed around her head, and leaned slightly forward.

"I don't know who you are, mister, and the thought of pursuing any sort of acquaintance makes me want to call for the conductor, but let me tell you this, my sister is not a hoyden, and whatever she has done to affront you cannot begin to compare to the effect you are having on me. Now, you will speak to me in a gentlemanly way and start with minding the manners that I am sure your mother, God rest her soul, tried to instill in you.

Your hat, sir—and I use the term lightly."

"Ah, I . . ." He jerked the hat off his head and held it with one hand.

"And I am sure she would not approve of you accosting a lady with that noxious weed hanging out of your mouth." The words could have set fire to the tip of said cigar had it been necessary.

With his cigar now clenched between two fingers of the hand also holding his hat, he started again, disgruntlement bristling from his walrus mustache and gray-shot beard. "That . . . that . . ."

"Child."

"That child was . . . I was sound asleep, minding my own business—" He hawked and spat a glob on the floor—"when . . ."

Ruby closed her eyes, at the same moment putting a hand to her throat. "I am sure there are spittoons for such as that"—she shuddered—"oral excrement, and I demand that you use one. I can tolerate your crudity no longer. I will speak with my sister to ascertain her part in this."

"You are dismissing me?" His voice skidded on gravel and cracked midword.

"Yes, she is." A male voice, steely with menace, coming from the regions of the roof of the car whipped Ruby's attention toward her left.

Her rude assailant turned as well. "Why . . . why, you . . . you are butting into business that is none of—"

"Anytime I see someone mistreat a lady, I make it my business."

Ruby catalogued her would-be rescuer in a swift glance. Dark hair that swept back from a broad forehead bisected by a line dividing tan from white skin, eyes that flashed daggers or perhaps arrows. Nose, cheeks, and chin seemed carved in stone, and his mustache brushed the top of chiseled lips. Shoulders that reached from seat to seat filled out the black coat that hung open to reveal a gold watch fob dangling flat in the loop from pocket to pocket. If this was what she'd heard called cowboy, no wonder the Indians always lost.

He flicked a glance her way as if asking if she was all right, and she nodded in return.

"Thank you, sir, but I believe I am capable of handling this gen—" She started to say gentleman, but changed her mind since he in no wise resembled any of the gentlemen she had ever known and finished, "—ruffian."

"As you say, miss." But instead of leaving, he took a step forward, his gaze never leaving that of the loudmouth.

The offensive man took one step back, then another. "This ain't over yet."

"Oh, I think it is." His voice kept an even beat, reminding Ruby of Mrs. Brandon when she was making a point with one of her children over a behavior that had been less than mannerly.

Ruby watched as the gentleman stalked the scoundrel with an easy grace that made her think of the cat she used to watch on the prowl for bird or mouse. At a sound from the other seat she glanced over to see Opal, eyes round as her mouth, watching the men.

"Is he a cowboy?" Opal whispered.

"Why do you ask?"

"Look at his boots."

Ruby glanced toward the floor. Sure enough, he wore boots with heels and pointed toes, exactly as she'd seen in a magazine. She watched as the once-attacking man backed into his seat and sat. While she couldn't hear what transpired between them in their brief exchange, she was grateful not to be on the receiving end. When the cowboy returned, she rose from where she had seated herself by Opal.

"Thank you."

"You are welcome." He nodded to her and then to Opal. "Much nicer for young girls in here than . . ." He nodded toward the car behind them, the one where the men played cards and smoke turned the air gray. Without another word, he strode on back.

Ruby chanced a peek around the seat back, then turned her attention to her sister, who shrank into the corner.

"I didn't do anything bad."

"Opal, I . . ." Ruby took a deep breath and sat back against the seat. "Just tell me what you did and why, and let me be the judge of that."

"Well, I was sitting here minding my own business when I heard a lady up there"—she pointed toward the front of the car—"say that a man was dead."

"Opal."

"Well, something like that . . . So I went up to make sure he was still breathing. I was looking at him when his mustache moved, so I was sure he was all right, but then he woke up and . . ."

"And?" Ruby considered what her sister had said. "And how close were you to him when you saw his mustache move?"

Ruby closed her eyes to think better, create the picture in her mind. She could feel her own hands moving, two feet apart, eighteen inches? She opened her eyes as Opal held her hands about twelve inches apart, then cut the distance in half.

The inner picture made Ruby flinch. She rolled her eyes. *Lord preserve us.* "Wouldn't you say that was a bit rude?"

"But what if he had been dead?" Opal threw her hands out wide and gave her sister a pleading look. "Or dying and no one paid any attention?"

Ruby leaned her head back and closed her eyes. Always an excuse came for which she had no answer. Opal had a heart of gold that always got her into trouble when she acted out her inherently good intentions. The thought of that man waking up to Opal peering into his face made Ruby smile, nay, nearly laugh out loud. What a shock that must have been. She peeked at Opal, who was watching her with all the intensity of one about to be shot for her transgressions.

Ruby tried to keep from laughing. She ordered her lips to narrow into rigid lines, but instead they turned up at the corners. She ordered the chuckles bubbling up to cease and desist, but instead they seeped out and floated around like iridescent soap bubbles. As the bubbles popped, the laughter invited more, and when Ruby, shaking her head, finally could keep from looking at Opal no longer, the two of them laughed together, hands over their mouths to stifle the hilarity.

"I really didn't mean to offend him," Opal finally said when they could catch their breath.

"I know. But Opal, dear sister, you must learn to think things through before you embark on them. I'm afraid that one of these days something serious will happen. Then what will we do?"

"I'll try, Ruby, really I will." Opal slid over in the seat to cuddle next to her sister's side. The two rocked together for a time, Ruby with both arms around her charge and resting her cheek on Opal's soft hair.

When Opal's stomach announced it was past a meal time, they dug into the basket at their feet. Bread, cheese, and cookies were all that remained.

Ruby wished for a cup of coffee or tea, but she'd tried the sludge on the stove and found it totally unpalatable, even with the addition of water. Shame there wasn't a teapot or a plain kettle to heat water to go along with the packet of tea Cook had provided.

As they settled down to sleep, Ruby thought ahead. What was waiting for them at the end of their journey? Wouldn't it be wonderful if their loving care could bring their father back to health?

CHAPTER FOUR

Dear Mr. and Mrs. Brandon,

We are still on our train trip west, and I must thank you for your generosity. I could not believe my eyes when I counted the amount you included in my pay envelope, not only paper money but a gold piece too. I shall sew that into the lining of my coat so that it is safe for an emergency, as you suggested.

We have changed trains for the final time in St. Paul and are nearing Fargo. There is still snow on the ground in places. April here on the frontier is not as warm as April in New York. We have in fact seen snow flurries, although green grass is covering the land, land so flat that I'm sure God spread it out with a giant-sized rolling pin.

We had a bit of excitement a few minutes ago, and this time it was not of Opal's doing. Two men got in a fight in the men's car and came bursting through the door into our car, grunting and pounding on each other. One of the lady passengers in our car let out a shriek that jolted some sense into them, and they returned to the other car with arms over each other's shoulders and laughing like they'd just shared the best joke. One was wiping blood from his nose and the other wiped a cut near his eye. I shall never understand the male of our species.

Ruby went on to describe Opal's brush with the mustached

sleeping man, all with the intent of entertaining her New York family who had provided for them so generously.

> I cannot thank you enough for the years we enjoyed so safely and lovingly cocooned at the Brandon mansion. I will write more when we know more.
>
> Your loving servant,
>
> Ruby
>
> PS: Opal too sends her love and wishes the children were here to play with. R.

The train left the station at Bismarck when the sun slipped behind the horizon, setting the clouds and sky on fire.

"Oh, look, Ruby, have you ever seen such colors?" Opal sat with her nose flattened against the windowpane so as not to miss a moment of God's glorious display.

Ruby leaned as close as she could without encountering the coal-dusted glass. She dug out a cloth and wiped the window clean, then spit on the corner of the cloth and, clamping Opal's chin in one hand, firmly scrubbed the black off Opal's nose and chin with the other.

"I hate that," Opal squeaked when finally freed.

"Then keep your face clean." Ruby put the cloth back and watched the changing hues as more lavender and purple overlaid the flaming vermillion and orange.

"How I would love to have a dress just that pink on the second layer of clouds." Opal's wistful sigh tugged at Ruby's heart. Her young sister wished for things so seldom that she tried to bring them about when it happened. Wishing for a dress of a certain color, now that was almost in the miracle category. How would she ever find lovely or even serviceable dress goods in this wasteland? As each turn of the wheels took them farther from New York, then Chicago, and finally St. Paul and Minneapolis, she felt that civilization as she knew it might never be seen again. Fargo had brick buildings, some of which surely housed sewing supplies, millinery, unmentionables, and boots for when Opal outgrew hers, which she was wont to do on a regular basis. But after leaving Fargo, not only were there no business establishments, she'd not seen the friendly roofline of house nor barn for more miles than she cared to speculate. Even the most glorious of sunsets could not begin to settle her unease. What in the world were they getting into? What had possessed her to leap to her father's bidding without exploring the ramifications? What had possessed him to ask them to come to this barren land?

But he sent the tickets, she consoled herself. *And he mentioned Dove House.* Even the name brought forth pictures in her mind of a more prestigious building than some of the hovels she'd seen along the way. Why some of the people out here lived in houses made of dirt—soddies, she'd heard them called. Someone else talked about dugouts, and when she asked what dugouts were, only through extreme strength of will could she keep from shuddering. A dugout was just that, a room-sized hole, if she understood right, dug into the side of a hill or a rise and faced with logs or bricks of sod. The speaker's description of building a soddy or a dugout had been graphic indeed. Opal's squeal in delight at no floors to polish had not elicited the same response from her sister. And when she learned what was used to create a hard surface on a dirt floor, she'd had to fight the gagging and had hurriedly retired to the necessary. The two women had been discussing the merits of blood and water over fresh cattle dung, called manure, also mixed with water and then made into a slurry with local clay if available, otherwise with local dirt, and then spread over a hard-packed surface.

Just the thought brought bile up from her stomach.

Surely Dove House had wooden floors and walls, at least. But by that time she was afraid to ask for any more details.

At least her cold was on the wane and she could sleep without feeling she was either drowning or smothering.

"Dickinson, next stop Dickinson," the conductor called, stopping at their seat. "We'll soon be crossing the river to Little Missouri. You positive someone will be waiting for you there? It's mighty primitive."

Ruby nodded. "Though my father is very ill, I am sure he will have someone there to meet us."

"I certainly hope so, for there ain't no real station there. Just a shack. We shoulda been there hours ago but for that herd of cows that didn't care to move. Sometimes we get stopped by snowdrifts, but what's coming down now won't stick." He peered out the window into a sea of black with white swirling dots hitting the glass pane. "I'd feel a whole lot easier if we knew for sure your telegram had gone through."

"They said they would try again later." *Please, Lord, let it be so.*

He straightened. "Sometimes something takes out a pole for the telegraph line, and then they have to go out looking for the problem afore they can repair it. Telegraph is mighty amazing, but give me a plain old handwritten letter any day." He touched the hard bill of his hat and swayed on up the aisle. This conductor had joined the train in Fargo and been real generous in answering Ruby's and Opal's questions. He'd said that *all* children here in the West, what few there were, did not have horses but indeed some did.

Ruby still wasn't sure why she hadn't asked him about Dove House, but something kept her from doing so.

Opal leaned against Ruby's shoulder. "Tell me another story of Papá."

Ruby closed her eyes in thought, clicking through memories, sorting for a new one that was appropriate for young ears. She couldn't tell Opal that their father was an accomplished gambler. She'd not learned that herself until one time they had to move rather quickly because he'd lost their house in a poker game. That little escapade had really made their mor cry. Mor never liked to play cards after that, not even whist. Through the years Ruby had regaled Opal with memories of their mother, but because Far had often been away from home—working or some such thing—she hadn't as many memories of him.

"I remember when he brought me a kitten, a lovely soft gray-and-white kitten." Ruby thought back to the rumbling purr that came from that tiny body. "I named her Misty, for she reminded me of the fog that came in, sneaking over rooftops and around corners." They had lived in Baltimore then, before the final move to New York City. "She loved to play, batting at strings. Far brought me a leather string with a bit of fur to the end. Misty would play with that by the hour."

"What happened to her?"

"She ran away after we moved in with Bestemor. I called and called, searched and searched, but she just disappeared. Bestemor thought sure someone else took her in, but . . ." Ruby's shoulders lifted and dropped in a sigh.

"Perhaps Papá will give me a kitten, and I will share it with you."

"Perhaps." Ruby pointed under the seat. "Will you be a good girl and make sure we have left nothing under there?"

Opal did as asked and came up with only a paper wrapper, which she put in the trash container by the door.

"All right, you read your book, and I shall write in my journal. It won't be long now."

The train stopped and started again in Dickinson, leaving behind the warm lights of the station and buildings around it. She could hear the change in sound when they crossed the trestle and finally slowed to a stop.

"Little Missouri, miss. Here, let me help you with your things. Your trunk will be waiting for you on the ground."

Ruby and Opal picked up their satchels, and with Ruby also carrying the now empty food basket, they followed the conductor to the exit and allowed him to assist them to the ground.

"There you go, miss, but I don't see any wagon here to meet you."

Another man came up with their trunk on a handcart and set it down beside them.

Ruby took several steps, still feeling as though she were on the swaying car. She put out a hand to the trunk to steady herself.

"It won't take you long to get your land legs again." The conductor reentered the train and brought out their final box to set on the trunk.

Ruby stared around. As he'd said, there was only a dark shack for a station building, but she could see lights not far off. However, there were no streetlights to lead the way and, as the conductor had feared, no one to meet them.

"I sure hate to leave you like this. Even snowing a bit. Just not right."

"We'll be fine, sir. As you said, the town isn't large."

"If you could call it a town. More like a settlement."

The train whistled twice, calling the man back aboard. He took up his red lantern and, with one last worried "good-bye," put the stool back up and mounted the train.

Ruby and Opal watched the train pull away, leaving them

there all alone in the darkest night she had ever seen.

Snowflakes drifted down lazily, as if they couldn't make up their minds whether to settle or scamper off.

Opal sneaked her hand into Ruby's. "What are we going to do?"

I wish I knew, Lord. I wish I knew.

CHAPTER FIVE

The red glow of the train's lantern dimmed in the distance.

"Will someone steal our things if we leave them here?" Opal asked.

"I doubt anyone will see them until morning. Right now we'll take what we can carry and go looking for Dove House." Ruby fought back the desire to sit down on the trunk and cry. Only the fear that she would never stop kept her from the easier action. Instead, she picked up a carpetbag in one hand and handed the basket to Opal. "Can you carry anything else?"

"No. I have the basket and my satchel." Opal sniffed. "How are we going to see anything?"

"Once our eyes adjust to the dark, we will do fine. Those lights don't look too far away."

Ruby could hear a piano playing somewhere and a dog barking. "The conductor said that there is a military cantonment near here too. Surely someone will know where to find Dove House." She liked the name Dove House. Doves were gentle creatures, their cooing and burbling noises most soothing.

"Follow me, Opal." She didn't finish with *If I fall first, you won't get hurt*. Not that her sister could pick her up, but she could run for help. A bush at the edge of the platform snagged at her skirt like unseen hands, reaching out to trip her. She took a step into air.

She teetered, windmilled her arms, stepped back—and

bumped into Opal. Her valise thumped her on her side as she clutched at air.

"Ow, you smashed my toe."

"We're lucky that's all that was smashed." Ruby stood panting, her heart racing, and clung to her sister. "I'm sorry. I felt like I was falling off a precipice."

Opal disentangled herself and moved to the edge.

"Careful."

"It's only a little way to the ground. You can make it easy." Opal stepped back up and picked up her things. "You have everything?"

"I think so."

"All right, this time I will lead. I bounce easier than you."

Ruby gingerly set one foot down on solid ground, grateful for the darkness that covered the mortification she could feel creeping up her neck and face. Surely she had let out a shriek too. That might be what set that dog to barking again. It sounded like a big dog. What if that dog attacked them? Her heart picked up the pace again, now slamming against her ribs.

God, if we ever get out of this mess, I will be your servant forever. Please, be our eyes and ears, for the darkness is as light to thee. As it is to that dog. Would that thought negate the prayer? Trust, that's what faith was all about. She'd heard that message often enough from the pulpit of the church they'd attended with the Brandons. But saying she had faith while sitting in church or in a warm parlor was entirely different from walking in a strange place in total darkness.

Doesn't do any good to listen for the scratch of dog's feet on the dirt. My heart is pounding so loud, I cannot hear myself think.

"We're almost there." Opal's voice floated out of the darkness, her body only a hint of a shadow, her nearness more felt than seen.

"Good thing." She couldn't see a thing except the light that appeared to be coming from a window in a house. A house with real live people. Surely they would be able to help these two sojourners in the wilderness of the night.

The gate Opal opened creaked, setting off another dog, closer this time.

The piano music was closer too. In fact, now they could see

a string of lights, perhaps houses in a row, not very close together but not miles apart either.

Ruby breathed a sigh of relief when they mounted three steps and the porch roof shielded them from the drifting snowflakes and bantering wind.

"If it is this cold in April, what must the winters be like?" She shivered as she muttered and reached to knock on the door.

"What?" Opal stood outlined against the light flowing from the window beside the door.

"Nothing." Ruby made sure her mouth was smiling as the door opened. A man stood in the doorway.

"Can I help you?"

"Yes. We just arrived on the train, and I was hoping you could tell me how to find Dove House?"

"Dove House! Up the street!" The censure in his voice slammed as loud as the door.

Ruby and Opal exchanged looks of absolute amazement. They shrugged and turned back to the dark. Was this an indication of the reception they could expect from all the people in Dakota Territory?

"I thought people in the West were supposed to be friendly." Opal picked up her parcels and started down the steps. "He sure wasn't."

Not far ahead light poured from several windows and filtered through slits from others that were draped on the second floor. As they drew nearer, the music grew in volume, along with laughter and shouting.

A wide porch faced the street, but as they climbed three steps, Ruby had a feeling this was not the kind of place for a young woman and a girl of their sensibilities.

"Come, this is not for us." She headed back down the steps.

"But why not? Surely they know where—"

"Come along now." Ruby interrupted her sister. "Opal, I said now!"

"But I—"

"We'll try the next place."

The wind seemed to be picking up, no longer just teasing them but tugging at Ruby's hat, forcing her to set her satchel down to clamp a hand on her hat to hold it in place. She tucked her parcel under her arm and picked up the satchel again with the same hand, leaving her hat-saving hand free to do just that. The traveling outfit of which she'd been so proud was certainly not sufficient this night, even though she wore a fine wool coat over it.

They staggered on up the street, at one time stepping into a mud puddle that not only soaked their shoes but also stained the hem of Ruby's dress. How would she ever get that out?

They finally made it to a lighted house again and knocked at the door. This time a woman answered. She peered out the door, caught sight of Opal, and said, "Oh, you poor dears. Come inside this minute." She stepped back and beckoned them in. "What are you doing outside on such a night as this. Why, spring has been here, but I think she bowed to winter and retreated for a spell."

Ruby remained by the door, not wanting to soil the floor with muddy shoes. "Thank you, ma'am. We arrived on the train and there was no one to meet us. I had sent a telegram to my father at Dove House, and he—"

"Dove House! Surely you can't mean that." The woman drew herself up and took a step backward.

"Our father is Per Torvald, and he—"

"Well, I never. That man . . ." The woman made fluttery motions with her hands. "You must leave. I cannot have such truck here in my house."

"But . . . but . . ." Ruby stepped back, shaking her head, feeling as though she'd been badly scratched by her favorite cat. "Could you at least tell me where to find—"

"Don't even say that word. Not in my house!" Her mouth pursed like she'd sucked a gingerroot. With one hand she pointed back the way they had come.

Ruby and Opal found themselves out the door and hearing the resounding slam for a second time that evening.

"I don't think she liked Papá. Or maybe she thought we meant someone else?" Opal looked over her shoulder. "She seemed so nice at first."

Ruby rubbed her forehead.

"Are you all right?"

"I will be. Guess my cold isn't all gone after all." She sneezed once, twice, and a third time, wishing that she could change the thought that was quickly turning into a fear. The only place between this slamming door and the other was the two-story building where men were gathered, laughing and, if she could believe her senses, drinking and most likely playing cards. The music did not indicate a genteel gathering, and the smell of smoke that rolled from the place in waves strongly suggested cigar smoking, many cigars smoking.

Surely Dove House did not harbor a saloon.

"What are we going to do?"

Ruby could feel her sister shivering as she leaned close against her side. *I don't know* screamed through her mind. *I don't know anything, and I'm cold and frightened, and I want someone to tell me everything is all right and draw me up to a warm stove and place a cup of hot tea in my hand, and I ... I want to go back to New York. Right now!*

She sucked in a deep breath, which set her to coughing this time, one step down from sneezing. "We are going back to that building in the middle and ask them if they know where our father is. I think, though, we'll go around to the back." There was no way she could take herself, let alone her little sister, in through that front door. Surely there would be a servant or someone in the back who could tell them what to do.

Ruby squared her shoulders, picked up her things, and chin in the air, strode back to the street and turned left. This time they would keep to the side where there was less chance of encountering puddles.

Back in front of what appeared to be a rather large building, they followed the porch around to the back. Horses dozed where they were tied up to a hitching rail alongside the building, further reinforcing her idea of the nature of the place. A saloon for sure, and judging by the number of horses, there were more than two or three men in there.

They'd just reached the back corner when two men rounded the front and headed for their horses.

Ruby pushed Opal, who had stopped to see the horses, ahead of her, hoping the men had not seen them. She stood in the darkness until she heard the jingle and clop as the horses trotted up the street. Relief made her feel almost warm.

They located a back door, and Ruby turned the handle. It

was not locked, an answer to a prayer she'd not quite articulated.

She led the way into a room lit only by the light sifting under a door across the expanse. Wishing for a candle but grateful just to be in a warmer space, Ruby closed the door behind Opal, making sure that the snick of the lock was only that. Although with all the noise from the other room, she was sure no one heard them enter. *So now what do we do?* She waited, hoping for some sort of inspiration, but nothing came.

"I'm hungry," Opal whispered.

"I know. Me too." Her stomach rumbled just in time to corroborate her statement.

Opal giggled, one hand hiding her mouth as if to trap the sign of merriment.

Ruby put one finger to her lips in the eternal signal of silence, then realized her sister couldn't see her so she uttered a "shh." A raucous burst of laughter, the sound of a hand slapping a table, and a string of expletives made her want to cover her own ears but she used her hands to cover Opal's instead.

Cigar smoke filtered under the door in addition to the light. Now that her eyes had adjusted, Ruby could see stacked boxes of what she presumed to be liquor. Bags and barrels might hold flour and other staples, but she was in no mind to go searching. She sniffed. Someone, somewhere, was cooking something.

Both their stomachs grumbled, in unison this time, eliciting another giggle from Opal.

A woman's voice sounded right outside the door, and along with her laugh the door flew open.

"You want one or two?" she called, pausing in the doorway, her buxom form outlined by a tight red gown.

Ruby wished she were close enough to cover Opal's eyes this time. One hearty cough or even a slight sneeze would surely pop those ample bosoms right out of the indecently low neck of the gown, which was sleeveless and missing most of the skirt. Gathered lace hemmed the skirt right up the divided front to the waist. A long red feather protruded from her high-piled hair and curved over one cheek.

Ruby laid an arm across Opal's chest and did her best to disappear into the stores, at the same time hoping and praying the woman would change her mind and return to the party.

"Hand me that lamp, will you, honey?"

"I'll hand you anything you want, darlin'." The man's voice sounded slurred. "I'll even carry it for you. Perhaps we can find something even more important in that there storeroom."

The man held the lamp high as the two of them continued on into the room. "Now what in the world do we have here? You been holding out on me, Belle?"

"Who the blazes are you?" The woman named Belle stared, red-painted mouth open, at Ruby and Opal.

Ruby gathered what dignity she could find and stood forward. "I am Ruby Torvald, and I am here at my father's request."

"Your father?" Belle's eyes slitted. "And who might your father be?"

"Per Torvald. He said we were to come to Dove House." Ruby nearly said "to gain our inheritance," but she stopped herself before the words got to her lips. "So, if you please, could you take us to see our father?"

"Well, can you beat all that. Per has a daughter that looks like this?"

"Keep your tongue in your mouth, Jake. These young ladies came clear from New York City, and they won't have anything to do with the likes of you." The sarcasm in her voice penetrated Ruby's fog. Surely this couldn't be happening. But if this were a bad melodrama, who would be there to yank them off the stage?

"I want to see my papá now." Opal stepped out from behind her sister.

"Papá. Did you hear that?" He repeated the papá, putting the emphasis on the final syllable as Opal had. Jake's guffaw threw kerosene on the embers of Ruby's long-damped rage.

"You thundering half-wit, picking on a child like that. I hope to heaven that when you are not three sheets to the wind, you have some kind of manners, for you certainly aren't exhibiting any now. And you, ma'am, from the look on your face I feel certain you know where my father is and how to take us there, so I suggest you do so immediately." *God, you shut the mouths of the lions facing Daniel in their den. Can you do the same here for us?*

CHAPTER SIX

"Ah, ain't she a looker!"

Ruby ignored the laughter and the comments as Belle led her and Opal through the smoke-hazed room and up the stairs. She wanted to keep her hands over Opal's eyes and ears, but that was not possible. No young girl should be subjected to this ... this ... She could not for the moment think of a word for the miasma of horrified thoughts that assailed her. She kept her eyes straight ahead, on the part in Opal's hair, created with such love and caring each morning when she braided her sister's hair. But like the flyaway wisps that glowed with a red fire in the lamplight, her attention careened around the room, sensing the men staring at them, realizing that Belle was prolonging the agony instead of protecting them.

Nay, surely not. Ah, but true. Up ahead she could see Belle's hips sway from side to side as she took each step of the carved oak stairs deliberately. Each hip would bump the side of a normal doorway, the sway was so pronounced.

A wolf whistle came from the room behind and below her. She saw Belle send a saucy look over her shoulder. She was enjoying every moment of this humiliation.

Surely this isn't the way our father would have his daughters treated—humiliated at the hands of these ruffians. If this was any picture of the men of the West, the romantic stories she'd read about cowboys were not only highly overrated but downright lies. A picture of the man on the train flashed through her mind.

What a difference. So which was true? She reached the top step and followed Opal, who followed behind Belle.

Ornate red wallpaper lined the hall with dark oak doors set at intervals. She heard a giggle behind one they passed and a man snoring from another. When Belle stopped and knocked on a door on the street side of the building, Ruby sucked in a breath. Were they about to meet their father? Must be since Belle had said nothing about his passing away. She laid a hand on Opal's shoulder.

"Wait here."

"But, Ruby—"

"No, let me go in first."

"Take your time, ladies, he ain't goin' nowhere." Belle's voice had lost the purr she used when men were around. And her smile didn't begin to reach her kohl-lined eyes.

"Th-thank you. You may go now."

"Don't you want me to introduce you?" The beauty patch at the side of her mouth moved when she talked, a trait that seemed to entrance Opal. She kept staring at Belle as if to memorize every inch of her, and in some areas the inches were considerable.

"If you like." Ruby wished she'd kept the words inside the moment she said them. She didn't need anyone to introduce her to the father she had at one time adored. They crossed the dimly lit, sick-smelling room.

"Per. Per!" Belle shook the shoulder of the skeleton lying in the bed. She leaned closer and called his name again.

Ruby glanced around the high-ceilinged room, wondering if she could turn up the lamp. Weren't there any candles available, or was the only light source the kerosene lamp nearer to the door than to the bed?

"Ruby," Opal whispered from the doorway, shielded from the sight of the bed by a short wall. "Can I come in now?"

Ruby shook her head, then whispered back. "No, you wait there." Surely this caricature of a man lying in the bed could not be their father. But he had said that he was dying, and from the looks of this man, he'd been dying a long time.

"Per." Belle shook him again, seeming with a touch of violence that Ruby found truly abhorrent.

"Be careful with him." The words slipped out without her volition, which seemed to have happened a lot in the last couple of days. Where had her manners gone? Even in the dimness she could both see and feel the malevolent look Belle flashed over her shoulder.

Ruby stopped slightly behind Belle. "How long has he been like this?" She kept her voice low, but even so the man turned his head slightly, and she recognized the finely arched eyebrows and the nick at the corner of his right eye, which he'd gained in some daring escapade, according to the stories she'd heard sitting on his knees.

Now he had barely enough skin to cover the bones of the hand that he slowly raised toward her.

"Ruby?" The word would not be heard much further than where she stood.

"Yes, Far. We have come." She knelt by the bed and took his hand in hers.

"Opal?"

"Waiting in the hall."

"Ah." He slightly nodded. A smile tried to move his lips, dry lips that needed something to soothe them.

"I'll leave you then." The tone of Belle's voice had lost its edge and, if Ruby was right, held a semblance of caring.

"Who has been taking care of him?" Ruby glanced up over her shoulder to see Belle outlined by the dim lamplight.

"We all take turns, but I take more turns than the others. I didn't really think you would come."

"We left the day after we received the letter and tickets." Ruby held his long-fingered hand to her cheek. He'd so often stroked her young-girl cheek, telling her that only angels had finer skin than she. When she'd laughingly asked about Mor's skin, he'd said he was twice blessed. What other man than he had two angels in his house?

A tear found its way past her resolve and dampened his fingers.

"Please . . . don't cry." Each word came haltingly, as if he had to go somewhere deep inside himself and search for strength to speak. "The . . . letter."

"In the morning, Per." Belle took a step backward.

"No. Now." The force of his words sent him into a paroxysm of coughing.

Ruby was certain he was never going to recover enough to breathe again, let alone talk.

"All right. All right." Belle crossed the room to a trunk, lifted the lid, and took out an envelope to hand to Ruby. "He said I was to give this to you if you came after he died."

"But you didn't think I would come."

"No. We sent the letter over a month ago. What would you think?"

"I would have come sooner had I known." She laid the letter on the bed. "Could we have a bit more light in here?"

"He likes it dim. He says it is easier on his eyes."

"Could we open the windows?"

"Whyever would you do that? You wanting to kill him off right quick?"

"No, but some fresh air might make his breathing easier."

"Ruby!" By the tone in her voice, Ruby knew Opal had grown tired of waiting.

If only there were some way she could clean Per up first. No one had shaved him, and his once-thick hair was matted and sticking out every which way.

"You best let her come in. You never know when he will draw his last breath." Belle's voice was harsh, but Ruby thought she noticed a hint of sadness.

"And yet he has hung on for months?"

"Wanted to see his two daughters and was too stubborn to die until—" Belle clamped off her comments. "I best get back to work. When you want us to show you where you will sleep, you pull that bell rope. Someone will come."

"All right. Thank you." While Ruby knew she was thanking this woman for more than showing them up the stairs, the memory of that degrading experience faded with the urgency of the moment.

But the way Belle turned on her heel with a huff said she thought she was being dismissed. Her high-heeled shoes snapped their comments too as she flounced out the door.

Too tired to try to repair the misunderstanding at the

moment, Ruby let her go. When Opal peeked around the corner wall, Ruby beckoned her over and curved an arm around her.

"Far, this is Opal."

His eyes fluttered open, and he stared at them both, his gaze more clear than it had been up to that moment. "Pictures . . . of . . . your . . . mother." His hand gripped Ruby's with more force than she thought he had in him. "Come . . . closer."

Ruby motioned for Opal to sit on the edge of the bed and laid her hand in her father's. "You can talk with him," she whispered in Opal's ear.

"Papá?"

A smile twitched the fine skin around his mouth. "Far."

"Yes, Far." Ruby nodded for Opal to use the Norwegian word rather than the French.

"Far."

"Tell him something you like." Another whisper.

"I liked the train ride. Thank you."

"You . . . came . . . a . . . long way."

"Yes, from New York City." Opal studied the face so dimly lit but stark in its whiteness. She cleared her throat, cast an imploring glance at her sister, and asked, "Are you really my father? Did I ever see you?"

Ruby inhaled a gulp and coughed accordingly. "Opal." Her hiss was meant for little ears alone, but Far smiled—if the grimace that stretched his mouth to the sides could really be called a smile.

His gaze drilled into Opal's. "Yes, I am your far." He spoke with more strength than at any moment since they'd entered the room.

Opal nodded. The silence stretched, broken only when Far coughed, a dry hacking sound that grated on Ruby's ears.

"Then why did you never come for us?"

Opal's question made Ruby stifle a gasp. Her hand tightened on Opal's shoulder. Leave it to her to cut right to the bone.

Far stared into his younger daughter's eyes, and she returned the favor.

"I . . . wish . . . I had. But the frontier was no place . . ." He paused and coughed again. His voice when it came was weaker. "For my treasures."

But you brought us here now. Why? What kind of inheritance did we come all this way for? Why didn't you just send it in the mail?

But Ruby knew they would have come anyway, even had there been no promise of an inheritance, even if she had to buy their tickets. Yes, she would have come anyway. Just to see her father one last time. Although the man in the bed bore little resemblance to the man she remembered, the man she had adored and all her life wished Opal had known like she did.

"Turn up the lights." His whisper made Ruby draw closer to the bed.

"The lights?"

He nodded.

She went to turn up the wick on the lamp and saw a packet of spills on the dresser by the base. Taking one, she stuck the dry slender stick down the lamp chimney and, once it was lit, crossed back to lift the chimney and light another lamp on the small chest nearer to the bed.

"That better?"

"Yes." He patted the bed beside him, and Opal sat, her stockinged legs hanging over the edge. "Your trip, tell me."

While Opal recited their adventures, Ruby glanced around the now more visible room. Women's dresses hung in the chifforobe, unmentionables draped over the doors, the exotic three-paneled screen across the corner, and puddled on the floor. His wife certainly was not a good housekeeper. So where was his wife? Was he married to Belle? The thought sent a shiver through her. How could he marry someone like her after having loved Mor? The two were as different as the moon and the sea. Her mother had been a lady in the gentlest and finest of terms, and Belle? Ruby refused to allow that thought to continue and went back to studying the room. Two tall windows would let in air if they weren't so heavily shrouded by floor-length red velvet drapes. Gold tasseled cords hung ready to pull them back. She tuned back to what Opal was saying.

"I can read and write. Ruby is a very good teacher. She could make even Jason want to do his lessons."

"Jason?"

"He is the oldest Brandon son. Bernie is the baby."

"When. . . ?" Per shifted his gaze from Opal to Ruby.

"We moved to the Brandons' when Bestemor died five years ago. I wrote you that. Did you never get my letters?"

"Some . . . not that."

"I needed to work, and they allowed me to keep Opal with me. We have been well cared for and happy there." *And wish we had remained there instead of coming on this wild trip to . . .* She cut that thought off and sank down on the bed. Standing was suddenly more than she could manage. Tired or weary did not begin to describe the fatigue that pulled at her bones, the despair that dragged at her heart. Surely there was no way this man could regain his health. With every slow breath, she doubted he would take another. But he'd held on this long, so who was she to question the ways of almighty God. Surely He had a reason for bringing them out from their comfortable home to this land of . . . of what? She'd know more in the daylight, but the memory of doors slamming in their faces did not elicit a sense of joy about the inhabitants of the town.

A burst of male laughter from down the hall caught her attention.

"Ruby."

"Yes, Far." She ignored the ruckus in the hall and bent closer to her father.

"The medicine . . . there on the stand . . ."

"This brown bottle?"

"Yes."

"Two." Two fingers on the hand that had been holding Opal's spread in indication.

"Two." Ruby looked for something to measure with and located a large silver spoon. "This?" She held it up and at his nod pulled the cork out of the bottle and poured a spoonful. She held one to his mouth and then the second.

"A drink."

She looked around for a water pitcher but saw only a crystal decanter with caramel-colored liquid—liquor. She touched a finger to the crystal stopper. "This?"

He nodded.

"Is there no water?"

His wrinkled nose told her what he thought of that idea.

She poured a minuscule portion into a cup standing by and held it to his mouth.

Per inhaled, closing his eyes as if to make it last longer, then downed the draught, expelling his breath on a long sigh. He lay still for a long moment, then said, "Envelope."

"Our letter?" This guessing game was getting old quickly.

He shook his head and pointed toward a chest of drawers against the far wall. All the drawers were closed, silver-backed hair brushes and a comb lay on a silver tray that graced the top.

"Second drawer."

"For whom?"

He pointed at each of them, his eyes fighting to close.

Ruby crossed the room and pulled out the second drawer. Only neatly folded piles of men's underthings filled the drawer. Feeling like an intruder, she felt beneath them. Nothing. But he'd said it was here. Perhaps he was confused. After all, taking pain-killing medicine followed by a shot of whiskey would mix up anyone's mind, let alone someone as ill as he. But instead of returning to the bed, she felt along the sides and the back of the drawer. Sure enough, the crinkle of paper. The fat envelope she pulled out was addressed to the Misses Ruby and Opal Torvald.

She brought it back to the bed, only to find him sound asleep with Opal curled up like a kitten at his side, sleeping like the innocent she was, her father's hand still resting on her head.

Ruby leaned over to kiss his forehead, something he used to do for her every night when he'd been home to tuck her into bed. His eyes fluttered open.

"Take . . . care . . . of . . . the . . . girls." He grasped her hand.

"I always do." *Who does he think has been taking care of Opal all these years, and I learned early how to take care of myself.*

"The girls, take care of the girls." He strained to add emphasis to his words.

"Yes, Far, you rest now, and we'll talk again in the morning."

"Promise?"

"Yes, of course."

"Good. I . . . I . . ." He looked directly into her eyes, as if searching her soul. "I love you, datter."

"I know and I love you."

"For . . . give . . . me." The words were barely discernable, as if he'd used his last ounce of will. He mumbled something that she leaned closer to hear. "*Buksbom*. See . . . the . . . buksbom treasures."

"Yes, I forgive you." But she wasn't sure if he heard her or not, for a slight snore puffed his lips. And had she heard right? Buksbom. What did that mean? She thought hard for a moment. Oh, that was the word for box. Box? What box, and what treasures?

She sat in the chair she brought over from the desk and watched them both sleep, fighting the weariness that descended upon her, weighting her down in the chair as if her bones had turned to mush. As she felt her eyes close, she heard the tapping of high-heeled shoes in the hall, and Belle entered the room.

"How is he?"

"Sleeping again." She watched as Belle laid the back of her hand along his cheek, then adjusted the sheet, smoothing it across the once broad chest. "Did he talk with you?"

"Yes, although strained."

"Good. He wanted to." Belle turned. "If you bring your sister, I will show you to your room. Do you have any more baggage than that?"

"A trunk and boxes down at the train stop." Ruby pushed herself to her feet, not sure for a moment if she would make it.

"I'll send Charlie down for them first thing in the morning." Belle picked up the two valises. "Come along."

Guiding Opal with one hand and carrying the remainder of their things with the other, Ruby followed Belle down a hall that seemed to lengthen as they walked. Would they never reach the end?

"Here, this one is yours. You better not go wandering around in the night. There's a pot under the bed."

"Where is the bathroom?"

Belle snorted. "The outhouse is out back. We haul in a tub for bathing. Anything else?"

Pot? Outhouse? Ruby's mind refused to function. "You will call me if my father needs me?"

Belle planted her hands on well padded hips. "Look, I been taking care of him for months now. I can make do another night."

"Oh. Of course." Ruby rubbed her forehead with weak fingers, too tired to argue. "Thank you, then, and good night."

Belle left with a nod that seemed curt rather than courteous.

Ruby turned to find Opal flopped on the bed. She pulled a nightdress out of the valise and, after undressing her sister, settled the garment over her head. Folding back the cover, she rolled Opal over to the side and tucked her in.

Once in her own nightclothes Ruby belted her wrapper and crossed to the draped window. While this room was sparsely furnished compared to her father's, the drapes kept out the cold. She parted them to look outside into total blackness. It was never this dark in New York City, where gaslights lined the streets, and even with a foot of snow on the ground, the streets of New York were never this silent. The only sound she heard came from the saloon downstairs, and even that was muted. Dark, quiet, what else had she to learn of Dakota Territory? She cupped her hand around the glass chimney on the lamp and blew out the flame. The acrid smell of smoke followed her as she climbed into bed and snuggled under the quilt. Sleep overtook her before she had time to adjust the pillow or say her nightly prayers.

Something pulled her awake from a deep sleep. Had someone called her name? It seemed so. But Opal breathed the gentle sleep of a child. She had not called.

A cry rent the night air. Ruby threw back the covers, snatched her wrapper, and headed for the door, stumbling in the blackness.

CHAPTER SEVEN

"My father! Is it my father?" Ruby met a strange young woman in the hall.

"I'm 'feared so. 'Twas Belle what cried out." The two rushed on down the hall, and Ruby entered the room first.

Belle knelt beside the bed, her head resting on Per's hand as it lay at his side. He looked only as if he'd fallen asleep and was resting peacefully.

Belle's sobs rocked her entire body. She reached with one hand to caress his cheek, then glanced up when she sensed Ruby beside her. "I . . . I didn't get to tell him g-good-bye." Black trails of kohl streaked her cheeks, and her hair hung in loops. The combs that had been holding it piled high on her head now dragged and drooped. She'd changed from her fancy dress to a wrapper, belted loosely over her corset and camisole.

Ruby ordered her attention away from the sobbing woman and onto her father. She didn't need to listen for his breathing. She could tell he was gone by the immobile way he lay. Even when sleeping, he had been moving, an eye twitch, a hand restless on the quilt.

Ruby closed her eyes and thought back. One of the things that stood out in her memories of her father was his energy, a force of life that picked up those around him and swirled them along with him. Even as ill as he'd been earlier this evening, that force had caught her, both her and Opal, and had made her love him all over again.

And now he was gone. *Lord, will I see him again in heaven?* The thought snagged at her breath. Surely her father knew the Savior. Hadn't he gone to church with them, nay, *taken* wife and daughter to worship on Sundays?

But if he believed, how could he have deserted us like he did? She caught the change in her thinking. Rarely had she used the word deserted, instead she had made herself think of him as leaving them, but only for a time. She had told herself that any day he would come striding and laughing back into their lives. She'd hoped he'd come and make Opal love him as she once had, by tossing the little girl in the air, telling her stories about a tiny girl named Opal who could live in his pocket: A tiny playmate who loved secrets and giggles and who would sneak over into her pocket if she wanted.

Ruby almost checked her own pocket to see if that tiny Ruby of long ago still lived there.

Tears rained unchecked as she thought back, wishing for what might have been but now had no chance of becoming. Their tie with him had made her hope grow again.

But now all was lost.

She laid a hand on Belle's shoulder. While she didn't like her much, Ruby recognized grief and realized that Belle had loved Per.

How fortunate you were, Far, to be loved by three women, your two wives and me. Opal, too, would have loved you had she known you.

Ruby turned to see two women, also in wrappers, and a man who looked to have risen from bed as a result of the crying. Perhaps he was the man she'd seen behind the counter in the saloon downstairs. Her quick glance at the premises when she followed Belle up the stairs seemed burned on the back of her mind. Had one of these women been playing the piano?

If the amount of tears was any indicator of the esteem these people had held for her father, he was deeply loved. But who would be in charge now? Was it her duty to take responsibility for getting her father buried? Surely, as his wife, that duty belonged to Belle. But grief affected some people so as to make them ineffective, like Per when his wife died. Was Belle like that? Somehow it didn't seem to fit the picture she'd formed of Belle.

She glanced back to find the others staring at her, not at Belle, but at her. She wiped her eyes with the pads of her fingers and took in a deep breath.

Letting it out, she straightened neck and shoulders and began. "It seems to me that, since there is nothing to be done here tonight, we should all return to bed and see to things in the morning. I . . . I . . ." She rolled her eyes upward to stem a new onslaught of tears. "I thank you all on my father's behalf for . . . for your friendship and . . ." *Did you all work for my father or were you his friends?* Who could she ask the many questions bubbling just below the surface of her mind?

The older of the two women came and put an arm around Belle's shoulders. "You come and spend the night in my room, honey."

Belle melted into her arms, and between the two of them, the women got her on her feet and out the door.

Ruby breathed a sigh of relief at the silence that grew as the others moved farther down the hall.

"What do you want I should do, miss?"

"I wish I knew. What is your name?"

"I'm Charlie, miss. Charlie Higgins. I tend bar and do whatever else needs doin'. Me and Per go back a long way." He took a few steps closer to the bed. "He been holdin' on just for you. Said he wanted to see his girls before he took the train to glory. Good thing you come when you did."

"He's been sick a long time." Just looking at the skin-wrapped bones that had once been a vibrant man told her that.

"I knew he was ailin' long before he told us."

"I see." While the thought of pumping this man for information since he seemed willing to talk was a strong one, her need for sleep won out. "Thank you for talking with me, but I'd best return to my room before Opal wakes up and becomes frightened in a strange place. I'm sure I will have many questions in the morning."

"Yes, miss." Charlie leaned over and pulled the sheet up over her father's face. "Rest in peace, my friend." His voice choked, and he turned away to blow his nose. Finished, he motioned for

Ruby to precede him out of the room, blew out the lamp, and shut the door behind himself.

"Thank you again." Ruby nodded and made her way down the hall. She could hear two women talking behind one door on the way down and assumed it to be Belle and . . . She shook her head. How rude not to have asked for their names, to have introduced herself. But then, they all knew who she and Opal were if Per had talked about them, as it seemed he had from her conversation with Mr. Higgins.

After nudging Opal over to her own side, Ruby climbed back in bed, certain that she would lie awake wondering about the group of people she'd met here at Dove House, about her father and the life he'd lived since he came west, about when she and Opal could return to New York and their life with the Brandons. Instead, she remembered no more of her prayer than "Please, God."

She awoke with the same thought, but "Please, God," what? And where was Opal? Throwing the covers back, Ruby dressed more quickly than she ever thought possible, bundled her hair into a snood, and rushed out the door.

The empty hall stretched dark but for the windows at either end. All the doors were closed, and she heard no sound. Surely others were up and about, not just Opal. Gray clouds obliterated the sun that surely must have been up for hours. It felt like midmorning. How had she ever slept so late?

As she drew closer to her father's room, she could hear someone moving around in there, opening and closing cupboards and drawers. She knocked, waiting for a response, and when the noise didn't abate, she pushed open the door. Belle, wrapper-clad and with hair flying every which way, was searching for something. Clothing dangled from half-open drawers, as if the searcher was in too much of a hurry to put everything back—or didn't care.

Ruby cleared her throat. "May I help you?" She glanced over to see her father's body lying where they'd left it.

Belle spun and took a step back, hand to her throat. "You 'bout scared the wits right outa me."

"I'm sorry. I was looking for Opal and heard someone in

here. I could help you look for whatever it is you are not find-ing."

"What I'm looking for is none of your business."

The snarl caught Ruby totally by surprise. "Pardon me." She kept her voice even with effort. "I just thought to be helpful."

"Best help you can do is get back on that train and head east to whatever life you lived before . . . before . . ." Belle glanced at the bed and dissolved into a sobbing, grief-stricken woman. She sank down into a chair, crushing the pile of petticoats that had been thrown there.

Ruby fought the tears brought on by seeing Belle's. "I have to go find Opal." She left the weeping woman and, resisting the urge to open every door along the hall, made her way down the stairs. Windows covered by thick drapes left a gloom broken only by slivers of light from around the curtains and from two open doorways. The saloon reeked of cigar smoke, spilled liquor, and cheap perfume. She wished for a handkerchief dipped in rose water to hold to her nose. The miasma hung thick enough to chew. She followed the light and a tinkle of sound down a painted hallway that opened into a kitchen where Charlie pre-sided over a cast-iron stove that was providing both welcome warmth and the aroma of frying ham.

Ruby's stomach rumbled in anticipation.

"Opal Marie Torvald, you scared me out of two years' growth." Ruby rounded on her little sister who was sitting at the table, spooning applesauce.

"But you were sound asleep, and I didn't want to wake you. You looked terrible tired." She smiled at the man who grinned back. "Charlie asked if I was hungry and I sure was and you say not to lie and so I didn't and he said he would make me some-thing to eat and so I came down here and. . ." She took a deep breath, and her smile grew beatific as she finished. "And you found me and so all is well." She sucked the sauce off her spoon. "Charlie is a real good cook too."

"Mr. Higgins. You call him Mr. Higgins."

"But when I asked him his name, he said Charlie, that I was to call him Charlie and I like that, so I did."

Ruby felt like taking a step back before the wall of words pummeled her.

"I did tell her that, Miss. No one ever calls me Mr. Higgins." He hefted a cast-iron skillet. "You want some ham and eggs? They be ready in a jiffy. You could start with applesauce like Miss Opal there."

Ruby sank down on a chair and nodded. "Yes, I'd love some breakfast. Is there something I can do to help you?"

"Help me? Why whatever for? Per, he would take a hunk outa my hide if I didn't take good care of his darlin' daughters."

Ruby thought back to the conversation with this man the night before. He'd said he did whatever needed doing, and obviously at this time of the day, putting food on the table fell under his jurisdiction.

"Do you cook for the hotel guests also?"

"Hotel guests?" Confusion darkened his already deep brown eyes even further.

"You know, the people who stay here?"

"Oh, you mean the girls? They don't usually want breakfast, you know. They pretty much sleep until noon. We don't open again until about two. Then there's Milly. She does the laundry. You got anything that needs washing, she's out back."

Take care of the girls. Her father's words echoed those of Charlie Higgins. Why did she feel as though she'd come in on the second act of a play and everyone else knew the lines but her?

"Here you go." Charlie slid a slice of ham and two fried eggs onto the plate in front of her, then did the same for Opal. "Hot biscuits coming right up." He returned to the stove, drew a pan of biscuits from the oven, brought it over, and set it on the battle-scarred pine tabletop. "There's butter and jam here and honey in the jar there." He pointed to a squat round jar filled with gold. "Can I get you anything else?"

"Coffee, please?" Right now her system needed a dose of something strong and hot.

"I'm sorry. Shoulda brought that first. Your father always wanted his coffee first too. Said it got the juices flowin' in the morning. Not that he was an early riser either."

Pleased on one hand that she had something in common with her father and sad on the other since he was no longer with them, Ruby laid a hand on Opal's arm. "Did you say grace?"

Opal laid her fork back down. "No, sorry."

"Well, just because we are living on the frontier now, doesn't mean that we will change the things we know to be proper. Is that understood?"

"I guess." Opal bowed her head. "Thank thee, Lord, for these gifts which we are about to receive, for food and strength to do thy will. Amen." While hurried, the words could be understood if one listened with intense concentration.

Ruby glanced up to see a look of confusion on Charlie's lined face. The light in his eyes and friendly smile beneath his brushy mustache made her feel she might have a friend in this world. And he had helped her during the night and was now treating young Opal like a princess. Who and what was this man?

"I'll take care of the boss when we're done here. The others most likely won't be up yet."

"Belle is. I saw her tearing the bedroom apart, looking for something, I presume."

He stopped and turned, holding a pancake turner in the air. "How'd she seem?"

Ruby paused before answering. A strange question. She thought back to the scene in the bedroom where Belle had had no respect for the dead man and then torrents of grief. "Undone, I believe." Snappy, she'd been, before the tears. But what would she know? How many people had she ever known who'd just lost someone they loved?

"Had they been married long?"

Charlie spun around. "Married? Who?"

"Why my father and Belle. I assumed—" She stopped at the look of consternation that made his mustache twitch. She glanced over at Opal who was taking in every nuance while eating healthy bites of eggs and ham.

"We will talk of this later."

"Ah yes. Good idea. Can I get you more to eat?"

Ruby stared down at her half-finished plate, wondering where her appetite had suddenly disappeared to. She finished off a biscuit that now needed dunking in her coffee, its dryness making swallowing difficult. Or was it her throat that was dry? She drank several swallows to alleviate the distress. What was going on here? The saloon was bad enough, but undercurrents seemed far more dangerous than the serving of liquor and men playing cards. Why, Mr. Brandon had sometimes gone to his club for the same pleasures. Were things any different here on the frontier?

"Will you contact the minister then for the funeral?"

"Minister? Funeral?" Charlie's eyebrows joined the twitching of mustaches.

"We are going to bury my father, are we not?"

"Ah yes. I'll get someone to dig the hole over in the graveyard. Then whoever wants can say some words over him. That's about all we do out here. And put some big stones on top so the wild critters don't drag 'im off."

Ruby schooled her face to keep from the grimacing and shuddering that threatened to overcome her. "There is no man of God to . . . to conduct a proper burial, then?"

"No. Sorry. We do the best we can." Charlie wiped his hands on the dish towel he had tied around his middle, untied it, and tossed the stained article on the back of a chair.

"I'll be back." He took his bowler hat off the peg on the wall by the door. "Oh, and I would stay out of Belle's way for a while."

Ruby didn't bother to ask why, certain she really didn't want to know the answer.

— ✥ —

The more copious Belle's tears as they laid Per in his grave, wrapped only in a blanket, no box having been made, the drier Ruby's eyes grew. Opal clutched her hand, bonding herself to her sister's side.

Other than those from Dove House, only men joined with the mourners. One of them was the grave digger, who leaned on his shovel handle and waited for them to leave so he could finish his job. Others wore the blue uniforms of the U.S. Army, one in full dress, including shiny gold buttons and a saber at his side. Some men looked as if they'd been dragged through a dirt bank.

Charlie took off his hat. "Per Torvald was a good man, he took care of his own and reached out a helping hand to those around him."

Took care of his own? Ruby kept her eyes straight forward. *What about us?* Across the mound of dirt rose a hill striped in the wildest colors she'd ever seen, most of which she would not normally apply to dirt or rock. Tan, dark brown, gray, purple, and a shading from orange to red that usually one saw only in a sunset. The cliff rose straight up as if someone had carved it out with a gigantic cake knife. Rocks at the bottom attested to continual change, unless they had been there for millennia. What kind of world had they come to? The train trestle stretched back across the river, a sign that man had indeed arrived and put his stamp on the land. Ruby planned to put that trestle to use as soon as possible, heading east.

"You got anything you want to say, miss?" Charlie's voice cut into her reverie.

"Ah no, I don't think so." She bit down on her quivering lower lip, almost losing her control when she heard Opal sniff and whimper.

"Belle?"

Belle removed her soaked handkerchief only long enough to shake her head.

"I do." An army officer stepped forward, his voice as commanding as his uniform. "Per Torvald was a good friend. His building of Dove House has been good for the town. He had a friendly smile for everyone, and if someone was in need, Per would be the first to offer assistance. We will miss him. Rest in peace, my friend."

"Anyone else?" With no other volunteers, Charlie nodded to the man with the shovel, shepherded the women in front of him, and headed back toward Dove House.

"Whether they came to the buryin' or not, they'll show up for the wake," Charlie offered.

"The wake?" They used so many terms that she did not understand.

"We'll be servin' drinks on the house."

"Why?"

"In honor of Per Torvald. As you heard, he has friends here."

Ruby glanced down to see Opal's chin quivering. Knowing how her little sister hated to have anyone see her cry, Ruby picked up the pace, and instead of going in the front door like the others, she took Opal around to the back. Once they were in their room, she held her little sister until her sobs subsided.

"H-how c-come we finally get to meet our f-father, and he goes and d-d-dies?"

"I wish I knew, dear one. I wish I knew." Ruby stroked the damp hair back from Opal's face. "But I'm glad you were able to meet him and talk with him. Now when I tell you stories of life when I was a little girl, you will know whom I am talking about." *Lord, I hope she doesn't always remember that skeleton in the bed. Our father was so handsome when he was younger and in good health.*

"What are we going to do?" Opal asked when she finally quit crying.

"Go down to the kitchen and prepare us some dinner, I expect." Ruby went to the window and stood overlooking what could barely be called a street. At least the dirt track between the scattered buildings had none of the silver gray bushes that covered the rest of the land. Every once in a while men would ride up, get off their horses, and enter the saloon. Mostly they wore flat-brimmed hats and leather gloves. Some wore long coats open halfway up the back so it would split when they sat on their horses.

A faint sun tried to scare off the clouds, but the wind that kicked up just moved more in. The wind sneaked in around the ill-fitting window frame, causing Ruby to cup her elbows in her hand and wish for a shawl. Mostly she wished for the newly leafed out trees that bordered the streets of New York, the wagons, buggies, and carriages that clattered by on the cobblestones, the huge houses set back from those streets and fronted by green grass and bulbs already blooming through the neatly tended soil. She would take the children to the park to swing or watch a ball game. She closed her eyes to remember better times, and when she opened them, she nearly cried.

Now then, she ordered herself, *there will be no more weeping here. You will learn what your inheritance is, take it, and be gone. You will be back in New York before the month is out. So think how Mrs. Brandon would act and do the same.*

Opal came to stand beside her. "Everyone has a horse here." She looked up at her sister. "I sure hope there is a horse here for me."

"Opal, we can't stay. As soon as I find out what our inheritance is, we are taking the next train east."

"Oh." Opal sighed a huge sigh that took in her entire body. She stared at the floor, her brows knit in thought, her chin starting to jut out. But when she looked up at Ruby, a smile sent the jaw back and unknit the brows. "Maybe I can ride a horse while we are here. I'm going to ask Mr. Charlie." The door slammed behind her before Ruby could do more than stutter.

"His name is Mr. Higgins!" Ruby called after her. Hand on the knob, she stopped, took a deep breath, thought of Mrs. Brandon and, chin lifted, back straight, soft smile in place, opened, passed through, and closed the door gently behind her. When she reached the end of the hall, she turned left toward the back staircase, since the loud music, laughter, and clinking of glasses told the tale of what was happening at the wake in the saloon below her. Smoke drifted up the stairs.

"Hey, little girl, what you doin' on these stairs?"

Opal. She'd not gone down to the kitchen after all. Ruby whirled around in time to see one of the women she'd seen at the graveyard coming up the stairs, a man right behind her.

"I was . . ." Opal had no time to finish her comment before she was snatched by the shoulder of her pinafore and almost dragged up the three stairs.

"Opal Marie Torvald, you come with me *now.*" Ruby hissed the words, kept her eyes from those of the other woman, and hustled her sister toward the backstairs.

"But, Ruby, I wasn't doing anything wrong."

"You were to go to the kitchen."

"But—"

"And we are going to the kitchen now, and you will not look down into that den of—that room again. That is no place for women."

"But Belle and the others are there, and—"

"March." Ruby clamped her lips together and placed her hand on Opal's shoulder.

They'd just finished eating their meat and cheese sandwiches when the door swung open and Charlie stepped inside.

"I'm hating to bother you, miss, but did your father give you an envelope?"

Ruby finished chewing the food in her mouth before replying, "Yes, why?" *Actually, he gave me two.* "Belle gave it to me."

"Well, you remember you said you saw Belle tearing the bedroom apart and seemed to be looking for something?"

"Yes."

"Well, perhaps it was another envelope. You read Per's letter she gave you yet?"

"No. But it is here in my pocket."

"Ah, good. I think you better read it and do whatever it says before you go to sleep tonight."

"But—"

"Miss, we ain't got no law here in Little Missouri, but we try to do what is right. At least some of us. So, please, listen to what I say and—"

"You are saying Belle would—"

He held up a hand. "I didn't say nothing, you understand. But please . . ."

Ruby nodded. "I will. You want to come back in a bit and—"

"No. Just do what it says."

Ruby and Opal exchanged confused glances after Charlie slipped out as quietly as he slipped in.

Ruby felt the crackle of paper from both envelopes in her pocket. Whatever could be so important as to cause consternation like this? And no law officers? What kind of man had their father been to have brought them to a land so wild? Whatever had he been thinking?

CHAPTER EIGHT

My dearest Treasures,

If you are reading this, either you made it to Little Missouri before I died and I gave it to you, or Belle lived up to her word and mailed it. Knowing Belle as I do makes me seriously doubt it was the latter. I couldn't wait any longer to write this, as my strength has been fading each day. Forgive me that my handwriting looks like that of an old man. Each day I feel older, and the pain is no longer tolerable, so I take the morphine when I can no longer stand the pain without screaming. But then I sleep all the time. Nothing kills that which is eating at me.

I know you must be shocked at what you found here, but Dove House is a thriving business. There are always military men, railroad men, and cattlemen who appreciate a good drink and an evening's entertainment. We don't serve rotgut like Williams does up the street. I heard he uses old cigar butts, sulphuric acid, and firewater. Amazing the men don't die from it.

I know this isn't the kind of business a young woman of your sensibilities should be running, Ruby, but short of selling out and sending you the money, there was nothing left for me to do. I plumb ran out of time.

The second sheet is the deed to this place, made out to you and signed by me while folks could still read my signature. More folks will be moving west, and these rich bottom lands will become settled. Dove House is well built and will make a fine hotel.

I do ask, though, that you take care of the girls. Belle will most likely try to take this from you. That is why I have transferred this title legally. But the other girls need a break. Life hasn't been kind to them.

Charlie will be a big help to you, a kinder man I've yet to meet. There are some scoundrels here in town but also some fine men and a few women.

I had hoped to leave Dove House to you free and clear, but there are some accounts that need to be settled. The business ledgers are in my room. Charlie has what cash we take in, and there is an emergency stash taped to the back of the second drawer in the tall chest and, of course, what is in the box. Charlie will explain how we run the business here.

God bless you both, my dear daughters. I know I don't deserve it, but thanks to Jesus I am going home soon to see my beloved Signe.

Your Far,
Per Torvald

Ruby wiped her eyes with the edge of her apron. If only she had taken the time to read this while he was still alive.

"Is it bad?" Opal stared at her sister with sorrow-filled eyes.

"No, really it is very good. Far has deeded Dove House to us."

"So we will stay here?"

"Until we sell Dove House."

"Who will buy it?"

"I don't know." Ruby read the letter again. *Take care of the girls.* He'd extracted that promise from her before he died. Why would she have to take care of the girls, and what had happened in their lives that made him request that of her? After returning the slim envelope to her pocket, she removed the other—it was Far's last will and testament. She sucked in a gasp and quickly put it back in her pocket. Where would she keep it?

Feeling she had more questions than answers, she washed up their few dishes and set the kettle on the stove to heat water for tea. Thanks to Mrs. Klaus's provision she could at least enjoy a good cup of tea. But maybe there was tea in the storeroom. Did people drink tea out here in the West?

With her cup in hand, she and Opal made their way back to the room they'd first entered upon their arrival at the hotel. Raucous laughter and the song of a hard-used piano played a backdrop all the time, sometimes swelling louder, then almost quiet but never silent.

They set a kerosene lamp on a table in the middle of the room and, starting in the right-hand corner, set to exploring. They found whiskey, sugar, flour, other staples, more bottles with corks, a box of glasses, one of candles, two broken-down chairs, and boxes that she didn't take time to look in.

Opal dusted off her hands. "Dirty, that's for sure. Mrs. Brandon would make us all help clean this place like she did the attic, but I still don't think cleaning up a mess builds character."

"Be that as it may, we will be cleaning so we know what is here and what we need. Come on. Right now we need to look upstairs." Together they mounted the backstairs, and when Opal glanced with longing at the other stairs that led down to the saloon, Ruby steered her on around the corner and down the hall.

The door to her father's room was closed, so she tapped on it before entering.

"What a mess." Opal stared around the room. "Doesn't she know how to put her things away?"

"I think Belle was distraught." Ruby remembered the look on her father's face when her mother died, like the life had gone right out of him. But then, as Mrs. Brandon once said, grief attacks some folks differently than others.

"Let's try to be real nice to Belle, help her through her grieving."

"I guess." Opal fingered an ostrich feather that curved over the center of the three-paneled screen. "I don't think Belle likes us much."

Ruby pulled out the second drawer of the tall chest drawer and felt under it. Nothing. But when she pulled the drawer all the way out and felt behind it, sure enough, there was another envelope there. She quickly pulled it loose and stuck it in her pocket, ever mindful that Belle could come in any minute. She quickly looked around to determine where the ledgers might be stored. No matter that this was her father's room, she felt like a sneaky thief. Should she take her father's things out of the room? No, that was a wife's duty. Wasn't it? *Should I be kind and clean up the mess?* She sighed.

Yes, they should be kind. After all, Belle had taken care of their father. But she was Per's wife, wasn't she? So of course she should have taken care of him.

The thoughts dove and zipped around her mind like bees on the attack.

Far as she knew, Belle had not slept in here since Per's death. So . . .

"Help me fold these things and put them away. Then we'll scrub the bed and remake it if Milly has the laundry done."

"I saw her take stuff out back where there's a big pot on a fire. You think we have to wash our clothes that way?" Opal stroked the underthings she was folding. "These sure feel pretty."

"Humph. You hang up the dresses, and I'll do that. Put them in that armoire."

"But Papa's clothes are in here. How come they have such fancy clothes?"

"I . . . I don't know." Ruby lifted a pile of drawers, camisoles, and petticoats off the top of the screens. Who'd ever heard of unmentionables being black silk? With so much lace they had a life of their own. And that life did not want to be imprisoned in the remaining drawer space. She smashed the rioting masses down and slammed the drawer.

"There aren't enough hangers."

"Then put the remainder on hooks." Ruby stared around the room, looking for a row of pegs or hooks along the walls. "There must be some in the armoire."

"I can't even see in there."

Ruby made a sound of disgust or frustration, the two emotions being so intertwined it was hard to tell the difference, and joined her little sister in front of the carved walnut doors that hung wide open and looked to never making it closed.

"See?"

Ruby huffed a sigh. "You sure Far's clothes are in there?"

"In the back."

"If we push them in, they'll be all wrinkled." Visions of the closet space at the Brandons' shot her with a pang of homesickness. She fingered a wine watered-silk dress and frowned at the stains along the hem and the lace at the sleeve hanging loose. Belle might have beautiful things, but they wouldn't last long without better care.

"What won't fit in there we will leave draped over the screen. At least things look tidier." Her gaze kept returning to the bed where her father had drawn his last breath. How long had he been bedridden? She followed an urge to draw back the velvet drapes and open the windows. This room needed a good airing. The rugs begged for a beating and the floor a scrubbing. Near as she could tell, the entire place needed housecleaning from top to bottom. Who would do that?

Milly, the chambermaid, looked to have her hands full already. Ruby stared down at her own, fingers spread. Capable hands, she had always called them, with fingers squared off, palms broad, not lovely and tapered like her mother's, but with a notable lack of calluses.

"Aren't we done now?"

"I guess so." They made for the doorway only to meet Belle coming in.

"What are you doing in my room?" Belle, hands on hips, arms akimbo, took up the doorway.

"Cleaning it up some, looking for the ledgers Father said were here." She laid a hand on Opal's shoulder to keep her quiet.

"How do you know—" Belle cut off her sentence. She took a step forward, her eyes slitting. "I'm telling you only once, stay out of my things."

"We were only trying to—"

Ruby tightened the hand on her sister's shoulder, cutting off her words. "If you will tell me then where the ledgers are."

"Don't know. Suppose Charlie has 'em."

"I see."

"How'd you know about the ledgers?"

"My father's letter."

"Oh." Belle slumped slightly, then gathered herself for the attack. "You two better be thinkin' on leavin' soon. After all, this is my place now, and I got no truck for freeloaders."

"But, Ruby. . . ." Opal stopped at the look on her sister's face and the pinch at her shoulder.

Ruby wanted to duck and run. But instead she pulled herself up by sheer will. "I will read my Father's final letter to everyone this evening."

"No way can we close the doors this evening, nor any evening. Men around here expect Dove House to be open for business, and open it will be."

"Surely they can go without drinking for one night."

"Honey, it ain't only the drinkin' that pays the bills here."

"But there are no meals—"

" 'Course not. We got the best doves in the county. That's what brings the men in."

"Doves?"

"You know, us workin' girls. You're welcome to join us." Belle's laugh hooted her derision. "Dress you up in some color, you might not look too bad." She reached over and fingered Ruby's cream waist with leg of mutton sleeves. "Not this drab—"

Ruby jerked back as if stung by a wasp. "I've been working all my life, or most of it, and . . ."

She slowed to a stop when Belle burst out laughing as if she'd just heard the funniest joke of her life. She waved to a man coming out of the room across the hall.

If Ruby remembered right, that was the room belonging to Cimarron, the redhead. Whatever was he doing in her room?

"See here, Slade, these two youngsters are Per's daughters. You think the older there could be a workin' gal?"

He finished tucking his shirt into his pants as he studied Ruby.

Ruby wanted to clap her hands over Opal's ears and eyes and hustle them both from his scrutiny. She'd read once how men inspected the slaves in the south before they bought one. Right now she was sure she knew how they felt.

"Ah, Belle, honey, she most likely could if'n you took her under your wing and made a real woman out of her." He dodged the elbow Belle aimed at his ribs and ambled on down the hall, his laughter floating over his shoulder.

"We shall discuss this later." Ruby glanced down at Opal,

who had yet to close her mouth, and back to Belle, hoping her sister got the message.

"Anytime, honey. Anytime."

Why did the glint in Belle's eyes make her doubt the sweetness of her words? Honey. Cloying sweetness but made by bees with a real sting. What had her father said about Belle's principles?

"I better get on back to work. Someone needs to start dealing down there before a fight breaks out. Hard collecting for the broke-up tables and chairs and such when a brawl cuts loose."

Ruby snapped her mouth closed. "They have brawls in Dove House? Down there?" Ruby clamped her hands on Opal's shoulder. "Excuse us, please." She'd mind her manners no matter what.

"Of course." Belle stepped aside to let them pass and chuckled as she entered her room.

"What was she talking about, Ruby?" Opal plopped down on the edge of their bed. "I really don't think she likes us at all." She rubbed her chin with one finger, a motion Ruby remembered their father doing. "But then, I don't think I like her much either. Charlie is nice and so is Cimarron."

"How do you know that?"

Opal shrugged.

"Opal . . ."

A crash sent them both running to the window to see a man take a header from the porch of Dove House and out into the street. He lay in the muddy ruts for what seemed like forever.

"You think he's dead?"

The young girl headed for the door. Ruby missed Opal's shoulder, but caught her pinafore. "No, Opal, you may not go down and check his mustache. Stay right here."

"But, Ruby, I . . ." Opal's lower lip stuck out, but she returned to watch at the window, arms locked across her chest.

Ruby fought to keep herself from charging down the stairs. Far as she could see, there was no blood, and she'd not heard a gunshot. "Oh, Lord above, I hope not." She felt her heart hammering in her throat.

The man finally pushed himself to his knees and staggered to his feet, swaying as if the ground shook beneath him.

"He looks hurt bad."

Or drunk. Ruby couldn't remember ever seeing a person sway like that unless they were terribly sick. Vomiting did that to one or a bad case of *la grippe.* Or getting hit on the head real hard. Did any of those things apply to the man below?

He reached down, stumbled forward, picked up his hat, and slapped it against his leg before settling it back on his head and striking off to what constituted the remainder of the town.

Ruby closed her eyes. *Lord, what have we gotten into here? Is all of this indeed your will for us? Or are we wandering in some desert?* She shoved her hands in her apron pockets and felt the envelopes she'd hidden there. Her father's letter and his will and testament in the left and the envelope of money in the right.

They couldn't just stay in their room. She had to find the ledgers and make some sense of all this. But when she thought of leaving Opal in the room alone, she almost laughed.

What would Mrs. Brandon do in a situation like this?

Mrs. Brandon would never be in a situation like this. Ruby most certainly agreed with that thought. *Think, Ruby, think. What is it I must do first? Crawl into bed and pull the covers up over my head? Take the gold piece Mrs. Brandon gave us and buy return tickets to New York City?* After all, what was keeping them here? She could just take the money in the envelope and call that their inheritance.

"Take care of the girls." Her father's voice rang in her ears. *"You promise?"* And she had. She had given him her word that she would see to the girls. But if one of "the girls" was Belle, she certainly didn't want or need any caring for, and it didn't look like the others did either. Except for Milly, the chambermaid, who didn't look old enough or strong enough to be taking care of anyone.

"Ruby, I'm hungry."

"All right. Let's go prepare something for supper." She started to put the envelopes in one of their carpetbags but stopped when she remembered how her father's room looked when she and Opal went searching for the money. *But surely no one would come in our room. You are getting far too suspicious.*

Ha. She made sure the envelopes were secure in her deep pockets and guided Opal ahead of her out the door, a door to which, while it had a lock, she had no key. She'd ask Charlie where to find it when she saw him.

"Ah, Milly?"

"Yes, miss?"

They'd met her just going into Per's room with fresh sheets and a quilt in her arms.

"Do you want some help with that?"

"What?" Milly stared around, then glanced from the bundle in her arms to Ruby. "I'm just going to make up the bed like Belle told me. I washed everything real good."

"I'm sure, but an extra set of hands always makes a job easier."

"You would help me?" If dumbfounded had a look, the girl wore it.

"Why not?" Ruby reached for the quilt, a lovely crazy quilt done in velvets, with intricate overstitching. The jewel tones glowed in the light from the lamp on the hall wall.

"Opal, you put on the pillowcases." She turned to Milly. "Do you usually iron these first?"

"Iron pillowcases?"

"I see." Life had indeed been different at the Brandons'. She went on around the bed so as to let Milly set the pace. Together they spread and tucked the sheets before Ruby asked another question. "How long have you been working here?"

"Two years or so."

They smoothed the top sheet in place.

"Do you have any idea how long my father and Belle were married?"

"Married?"

Ruby stopped in centering the quilt and stared across the bed at the young woman. "Yes."

"They wasn't married. Belle talked about it some, but . . ." She shook her head and jerked on the quilt.

Not married? So that's what Charlie was hinting about. Ruby kept from looking at Opal, who she was sure had plenty of questions. "I see." Perhaps that explained some of her father's comments in the letter.

"But my Papá's clothes and Belle's things are—"

"Opal."

"But—"

"That is enough." Ruby came around the end of the bed and took her sister by the arm. "We'll be in the kitchen making supper, Milly. Please come down as soon as you finish here."

— ༃ —

"Ah, there you are, Miss Torvald." Charlie greeted her with a smile when she entered the kitchen. "I have someone who wants to pay his respects."

"Oh, well, of course." Ruby's hands automatically went to smooth back the tendrils of hair, and she wished she had glanced in a mirror before coming down.

The door swung open and Charlie ushered in the officer she had seen at the graveside.

"Miss Torvald, Captain Jeremiah McHenry."

Even in the dim light from the kerosene lamp, his buttons gleamed as if lit from within. She followed the button trail upward to a cleft chin and a smiling mouth bracketed by deep grooves. His hazel eyes smiled easily, the lines radiating from the edges, a mute testimony to a man that saw far distances and enjoyed the journey.

"Miss Torvald, I just wanted to offer my personal condolences on your father's death. I know coming here must be a shock, and I hope you will let me know if there is anything I can do to make your stay easier."

"Thank you, sir. I appreciate your offer. My sister and I have a great deal to become accustomed to here."

"Do I take it that you will be staying?"

"For a time, anyway. Would you like to sit down?" Ruby glanced toward the table to see Opal standing just inside the door to the staircase. "Captain McHenry, this is my sister, Opal."

"I'm glad to meet you too, miss." He turned back to Ruby. "Remember, if there is anything I can do to—"

"Do you have horses?" Opal crossed to stand by her sister.

"Why, yes. At least I have access to army horses. Why?"

"Opal has always wanted to ride and was hoping she could while we are here."

"Now that is an easy wish to grant. As soon as we return from patrol, I will bring a horse for you to ride."

"You really will?" Hero worship wrapped Opal's sigh in awe.

"Yes." He turned back to Ruby. "If you will excuse me now, I need to return to the cantonment."

"Thank you."

"You are most welcome." He clicked his heels and, with a slight bow, left via the swinging door that led to the saloon.

"Opal, that was not very mannerly."

"But he said to ask if there was something he could do, and so I did." Opal squared her shoulders. "I said please and thank you."

"That you did. Let's see what we can find for supper." *Perhaps one of us will get a wish come true out of this ... this ...* She couldn't think of an adequate word.

Ignoring the sounds from the saloon, Ruby found a bag of potatoes and set Opal to peeling them while she sliced some of the ham she had discovered in the pantry. When Milly joined them, Ruby set her to making biscuit dough.

"Who does the cooking here?"

"Mostly me and Charlie."

"And the others?"

"By the time they take care of themselves and their clothes and things, there ain't a lot of time left. That's what your pa hired me for, and that's *all* he hired me for."

"I see." But she didn't see at all.

When supper was ready, the three of them sat down to eat.

"What about the others?"

"I usually leave some things out, and they help themselves when they want."

"I see." *I'm beginning to sound like an echo. What is going on here?*

"Do you have a horse?" Opal looked up from cutting her potatoes.

"Nope."

"The captain says he has one."

"Oh, the army has lots of horses. But if you need one, you can rent 'em over to the livery."

"No," Ruby stared at her little sister.

"I didn't ask yet."

"I know."

"Gets right purty here in the spring. Grass greens up and flowers bloom near to everywhere."

Ruby smiled across the table. "Really, Milly. How nice."

"Maybe we can stay awhile, Ruby? Maybe if the captain takes too long, we could rent two horses and go out riding to see the country. Maybe we'll see buffalo. There was a picture of one in a book I saw."

"Nah, there ain't too many of those left, but you can see deer and elk. Some folks have brought in cattle too."

Ruby listened to the two talk with one ear while she puzzled out how to find the ledger books and how to set up a meeting with everyone at once so she could read her father's last will and testament.

"Do you know where the ledgers are kept, Milly?"

"Ledgers?"

"The big books that my father kept his records in."

"Oh, Charlie has those."

"After supper, could you ask Charlie to bring them in here?"

"I s'pose." The look she gave Ruby clearly asked why she didn't do that herself.

Ruby ignored the look. "Opal, when we are finished, you can wash the dishes."

"Oh, I just leave 'em in a pan of soapy water on the back of the stove." Milly offered.

"I see." Ruby nodded and swallowed. Getting the kitchen cleaned up might be her first order of business, after the ledgers of course. And after they all had a meeting of the minds.

"I think I'll write notes to everyone and set up a meeting time. You can slide them under their bedroom doors."

"Notes? Like in writing?" At Ruby's nod Milly shook her head. "Belle and Charlie are the only ones who can read."

"Oh." Despite all her good training from her mother, her grandmother, and Mrs. Brandon, Ruby leaned her elbows on the table and rubbed her forehead with her fingertips. Was nothing possible here?

"Please ask Charlie to come in here. Tell him it will only be for a moment."

"Yes, miss." Milly resumed her distance.

"Opal, you wash the dishes while I go over the ledgers." Unless of course, Charlie refused to bring them to her. Then what?

CHAPTER NINE

"Who do you think did it?" Opal asked.

Ruby stared from her sister to the unmitigated mess of their room. Drawers pulled out, valises gaping open, their trunk riffled, dresses and underthings tossed like a big wind had blown through.

"I don't know. But I have a good idea." *Who but Belle would do such a thing?* Ruby rubbed her forehead again. The headache that had been creeping in now had taken up residence with a vengeance.

But if not Belle—and how could they accuse her without proof—then who? Milly had been with them most of the time. That left Charlie, Cimarron, or Jasmine. Or what if someone else came up from the saloon, or what if just anybody came in and it wasn't just their room that was riffled? With no locks on the doors, anything was possible. Ruby slumped against the post at the foot of the bed. Rubbing her forehead was doing no good, the resident hammer wielder refused to respond to such measures.

Opal sat down beside her. "You want I should make you a cup of tea?"

Right now a cup of tea sounded like a gift straight from heaven, but she daren't let Opal out of the room by herself— who knew what kind of trouble she could get into.

Whatever made me think we should come out here like this? We are on the verge of nowhere, no father, an enterprise that is feeling shadier by the minute, people who really don't want us here, people of questionable moral fiber, a town—She snorted at that thought, which made for a syncopation in the pounding of her head. Hamlet? Village? What would you call this place but a sinkhole bound to the land by the railroad?

"Perhaps some fresh air would help." She made her way to the window and, using every muscle God gave her, lifted the lower sash so fresh air could blow through and perhaps take her headache with it. She sank down on her knees and rested her crossed arms on the sill. Cheek on the back of her wrist, she tried to think of something besides the hammering in her head and their absurd situation. She heard Opal's steps crossing the room and felt the girl's hand on her head. With gentle fingers Opal stroked Ruby's hair, starting from the crown of her head and down the length of blond curls that had not been bound into their usual coil or bundled into a snood.

"Your hair is so pretty," Opal whispered, as if a regular voice would break the spell that was weaving comfort in the dimming day.

"Umm." Thank you was more than Ruby could manage. She let her eyes stay closed, in spite of a loud shout she heard from down below. This one at least sounded like a greeting rather than a beating. Had Charlie thrown the other man out or had someone else? And what could the man have done that warranted such action? Mentally she slammed the door on such thoughts and concentrated instead on Opal's generous gift.

"Would you like me to brush your hair?"

"If you'd like."

The brushing commenced after Opal located the brush—no simple task—removed the pins and ribbon that held the curls back off Ruby's face, and stroked the brush through the riotous strands. She heard the sparks snapping in the dry air.

"Could almost start a fire with the light flashes here." Opal's voice wore a dreamy quality, as if she were enjoying the brushing as much as Ruby.

Ruby was almost asleep when she realized she was getting chilled. She started to push herself to her feet, when Opal asked, "How's your head now?"

Ruby paused, halfway up and tilted her head to one side and then the other. "Why, it is gone. That's amazing. Thank you." She slammed the window shut, and hands on hips, stared around the room. "Let's get this mess back in order and then—"

"Then you could read to me."

Ruby started to decline, remembered the wonderful hair brushing, and smiled instead. "I think that is a very good idea." She took her blue ribbon from Opal and retied her hair. Getting the room back in order wouldn't take nearly the effort of cleaning it thoroughly or of determining who their assailant was. The motive was apparent, at least to Ruby. They were searching for either money or the letter. If it was money, everyone fit the bill. If the letter, that left Belle or Charlie. Unless, of course, Belle had told someone else about the letter.

With the thoughts chasing each other round and round, she could sense the return of the headache.

"Talk to me, Opal."

"Why?" The sunrise on Opal's face made Ruby smile.

"I know, usually I'm asking you to be quiet, but right now I don't want to think myself into a headache again, so tell me what you've learned about Dove House in your forays."

Opal folded up her nightdress. "Ah, there are mice everywhere."

"Wonderful."

"We could get a cat to take care of that problem."

"True."

"You mean it?"

"Did I say that?"

"Sort of. But can we have a kitten?"

"I'd rather have a cat that knows how to hunt." Ruby rehung two dresses in the armoire.

"Did you know there is a hen house out in the back?"

"No. How did you find that out?"

"I looked out the door and saw chickens in a fence."

"So now we know where the eggs come from. Was there a cow there too?" Ruby beckoned Opal to help remake the bed.

"Not here, but next door."

A knock on the door caught their attention.

"Yes?" Ruby plumped a pillow and set it back on the bed.

"It's Milly. I brung the big books."

"Thank you." Ruby crossed the room and opened the door. She took the leather-bound ledgers and turned to set them down.

"Would you like some hot water for washing?"

"Why, yes, that would be very nice."

"I, ah, want to thank you for supper tonight. It's nice to have a real lady in the house."

"But . . ." Ruby wisely skipped what she was going to say. "I'm glad you liked it. Tomorrow you will have to show me where things are kept."

"I will. I'll bring the water right up." Milly turned with a little wave and headed back down the hall.

Ruby glanced after her to see a man walking ahead of her, and it looked as if he came out of Jasmine's room. Could he possibly be the one who ransacked their room? Should she follow and accuse him? Or should she wait and ask Jasmine, whom she hadn't even really met yet, if anything was missing from her room? But perhaps she was mistaken, and he was one of the guests staying here at Dove House.

"Are you all right?" Opal joined her in the doorway.

"Yes, I believe so." Ruby closed the door. She and Opal had just settled themselves against the pillows to read when another knock came on the door. Thinking it Milly, Ruby called, "Come in."

Charlie stuck his head around the door. "You wanted to see me?"

"Yes, ah . . ." Ruby scrambled off the bed and shook out her skirts. She could feel her neck growing warm. *Do I invite him. . . ?* But a man in a woman's room? What would people think? Of course Opal was here too, but still . . .

"I can come back later if you want."

Oh, for a sitting room.

"No, I know how busy you are. We can talk now." She opened the door and motioned him in, leaving the door partway open. "Milly is bringing hot water."

"Good." Charlie nodded toward the ledgers on top of the repacked trunk. "I see you got them. If you have any questions, just ask. I'll tell you what I can."

"Ah, good. I plan to study them later tonight." She took in a deep breath. "But in the meantime, I believe our first order of business is to meet with everyone so that I can read them my father's letter."

"You are planning on staying, then?"

"For the time being." She studied him a moment. Could she trust him? Or was he in league with Belle? Or was she being too suspicious?

"Mr. Charlie, I—"

"Please, miss, just Charlie. I go by Charlie. That's all anyone knows me by here. Just Charlie." He cocked his head to the side and shrugged slightly.

So what kind of past was he hiding? Ruby'd not only read of men who went west to start new lives, but she knew one personally. Had anyone ever suspected Per Torvald had left two daughters in New York? What kind of life had he led since his wife died?

"All right, Charlie it is." She stared at the braided rug in the middle of the floor for a moment. "May I ask you a question?"

"A 'course."

"How many years did you know my father?"

Charlie scrunched up his face, ticking off thoughts on his fingers. "Five, six years. Met up with him when we first got to the Black Hills. We decided we was safer from the Indians or marauding claim jumpers if'n there was two of us. Been partners ever since."

"Partners?"

"Well, here I more or less worked for him, being as he had most of the money, ya know."

No, I don't know, but how I wish I did. She nodded. "Thank you."

"You can ask me anything. I'll tell you what I can."

Does that mean the truth or what you can get by with telling me and still hide what I need to know? Ruby Signe Torvald, either you are going to trust this man until he does something that destroys that trust, or you are . . . The thought wouldn't finish.

"Would you please tell the others of our meeting time?"

"Which is?"

Stopped again. "What do you recommend?"

"Well, we open at two, so I'd suggest half past noon or one o'clock. How long do you think you'd need?"

To read the letter and will? Five minutes. To fight off the attack? Who knows. She was absolutely sure Belle would go on the attack even before she was finished reading.

"Let's say twelve-thirty."

"Good. In the kitchen or the saloon?"

"The kitchen. We can eat and talk at the same time. Do you know if there is any meat besides ham?"

"Got some bacon. I'll ask Frank if he could get us a deer. Would help pay off his chit."

"Chit?"

"You know . . . his account."

"Men have accounts in the saloon?"

"Only for whiskey or a room. Cards and the other, they pay cash."

"I see."

"Most people here get paid only once a month or so or when the army or railroad pays. They pay us when they can, we charge 'em interest."

"I take it this is all in the ledger?"

"Back pages got a runnin' total."

"And what if someone leaves the area without paying?"

"Like Per allus said, you got to trust your customers. 'Course, some folks hereabouts don't have no chit here."

His jaw tightened just enough that Ruby noticed.

"I better be gettin' back."

"Thank you." What had he been referring to? Something or someone had caused his clenched jaw.

Charlie met Milly coming in as he was going out and said something to her that brought a real smile to the girl's pale face.

"Anything else I can bring you?" Milly set the full pitcher in the bowl and turned to catch a glimpse of the book lying open on the bed. "You can read?"

"Yes, of course."

"Me too." Opal turned from where she lay on her stomach on the bed, heels in the air.

"Really? Was it hard to learn?"

Ruby waited to see what Opal would say after all her years of muttering how difficult school was.

"No. Just takes time and a good teacher. Didn't you go to school?"

"Ain't no schools out here, and my ma couldn't read neither."

"Oh." Opal stared from the open pages to Milly and back. "I could teach you if you want to learn."

"You would do that?"

"Why not? We played school lots when I was little."

Ruby thought back to those play school days. Opal had begged so hard to be included that she was learning to read when she was four, not too long after they moved to the Brandon house.

"If we stay, that is." She cut a look to her sister.

"We'll be fixing a late breakfast for everyone in the morning. Oh, I should have started bread. You have yeast?"

"We have sourdough."

"Sourdough?"

"You know, flour and water or milk that you add more to, then use to raise bread."

"I see. Perhaps you will show me?"

"A 'course. I'll set it to risin' right now. It's a bit late but if'n I leave it on the warming oven, it should grow faster." She turned to leave, then paused. "Thank you."

Both Ruby and Opal answered at the same time. "You're welcome."

For what, Ruby wasn't sure, but the smile on the young woman's face made her look almost pretty. She usually seemed to fade into the woodwork and wore a permanent crease between her pale eyes. Pale and faded were two words that aptly applied to Milly—all of her.

— ✦ —

By the time Ruby finally blew out the lamp, she'd read enough of the ledgers to have a pretty fair idea of her father's business except for the source of income called Hospitality, below which Cimarron's and Jasmine's names were listed along with two columns of figures. Did they hold tea parties in the afternoons and charge for them? Or soirees at night? All she'd heard at night was raucous laughter, the tap of dancing feet, and some wild singing. Not the kind of hospitality she'd been raised on, that was for sure. And the word was entered often and for varying amounts, not like room charges, which were always the same per night.

She resolved to ask Charlie in the morning.

— ❧ —

The next morning Opal stormed into the kitchen from outside. "That mean old hen pecked me." The young girl held up her hand where a drop of blood marked the wound.

"I tried to warn you." Milly set a basket of eggs on the table. "She's already setting and don't want us to take her eggs."

"Setting?" Ruby turned from kneading the bread dough that already had a fine yeasty flavor, thanks to the sourdough Milly had instructed her in using.

Milly gave them both a questioning look. "She wants to hatch chicks so she is setting on the eggs. That's what hens do."

Opal looked at the eggs in the basket. "Are there chicks in there?"

Milly rolled her eyes in obvious disgust. "No, those are the eggs we eat."

Ruby and Opal exchanged baffled looks.

"I'll explain some other time. You want to come with me to get the milk?"

Opal glanced at Ruby for permission, then followed Milly out the back door. "We got ours in bottles from the milkman in New York. He delivered on Monday, Wednesday, and Friday."

"We get ours from old man Johnson. Sometimes, if he ain't home, I got to milk the cow."

"Milk the cow?"

"I'll explain some other time."

Ruby could hear them through the window she'd opened to let in the breeze that cooled the heat from the cookstove and the steam from the boiler where sheets were bubbling. Doing the wash over the campfire outside was not to be tolerated. She'd peeked in a couple of the rooms that weren't let and immediately ripped the beds apart. There would be clean bedding in her hotel, and scrubbed floors would be coming very soon.

Milly and Opal returned quickly, and the *girls* ambled in just as Ruby was setting the food on the table. And just before she went to knock on their doors. They wore wrappers and makeup left on from the night before.

Ruby swallowed the words that bubbled up like a kettle on fast boil. No sense getting off to a wrong start.

Belle yawned and scratched under one arm. "My, this does look good. Shame it couldn't be an hour later when I'd had time to get really hungry."

Ruby passed the platter of scrambled eggs and slices of bacon. She nodded to Milly to pour the coffee.

"Thanks." Charlie was the only one to use a kind word of appreciation, or any words for that matter. The others just fell to eating and made short order of the platters of food.

Opal's eyes rounded like the plates before them, looking from Ruby, who gave a slight shake of her head, back to the women who seemed to be making Opal a believer in the value of manners.

Ruby felt like the inside of her mouth was all in tatters from biting her inner lip, her cheeks, and even her tongue. When the plates were empty and the coffee cups refilled, she took the envelopes from her pocket and stood at the head of the table.

"I know you are all very curious as to what will happen next here at Dove House, so I would like to read my father's last will and testament. He gave me this before he died, and . . ."

She almost mentioned the promise he had extricated from her but held back. When she caught Belle's glance, she knew the meaning of the phrase *evil eye*. If she'd not been fortified by tea and prayer, she knew she would have withered away.

She kept the personal letter and deed separate and read the will.

"I, Per Torvald, being of sound mind write this as my final will and testament. While I know this will make Belle furious because she believes this place should be hers should I pass on, I will Dove House to my daughters, Ruby and Opal. I have sent for them, and unless I hear from them otherwise, this property belongs to them. Should they not come to Little Missouri to claim their inheritance, then, Belle, you will have your chance.

"But no matter who is in charge, you must take care of the girls, making sure they have a home for as long as they want. To Charlie I leave the gold nugget we dug out of the Black Hills and the right to run the saloon here at Dove House.

"Thank you all for being my friends, and may you remember me with favor.

"Per Torvald, March 29, 1882

"Dakota Territory in the United States of America."

Ruby looked up from the paper. "As you can see, we did arrive in time to talk with our father, and according to this will, my sister and I are the owners of Dove House. Far as I can determine for right now, we should continue with business as usual, even though I hate the thought of a saloon. I have gone through my father's ledgers and—"

"Who's going to help you run this?" Belle stood, leaning toward Ruby as if to snap at her.

"I . . . I said, business as usual."

"Are you going to deal?" Belle stabbed the air with a finger.

"Cards?" Surely they didn't play whist.

"That's what your father did, along with taking in the money. Or, if Charlie was dealing, Per took care of the bar."

"I see." *God, I sure do need your help here.* "Perhaps then you should each tell me what you do here. Outside of Milly, for I know her position."

Ruby looked to Cimarron, her red hair all a tumble, who leaned back with one arm draped over the chair. "And what is it you do?"

"I'm a singer and dancer and one of the doves."

"I see." *What is a dove? Is she trying to make fun of me?* "And you, Jasmine?" She turned to the dark-haired woman, who had yet to speak.

"Like her." Jasmine tossed her head. "I sing, dance some, I can play the piano when Belle is busy, and I'm a dove." She and Cimarron exchanged winks.

"I see. And men pay you to dance with them?"

"Guess you could call it that if'n you want to."

Ruby looked toward Charlie. "In the ledgers, there is a constant reference to hospitality. Are all of you part of . . . hospitality?" She said the word with hesitation.

Charlie shook his head, his eyebrows caterpillaring across his brow. "Not me. I just pour the drinks and knock a few heads together and throw 'em out the door if they get too rowdy. We keep a safe place here."

"Oh." She turned to glare at the three women who were snickering to each other. *What do they think is so funny?* She drew up into her schoolmarm self, the persona that could keep the three older Brandon children under control even when Alicia and Jason ganged up on her.

"Is there something I should know that you would like to tell me?"

"You haven't asked what I do." Belle raised an eyebrow, her eyes anything but friendly, something like a rat that she had cornered near the feed bin in the carriage house one time. Ruby still shuddered when she thought of the malevolence of the creature.

She expected Belle to twitch her whiskers at any moment.

"Pardon me. Belle?"

"I been with Per for five years, we met up in Deadwood. I play the piano, deal some, and while I watch out for the girls, I ain't been a dove since we came here." She dug a thin cigar from the nether regions of her bosom, and Charlie rose to take a spill, light it in the stove, and then light her cigar.

Opal stared with utter fascination as Belle blew smoke from between pursed lips.

Oh, Lord, preserve us.

"Ruby, what's a dove?" Opal leaned forward to ask.

"A dove? Why you've seen doves in the park, not much different than a pigeon, only prettier."

"But . . ." The two sisters stared at each other, then the women as they burst out laughing.

Belle waved her cigarillo, the end of it now lodged in a long stem sort of attachment. "We ain't the pigeons, sister."

This brought on another wave of laughter.

Ruby looked at Charlie, who was fighting hard to keep a straight face. He gave a slight shake of his head when he caught her eye, but she had no idea what he meant.

Ruby closed her eyes and counted to ten in double-quick time. While these people were adults, they had worse manners than children—at least the children she had known.

When Opal started to say something, Ruby laid a hand on

her shoulder. The squeeze meant not now. Opal subsided, muttering half under her breath. "So what's wrong with doves?"

More snickers and an outright guffaw.

Belle leaned forward like she was conversing friendly like. "Not just doves, dear, soiled doves."

Ruby rapped her knife handle on the table. "That is enough. Since you are taking such delight at our expense, this meeting is adjourned."

"Now, it ain't fair to ignore your baby sister like that." Belle drew in another mouthful of smoke and blew a thin stream out of the side of her mouth.

The rat was about to bite, and short of running out of the room, Ruby had no idea what to do.

"Some folks call us ladies of the night?" She waited to see if that rang any bells.

"That's enough, Belle." Charlie shifted in his chair. "Milly, why don't you pour us some more coffee? There's a good girl."

Belle hissed another term, then shook her head at the look of confusion on Ruby's face.

"I said, that's enough."

"You don't own me, Charlie boy, and don't you forget it." Belle pushed back her chair. "If she ain't smart enough to know what's going on here, this country's goin' to eat her up and spit out the bones to bleach on the prairie." She took her cup of coffee with her as she stalked out of the room.

Cimarron glared after Belle, then leaned forward. "Honey, you send your little sister out with Milly, and Charlie can go set up the bar. We got to have a little talk."

"I'll be upstairs." Jasmine headed out the door as if chased by a fire-breathing dragon, and Charlie rushed out too, presumably to set up the bar.

Ruby, her throat suddenly dry as the dust she'd seen under the beds, sent Opal out with Milly, then took the seat right across the table from the woman.

"Now, you know you got Belle by the ostrich feathers. She's mad 'cause she's runnin' scared."

"Oh?" *Belle certainly didn't look scared. I'm the one that's shaking in my shoes.*

"You know when you asked about that there hospitality?"

Ruby nodded.

"And we all was so rude and laughed at you?"

Ruby nodded again. *Lord, if this is what quicksand is like, please keep me out of it.*

"Well, we, ah, we do for men what their wives would do if'n they had wives. You get my meaning?" She waited. "At night, in bed."

Ruby could feel the heat flare from her chest to the ends of her hair. She was sure she could hear it sizzle. "Oh. Oh!" If only she could melt under the table and drain out through a knothole in the floor. *Lord, help me. What do I say? What do I do?*

"But . . ." She clamped her lower lip between her teeth.

"Then we gave half of what we earned to your pa. So if Dove House closes, we would be out of work, at least in a place as nice as this. We could go to the cribs, but that would be awful. Our line of work doesn't exactly make us popular with the other women in town. Not that there are many."

"I . . . I imagine not." The meaning of the short and brightly colored dresses they wore became clear to her. If only she had a fan. "If you'll excuse me, please." Ruby pushed back from the table. "Tell Milly to send Opal up to me. I'll be in my room." *Packing.*

CHAPTER TEN

"But, Ruby, you promised Papá . . . er, Far."

"Opal, you just don't understand." Ruby jerked another frock off the hook in the armoire and stuffed it into the trunk. *All those men—and the girls!* She laid a hand against the base of her throat. In the hall and . . . It didn't bear thinking about. And part of the horror was that she had brought her little sister into this awful place. And their father! Whatever had he been thinking? She poured herself another glass of water and downed it in one long gulp. A glass wasn't enough. She needed a pond or a lake.

"You always say I don't understand."

What would Mrs. Brandon have to say about such a mess as this? That didn't bear thinking about either. *Father God, how could you have let us—I mean, I was only obeying my earthly father. How could you let us. . . ? Why?*

"But, Ruby . . ."

"What?" Ruby jerked her mind back to see the consternation on her sister's face. She knew the word came out too sharply even before she saw the hurt in Opal's eyes. But as she watched, the hurt changed to a tightened jaw and flashing eyes.

"You said we always have to keep our word. And you gave Papá your word." The last was delivered with all the regalness of a queen confronting an errant subject.

But you don't understand. Ruby kept the words from her lips, took in a deep breath, let it all out, unclenched the fists at her sides, took in another deep breath, and collapsed on the side of the bed. She reached for Opal's hands and drew her close to stand right in front of her so they could look eye to eye.

"Opal, dear, there is so much here you don't understand. There's a lot here I don't understand either, and I think the best thing for us is to be gone, to get back on the train and return to New York."

"Best for us or best for them, the girls you promised to take care of?"

But they don't want us to take care of them. They are happy with the way things are. But were they really? Belle said she was, but what about the other two? Could they really be happy doing what they were doing with different men?

Would I be happy with that? How could anyone. . . ?

She clenched her fists against her mouth, bit down on her knuckles to drive the inner arguments away. Maybe if she hurt bad enough herself, she could quit thinking.

"Please, Ruby . . ."

"Opal, you don't know what you are asking." Ruby reached out and stroked the curly wisps of hair off her sister's forehead. Pulling her down beside her on the bed, she kept an arm around Opal's shoulders. "Yes, we should always live up to our word. It's not just me or Mrs. Brandon who says that, but God's Word says so too." *But how can I stay here to keep my word and live with myself?*

"Take care of the girls." What if they really don't want to be taken care of? *Would I want to be taken care of?*

Yes! If it is like the Brandons' home in New York. But didn't you wish for an opportunity to meet a fine young man and perhaps marry and have children of your own? Lord, what am I to do? What is your will in all of this? Are you listening?

Ruby had no answers.

"Can I go help Milly? She works awful hard."

"I better go downstairs too." Ruby took Opal's hands again. "You have to promise me you will not go into the saloon or into any of the girls' rooms."

"I promise."

"And you won't talk with any of the men who come here."

"I don't anyway. But what about Mister Charlie?"

"You can talk with him when he is not in the saloon."

"I want to gather the eggs again, and I won't let that old broody hen get me this time." She pulled away. "I'll ask Milly if she knows where we can get a cat. I ain't never had a cat before."

"Don't say ain't."

"The others do."

"We don't." *Lord, see it has already begun. All my teaching blowing away like the wind.*

Opal darted out the door before she could hear any more restrictions.

Ruby leaned her head against the bedpost. *What can I do, Lord, what can I do?*

She eyed the trunk. Packing and leaving would be so much easier than the only other possibility that lurked in her mind. She thought of the money in the envelope, a small fortune to one who'd never had more than five dollars at a time in her entire life.

"Why would I decide to stay here?"

Because you promised. The words rang in Opal's voice. Ruby crossed to the window and leaned her forehead against the glass. Down on the street, she saw two men ride in on horses, dismount, and flip the reins over the railing in front of the porch. While they disappeared under the porch roof, she could hear the thud of their boots and the jangling of metal. The door squeaked when they opened it, and the sounds she'd now come to understand as normal spilled out into the air, then dimmed again with the squeaking close of the door. A scruffy dog sniffed a clump of weeds and lifted his leg to water it before trotting off. Sunlight sparkled on the river as the Little Missouri wound its way between cliffs of preposterous colors and shapes. Trees along the river wore a haze of green, new buds just sprouting on their branches.

What would it be like to walk down by the river? To sit on a rock in the sun? To ride a horse up on the hills as Opal wanted?

She straightened and saw a clean spot on the glass where her forehead had rested. "Ugh." Dipping water out of the pitcher with a cloth, she rubbed her forehead clean again, and after straightening her hair and clothing, she donned an apron and headed out the door. Perhaps she would get a good idea or two while she was cleaning. And of that there was enough to keep her busy for weeks. Unless she could recruit some more help — from the "girls."

She met Charlie in the hallway.

"Can we talk a minute, Miss Ruby?"

"Of course." She gave him a smile that she hoped signified confidence.

"I . . . I need to apologize." He studied the lay of the floorboards.

Ruby waited, not sure what she should say.

"I . . . ah . . . I didn't know you didn't know. I mean, what we . . . we got here. I'm sorry we embarrassed you so."

Ruby could feel the red heat creeping up her neck again. What to say? "Thank you," she finally said.

"If'n there is any way I can help you, besides tending the bar, that is, I hope you will let me know."

"I will, and thank you again."

"I hope you stay."

She darted him a look of inquiry.

"I mean, no one has said nothing, but your leaving wouldn't surprise any of us."

"And that is what Belle is counting on?" She watched him closely to see if he would defend Belle or answer straight.

Charlie nodded.

"And you?"

He looked her straight in the eye. "I want you to stay. Your pa bragged about his two treasures, as he called you. He always wanted you to come west and be with him."

"Then why didn't he send for us sooner?" The words ripped out of her heart and flew across the brief space.

"He figured he didn't have a place for you, and then when things were gettin' better, like here, he started feelin' poorly. He didn't plan on dyin' so soon."

"No one does." She swallowed the tears that burned at the back of her throat.

"He carried a picture of you in his watch, you and your mother. All those years."

"I didn't see a watch in his things."

"It was gold. I don't think he ever gambled that away. You might ask Belle."

As if Belle would give me anything of my father's.

"Hey, Charlie, you're needed down here." Belle's voice echoed up the stairs.

"I better go. Please don't give up too soon. Think on it?"

"I will." She watched him head back down the hall, a slight limp on his right side. One more thing to think on—where had her father's watch gone?

She descended the backstairs to find the kitchen cleaned up again, the washed sheets hanging on the clothesline out back, and ham and beans baking in the oven. The aroma drew her to open the oven door and check to see what was cooking.

When she opened the pantry door, a mouse scampered along the counter and down the other, diving into a hole in the baseboard. She clamped her hand over the shriek and shuddered instead. *You silly, why didn't you take a broom after the filthy thing? Because I don't even know where the broom is kept, but I sure am going to find out.* She began opening cabinets, pulling out drawers both in the pantry and in the storeroom they'd started cleaning the day before. She found a broom and a bucket on the back porch. Opal was coming back from the necessary that stood out behind the chicken house.

"You want to see the chickens?"

"No, thanks."

"Milly showed me where the garden was too. We could plant lots of stuff there pretty soon."

"Is it dug up?"

"No, but we're going to spread chicken droppings on it before we dig it up." Opal screwed up her face. "Won't that make the vegetables taste terrible?"

"No. You remember Mr. Klaus used to spread straw and such on the gardens at home. He'd buy a load of manure from a farmer who brought it to town."

Opal made a face.

Ruby returned the grimace. "I just saw a mouse."

"Did you kill it?"

"With what?"

"Cook used to use a broom. She broke a teapot one day when

she missed on a swing." Opal acted out Mrs. Klaus flailing at a mouse. She came to Ruby's side and looked out over the hills. "Sure is pretty here, don't you think?"

"More like a strange and terrible beauty." Ruby knew she was quoting someone but had no idea whom.

"Sure different than New York."

It was Ruby's turn to nod. "That is the truth."

"Milly said Mrs. Fitzgerald and Mrs. McGeeney are the only married ladies in town, and they don't even speak to each other. No one even knows why. Strange, huh?"

"What other bits of interest has Milly poured in your oh-so-willing ears?"

"Well, the army is housed in those buildings down the street. They call that the cantonment. Some of the soldiers are regulars at Dove House."

"Opal!"

"Well, they come to play cards most nights. That's what Milly said." Opal stepped off to the side in case she needed some space to keep from getting her arm grabbed.

"Most supplies come in on the train. There's only a small store here, owned by someone named Johnny Nelson. Seems there ain't much here . . . er, isn't."

"Thank you."

They studied the landscape in silence. "We are going to stay, Ruby, aren't we?"

"We shall see. Where's Milly?"

Opal shrugged. "She said she had some mending to do. She takes care of those fancy dresses the girls wear. Wouldn't you like a pretty dress like some of those Belle wears?"

"Opal!"

"Not clothes they wear in the saloon but like that beautiful aquamarine silk we saw hanging in the armoire. Blue always looks good on you."

"Well, right now I wish I had more serviceable skirts like my black wool. Clothes for cleaning is what we need. Most of our new things are too nice for that." She turned and went back in the door. "You coming?"

"I guess."

— ᘒ —

That night Ruby found herself turning and sighing, tossing and sighing again. The noise from downstairs made sleeping nigh on to impossible, but even after that all shut down, she couldn't close off the thoughts chasing through her mind. If she could only take a broom to them like she should have taken it to that mouse. Finally she slipped out of bed and relit the lamp, carrying it over to the table where she had the ledgers spread out. Now all the entries made sense, horrible sense in her estimation. She stared at the notes and numbers until her eyes went out of focus and they all jumbled together.

How could she take care of the girls without the saloon and the other business? She didn't need to add all the figures to see how much the girls contributed to the coffers.

"Do all to the glory of God." The piece of a Bible verse floated through her mind. *So what could Dove House become that would be to the glory of God?* She removed her father's letter—now permanently wrinkled from the many readings—from her pocket and reread it again. Hotel—that's what he'd written. Dove House would make a fine hotel.

"Good food and a clean place to sleep." That's what she would want. But these men out here on the frontier didn't seem to care about a good bed. They'd rather have a place to drink and carouse around. So was playing cards wrong?

She shook her head. "I don't know." Could the men play cards and drink coffee? Would they?

She could feel the ideas coming together like butter in a churn.

If they turned the saloon into a dining room, moved the card room off to the side, used the bar for checking in those who would rent the rooms—for sleeping only. The girls could be waitresses; she and Charlie could do the cooking. Ruby ignored the voice that said she'd never cooked a full meal in her life. Not to mention preparing three meals a day. Could Charlie cook that well? He seemed to know his way around the kitchen. And Milly seemed to know something of cooking too, and the cleaning.

Where do we get the supplies?

Off the train, of course, but where was a town big enough to provide what they would need? Charlie would know.

Perhaps Belle would like to be in charge of the card room. She wrote down ideas as they came to her, filling up two pages of the ledger before she realized she was running out of both kerosene for the lamp and stamina for her eyes.

— ❧ —

"Don't you ever sleep?" Ruby asked Charlie when she found him already downstairs after the rooster had crowed only once. Her many new ideas had awakened her after only an hour or two of sleep.

"You look mighty perky this morning too." He leaned back in his chair. "'Sides, I like the early mornin'. 'Specially now, when spring is here and summer on the way. Step outside, you can smell the world changing, coming alive again."

"Charlie, how good a cook are you?"

He blinked at her, shrugged with one shoulder, and sucked through the slight gap between his front teeth. "Passable. Why?"

"You must know that in order to remain here . . ." She sucked in a stiffening breath. "I cannot abide what is going on . . . with the girls, I mean. So I got to thinking, what if we turned Dove House into a good hotel and place of dining? We could have a cardroom for the men for now, but there would be no liquor."

"None?"

She nodded as he shook his head.

"They wouldn't have to pay for the coffee."

"What would the girls do?"

"Wait on the customers, serve the food, help with whatever was needed in the hotel. We could have more rooms to let if we used the attic for rooms for all of us who work here. There is an attic, isn't there?"

"Body could freeze to death up there in the winter."

He hadn't said no, but he hadn't said yes either.

"What do you think?"

"I think you'll lose your shirt. There's no call for a eatin' place. Mrs. McGeeney down the road offers that. The rooms we have ain't ever full. And no spirits for drinkin'. . . ?" He kept shaking his head as he listed the reasons why it wouldn't work. "Besides, if Belle can't get her way here, she'll take the others and open up a place of her own. She's been thinkin' hard on that."

"Oh." Ruby sank down on the nearest chair and propped her elbows on the table so she could hold up her chin. All of a sudden the need for sleep nearly drowned her. She covered a yawn with one hand and used her tongue to rub her teeth. "How come it sounded like such an excellent idea in the wee hours of the night?"

"Most anything can sound like a good idea at that time, even if you ain't been drinkin'."

"If I decide to do this, would you help me? I'd pay you." *Not much, but we can work out something.*

Charlie shrugged. "Ain't got nothin' else beggin' me to join in right now. Guess I would."

"What about the others?"

"You'll have to ask them."

"Or tell them?"

"It's gonna be a shock." He rocked the chair back on two legs. "You give any thought to the men who come here all the time?"

"They can play cards and drink all the coffee they can hold. And if they want to spend the night, the cost will be seventy-five cents, twenty-five cents more for a bath. And no bed partners unless they're married."

She rose and went to the stove to put in more wood. "We got any black paint?"

"Don't think so."

"Any paint at all?"

He shook his head again.

"Do you think anyone in town has any?"

"Maybe some over at Johnny Nelson's store. Never know what he has in there."

"Good. Would you, please, check into that soon as you can? We need to make some signs. The first one will say Closed for Renovations."

"Renovations? What's that?"

Ruby sighed. "You think they can all understand Closed?"

"Most likely, 'specially if the lights is off."

By the time the girls yawned their way downstairs, Ruby had

Dove House trembling in the winds of change.

"What is all that pounding goin' on?" Belle raised her voice to be heard above the noise.

"Charlie is building some shelves in the storeroom." Ruby looked up from kneading another batch of bread, one of the few things she did know how to do in a kitchen.

"Couldn't he wait till we got our sleep? Just 'cause he don't need enough to keep a gnat alive, I—"

"Coffee's hot." Ruby flipped the dough over and began the pushing and turning rhythm once again.

Cimarron stopped in the doorway. "Sure smells good in here. What are you fixing?"

"There's fried potatoes, bacon, eggs, biscuits, and jam."

"Lawsy me, and here I thought we'd be havin' warmed up beans like usual." She took her place at the table, and Opal dished up a plate and set it before her.

"Thank you, honeybun, and with a smile no less. Things are lookin' up here at Dove House."

"Soon as you're finished eating, I have some things to discuss with you." Ruby gave the dough a last good thump, rolled it into a ball to set back in the big crockery bowl, and covered it with a clean dish towel, thanks to the good bleaching it got after being washed and hung on the line in the sun.

"Sun sure is bright this morning," Jasmine said after drinking half a cup of coffee.

"That's because Milly washed the windows, and now you can see out of them."

"Where'd the curtains go?"

"In the wash."

"Better be looking out, or we'll all be in the wash." Cimarron laughed at her own joke.

"Cimarron, is that your real name?" Opal brought back the coffeepot and carefully filled each cup.

"Yes, indeed. My mamma loved that song about the Cimarron Trail, and when I had kind of cinnamon colored hair, she just tacked that moniker right on to her bitty little baby girl."

"I think it's pretty."

Cimarron set her cup back down on the table. "Why, thank you, honeybun. You know how to make a body feel real good."

When they'd nearly finished eating, Ruby nodded to Opal to go get Milly and Charlie, who were both working in the store-room. When they all sat down, the women shared questioning looks between one another.

"Looks to be serious." Jasmine nudged Cimarron with her elbow.

"All right, what's going on here?" Belle dug out her morning's cigarillo and set it into the holder before holding it out for Charlie to light. When she'd leaned back to blow out her first line of smoke and appeared to be relaxing, she looked to Charlie who shrugged and nodded to Ruby.

Only the whisper of falling coals in the stove broke the silence. Ruby sent a prayer heavenward for guidance. She straightened her spine and plastered a smile on her face. "I've decided to close Dove House . . ."

Hollers of shock drowned out her final words, ". . . as it is."

CHAPTER ELEVEN

"You want me to what?"

"Belle, we can discuss this without gettin' all riled up." Charlie got up to pour himself another cup of coffee before crossing the room to stare out the window.

"I've seen the books, big man, and this place don't have a chance in a million of making it without the workin' girls. That's what makes us different from the pigsty down the street."

"And our drinks don't go killin' people." Cimarron studied her nails, then shook her head, staring at Ruby. "She's right. I don't see how you could make it."

"You gonna make for some real mad hombres out there. They been real happy comin' here before they set out hunting or trying to build something or keeping the peace." Jasmine propped her elbows on the table to hold her cup at mouth level.

"Times are changin' here. You got to keep that in mind." Charlie lifted his bowler hat and smoothed his hair back before resetting it on his head.

"I heard there are more easterners coming here for the hunting. They like to have a bed and a bath and good food. That's what they're used to." Ruby kept from looking at Charlie, who'd been her informant.

"They like our entertainment too." Jasmine gave a knowing smile.

"But they don't go upstairs much, unless to their own rooms."

Milly spoke from the corner, and everyone jerked around to see who said that.

"I s'pose you"—Belle pointed a finger at Milly—"are all jumped up about this change. You think you're so much better than us just because—"

"Belle!" Charlie nodded to where Opal was pushing open the door from outside.

Belle had the grace to shut her mouth, which brought her up a notch, albeit a small one, in Ruby's estimation. But perhaps it would be better if Belle left like Charlie figured she would. And if the others went, well, so be it. The four of them could manage for a while at least, until the folks who rode by on the trains knew about the new place in Little Missouri. Or rather, the newly refurbished place.

"Well, we better get ready for work." Belle started to stand.

"There won't be any work of the kind you are thinking, today or any day. The doors are closed, and we hung a sign that says so."

"You mean you're startin' right now?"

"I thought I made that clear."

"Come on, girls. We need to talk. In my room." Belle stared both Cimarron and Jasmine down so that they rose and, with an apologetic smile in Ruby's direction, followed Belle from the room.

Opal came to stand by Ruby. "They aren't too happy, huh?"

"No, they most certainly aren't." Ruby laid her arm across Opal's shoulders. "Well, as Caesar or Alexander the Great or someone from way back said, 'The die is cast.'"

"What's a die?"

"I'm not sure, but it sounds good." *And if there is any turning back, it won't be to the former—not if I have anything to say about it. If I only knew what was in the buksbom—if that is indeed what Far had said. What box was he referring to?*

"What do you want me to do?" Opal looked up at Ruby.

"You can help me in the pantry. We're going to scrub it from top to bottom. And after we finish the pantry, we'll go put supplies up on the lovely shelves Charlie is building and finish scrubbing in the storage room. Charlie, we need to count up the stock of liquor, and then you can go ask the man down the street if he wants to purchase it. Cash only, but we'll give him a fair deal. I need to know who my father dealt with at each of the places he did business so I can call on them in the next few days."

"You'd go to Dickinson? All by yourself?" The shock of her words nearly choked him.

"Why not?"

Charlie's head swung like a pendulum. "They won't do business with a itty bitty girl like you. Better if Belle went. No, that won't work. Me, then. I done most of the buyin' since your pa took sick."

They'll learn to deal with me if I'm the owner here. Ruby kept her thoughts to herself and only nodded. "If Mr. Williams doesn't want the liquor, you can return it when we go shopping in Dickinson."

"Beats his Forty Mile Red Eye, that's for sure." When he saw the confusion on her face, Charlie added, "That's his own brand. Makes it himself out of sulphuric acid, cigar butts, bad gin, and worse rum." Charlie shuddered. " 'Bout takes off the top of your head if it don't blow out your belly."

"Is that what they call 'white lightning'? I read about that somewhere."

"Na-a-a. They make white lightning down in the south, out in stills in the woods." Charlie slapped his leg. "Men can make alcohol outa just about anything if'n they got a mind to. Why I heard tell—"

"Charlie . . ."

"Oh, sorry." He smiled his apology to Opal, who'd been staring at him with eyes round as the coffee cups.

"Charlie sometimes exaggerates," Milly informed them, at the same time casting a tolerant smile his way.

"Not this time. Best get back to my shelves. Maybe tonight we can sit down and make me up some kind of shopping list, eh?"

Ruby tied a cloth around her hair, shaved soap off a bar into a bucket, then poured boiling water over it. Broom, brush, and rags in hand, she motioned to Opal. "All right, let's get started. Oh, you better tie something over your hair too. No telling what we might sweep down."

She popped back out of the pantry. "Charlie, could you bring me something to stand on, please?"

Charlie brought a box and set it on the floor. "I think you better let Miss Opal climb up on the counter. She can reach the top shelf from there, lest you want me to do the tops?"

"No. Shelves are needed in the storage room the most. And I

can't do that." *Unless I have to. Then I would learn.* While she watched, Opal scrambled up from the box to the counter.

"Hand me a washrag. I can't see up there, but I can reach." She took several tins out and handed them to Ruby.

"You be careful now."

"I am."

The hammering started again in the storage room as Ruby set the tins on the opposite counter. She stepped back as dust and debris filtered down from Opal's industrious scrubbing.

"What's in those?"

"I'll see." Ruby wiped the dust off the lids and pried them open. "Raisins in this one and . . . *pew.* Rancid lard." She set that one out in the kitchen to be emptied later.

They'd finished the top shelf and started on the next when Opal let out a small shriek. Ruby looked up in time to see a mouse land on Opal's shoulder. It jumped down to hers, from there to the floor, and then disappeared in the hole in the wall.

Ruby screamed, flailed at the mouse, and shuddered, glaring at her sister, who nearly dissolved in giggles.

"What happened?" Charlie burst through the half-closed door.

"Ahh! Another mouse." Ruby brushed off her shoulders and shook all over.

"A mouse jumped from me to her, and . . ." Opal, still laughing, pointed to the floor.

"Opal Marie Torvald, I do not find this funny in the least. Ooh." Ruby shuddered again.

"You want I should do this?" Charlie waved a hand to indicate the remaining cupboards.

"No. We will manage, thank you." Ruby drew herself up straight. No mouse, or rather most likely mice in this case, was going to intimidate her. It wasn't exactly that she was afraid of mice; she just didn't like them to surprise her.

And that one had definitely surprised her. Her heart still hammered in her chest.

"We need a cat!" Opal looked down at Charlie. "You know anyone who has one to give away?"

"Not right offhand, but let me think on it. But I'll warn you, cats are at a premium out here. Breeding cats might be a good side business."

Ruby could tell Charlie was fighting to keep a straight face. "You ever had a mouse jump almost in your face?"

"Nope. Can't say that I have." He backed out of the pantry without laughing, but she was sure she heard a snort as the door swung shut again.

"Good thing it was me up here and not you, huh?"

"Good thing."

"You would have fallen down to the floor, huh?"

"Opal, just clean the next shelf."

"What if another mouse jumps out?"

"What if I make you wash dishes for a week? Or perhaps a month?"

Opal groaned.

They wiped and dusted in silence for a whole shelf before Opal squealed, "Ooh, lookie."

"Now what?"

Opal carefully pulled out a pile of what looked like torn-up paper and cloth. She held it carefully in both hands and lowered her burden for Ruby to see. "Baby mice. Look how tiny they are."

"Ugh, won't be long before they can jump and run too. Throw them in that box of trash."

"But, Ruby, they'll die."

"Yes."

"You think that was their mama who jumped out?"

"Opal, I don't have the time or desire to figure mouse lineage."

"But, Ruby . . ." Opal touched one of the hairless little creatures with the tip of her finger. "How can we get them back to their mother? Leave the nest in here?"

"No!"

"But we can't just let them starve to death."

No, I can think of a much swifter demise than starvation. But the look of awe and delight on her little sister's face prevented her from saying what she thought.

"What if the mama mouse comes looking for them?"

Ruby picked up a bowl from the counter. "Put them in here, and we'll think on what to do."

As they finished the cupboards, they saw plenty of evidence of mouse habitation but no more actual encounters. Ruby called Charlie to bring hammer and nails and cover a hole they found at the back corner. Now surely, if the doors were kept closed, they would have no more mice in the cupboards.

"They can get through a pinhole, I declare," Charlie said after he finished hammering.

"I don't care if they live outside, that's where they belong, but not in my cupboards and kitchen."

"You want I should put these outside?" He indicated the nest. He glanced at Opal. "I'll put them in a box right under this window, and most likely the mother will find them there."

Opal looked from the nest to Charlie and then to her sister. "I hope so. Or maybe we could pry off that board and put them in the wall. That's where she went. She'll be awful sad without her babies."

Lord, help me. Ruby patted Opal's shoulder. "A tender heart is a good thing to have." *But does it have to apply to mice?* "Put them outside, Charlie, and thank you."

Ruby set the leftover beans to heating and sent Opal up for the girls. She'd had to argue with herself over what to expect from them. If they didn't help out with the cleaning, why should they eat? After all, even the Bible said that if people were too lazy to work, they shouldn't expect to eat.

Opal came back down. "They said they aren't hungry."

"That answers that." Ruby scooped out bowlfuls for the four of them and set them on the table where a stack of sliced bread already waited. Simple fare but filling. And quick.

At about the usual time for the saloon to open, they heard a pounding on the front door. Ruby and Charlie exchanged looks and shrugged. Whoever it was would go away.

Sometime later, the pounding started again.

"Can't they read the sign?" Ruby wiped the perspiration off her forehead with the back of her hand.

"Most likely not." Charlie rolled a barrel of flour into place. "You want I should go tell them? Word will get around real quick."

"They can go do their drinking down at Williams'."

"But . . ."

"I know—the girls."

"Not only that, but he don't have room for them to play cards. Men hereabouts like to come over in the evening to play."

"Fine, you go tell them we are closed now but we will be open for meals and cards in three days. You said you knew someone who hunted and might get us a deer? If you see him, will you please ask?"

"Sure enough."

— ❧ —

That night Ruby was so tired she could hardly climb the stairs to her room, let alone carry the bucket of hot water. Opal helped her.

As she looked down at the washbowl, nothing sounded more wonderful than the bathtub they'd had at the Brandons', where she could sink down in hot water with bubbles up to her neck. They'd just poured some of the water into the washbowl when a knock came on the door.

"Come in."

Cimarron peeked around the door. "It's me. Do you have a minute?"

Ruby stifled a sigh. "Of course. Come on in."

Cimarron closed the door and leaned back against it. "I just want to ask if . . . you know . . . talk about . . ." She clutched the sides of her skirt with shaking hands.

"Go on."

"Well, did you really mean it that there won't be any more, ah . . ." She glanced over at Opal who smiled back at her.

Ruby thought longingly of the hot water in the washbowl. "We will be serving food and coffee. If you stay, you will be a waitress and at times a maid, depending on where the work is most needed. We will close all but the cardroom, where we will serve coffee only, until ten or so. No more late nights, but we will serve breakfast starting at six."

"I see."

Ruby waited until she saw indecision replaced by relief.

"Can I stay?"

"Can you sew?"

"Somewhat. Actually yes, I just haven't in some time."

"Good, we'll all need new dark skirts and waists. I'll have Charlie bring back dress goods from Dickinson."

"So that means I'll still be working at Dove House. Oh, I

mean . . . well, you know what I mean."

"Yes, and if someone you serve leaves a tip, that will be yours to keep."

"All of it?"

"All of it."

"Belle's going to be spittin' mad."

"That's up to her."

"She wants me and Jasmine to come with her."

"We'll see you downstairs, ready to work, in the morning at six."

"What should I wear?"

"Something to scrub in because getting this place clean is our first order of business." Ruby refrained from asking about Jasmine and nodded when Cimarron said good-night.

Ruby slipped behind the screen and had disrobed down to her drawers and camisole when another knock came at the door.

"Would you answer that?" she whispered to Opal. Dipping the cloth in the now warm water, she buried her face in it and, water slipping down her arms, inhaled the dampness and washed the grime from her face and neck.

"Ruby, it's Jasmine. Shall I tell her to come back later?"

"No." Ruby huffed a sigh. Why was it so difficult to get time to even wash? Why couldn't they have come earlier?

She dried her face and shoved her arms into the sleeves of her wrapper, belting it as she came around the screen.

"Sorry to bother you." Now Jasmine leaned against the door. "Would all the stuff you told Cimarron be the same for me?"

"If you want to stay."

"I do."

"Good. I'll see you in the morning at six, ready to scrub."

"I only got my wrapper and fancy clothes."

"Wear your oldest and most decrepit."

Her eyebrows turned into question marks. "I'll see if Cimarron has anything."

"Can you sew?"

Jasmine shook her head, her dark hair catching glints in the lamplight.

"Guess you'll be learning then. What can you do besides . . . you know."

"I can sing and dance."

"I know that, but what about cooking, ironing—"

"I can do that—ironing, I mean. But other stuff, I learn quick."

"Good. I'll see you at six."

"I can stay, then?"

"Yes."

Jasmine turned to leave, then stopped. "Ah, can I change my name back to my real name?"

"I don't see why not. What is it?"

"Daisy, like the flower. Daisy Whitaker. Belle said daisies are common old weeds, and she wanted something fancy for her girls."

"Daisy sounds quite lovely. Oh, and there'll be no face painting. Tell Cimarron too."

" 'Night."

I hope so. Ruby returned to tepid water and her ablutions. "You have to wash before you can get in bed, Opal." She came from behind the screen, hairbrush in hand.

"I'll brush your hair for you."

"Wash first."

"Ah, Ruby, I'm clean enough."

Ruby held up Opal's hand and showed her the streaks of dirt on her arm. "Down to your drawers."

While Opal splashed behind the screen, Ruby took out her writing case and uncorked the bottle of ink.

Dear Mrs. Brandon,

We are settling in here. My father died the same night we arrived, but we were able to talk with him, weak as he was. Our inheritance is a hotel called Dove House located in Little Missouri. We are in the process of cleaning it from attic to basement so that we can offer travelers both clean beds and good food.

Since there was no way she could describe what things really were like, she chose her words carefully.

Some of the people who worked here before are leaving, but some will stay. How I wish I had asked Cook for some of her recipes. If you would be so kind as to do that, I would be even further in your debt.

The country has a certain wild beauty, but we have not had time to go riding out in it like Opal wants. I have yet to see any other children here, but all she asks for is a horse.

Oh, you would have laughed when she learned how broody hens act. She said the hen attacked her, and the scratch on her hand proved it.

I will write more later. Please know that we miss all of you dreadfully. While I would rather get back on the train heading east, I have promised my father to give this a try.

Faithfully yours,
Ruby Torvald

She closed up her case and let Opal do her one hundred nightly strokes for healthy and shiny hair, something Ruby had learned at her mother's knee.

"Now I'll brush your hair while you read our verses for today." She handed Opal the Bible she kept on the stand by the bed.

"Where should I read?"

"How about from the Psalms? I think we need to be reminded how important it is for us to praise God."

"You didn't praise Him for the mouse today."

"No, I most surely didn't." She flinched at the memory. A chuckle started. "I didn't know anything could move so fast."

"Scared me too." Opal giggled as she flipped pages.

Ruby leaned her forehead on the top of Opal's head as they laughed softly. "I wonder what will happen next?"

— ✹ —

She found out the next afternoon when a furious pounding came at the front door. "Open up!" The man's voice sounded anything but friendly. And he wasn't begging.

CHAPTER TWELVE

"Can't you read the sign?"

"Yes, I can read, and if you don't open this door, I'm going to break it down."

Where are you, Charlie, when I need you? "If you want to talk with me, you may come around to the back. This door is locked, and I don't have the key."

The heels of his boots thudded against the porch floor all around the building, accompanied by a jingling sound.

"That's his spurs," whispered Milly at the question Opal didn't get to ask. "Spurs is what they wear on their boots to make the horse go faster."

"Oh."

Ruby tucked a strand of hair up in her bun and smoothed the sides. Stubborn little strands refused to lie down, something like the way she felt right now. Who did this man think he was anyway, giving orders like that?

Most likely one of the girls would know him, but she'd seen Belle leave early in the morning, all togged out in the styles sure to catch a man's eye. Cimarron and Daisy were up in the attic scrubbing it down so they could move all of their beds up there in preparation for reopening the hotel.

That left her, Milly, and Opal, whose eyes danced in delight at this interruption.

Ruby knew with every sense in her body that this was not

going to be pleasant. *So, do what Mrs. Brandon would do: straighten up, put a smile on your face, and speak softly and gently.* Straighten up was the easy part. Smiling was more difficult because her lips trembled, and speaking softly? Well, getting any words out at all might be part and parcel of a good miracle.

If only Charlie were here. *You better learn to handle these men, Ruby Torvald, or you will be run right out of town. Or they'll run your hotel into the ground, whichever comes first.*

He stepped through the door, and her breath caught in her throat. Their hero from on the train. The cowboy who took all the bluster out of the man who'd been so angry at Opal. Took it out so much that the drummer didn't even look their way when he left the train.

She felt Opal's hand seek a home in hers.

"Ruby, it's him," she whispered.

"I know." Ruby stepped forward, a smile in place. *"A soft answer turneth away wrath. A soft answer turneth away wrath."*

"Good afternoon, sir. How may I be of help to you?"

"Who in blazes are you?" He looked her up and down, then obviously dismissed her as being of no account. "Where's Belle?"

"One question at a time, please." Ruby clenched her fists in the folds of her skirt. The nerve of the man. "I am the new owner of Dove House. Per Torvald was my father."

He narrowed his eyes, studied her first, and then glanced at Opal beside her. "I've seen you before—I know, on the train." His jaw clamped. "What are you doing in a place like this?"

A soft answer . . . "As I said, I am now the proprietor of Dove House, and we are closed for several more days while I—we put things in order."

"My men came to town for their normal—" He clipped off his words and belatedly removed his flat-brimmed hat.

"When we reopen, we will serve three meals a day, have rooms to let, and there will be card playing in the west salon."

"Salon? Lady, this is Little Missouri. We don't have salons here, only saloons, where the liquor flows, and in Dove House the—" He stopped and glared at her. "How come you have your little sister in a place like this?"

"I assure you, Mister. . . ?" She waited for him to answer.

"Rand Harrison of the Double H."

"Double H?"

"A ranch southwest of town. Now see here, Miss Torvald, Dove House has been a good clean place for my men to come and let off steam. They come home in a good frame of mind and ready to work again. I can't say what's going to happen next payday if they get riled and—"

"Are you threatening me, Mister Harrison?" Ruby kept her voice at a tone that might have said, "would you like a cup of tea?"

"Where did you say Belle went?"

"I don't know. She no longer works here."

"Works here? She was half owner."

"Not really." *She just acted like it.*

"What about Cimarron and Jasmine?"

"They'll be serving food in our dining room." She put the emphasis on food.

"Food?" His dark eyes narrowed again.

Her attention was drawn to that line that bisected his forehead, leaving white to his hairline and suntan to his shirt collar. Even after winter the line was still there.

"I'm sure your men would like a real meal. I invite you to bring your wife to supper here. She might enjoy not cooking for all of your men."

"We have a first-rate cook out at the ranch, so you can forget about any customers from the Double H." He slapped his hat against his thigh, settled it back on his head, and spun on his heel to head back out the door.

"Good day, Mr. Harrison."

The slamming door was her answer.

Her knees, softening like jelly in the sun, forced her down on a chair at the table. Her heart felt as if it would leap clear out of her chest.

"Water, please?" How the words got past the rock in her throat she had no idea.

Opal took a cup to the bucket, used the dipper to fill it, and set it next to Ruby's hand.

"He was so nice on the train."

"I know. Shows he does have manners when he wants to use

them." She swallowed half the cup at a gulp, wiping off the bit that dribbled on her chin.

He was better looking than she had remembered.

— ⊰⊱ —

Rand Harrison glared one more time at the sign that barred the front door. Closed! Whatever convinced a young woman like her that she could run Dove House? And not only run it, but change it completely around? He would bet his last dollar that, when he saw her on the train, she'd not had any idea what went on in a place like Dove House. Dove House, home for soiled doves and the comfort they provided for lonely single men, men like most cowboys on the western range and the military and railroad men. Hadn't someone explained it to her? He swung aboard his horse and reined him around to head down the street. Now, where would Belle be holing up? Perhaps she planned on starting another place of her own. But where?

He tipped his hat to Mrs. McGeeney as he rode alongside her boardinghouse. "Good day, ma'am."

Hair bound under a kerchief, she looked up from sweeping her front porch. "Howdy-do, Mr. Harrison. You wanting something to eat?"

"Not right now, but thank you. I may be back later." He crossed his arms on his saddle horn. "Can you catch me up on what's gone on around here?"

She left her broom leaning against the wall and came closer. "You know that Per Torvald died? Buried him several days ago."

"I do now. I would have come to the funeral had I known. He was a good man."

Mrs. McGeeney rolled her eyes. "If you're meaning he weren't violent, you'd be right, but the goings on over to that place . . ." She shook her head, setting her third chin to wobbling.

"Leastwise, there weren't too many shootings there, and the cards were dealt straight. Charlie keeps things pretty much under control."

"You heard about the new owner? Torvald's daughter? Now what kind of man would bring his daughter into a situation like that, unless of course, she's one of them." Mrs. McGeeney dropped her voice on the last word as if afraid to soil her lips.

Rand Harrison looked over his shoulder to the three-storied Dove House and back at the pug hound woman near the shoulder of his horse. "Oh, I think a real lady has come to town, and we're all goin' to pay the piper." He touched the brim of his hat. "Good day." His horse twitched his tail and moved forward at the touch of the spurs.

His thoughts returned to the encounter in the kitchen of Dove House. *Spunky little thing*. But then he'd noticed that on the train too. Just never in a million lifetimes had he thought to see her again—and least of all at Dove House. *Have to admire her—for doin' what's right—but I'm gonna have my hands full keepin' the men in line*.

At each of the next places he asked if anyone had seen Belle. She'd been to Johnny Nelson's store but had gone on. No, he hadn't noticed where. There weren't that many places in town. The cantonment? Perhaps McHenry knew where she was.

He found her at Bill Williams' dingy saloon, sitting with Jake Maunders, one of the first unsavory characters to settle in town. She was having a drink and looking like she owned the world. That was Belle all right.

"Howdy, Bill. Maunders."

He joined her at the table, setting his hat down first. "I'll have a cup of coffee, Bill."

"Coffee?"

"Unless you got some good stuff?"

"I do. Bought it off Charlie this morning. Got a good deal on it too, but only going to offer it to my best customers." Williams' long teeth glinted through his bushy red beard, giving him the appearance of a fox with a swollen nose.

"What was Charlie doing peddling whiskey?"

"You want some or not?"

"Yeah, I do. Now you didn't go mixing it with that rotgut you usually serve, did you?"

"No, I didn't." Bill Williams looked aggrieved, as if Harrison had hurt his feelings doubting him like that. Aggrieved was a look he did well. "That'll be fifty cents."

"Fifty cents?"

"You wanted the good stuff. Only place in town you can get

it now." He held out a hand that had needed a good scrubbing for as long as Rand could remember.

"So now you know." Belle tapped Rand on the arm with her closed fan. "Just give us a couple of months, and that high-and-mighty girl will be hightailing it east again, back to where life is easy. Maybe only weeks."

"So what are you going to do in the meantime?" He glanced around the long narrow room with its unpainted walls darkened by smoke. "No piano here. Can't be room for more than one card table. And no upstairs. Besides, Belle, you ain't been a workin' girl for all the years I've known you."

Belle blinked several times and looked toward the low ceiling. "Might as well've been married to that man. Never thought Per's going would leave such a hole." She sniffed. "My land, but we had good times before he went and took sick."

"The two of you sounded real good singing together. Like the shows I've seen sometimes in the big cities."

"He had the voice and the smile of an angel. Never could tell him no when he got to really wanting something." Her jaw tightened. "And then he up and deeded our place to them two girls of his. Guess he had an attack of conscience or something. Rand, Dove House was supposed to be mine."

"So what are you going to do?" He took a swallow of his drink and nodded to Williams, who'd gone behind the bar.

"I thought to bring the girls along and open up a place of my own, but there's nowhere in town to do such. I ain't going back to living and working out of a tent. Did that back when I was younger, and I ain't goin' to do it again." She took out a slim cigarillo and set it into a holder.

"Hey, Bill, the lady needs a light."

"Be right there." In a minute or so the man brought a spill from the kitchen and lighted the cigarillo.

Belle drew in a deep breath and released the smoke in a thin stream, her eyes slitted like a contented cat's. "That fool girl has no sense what is needed here. We was doing just fine, even after Per took sick. Went on with business as usual. Even if she just came and left things alone, she'd a had a good living. And the rest of us too." She knocked the ashes of her cigarillo off onto the floor. "What are our regulars going to do?"

"They can gamble here." Williams brought the bottle over, but Rand waved it away.

Yeah, so you and your reprobate partner, Hogue, can cheat 'em clean to their teeth.

"I got to get back to work." Rand rose and pushed his chair back in to the table. "Let me know what you decide, Belle. If'n it were me, I'd lay low and play the waitin' game."

"Easy for you to say. What am I supposed to do? Pay for my room and board there?"

"That's not a bad idea, you know."

"If you was the southern gentleman you claim to be, you'd invite me out to your ranch to stay."

"My ranch, as you so grandly put it, is a two-room log cabin, and I know you wouldn't want to bunk with the boys."

"Teach 'em some manners, maybe?" The glint in her eyes told him she was teasing.

Rand touched a finger to his forehead and headed out the door, settling his hat on his head as he went. Change was coming to the Little Muddy, and a certain young blond woman was at the heart of it, whether she wanted to be or not.

Grass is comin' up so fast, you can watch it grow, he thought as he rode out along the river toward the Double H. He glanced up as an eagle's scree echoed from high above where the big bird lazily drifted on the winds. Spring was coming to Dakota Territory, and no other place on earth equaled it, least not the places he'd been. Spring in Missouri held a place in his heart, but the violence of a Dakota winter made warm breezes and sprouting grass and wild flowers even more appreciated. And the amazing thing was it could change overnight. Go to sleep with the north wind trying to freeze your nose off and wake to the icicles dripping off the roof and the chinook wind inviting you to leave your coat behind.

Restless and unable to settle at home in Missouri after the destruction of the war, Rand had followed what he heard about the abundant grass for hay and cattle in the last frontier. Range land, wild and free, and a place to start over with no laws to speak of and no one inquiring into your past was just what he had been looking for. Though he was fairly certain some of his men had plenty to be hiding from in their past, he had nothing to hide.

Unless, of course, someone reminded him of Isabelle. The eagle cried again, a primal sound that, like the bugling of a bull elk, ate its way into a man's heart and soul to take up permanent residence, unlike those of the female gender who promised and left.

He stopped at a slow shallow pool to let his horse drink and stared off across the river to where a flock of Canada geese grazed on the sprouting grass, the honking of the guard goose letting the others know there was danger in the area. Shame they weren't on his side of the river, where he could bag a couple for supper. Something other than venison and rabbit would be a welcome change.

Thoughts of Miss Torvald made Rand clench his teeth, the tension running out his hands, causing his horse to toss its head at the tightening of the reins. She was causing more trouble than she knew. "I hope she does get back on the train like Belle said. Save us all a pile of grief." The buckskin twitched his ears and snorted as his rider added, "But she sure is a pretty little thing."

He crested the final hill before home, his heart picking up as it always did when he saw his low cabin, sheltered by cotton-wood trees along the creek. He'd known this little valley was home the first time he'd ridden over the hill. Elk had been graz-ing the flatland on grass just going to seed with the greens and golds mixed with nodding white daisies and a blue flower that looked like bits of sky had been trapped and were being held prisoner in the grass. Ducks had quacked on the river, and a crow had announced his arrival from the top of a cottonwood, sending the elk splashing through the shallows and up a steep bank on the other side.

Today Beans had red long johns, several sheets, and other clothes hanging on the line, a sure sign that winter was over. Rand had met Beans, who agreed to come cook for him, on his way west. The three hands he employed year around were two drifters and a cowboy who'd decided Texas was getting too crowded.

He watched a few minutes more, counting the calves that had started arriving in the last two weeks. His dream of buying a

Hereford bull to cross with his longhorn cows from Texas had yet to materialize.

He leaned forward and patted his horse's shoulder. He'd traded his blooded horse for the buckskin back in Kansas on the way west. Out here speed didn't count as much as endurance.

Harrison, you got a good life here, he told himself, *so stop thinkin' about that heifer back at Dove House. I don't reckon Miss Torvald is the one for the likes of you. Maybe Belle, then, now that Per was gone? Or one of the others?*

"Must be spring when all men's fancies turn to . . ." He snorted and nudged Buck forward. Beans had been heckling him lately to find himself a wife, but face it, there weren't too many women out here on the frontier to choose from.

Even if you did head back east to find a wife, what woman in her right mind would be willing to come this far west, to the brink of civilization?

CHAPTER THIRTEEN

The front doorknob rattled and the door shook from the force of a slamming shoulder.

"We're not open yet." Daisy stopped scrubbing the woodwork stained a dull ocher by the cigar smoke and shook her head. "How many times. . . ?"

Ruby glanced over from measuring the windows for their new curtains that Cimarron was about to cut out of bleached muslin. "Be polite."

Daisy shot her a disgruntled look.

"Sign said three days, and you been closed over a week."

"Sam, we won't have whiskey when we open, so go on down to Williams'." Daisy dipped her rag in the soapy water and wrung it out. Scrubbing the woodwork without getting the flocked wallpaper wet took special care.

"No whiskey?"

"You heard me. We serve food now instead."

As the man stomped off, Daisy looked over to Ruby and shook her head. She looked up at the wide white woodwork that emerged from the dingy yellow. "Looks good, don't it?"

"Yes, it does. Better than I thought it would. Charlie said he would paint the floor tonight."

"How you goin' to keep them men from spittin' on the nice new floor? They don't take to change easy."

"Who does?" came out on a sigh. "I ordered extra spittoons."

"I scrubbed this floor three times afore I got all that up with a scrub brush. Near to wore it out."

The grumbling tone grated on Ruby's nerves, but she bit back a retort. Daisy had borne the brunt of the scrubbing in here since Cimarron spent all of her time sewing and Milly and Opal worked together on the bedrooms. Not all of the rooms would be open at first, but if she believed the girls, that wouldn't be important, as no one would be staying.

Belle had been no help at all. More of a hindrance when she made her comments on the impossibility of success.

Keeping a civil tongue in her head took constant effort.

Daisy sighed and hefted her bucket of water. "Got to go change this. Don't look like I'll get any sewing done today."

"Get yourself a cup of coffee." *Maybe that will help. As if anything would help. Why, oh why, did I not get back on that train?* Ruby stared at her hands, now red, with one thumb cracking from the lye-soap water. Her skin felt rougher than the grit they'd used to scrub the floor. She rubbed the spot on her forehead that seemed to simmer constantly with headache warnings. *Far, how can I live up to my promise? I'm just too tired.*

— ❧ —

"That's too much money." Belle stood, hands on her hips, glaring at Ruby.

"That's what we're charging for that room. It's the best in the house. If you want to move to a smaller one, the price is seventy-five cents a night, breakfast included." Ruby forced herself to stand toe-to-toe with Belle, wondering if at any moment the discussion might turn to fisticuffs or hair pulling.

"But that room's been my home ever since we opened the doors at Dove House."

"Save the tears for the men, Belle. I have a heart of stone." At least she'd been working at toughening up her heart. Explaining to men in various stages of rage that Dove House would no longer have the same hospitality services as before either hardened one's heart or broke it. And she was determined hers would not be broken. Not by hard work or whining women or thundering men.

Both Cimarron and Daisy bemoaned the demise of their soft

hands due to all the scrubbing, water-hauling, and washing of curtains and braided rugs that had been inflicted upon them since the arrival of Ruby Torvald, despot and slave driver. But at least they worked, unlike the high-and-mighty Belle.

"Belle, my offer for you to run the cardroom still stands, and I am hoping we can offer some musical entertainment since we have the piano."

Belle leaned forward, her cigarillo-tainted breath nearly knocking Ruby backward. "You won't be open even two weeks unless you got money I don't know about stashed somewhere. A lot of money. And how you going to pay me?"

"One third of the receipts from the cardroom, like I told you."

"Half."

"Either take it or leave it, Belle. I'm not going to haggle with you."

"If I agree to run the cardroom at a third, can I keep my room?"

Ruby thought of the lack of customers desiring rooms of any kind, let alone the big room. Charlie had suggested she and Opal take that room, and she'd declined. But if she let Belle have privileges, that wouldn't be fair to the others who had worked so hard. The urge to rub her forehead twitched her fingers.

"No, Belle, I'm sorry, but that room needs cleaning too. You can have a free room up in the attic like the rest of us."

"You're up in the attic too?"

"Yes. And we *all*"—she stressed the all—"have pallets on the floor for now." Until we can make or buy some beds. Extra tables for the dining area had come in on the train just that day, but there was no money for beds. She thought of the funds in the envelope and the expenses so quickly slimming it down in spite of all her efforts at frugality. Dove House ate money like the stove did wood.

"I think not."

"That's your choice, but you must have your things out of the room today."

Belle threw four dollars down on the counter. "There. That gives me four nights. You got at least one customer." She glanced at Ruby. "And if I pay for my room, I get half the winnings?"

Ruby shook her head again. This was too much. Carefully

folding and putting Belle's rent in her pocket, she said, "Thank you. Breakfast is from six to eight."

"I don't get up that early, and you know it."

"There will always be coffee and bread or rolls for those who would rather sleep later." *Please, Lord, get her out of my hair before I tear it out.*

"Humph." Nose in the air, Belle marched up the stairs, her heels tapping out her displeasure.

Ruby stared down at the dirty apron that covered a skirt badly in need of a brushing. Her waist needed washing, and more than anything, she needed a bath. In a tub—with hot water. But there was no way she was going to lug all those buckets of hot water up two flights of stairs to the attic.

Thinking of a way to remedy that situation, she went in search of Milly. Together the two of them dragged the tin hip bath into the pantry. Carrying the buckets ten feet was a relief compared to lugging it up all the stairs to the attic.

"Why don't you go tell Cimarron and Daisy that, if they'd like to use the bath water, they are welcome to do so. I've heated enough water from the rain barrels for all of us to wash our hair and to bathe."

Milly took a step back. "You don't mean for me to get in that water, do you? Catch a chest cold is what you do if you take a bath before summer. 'Sides, that's what the bowls and pitchers are for."

Arguing took more energy than Ruby could dig up.

"Do you know where Opal is?"

"Last I saw her she was about done scrubbing the porch. She might be helping Charlie."

"Tell her she can have a bath too."

Ruby climbed the back two sets of narrow stairs to the attic to fetch clean undergarments. While she had a new skirt cut out, she'd not had time to sew it yet.

Daisy and Cimarron were sitting in the light from the window and stitching new aprons. They had finished their new navy-blue skirts, a white shirtwaist for each, and two aprons that pretty much covered their clothes. The cost of their fabric had been part of the drain on the money.

"You want I should start on your skirt?" Cimarron, much

quicker with the needle than Daisy, asked. "I'm nearly done with these."

"That would be good of you." Ruby leaned over the trunk in the small space she shared with Opal and retrieved her undergarments. "We've moved the hip bath into the pantry, and right now I'm going to take a bath. You are welcome to do the same if you like."

"Ah, a real soak in the tub?" Cimarron waved her hands above her head. "In the pantry—what a perfect idea."

"How close to done are you on the table linens?" Ruby asked the two girls.

"If we all work on them, we should be able to finish hemming the tablecloths tonight. The napkins . . ." Cimarron shrugged. "You know, Opal is real handy with a needle too."

"Opal is real handy with a lot of things. She fixed my window when it was stuck." Daisy looked up from her stitching, and immediately the wrinkles left her brow. "She's smart, that one, and not afraid of hard work."

Ruby felt as though she'd just been handed a gift, all opened and ready to enjoy. "I'll tell her you said so." Treading quickly back down the stairs, she couldn't wait to talk with her younger sister.

"Ruby, guess what?" Opal met her on the bottom stair.

"What?"

"Charlie found us a cat, only half grown but real pretty." She grabbed Ruby's hand and pulled her along. "Come see. We have her in a box. Charlie said female cats make the best mousers. He said her mother is a real good hunter." Her words tripped over each other in her rush to get them all out. She knelt by a wooden box with the lid held down by a rock. "She's so scared, being hauled around like this."

"Where did he find her?"

Opal looked up, questions marking her eyes. "I don't know. I forgot to ask. You think she will like it here?"

"She will if you get her a saucer of milk and some of that venison roast left from last night."

"Good. I will." She motioned Ruby to kneel down beside her. "I'll lift the lid, and you peek quick before she jumps out."

Ruby did as ordered and peeked in the box. A fluffy gray cat with a white spot on her head that took in part of one ear hissed back at her. Crouching in the corner, the cat glared back out of slitted green eyes.

"Oh, Opal, she *is* really pretty."

"See, I told you. Now we got to tame her. Wish we had a cage or something so she wouldn't run off."

"We could keep her in the pantry, soon as we get done with our baths."

"I don't want no bath."

"Any."

"Any bath."

"I know you don't, but sometimes we . . ."

" . . . have to do things we don't like."

Ruby cocked an eyebrow and stared at her sister. "I've said the same thing too many times, I take it. You even sound like me."

Opal scuffed the floor with the toe of her shoe. "Sorry."

"Bath after Cimarron."

Opal heaved a sigh, the kind of sigh that said she was only doing this terrible duty out of love for her sister. "All right."

Ruby tugged gently on one of Opal's braids. "And we'll wash your hair too." Chuckling at the woebegone look on her sister's face, Ruby headed for the pantry and the bliss of a bath.

— ✣ —

That evening, with Charlie baking a cake to serve for dinner the next day, they all gathered in the dining room to spread the tablecloths on the tables and set them for the morning. Opal laid the last knife and fork in place and stepped back to see that all was straight. Ruby had given strict instructions on how the tables were to be set, how those who came to eat should be served, and who was in charge of what.

Daisy pulled at the high neck of the waist she now wore. "Can't hardly breathe, this is so tight."

"Won't nobody come without booze behind that bar." Cimarron shook her head. "While I sure do hope this works, I don't have me a good feeling about it a'tall." She nodded toward the pounding that had started on the front door. "I'll get it." She crossed to the door and yelled back. "We're closed until six in the morning when we open for breakfast."

"Breakfast! I want a drink, and I want it now."

"Sorry, we will no longer be serving liquor. The cardroom will open at three."

"Cimarron, that you?"

"Yes, Johnny, it's me."

"I heard there ain't anymore . . . you know."

"You heard right."

"Well, whatever's a man to do?"

"See you at breakfast from six to eight."

They all listened as he stomped off, the words he threw over his shoulder none too complimentary, nor were they fit for young ears. Or any woman's ears, for that matter.

"Told you so," Belle called down from halfway up the stairs, where she'd been sitting and watching the goings on.

"Have you decided to run the cardroom yet?" Ruby asked.

"For now. But I ain't sleeping up in the attic."

"Suit yourself. You know the rate for the room." Ruby glanced around one more time. Hard to believe this had really been a saloon. It cleaned up mighty fine, just like the girls did. White cotton curtains were looped off the long windows with red tiebacks to match the red papered walls. The floor took two coats of blue-gray paint that set off the dark chairs amid the white-clothed tables. All the woodwork shone from scrubbing and a fresh coat of beeswax. The former bar now gleamed like the rest of the woodwork, ready for its new life as a desk for checking guests into the hotel. A shiny bell sat next to the box for cigars. Thinking the carved and inlaid box might be the buksbom her father had referred to, Ruby had cleaned and polished it herself, finding nothing but cigar dust and disappointment. She knew both Cimarron and Daisy had applied a little kohl, some rouge, and some powder to their faces, but she decided to let it go for now. Their suffering in the new garments was bad enough to hear about without having them grouse about looking like ghosts.

They were all set for their new customers. Now if only some would show up.

— ❧ —

That night, after the lights were all out and her stomach was knotted like the ball of yarn the cat had found to play with, Ruby realized how long it had been since she'd read in her Bible, how long since she'd really prayed. *Lord, how easy it is to fall away, please forgive* ... Sleep claimed her.

— ❧ —

6:00 A.M. No one.
6:30 A.M. No one.
7:00 A.M. Ruby went outside to make sure the open sign was still in place. Two of them, in fact. One nailed to the right front post read:

Breakfast 6–8, 35 cents.
Dinner 11–2, 75 cents.
Supper 5–7, 50 cents.
Cardroom 3 P.M.–1 A.M.

She had changed the cardroom hours from 10:00 P.M. to 1:00 A.M. at Belle's insistence. Was she charging too much? Wrong hours? She returned to the kitchen to join the others in eating their own breakfasts.

"Word just hasn't gotten around yet." Charlie set a plate of ham and eggs in front of her. "I'll go out later and call on every building in Little Missouri."

"What if you put up a sign at the railroad stop? For the people on the train, you know." Cimarron took a bite out of a cinnamon roll that looked and tasted both sinful and delicious.

Charlie continued to surprise Ruby with his cooking talents. If only everyone would realize what they were missing.

"Good idea. We'll paint one this morning."

"Milly and me could take samples around," Opal offered.

Ruby looked a question at her little sister. "Samples?"

"You know, like the man in the park used to do. 'Get your free samples here!'" She imitated the barker's call to the chuckles of the others at the table. "We could do that, huh, Milly?"

Ruby glanced at Milly too, hoping that she would agree. At her nod of agreement, Ruby smiled at Opal. "That's a good idea too. Anyone else?"

"Oh!" Charlie shut the door to the pantry a second too late.

Cat, as the young kitten was called since she had no name yet, streaked across the kitchen and into the storage room. Milly and Opal lunged off their chairs, too late to dive for the cat but quick enough to see which stack of boxes, barrels, and buckets the gray fluffy tail disappeared behind.

"Here, kitty kitty." Opal had already perfected the right tone of pleading. She'd spent a good part of the evening before sitting in a corner of the pantry trying to entice the cat to take a bit of venison from her fingers, all to no avail. However, anything put in the dish had been devoured. Their cat would not starve to death. Of course, with all that food available, she might not bother with the mice either.

"There are mice in the storeroom too." Charlie poured more coffee all around.

"True, but it will be more difficult to tame her if Opal can't find her."

"She'll come out for food."

"Now if that was a male cat, food would work, but for a female? Don't count on it." Cimarron stared at Charlie over the top of her coffee cup, one eyebrow raised.

"You saying males can be bribed with food?"

"If the shoe fits . . ."

At the man's guffaw, Ruby happened to glance at Daisy and saw a look of adoration aimed at the man teasing Cimarron. *Oh my, I hope that's not what I think I'm seeing.* Though inexperienced in the ways of men and women, she'd read enough books to recognize the situation. Daisy had a thing going for Charlie, and Charlie always treated her like his kid sister—if he paid any attention to her at all, other than being polite.

A bell tinkled. Ruby leaped to her feet and headed to the dining room. Someone had come in. She pushed the newly painted swinging door open.

"Good morning."

"Good morning, ma'am." The soldier who spoke removed a gray broad-brimmed felt hat. "Is Charlie here?"

"Yes. I'll get him. Would you like to have breakfast?" At the shake of his head, she added, "Coffee?"

"Sorry, I just need to talk with Charlie."

"All right." Ruby returned to the kitchen and sent Charlie

out. She'd hoped for at least one customer.

By evening they'd served no one in the dining room, but four men had gathered in the cardroom where Belle could be heard laughing as she dealt.

"Hey, Charlie, bring on the whiskey!"

Ruby looked up from the table where she sat going over the ledger and caught the look on Charlie's face.

He believes we should be serving whiskey. And if we were, we would have some money coming in today. I know that's what my father would have been doing, along with providing plenty of "hospitality." And he made money. Now here I am trying to turn this establishment into a place I needn't be ashamed to work in and where I can have my sister with me. God, I figured this is what you wanted me to do. If I'm wrong, I'd sure appreciate it if you would let me know before I lose every cent I have and this place, our inheritance, too.

"Don't you go gettin' discouraged now." Charlie stopped by the table on his way back to the kitchen. "It's just the first day. Tomorrow I'm going to take rolls and coffee over to sell when the train comes in. No one is used to getting food here, but we'll see how it goes. I baked cookies this afternoon too. If it goes well, this is another something that Opal and Milly can do."

"You think so?"

"Well, how often did you have to get off the train for food on your way west?"

"You're right." She thought a moment. "We could make up some handbills to hand out to the drummers." She flinched at the thought of the man she'd had the altercation with on the train. What if he came by? Not that there were many people in the town to buy anything from a drummer. Whatever possessed her to think she could. . . ?

"Now, Miss Ruby, there you go again."

"Is it that obvious?"

" 'Fraid so."

Belle's laugh from the cardroom stung like lemon on Ruby's nerves. Here all the rest of them had worked themselves to the bone, and Belle lay around complaining. Now she was having a great time while the rest of them were still working dawn to dark and later.

Ruby slammed the ledger shut, stuffed it on the shelf behind the former bar, and stomped off into the kitchen.

The three around the table looked up, guilt like red paint all over their faces.

"What are you doing?"

"I'm learning how to play poker, Ruby, want to join us?" Opal held up her hand of five cards. "Five card draw, and I won twice already."

Ruby closed her eyes, sucked in a deep breath, and unclenched her teeth.

Cimarron snatched the cards back. "I think we'll play hearts instead. You ever played hearts, honey?"

That's all I need. My little sister a cardsharp.

CHAPTER FOURTEEN

"Fool woman. Why'd she have to go messin' around with things?"

Thoughts of Dove House's new proprietress had plagued him day and night for the two weeks since he'd been to town. Buck's ears swiveled as he kept track of the terrain, his rider's muttering, the whisper of the wind in the sagebrush, and the tumbling creek.

Pretty little heifer, isn't she? Rand thought back to the spitfire he'd stepped in to protect on the train. In spite of having spent days on the train, she'd backed that fool drummer right up the aisle. Rand's own warnings had been helpful but not necessary. Still, it must have been a shock to wake up to a little girl staring you in the face.

He chuckled, then right out laughed when he put himself in the man's place. No wonder the drummer had been fit to be tied. And Rand was tied too, tied up in knots by a bitty young woman who'd most likely take on the world in defense of her little sister. On the train he'd thought the young girl might be her daughter, but Miss Torvald, as he now knew her to be, didn't look old enough to have a child that age.

While she didn't look so fancy in a dark skirt and white shirt, blouse, waist, whatever women called it, her backbone hadn't softened any. You had to respect her for that, even though she was totally foolish in making changes at Dove House. The odds on her making a living in Little Misery without the girls' services and the booze were slim to none.

Of course, that's what his family had told him about running cattle out here in the middle of nowhere. But then they hadn't seen the lush grass that grew so fast in the spring you could measure it each day, the rivers and creeks that provided water, and the breaks and valleys that provided protection from the cold in the winter and the heat of the summer. One needn't worry about neighbors getting in your way either.

And now that he had a snug cabin, steady help, and two hundred cows calving this spring, he'd decided one winter night that if he didn't start thinking of a family pretty soon, he might as well not think of it at all. Thoughts of sharing his bed and house with a warm and willing woman kept returning to him like butterflies to a patch of flowers.

He tightened the reins only a twitch, but Buck stopped immediately. Rand stared out over the greening plains that rippled and rolled far as the eye could see. If you didn't know the badlands were out there, one would think the plains went on forever until you rode up to the edge of the cliff and looked down and across the most incredible shapes and colors, unimaginable until you saw them yourself. Near as he could figure, God went on a carving and painting spree when He laid down the Missouri and the Little Missouri Rivers. He must have been having a right good time. After the horror of war, the wildness of the badlands—or Mako Sica, as the Indians called it—was a good antidote. Rand had not had time nor energy for feeling lonely up until this past winter.

The trip home to Missouri hadn't helped.

"Why don't you stay, Rand?" His sister Abigail had pleaded. "We could sure use some help around here."

"I know you could, but I got cows of my own to take care of. Spring roundup will start not long after I get back, and I gotta be there for that."

"Roundup?"

"We have free range. That means those cows can cover half a county or more."

"No fences? You must lose a lot of stock that way." Abigail paced the kitchen, alternately patting the baby she carried against her shoulder and stirring the squirrel stew she'd made for supper. She handed Rand the baby and set about beating an egg and adding the flour and milk for dumplings. After dropping the spoonfuls of dough into the simmering stew, she retrieved the now sleeping infant.

"How bad has it been?" he asked her.

"Well, we still have the place. As you can see, Mark Allen works dawn to dark in the fields, and most of what we make goes for taxes. If we could pay some of the Negroes to come back and work, it sure would help. This place is too big for one man. Though Benjamin helps as much as he can, he's only ten." She laid the baby down in the cradle near the stove. "But it's not big enough to support the two or three families needed to work it."

"I understand, but . . ."

He watched her. She'd aged far more than her letters had let on. They had three children now, and several small markers over in the family graveyard told of losses alongside of his mother and father. While his father died not long after the end of the war from wounds suffered in the battle at Sayer's Creek, his mother lived on until after Rand had left for the West.

"How are Jefferson and Sue Gail doing?"

"Hanging on like the rest of us. Too many women and not enough men to support them or keep the farms going."

Rand thought of all the land in the West, the free homesteading. But in the West one didn't have two-story houses with curtains and rugs or barns with stalls and neighbors within hollering distance. You didn't have churches and schools and roads, but then you didn't have taxes and the law breathing down your neck either.

"You could come west."

"We've been over that before. This is home, and here we'll stay."

The next morning he had kissed his sister good-bye, shaken his brother-in-law's hand, and offered them the freedom of the West once more before boarding the train. He hoped his next trip would be to take back the Hereford bull he'd found after visiting several farms up in Illinois.

Buck stamped a foot and tossed his head, bringing Rand

back to the present. On the valley floor a small herd of prong-horn antelope grazed, one buck keeping an eye on the horse and rider. Ponderosa pine trees, junipers, and elderberry and choke-cherry bushes lined the draw leading from valley to prairie. He would follow the cattle-and-game trail back down, most likely scaring up a mule deer or perhaps the doe with twin fawns he'd seen a few days before. Riding this range he called home always brought new sights, if nothing more than the way the buttes threw their shadows in the evening or the rising sun highlighted a slash of red stone. The *whee whee* of a canyon wren sang from the draw. He'd seen them, their tiny tails flicking upright with every motion, almost invisible as they dug in cracks and crevices, searching for insects. There were far fewer birds here than at home.

Mother would approve of her. The thought jolted him.

Buck tossed his head, his show of surprise or even resent-ment at Rand's movement. Rand knew his mother had only tol-erated Isabelle, warning her son more than once that his intended had a roving eye. Hard to admit she'd been right. He patted Buck on the shoulder and murmured an apology. Funny how thoughts could blindside you like that.

One rifle shot, then another—the universal call for help—echoed across the land. Turning Buck to the left, he headed over the prairie and to the ranch house. What could have happened now?

CHAPTER FIFTEEN

May 1882

Empty rooms. Empty tables. Empty pocketbook.

Ruby stared at her ledgers. Empty. At least on the income side. She hated to look at the other side. Good thing she couldn't write in red, or it would look as if someone was bleeding on the pages. How could refurbishing Dove House cost so much money? Although she wasn't totally out of funds, her resources were dwindling. If only she could find the buksbom. Surely there was more money in that.

"Ruby!" Opal's call jerked her out of her stupor.

She rose and followed the calls to the pantry.

"Look. Cat caught a mouse." Cat looked up at them, the half-eaten body clutched between her claws. Cat had become the name because they could not agree on a name for her. Fluffy, Spot, Ghost, Tippy—none of them fit as well as Cat. And besides, she'd quickly learned to come when someone called Cat. It never failed that a treat was waiting for her when she arrived.

Ruby felt slightly sick at the sight, but one less mouse in the pantry meant one less shock when she opened a cupboard door, although the mouse population had dropped after Charlie boarded up the hole in the cupboard and the other in the floor molding.

"Charlie says she caught one in the storage room too." Opal couldn't have been more proud had she caught the critter herself. "She's really smart, isn't she?"

"I guess."

"Well, just think. She figured this out all by herself, even without her mother here to show her how."

"I think cats are born knowing how to hunt."

"Well, how come people have to be taught to eat and get their food?"

"I imagine people would eat just fine with their hands. We teach manners and proper ways of doing things so that we can all get along better."

"Do you think if we had another cat, they would share?"

"Have you done your lessons for today?" Sometimes changing the subject helped when the questions got beyond her ability to answer.

"Well, Bernie didn't share well. He took Jason's toys whenever he could."

"Your lessons." And sometimes distractions didn't work at all.

A big sigh. "All right. But it's almost bedtime now."

"Opal." Ruby closed her eyes to calm the words that shouldn't be said, no matter how good the saying would feel at the time. She'd spent much of the day practicing to be like Mrs. Brandon.

Belle had tried to talk her out of making her pay for her room—again. Several of the cowboys from area ranches had complained at the changes in Dove House. Cimarron burned her hand on the flat iron. The men who came to play cards tracked in mud from the slick street, due to two days of rain. If allowed to dry, the mud had to be chipped off the floor. Never had she seen such hard stuff in her life. Milly had shown Opal how to slide across the top of the mud, something like skating on ice. After they'd slipped, she'd sluiced them both down with buckets of water on the back porch before allowing them to enter.

Charlie thought it was funny. She might have too if things weren't piling up high enough to choke her. Good thing every day wasn't like this one.

— ❧ —

The next morning Cimarron pulled Ruby aside into the storeroom. "I just want to tell you what I've found out."

"All right." Ruby waited, wondering if she should ask where the information came from.

"I heard that some folks in town have been warning everyone to stay away from Dove House."

"Stay away? Why?"

"So you will go broke and someone can come buy the place cheap."

"Who?"

"I don't know."

"Who told you?"

"I better not say."

"Is Belle in cahoots with this idea?" Cahoots was a new word she'd learned from Charlie. It seemed to fit well here.

"I don't think so."

"Why not?" Ruby could feel the heat beginning in her midsection, heat she'd felt far too often lately.

Cimarron tightened her jaw. "Because she's the one who told me, and if you let on you know, she'll suspect I told you, and then she won't never tell me nothing again."

Ruby rubbed her tongue against the back of her teeth, thoughts chasing after one another like Cat after her tail in the sunshine.

Speaking of which, Cat meowed from the top of a box, and when Ruby reached up to pet her, she commenced to purring. "Well, will you listen to that?"

"She's getting tamer every day." Cimarron rubbed under Cat's chin. "I better go. Charlie is teaching me to make bread this morning. I figured I might as well learn more about cooking too. After all, who knows what the future might bring."

"Good for you." Ruby kept on stroking the cat, the rumble feeling as good beneath her fingers as it pleased her ear. When Cimarron left the room, Ruby dug through a barrel and a crate looking for *the box*, as she'd come to think of it. Soon, when she ran out of places to look, she'd ask Charlie if he had any idea what box her Far had meant.

A jingle from the bell over the front door sent her scurrying into the dining room.

"Good morning." Captain Jeremiah McHenry pulled off his leather gloves to loop through the belt of his dark blue coat.

"Good morning, Captain, welcome back. How can I help you?"

"Are you still serving breakfast?"

While it was past the hour, Ruby nodded. No matter what

time it was, they finally had someone who wanted a meal. "Sit where you like, and I'll bring in the coffee."

His hat lay on the table nearest the kitchen door when she returned, and he was studying the changes in the room.

"Looks mighty nice in here. Has an entirely different feeling."

"Thank you. Charlie is making fresh coffee, so it will be a minute. We have ham and eggs with potatoes and a choice of fresh bread or sweet rolls." No sense letting him know that the girls drank the extra coffee so as not to waste it. It was better to let him think there had been customers earlier of sufficient numbers to drink it all.

"Sounds wonderful, especially the sweet rolls." His smile made her want to make sure her hair was neat, but she kept from fussing with the reminder that a lady didn't fidget. This time the voice was her mother's, and since fidgeting had been a problem for her daughter, she'd repeated the admonition every day, sometimes far more than once.

"I'll bring the rolls in."

"Could you join me in a cup of coffee?"

"Why . . . why I suppose so. Is there a problem?"

"Problem? I don't believe so." The look of confusion that flitted across his face told her he had no part in the revolting scheme. But since he came in, of course he didn't. She scolded herself as she returned to the kitchen. But who could it be? If it wasn't Belle, then who? That Bill Williams and his cronies? Could be. But who had voiced his disapproval most heartily?

That rancher — Rand Harrison, that's who! The certainty burst in her mind like a gunshot. She set the rolls on a plate and returned to the dining room.

"You said Charlie was making coffee. Is he your cook?" At her nod the captain shook his head with a chuckle. "He is most certainly a man of many talents."

"He's a far better cook than I am." Ruby held the plate of rolls out for him to help himself.

"I wanted to come by and tell you again how sorry I am on the death of your father." He bit into the roll and nodded. "Very good."

"Thank you." She took a roll and broke off a small bite.

"I hear you are from New York?"

"Yes, and you?"

"Ohio. I joined up on my seventeenth birthday in the final days of the war. My mother wouldn't allow it before then. I'd just joined my father as an adjutant when he was wounded during the siege of Petersburg. He died a few weeks later."

"I'm so sorry to hear that." She glanced up when Daisy arrived with the coffeepot and filled both their cups. "Thank you, Daisy."

"Your breakfast will be right out, sir." Daisy kept her gaze down, as Ruby had instructed her, and returned to the kitchen.

"How'd you find any young woman like that to work for you out here?"

He doesn't recognize her. The thought pleased her. Perhaps Cimarron could serve the tables too—no, Cimarron's red hair would give her away anywhere. And once anyone heard her laugh, they'd never forget it. But Daisy . . . Her new look along with a name change had made her unrecognizable. If what she'd heard about the lack of women out here was really true, perhaps some man would fall in love with Daisy and . . . Within heartbeats, Ruby had the story all worked out. Now if only life would help instead of hinder.

"Ah, here comes your meal. I hope it meets with your approval." *And I hope you will tell everyone you know that the food here is the best.* Best of what she wasn't sure, but something needed to happen soon if they were to stay in business.

"Sure beats military grub," he said after a few bites.

"How long have you been stationed here?"

"Two years." He took another roll. "I was stationed at Fort Laramie in Wyoming Territory before coming here."

"So you know the local people well?"

"Most of them."

Ruby argued with herself for a few moments. Would he be loyal to his friends, if that's what they were, or would he be honest? "Your family must enjoy being closer to a real town again."

He paused, set his fork down, and wiped his mouth with the napkin. "My ma and brothers and sister are still in Ohio. I thought of bringing Ma out, but this is still frontier country, and she likes having her family around."

So he'd say if he were married. But, still, I want to know about the folks here. "I have a question to ask if you don't mind."

"No, I don't mind, but I'll make it easy for you. I'm not married and never have been."

Her face flamed in a flash. "Pardon me?"

"Oh. Miss Torvald, please forgive me for my . . . my . . ."

Rudeness, presumption, ego, even if she had thought—oh, bosh. She didn't help him out but stared at her hands and wished for a fan, a breeze, cold water, anything to cool the heat. She took a sip of her coffee and finally looked back at his face. Good, he was as uncomfortable as she. Served him right.

"I was going to ask you for advice." At his now composed nod, she continued. "It has come to my attention that someone in the vicinity has requested or suggested that no one eat or stay at Dove House so that I will be forced to sell, supposedly at a greatly reduced price. Do you have any idea who that might be? The 'why' I can understand, since whoever this person might be would like to return Dove House to its former mode of business."

"Ah, I see." He drank from his coffee cup, staring at nothing, clearly running names through his mind. "Williams wouldn't have the money. He's always cash poor. Not Maunder's way of doing things. He'd cuss or cut you to death instead. Belle?"

"That was my first thought too, since she assumed Dove House would be hers when my father died."

The captain shook his head. "I can't see it being any of the ranchers. You considered someone outside of the area, like from Dickinson or Bismarck?"

"I hardly know anyone in town, let alone those places."

Daisy returned with the coffeepot. "Would you like refills?"

The captain smiled at her as he raised his cup. "Daisy, is it?"

"Yes, sir."

"Well, thank you kindly, Miss Daisy. And tell Charlie he makes a great breakfast."

"I will. You are most welcome, sir." She turned and scurried back to the kitchen.

Ruby caught him staring after her.

"She looks vaguely familiar. Where did you say you found her?"

"I didn't. She found me. So can you think of anyone else who might be involved?"

"Not off the top of my head, but if someone comes to mind, I'll let you know."

"Would you like more to eat?"

"Gracious, no." He drained his coffee and leaned back with a sigh. "It's been a long time since I had breakfast with a lovely young woman."

Again the heat flared. "You are most kind, sir."

"I was wondering if you might like to see more of our country? I haven't forgotten my promise to your sister that I would bring a horse by for her. Do you ride?"

"No, but both my sister and I are willing to learn."

"Your sister is how old?"

"Nine, but as she reminds me, almost ten. She dreams nightly of riding a horse and has suggested we have plenty of room behind the hotel to pasture said animal should I be willing to purchase one for her."

"She sounds like my little sister when we were growing up. She became quite a horsewoman." He leaned slightly toward her. "So am I understanding correctly—if I brought two gentle horses by, both of you would be willing to learn to ride so I could show you the country? We don't have too many roads for a buggy or wagon."

"I see." Ruby thought of Opal's coming delight. "Yes, Captain, we would be most happy to ride with you."

"I don't have sidesaddles. They aren't exactly army issue."

"Oh."

"Women around here, what few there are, wear divided skirts."

"Divided skirts?" *What am I getting myself into?*

"You haven't seen pictures of them?"

"No."

"Sometimes they are made of leather."

"Leather?" *What do I do with all my petticoats? I can't ask him things like this.* There came that heat up the neck again. *Mrs. Brandon, what would you do now?*

"I'll work something out. Thank you for the invitation." She pushed her chair back. "We'll see you tomorrow then?"

"Yes, for breakfast, and unless it is raining, we'll ride. That's thirty-five cents, right?"

"Yes." Should she say it was on the house since he volunteered to take them riding?

He handed her a dollar. "That nice little waitress deserves a good tip."

Ruby swallowed her immediate response of "no." If he wanted to tip the waitress, that was his choice. After showing him out the door and making change from the cashbox, she whirled around to head for the kitchen.

"See, you knead this way," Charlie was explaining to Daisy as Ruby burst through the door.

"Does anyone in this house have a divided skirt for riding a horse?"

Cimarron looked up from her sewing by the window. "I think Belle does. She and Per used to ride. Why?"

"Captain McHenry wants to teach Opal and me how to ride tomorrow morning."

"Ride? Me?" Opal dropped the plate she was washing back in the water. "I get to ride a horse?"

"Looks that way." Ruby oomphed as she caught Opal running full tilt to hug her. The change in her hand bounced on the floor.

"Oh, thank you, thank you."

"Don't thank me. Save that for the captain—not that you will thank him the same way, right?"

"Right." Opal squeezed even harder. "I get to ride a horse. Tomorrow can't come soon enough."

Ruby broke free and picked up the coins. She laid them on the table. "Captain McHenry said this tip is for you, Daisy, for doing such a nice job."

Daisy stopped kneading the bread and gaped at Ruby. "For me? Really? All of it?"

"Of course. Why?"

"Well, Per took half . . . I mean . . ." She stared at her hands, then back at Ruby. "Sorry."

"That's all right. It's yours." Ruby shook her head as if shaking off a fly.

"All right, tell me about divided skirts. I've never heard of such a thing."

Cimarron put down the napkin she was hemming. "You and

Belle aren't too different in size, if the waist is a bit big—"

"I thought we were talking about a skirt, not a waist."

"We are." Patience colored her words gently, but her smile was a teaser. "I mean the waistband. And if I remember right, Belle's is made of real soft leather, both skirt and jacket, beaded with a leather fringe. Per had a jacket like it. I wonder what happened to that jacket? Humph." She thought for a moment. "Wonder when I saw them last? But then Belle don't get rid of nothing, so we might find them. I could take one of Opal's skirts and remodel it for her."

"By tomorrow?" Opal went to stand next to Cimarron.

"If I start now. You bring me one, and I'll get right at it."

"Thank you." Ruby studied the young woman whose red hair was backlit enough by the window to look like autumn in all its blaze of glory. What a difference there was between who she had thought Cimarron was at their first meeting and this young woman sitting in the chair, so ready and willing to make Opal happy. And Ruby too, for that matter. She turned and glanced at Daisy smiling up at Charlie as she kneaded the dough.

What about Belle? Was there someone else lurking under that brash and brassy exterior? Someone who might come out if a bit of kindness was shown to her?

"You think Belle would loan me her skirt?"

"Never hurts to ask. And if she won't, I'll stitch faster."

"You think Belle is up by now?"

"Ain't seen hide nor hair of her, but it's early yet."

Ruby stretched around from one side to another. Often lately she woke with a backache. Her body still wasn't used to the heavy labor. It made no sense for all of them to sleep on pallets when all the beds in the hotel but one were empty. But any day now they could have a crowd of people wanting rooms, couldn't they?

"I been thinking . . ." Charlie brought her a cup of coffee.

"Thanks. About what?"

"About how to get more people to know about the changes at Dove House."

"Me too, but I hope you've come up with some ideas, because I'm fresh out."

"I think you should write letters to places of business in

Dickinson, Bismarck, and even Fargo. Or maybe write to the newspapers and ask if they'd like to make an announcement to their readers. The *Bismarck Daily Tribune* is always reporting on things here in Little Missouri."

"Good idea. Do you know to whom I should write?" She held up a hand. "Wait until I get paper and pen."

As soon as Charlie had given her a list, Ruby sat down at the table to write. She knew she could go in the dining room where it was quieter, but today she wanted others around. The laughing and talking in the kitchen reminded her of home at the Brandons' in New York.

After finishing one letter, she looked up, tickling her chin with the feather end of her quill pen. "I'm surprised we haven't gotten any business from the sign you put up where the train stops."

"Come to think of it, me too."

"I'll go look." Opal carried the dishpan toward the door. "After I dump this."

"When we get the garden in, all water goes on the plants. I'm thinking to put some roses around Dove House. Will look right purty."

Ruby stared at Charlie. That man was full of surprises.

"We had a garden last year, but this year it better be a big one. I will keep digging it up today. I already planted the peas and early stuff, 'cause when it's warm like this the ground heats up fast. Got seeds coming in on the next train, besides the ones I saved from last year."

"Charlie, you constantly amaze me." Ruby signed another letter and began addressing envelopes.

"Good morning." Belle swept into the kitchen, all dressed to go out, her lavender walking dress with black trim a sight to behold.

"You're going to get that hem all muddy out there." Cimarron glanced up from her hemming.

"No, I won't. I'll be riding in a wagon."

"Where to?" Charlie asked.

"You'll know soon enough." Belle poured herself a cup of coffee. "Are there any rolls left?"

"In the pan." Charlie nodded to the pan covered with a dish

towel and sitting in the middle of the table.

Belle helped herself and made appreciative noises with the first bite.

Ruby folded one of the letters and inserted it into the addressed envelope. Might as well get it over with. "Belle, I have a favor to ask."

Belle licked the frosting off her fingertips. "And what might that be?"

"You know your leather riding skirt?" Cimarron intervened. "Ruby needs it to go riding."

"Riding. Really? Who with?"

"Captain McHenry. He said he'll teach Opal and me how to ride."

"Well, well, well. I assume you have no riding costume?"

"No, I've never had a chance to ride before. Opal is ecstatic." *Please say yes before I have to beg.*

"I wonder where it is." Belle propped her elbows on the table to hold up her coffee cup. "I haven't seen it in a month of Sundays. Not since Per lost the horses gambling. Miracle he didn't lose the whole place." She took another bite of roll. "You got any idea where it is?" She looked over to Cimarron.

"Back of the armoire would be my guess. Unless it's in the trunk under the window."

"Must be there. I tore the armoire apart and didn't see it." Eyes slitted, she studied Ruby over the rim of her cup. "You find 'em, you can have them. Including that shirt of your father's if you'd like. Should be with the others." She turned her head to the side, watching Ruby from the corner of her eyes. "Of course, we might work out an exchange. Say riding skirt for rent?"

So much for Belle's generosity. "We can work something out, I'm sure."

Opal came through the back door, shouting her sister's name.

"What? Lower your voice, please."

"But the sign! It's gone. Someone took it."

Ruby glanced over at Belle but saw no guilt there. Either the woman was a superb actress or she really wasn't involved in the conspiracy. Which was it?

CHAPTER SIXTEEN

"Look, Ruby, I'm really riding."

Ruby would like to have been able to wave gaily and sing back to her precocious baby sister, "Yes. Me too," but she daren't take her eyes off the horse to which she clung with hands, feet, legs, posterior, ankles, toes, elbows, and any other portion of her anatomy with which she could maintain contact.

All but her stomach, which was ready to jump ship, or rather jump horse, at any moment.

"How are you doing up there?" Captain McHenry smiled over his shoulder as he led her mount gently around in a circle.

Is this really necessary? Surely a buggy would be better. Or walking. I'm a good walker. "Fine, I'm just fine." *Can he see the fear all over my face, or am I as good an actress as Belle? Why did I ever find this outfit? I could have had an excuse.*

"You look fetching in that outfit."

"Th-thank you."

"You know, if you relax in the saddle, it will pretty much keep you from falling off. We train our new recruits to relax and have them galloping in no time."

Her throat clamped shut.

"No, don't worry. I wouldn't do that to you. But this old horse, he's trained many a young rider. Here, let me give you the reins."

Her squeak must have changed his mind.

"All right. Once more around the circle, and then I'll stop and you can ride around me."

Ruby kept her gaze straight out between the two ears that swiveled and twitched with all manner of motions. Surely the horse couldn't see with his ears too, but that's what he seemed to be doing.

Captain McHenry stopped and flipped the rein over the horse's head to lie on the mane. "Pick up the rein. This horse is neck-reined, meaning when you lay the rein to the left, he will turn left and the right for right. See how Opal is doing? She's a natural rider. You'd have thought she'd ridden for years, not just minutes."

"I'm glad. She has looked forward to this day most of her life, but before it was only a dream." Ruby could feel herself relax now that the horse wasn't moving.

"Hold your reins gently and even. You'll think that Blaze here will almost read your mind, but really he's reading the way you move. Your feet and legs are just right. Sit straight and stay relaxed like you are now. Let yourself feel the horse moving."

She wanted to nod and smile, show her courage, but she couldn't find it. Where had it gone? She took a breath and let it out.

"See, Ruby, how easy it is?" Opal stopped beside her.

Captain McHenry had found a fairly small mount for her.

"You be careful," Ruby admonished.

Opal picked up her rein again. "Come, ride with me, Ruby,"

"All right." Ruby glanced up to catch a smile from the captain. She could do this, of course she could. She could also fall off and crack her head, and then who would take care of Opal?

"Just lean forward slightly, and your horse will walk out." The captain's smile gave her renewed courage. Why could someone brave enough to get on a train and head west to a place she had no idea what to expect panic at riding a horse around in a circle?

"Come on, Ruby. You have to ride here so we can go up the river."

"Oh, of course, go up the river." Ruby did as the captain had told her, and sure enough the horse moved smoothly forward, following Opal's mount, stopping and starting the same as she.

"All right, lean your reins to the left and turn in a gentle loop to go the other way. Good."

After once more around, Ruby realized she was actually enjoying the movement of the horse. She smiled over at the captain, who touched the brim of his hat with two fingers.

"Are you ready to go riding with us?" he asked.

"I think so. As long as we don't go any faster than this."

"We'll take it easy."

I sure hope you and I have the same definition of easy.

Single file, they headed south along the river. Long pussy willows wore a patina of yellow pollen, their bright green leaves sparkling in the sunlight.

"What's that sound?" Ruby stopped her horse to listen. A thrumming rose on the air, then abated before rising again.

"That's a grouse looking for a mate. He makes that sound to attract the females."

"Where is he?"

"Most likely up there in the brush. You can see them roosting in the trees come dusk. You mean no one has brought you any to eat?"

"Not that I know of. Charlie bought venison and antelope from a hunter."

"You ever been fishing?"

"No. There's not much call for fishing in New York City."

"Would you like to learn?"

"I would." Opal sat on her horse like she'd been riding for years.

"We could take a picnic and go to one of the best fishing holes, not that there are any bad ones, and fry our fish right there."

"Really?" Opal looked from the captain to her sister. "Can we do that?"

"Do we have to ride very far?"

"No, but it's faster than walking."

Ruby rubbed one hand down the soft leather covering her thigh. Without her petticoats, she felt a freedom she'd never known. She tipped back the flat-brimmed hat that had stayed on her head only with the help of the leather string under her chin. Now it swung down her back, and the breeze lifted the tendrils of hair that refused to stay bound in the bun at the base of her head. She looked up into a sky so blue she could think of no words to describe it. The light danced on the water, the current bouncing back sparkles like the crystals that glistened in the candlelight from the chandeliers in the Brandon home. Her gaze moved up the hills along the river, where a cowboy on a horse stood watching them.

"Do you know who that is?" she asked the captain.

"Looks to be Rand Harrison. He's the only man around here that I know of who owns a buckskin."

"Buckskin?"

"The dun color of his horse."

"Ah." Could he be behind the conspiracy? But she hesitated to ask the question. After all, even the captain could be involved.

The sight of the rider on the hill stayed with her as they rode back to what only euphemistically could be called a town. It was just a small group of buildings scattered down along the railroad tracks.

"Thank you, Captain." Ruby smiled his way and then stared at the ground. Now that she was going to have to get both feet back down there without embarrassing him or herself, it looked farther away than ever.

"Like this," Opal said, demonstrating the dismount. She swung her leg over the rear of the horse and, kicking her foot free of the stirrup, jumped to the ground. But Opal didn't have to worry about showing any more of her leg than was proper, whereas the divided skirt Ruby wore didn't cover her legs clear to her ankles.

"Did you have a nice time?" Charlie stood on the back porch of the hotel, his derby hat in place, as always. He snapped his suspenders. "I have good news for you."

"What?"

"Would you like some assistance?" The captain stood at the horse's shoulder.

"I . . . ah . . ."

"Just swing your right leg over while you hang on to both the front and the rear of the saddle."

"You make it sound so easy."

"Once you do it a few times, you'll find it so." His smile eased the panic setting her stomach to fluttering. "I won't let you fall."

"Good. The thought of suddenly sitting on the ground isn't appealing." She took a deep breath and followed his instructions. *Right leg over, strangle the saddle, but there's no ground down there.* She hung on the side of the horse.

"You only have a few inches from your foot to the ground, but if I assist you at this time, you will accuse me of being most forward." His voice came from just behind her, and she could feel the heat of him he was so close. "Just let go. You won't fall."

She shut her eyes and did just as he said. Both feet hit the ground. "I did it."

"Good for you, miss. Next time we'll devise a mounting block to make this easier."

He stepped back as she turned to leave. Her gaze traveled up the row of polished gold buttons to his chin, a fine square chin, clean shaven, a smiling mouth and eyes that held both warmth and a hint of laughter. In spite of his rank, he seemed a man who liked to laugh.

Her breath caught in her throat. What a fine man it was who stood right next to her. "Thank you again. We had a most pleasurable time."

"Tomorrow?"

"Tomorrow?"

"For the fishing expedition."

"Oh." If only she'd left her hat on to shield the heat she could feel blazing from her face. She must look red as a radish.

"We can go tomorrow, can't we?" Opal pleaded with every ounce of her being.

"Let me think a moment." Ruby stepped back away from the captain. Thinking was easier with a bit more space between them.

Charlie snapped one of his suspenders. He had waited patiently but obviously had news. "We have three guests who came in on the train today. They are talking with Frank Vine over at the post store about going on a hunting trip. But we can take care of them while you go fishing. In fact, fried fish would be a good thing to serve for supper."

Ruby nodded. "All right, Captain. We'll go fishing."

Opal leaped up the steps to the porch and then back to the

ground. "Fishing. We're going fishing!"

Ruby smiled up at the man near her. "I think she's happy."

Captain McHenry chuckled. "How old did you say she is?"

"Ten next week."

"What day?"

"May sixteenth."

"Ten is a big year. Perhaps we should plan something special."

"It's already in the works." She whispered so Opal would not hear. "I'll let you know the details later. Thank you, sir, for a very special day." She mounted the stairs and turned to wave as he rode back to the street, leading the other two horses.

"I like him." Opal leaned against the carved post. "Ruby, riding that horse was more fun than I ever dreamed it would be."

Ruby wanted to rub her backside but knew how improper that would be. If she was sore now, what would it be like to ride for hours?

She turned to Charlie. "All right, tell me about our guests."

"You'll meet them at supper. All are from the East—two from New York, one from Boston. They sure do talk funny. Have to concentrate real hard to understand them. It's their first time out here. I don't think they even know how to ride."

"Now *that* I can understand. What are we having for supper?"

"Roast venison."

"Good." She met Daisy at the door.

"That Captain McHenry, he is one handsome man."

"True, and so very mannerly."

Daisy leaned closer to ask, "Are you sure he wanted me to have that big of a tip?"

"He said so."

"But that's almost as much as . . ." Daisy looked away over her shoulder.

"And it's yours." Ruby laid a hand on Daisy's shoulder. "This is a new life, remember?" At Daisy's nod, Ruby added, "Besides, who knows when I will be able to pay you."

"Perhaps if you went back to the bar and the singing and dancing but not the . . . you know, that might bring in more money."

"You liked the singing and dancing?"

"We all did, except for when the fellas got drunk. Some of them were real mean. I had bruises lots of times from them pinching. But Charlie, he tried to keep that kind of thing from happening. Any of us gave him the sign, and he took care of the customer all right. Threw them right out the door, he did."

Ruby remembered the man who had been thrown out in the street soon after she and Opal arrived in Little Missouri. Now that she knew more, she wished he'd thrown out a lot of others too.

Opal ran to regale Milly with all the details of her ride, and Ruby followed Charlie into the dining room.

"I put them in the first three rooms on the back side."

"Good. Those are the nicest."

"The men will be here three nights now and also when they return from their hunting expedition. They agreed to pay for the rooms as long as their luggage was there, so . . ." He touched the brim of his bowler at Ruby's beam of delight. "I try, Miss Ruby, I really do."

"I know you do, Charlie, and I can't begin to tell you how grateful I am. We couldn't manage without you."

"Thank you. We might have more customers soon. I talked to one of the drummers heading west, and he said he'll pass on the information. Rumor on the line was that Dove House was closed up permanent-like, so I told him different. Got a new sign up too."

"And the garden plot spaded up?"

"Not all of it but enough to get more seeded. Cimarron's been making noodles to go with the venison roast. And Milly is doing the biscuits. We'll put out a good spread, not like fancy hotels back east, but if they aren't happy, they can try down to Mrs. McGeeney. Three in a room and no clean sheets. Or sleep on the floor at Williams'."

"Why, Charlie, you make a right good salesman."

"Now for the bad news."

Ruby sighed. "Why would I ever think we could have all good news in one day?" She glanced down at her clothing. "Tell me what it is so that I can go change before I help with supper."

"We got a letter from the mercantile in Dickinson."

"Letter or a bill?"

"Since it was addressed to you, I thought I better not open it. No way it can be good though. We owe them a lot of money."

"I know." She took the letter and slit it open with her fingernail. Unfolding the sheet, she read swiftly, then went back to the top to read it aloud.

"Dear Miss Torvald,

"I am sorry to be forced to these desperate measures, but unless I receive a sizable payment on your account by the end of May, we will be forced to operate on a cash-only basis. I hate to lose the business of Dove House, but with the changes you have implemented, we believe that your hotel will soon be bankrupt.

Sincerely,
Mr. Boyd Rumsford,
Proprietor"

"What are you going to do?"

"I don't know, Charlie. I just don't know."

CHAPTER SEVENTEEN

"Ready to go, Boss."

Rand looked up from filling his tin canteen, one of the few useful mementos of his father's time in the war. Riding the arroyos and buttes looking for cows was a hot and thirsty business even in May. He checked the cinch on his saddle and mounted. Buck waited for the signal and moved forward as Rand gave final instructions to his men.

"Joe, you and Chaps cross the river. You, Joe, take the south, and Chaps, you go north. Bring in any cows you find. You can leave the steers and heifers out there. Beans, you go north on this side, and I'll go south."

"Sure, Boss, but I got to cook supper too."

"I know." One more hand would sure be a help. Someone to keep the fire going under the stew. "Let's bring 'em in."

He watched as the other three headed out. For the two crossing the river, the river was belly deep on the horses, so the cows and calves would have to swim a short way. However, most of the stock would be on his side of the river. He hoped.

By the time the sun was straight up, he'd found fifteen cows, only one without a calf. He started them back toward the ranch, riding down into the arroyos, checking out the shade where the cows could lie to chew their cud during the heat of the day. He stopped at a tumbling creek to wet his bandana and give Buck a quick drink. Other than the bellowing of the cows as they called their calves and the laughter of the creek, sounds seemed swallowed up in the immenseness of the prairie. He remounted and swung the loop of his rope to get the now grazing animals moving again. One calf bawled at his mother when she started walking before he finished nursing.

He heard a rifleshot and waited for the second one of a distress call, but none came. Not like just days earlier when Mrs. Robertson sent out the call and they went to help her find her youngest daughter. The little girl had wandered away, and if it hadn't been for a snag of blue fabric on a stick, they might not have found her, having tumbled down into a gully as she did. Mrs. Robertson said she was going to put a leash on the girl and tie her to the clothesline for the summer.

Rand picked up two more head and drove them all into the home valley as the western shadows started to paint the valley floor. Beans had found only eight but carried the carcass of a yearling buck tied behind his saddle, and Joe and Chaps were nowhere in sight. Rand drove the cattle over to the river to drink and then let them spread out and graze. He sat easily on Buck, one leg crooked around the saddle horn as he studied the cows for signs of injuries or illness. With hides varying from red to white to black and all variations of spots in between and their horns lengthening by age, the cows made a good showing against the green of the meadow. By keeping all his heifers, his herd had doubled in the last two years. The Hereford bull he hoped to bring back from Missouri soon would make a big difference in the quality of the steers he would have for market over the next years.

When he heard whistles and calls from across the river, he rode back down to the bank in case some of the calves needed help. The older cows knew enough to swim downriver from their calves, but the younger ones could easily lose a calf in the current, even lazy as it was.

"Lookin' good," he shouted as Joe and Chaps hupped the cows into the Little Missouri. But sure enough, one calf started drifting downstream, bawling for his mother and half drowning in the effort.

Rand flipped his loop larger and nudged Buck into the water. Swinging the lariat above his head, he tossed it over the bobbing little red head. His noose landed with a splash, right on target. He tightened the rope and dragged the calf until he got his feet back on the ground. But as soon as the calf could stand, he tried to run for his mother and slammed against the length of the rope. Buck followed the calf so Rand could get close enough to loosen the rope and let the scared little fellow go running back to his mother, who bellowed and shook her horns in her disgust at the rude way her calf had been handled.

Rand shook his head. "You'll really be mad day after tomorrow, old girl, so rest up good tonight."

— ❧ —

"You're going fishing? Ugh." Cimarron made a face.

"Have you ever gone fishing?" Opal stood at the dry sink washing the breakfast dishes while Milly tidied up the rooms of their guests.

"No, but my brothers used to. You can believe they scaled and cleaned them too—I wouldn't touch them."

"But you like to eat fish?"

Ruby looked over to her sister. What was going on in that head behind the innocent face?

"If I go catch the fish, can we say I am repaying you for making my skirt a divided one?"

"If you'd like."

"And if I caught lots of fish, you might be willing to fix another skirt?"

Cimarron laughed, an unmistakable laugh with half a horse whinny in it. "Opal, you don't have to pay me for sewing for you. Your sister is doing that."

When she can. The thought sent Ruby's mind off on the track of trying to figure out a way to bring in enough money to stay in business.

Cimarron glanced out the window overlooking the hen house and garden. "I see Charlie is hard at it. Since you came, Ruby, he's been going like a barn a'burning."

"You mean he wasn't always this way?"

"Nope." Daisy flipped the bread dough over and kneaded from the other side. "He did a garden last year but not with all the hummin' and whistlin' I hear goin' on."

"Why do you suppose that is?" Ruby asked.

"No idea, unless he feels like all of us do. You make us feel needed, even important."

"Oh."

"Whole place feels different."

Yes, it feels empty. But the men had played cards until long after she went to bed and seemed to be having a good time, even without the liquor. Charlie had dealt at the second table.

Opal took her dishpan to dump the water in the barrel outside. "Charlie is ready to plant, and I'm going to help him." She clattered the pan onto its nail on the wall behind the stove. "Milly, you want to come help me?"

Milly glanced at Ruby to catch her nod.

Cimarron watched the girls leap from the porch, calling to Charlie. "You know, I think that Milly likes Charlie." She raised her brows to indicate her meaning.

"Nah." Daisy shook her head as she thumped the bread over again. "He's too old for her."

Ruby looked up from her writing to catch Cimarron's raised eyebrow. "She's too young to be interested in men."

"She's fifteen."

"But that's . . ." Ruby stopped to think. Back east Milly would still be a schoolgirl, but out here, she'd heard of girls marrying by fifteen. "You think Charlie realizes it?"

"Nope, he's been eyeing me for the last two years." Cimarron snipped the thread with her scissors. "He hides it well but a couple of times I caught a look in his eyes. Shame, 'cause I don't feel that way about him at all." She held her needle up to the window to see the eye better.

Daisy was silent but was kneading the bread with a little more gusto than Ruby thought was necessary. *And Daisy has feelings for him too. Oh, for the wisdom to handle all this.*

Daisy set the bread to rising. "I'll go clean out that cardroom now. You'd think those men could hit the spittoon more often, wouldn't you? It's not like we don't have enough of them around." She picked up a bucket, dumped hot water in it, shaved in some soap, and with broom and wash rags, headed out the door.

Ruby caught the look Daisy daggered at Cimarron. One

more place to watch out for trouble. As if money, or the lack thereof, wasn't enough of a headache.

At the same moment, the bell tinkled from over the front door.

"Good morning, Captain," Daisy greeted.

"And to you, miss."

Ruby rose and followed Daisy out to the dining room. "Good morning, Captain. Would you like a cup of coffee? It will be ready in a minute."

"That would be just fine, unless of course there are any of those delicious rolls left."

"You make yourself comfortable, and we'll rustle up something." *My land*, she thought, *I'm beginning to sound like the others around here. Rustle up, indeed.*

"I hear you have some guests." He pulled out a chair.

"Yes, they're out settling things with Frank Vine. Planning their hunting trip. Does he do that a lot?"

"Frank does anything that will earn him a dollar."

"Are you saying that he is . . . ah . . . shady in his dealings?"

"You might put it that way." He laid his hat on the table. "Frank hasn't let too many scruples grow under his feet. But then, that's not too unusual for the folks of Little Missouri."

"I see." As she returned to the kitchen she wondered if the captain had included her father in that none too savory assessment. Would Frank Vine have enough money to buy Dove House? Could he be in league with Belle?

She left Cimarron to serve the captain and hurried upstairs to change, grateful all over again for her soft leather riding skirt and jacket. That she had hat and boots also was certainly providential, even though they came by way of Belle, who had claimed more rent-free days as payment. She dressed quickly and returned to the kitchen.

"That surely does become you," Cimarron said, setting the coffeepot back on the stove. She raised her now full cup in salute. "Go forth, have fun, and bring home plenty of fish."

Ruby glanced into the dining room where Captain McHenry had made three rolls and two cups of coffee disappear. "I'm ready when you are," she called out to him.

"Good, I'll bring the horses around to the back."

Moments later, Opal charged through the door. "The captain's here."

"Yes, so you better go wash your hands."

"To go riding?" Opal held up dirt-crusted fingers. "We got worms for fishing too. And I planted the beans." She ducked around Ruby, sloshed her hands in the pan of soapy water on the reservoir, and hit the door, wiping her hands on her skirt.

Ruby pulled on her gloves as she went out the door. "Oh, I forgot the picnic."

"Not a problem. I brought what we need." Captain McHenry stepped to the ground in such a fluid, easy motion that Ruby sighed. Would the day ever come that she didn't feel like a top about to tumble when mounting and dismounting?

She stopped at the steps. Charlie was setting a box down by the hitching rail. "What's that?"

"Your mounting block. It will make getting on and off much easier."

"Charlie, you think of everything."

"McHenry asked me to build one." He stood back. "Opal, you want to bring your horse over here? Makes mounting a long sight easier."

Opal did as Charlie showed her and was on her horse in a twinkling. "Thanks."

Having seen how to do it, Ruby took the reins from the captain, led her horse over to stand in the right spot, stepped up on the block, put her left foot in the stirrup, and with hands only half strangling the saddle, got her leg over the horse's rump and half sat, half fell into the saddle. But at least she made it with her dignity intact and her legs decently covered.

"Very good," said the captain. "Now, I suggest you dismount and mount again. Each time will be easier."

"But I . . ." She gave him a disgruntled look and dismounted. The mounting block definitely made a difference. By the third remount, while Opal was being taught to post, Ruby settled in the saddle comfortably. She picked up her reins and, after giving Charlie a pleased wave and smile, nudged her mount forward. *Why don't they make these saddles with some padding?* A pillow would be a welcome addition.

"Comfortable?" Captain McHenry rode up beside her.

Well, endurable. "Yes, thank you."

"Good. Let's go fishing."

They rode out along the west bank of the river, following the same trail as the day before. A birdsong rose and danced in the air like the sound of an opera singer practicing her scales.

"That's a meadowlark. We have a lot of them around here." The captain turned in his saddle to tell her. Another answered from across the river. "There, he's flying. See that flash of yellow?" When he pointed out the bird, Captain McHenry dropped back to ride beside Ruby. "You'll find lots of new birds out here. You've seen the flocks of ducks and geese heading north? They look like long V's in formation."

"I thought I heard quacking."

"And honking. That's the geese. Easy out here to have plenty of goose down for pillows and bedding. You could most likely get one of the local men to hunt anything you'd like. Although I wouldn't recommend rattlesnake. Some like it, but I don't much." He glanced over and chuckled at the look of horror on Ruby's face.

"Surely you are teasing me."

By the time they'd ridden about a half mile up the river, the captain announced they would stop and fish there. They tied their horses under several cottonwood trees, and McHenry slung his saddlebags over one arm.

"First thing we need to do is cut three willow branches for poles." He handed Opal the saddlebags and drew a knife out of the scabbard attached to his belt. Then choosing a long straight branch from willow brush, he cut the first one and handed it to Ruby before cutting the other two. After trimming the branches off them, he handed them around. "There you go. Opal, do you have the worms?"

"Yes, sir." She drew a pouch made from one of Charlie's handkerchiefs out of her pocket. "We gave 'em some dirt so they wouldn't dry out."

Ruby knew Opal was quoting Charlie again. According to her, Charlie knew everything worth knowing about life in the badlands. However, even the thought of carrying a pouch of worms in her pocket made Ruby shiver.

The captain opened the flap on one of the leather saddlebags and pulled out three corks with a fishhook imbedded in each, a ball of string, and three round peas of lead.

"What's that for?" Ruby eyed the lead.

"The cork is for a bobber and the lead is a sinker to take the worm down to fish-eye level. Watch." He pulled some line off the ball of string and tied one end to the top of the pole. About two feet from the other end, he tied the string in the groove cut in the cork. Another eighteen inches down he did the same with the lead, then tied the hook on the very end. "Now, Opal, you do just as I do, and we'll get the other two ready. In this country you always travel with a hook in a cork and some string, and you'll never starve to death."

"How would you find worms all the time?" Opal was tying her string to the pole as she questioned.

"Wait. Let me show you a proper knot." He demonstrated a half hitch and a slipknot, which Opal copied quite deftly on the second attempt. "Very good."

"What would you use if you didn't have worms?" Ruby's curiosity got the better of her.

"Oh, grasshoppers, most any bugs, grubs from under rocks. The fish are so thick here I think you could throw out an empty hook and snag something."

He took a worm from Opal's pouch. "Now, you thread it on like this."

Ruby turned away.

"You need to know how." Opal looked up from copying every move the captain made.

"I'll learn that part another time." Ruby took the pole handed to her.

"Then you choose a rock to sit on, always watching out for rattlers —"

"Out here?" Ruby shivered.

"They like the sun in the spring like this. Snakes are cold-blooded creatures and need a warm rock and the spring sun to get them going."

Ruby stared at all the rocks around them. "If I'd known we could see a snake, I'd have stayed at Dove House," she muttered as she looked for an empty rock to sit on.

"You sit here, and I'll show you how to toss your line out."

The captain flipped his line out gently, and the cork landed with a slight plop, sending concentric circles rippling out. "I like fishing in the pools like this. Some like—" His cork disappeared and with a flip of the wrist he jerked the pole and a fish went flying out behind them and landed smack on the bank.

"Oh, did you see that?" Opal's eyes were as round as her mouth.

While his fish flopped around, the captain motioned to Opal. "Get your line out there, the next fish is yours. Miss Torvald, you can't catch fish unless you throw your line into the water."

Ruby tossed out her line, enjoying the circles waving out. She turned to look at Opal's shriek and missed her own cork go under. But she felt the tug on her line and automatically jerked it. The fish flew up, missed the captain's head by inches, and landed with a resounding smack.

"I nearly got kissed by a fish there. Better watch out for the two of you."

Ruby clung to her pole. *I caught a fish!* She wanted to whoop like Opal, but whooping was definitely not on the list of ladylike things to do. So she giggled instead.

"Come on, you got to take the hook out of the fish's mouth so you can fish again."

Ruby stopped all forward motion. She watched as McHenry showed Opal how to grasp the fish in one hand and slip the hook out with the other. Then he strung a line through the gill and tied the line to a stake he stuck in the bank, sliding the tethered fish back in the water.

"That's to keep them cool so they don't spoil before we head back to town. Unless you'd like to cook them out here. I brought fire starter."

"I think I'd rather take them back for everyone to enjoy."

Ruby shuddered as Opal threaded another worm on her hook and returned to the riverbank. She turned back to catch the captain staring at her.

"What?"

"Do you know, Miss Torvald, how lovely you are?"

Ruby wished she could pull her hat down to cover the fire burning up her face. "Th-thank you." Catching her breath took a moment. Now she didn't dare even look at him. *Oh, my. What do I say now?*

"Would you like to fish again?"

She nodded.

"Can you bait the hook?"

She shook her head, accompanied by a shiver that ran clear to her fingertips.

Another of Opal's fish flopped at their feet. Ruby stepped back so it wouldn't smack her boots. She took the rebaited pole offered and returned to her rock.

Within an hour they had three strings of fish. The captain dismantled their poles while Ruby set out the sandwiches, cookies, and a jug of water from the saddlebag.

"Not very fancy I'm afraid, but I was really planning on having fried fish."

"I had no idea we would catch so many so fast." Ruby unwrapped her sandwich. The first bite told her how famished she was. "Are there other places like this for fishing?"

"You can catch fish about anywhere on the river and in most creeks, but this is one of my favorite spots. Sometimes if you are real quiet in the early morning or the evening, you can see deer come down to drink. I've seen fox and coyote. And cattle too."

"You ever see any buffalo?" Opal swallowed quickly when Ruby caught her talking with her mouth full.

"I've seen them, but there aren't very many anymore."

"Indians?"

"Of course, but they're on the reservations now."

"See out there on the water where the circles are?" He pointed toward the middle and slightly upriver where the water eddied and quieted below the rocks. "That's a fish come up for a bug."

"They're hungry, huh?"

"They sure are, especially in the spring like this. They hide on the bottom of the deep pools during the winter."

"All winter without eating?"

"That's right."

Ruby picked up a piece of wood and tossed it into the water to watch it float downstream. One of their fish on the string flopped, tail flapping the water. A horse stamped and snorted.

How easy it would be to lean back against the log, close her eyes, and let the sun soak deep into her bones.

The voices seemed to come from afar off.

"Miss Torvald!"

"Ruby."

She blinked to find both Opal and the captain staring at her. "What? What's wrong?"

"Nothing, but we need to get going before you two get sunburned out here."

"You fell asleep," Opal whispered.

Sunburn or not, her face flamed again, and she scrambled to her feet.

"When the water warms up, this is a good place to go swimming." Captain McHenry finished packing his saddlebags and turned to smile at Ruby. "You know how to swim?"

She shook her head.

"You could learn."

"I—I—we better be getting back, like you said." Substituting a convenient log for the mounting block made getting into the saddle easier than she expected.

Captain McHenry handed her one string of fish. "Loop it over the front of your saddle or tie it to one of those rings." He waited while she looped it in place. "Good. You two are quite the fisherwomen."

After Ruby had dismounted back at Dove House, this time with somewhat relative ease, the captain said, "I'll be leaving on patrol again in a couple of days. I hope you had a good time."

"We had more than a good time. We had an adventure we'll never forget." Ruby nodded toward the three strings of fish he'd handed to Charlie, who immediately set to cleaning them for supper.

"I should be back before Opal's birthday. Perhaps we can ride again?"

"I'd be pleased. Thank you, Captain. You made one little girl happy beyond measure."

"And her older sister?"

Ruby looked up at him from under her hat brim. "Why, Captain, if I didn't know better, I'd say you were flirting with me." *As if I know what flirting is.*

"Would that be such a terrible thing?" His voice deepened.

Surely just getting off the horse wouldn't speed up her heart rate so. "Good-bye, Captain McHenry. I hope you have a good trip." She dropped her voice. "And that you get back in time for Opal's birthday." If she took the steps a bit faster than necessary, it wasn't because she was running away—at least that's what she told herself. When she entered the kitchen and caught Cimarron watching her with one eyebrow cocked and a knowing smile, her face flamed yet again.

"Must have been too much sun."

"Uh-huh."

— ঙ৽ —

Chaps wiped his mustache clean with the back of his hand as they sat around the table replete with the stew and biscuits Beans had made. "Saw a carcass out there, or what was left of one after the vultures took their fill."

"How many with other brands?"

"Oh, ten, fifteen."

"The men from the other ranches will be here day after tomorrow for the branding."

"The steers look pretty good for so early in the season." Chaps dug at something caught in his teeth.

"Winter wasn't bad." Rand looked to Joe. "You see any sign of predators?"

"Only that one I told you. Might be some missing, but we won't know that till the branding's all done."

"Turner said the Indians took some of his." Beans looked up from sopping the last of the juice off his plate with a biscuit half.

"If they'd let 'em off the reservation to hunt elk and deer, the Indians might not take the beef." Joe pushed his tin plate back.

"Well, if the beef range on Indian land, they got a right to take 'em, far as I can see."

"So how you gonna tell a cow, 'There's the line. Don't go no further'?" Chaps shook his head. " 'Course, why don't the Indians range their own cattle?"

Rand poured himself more coffee and raised the pot. The others shook their heads. "Because they're hunters, not farmers."

"You wasn't a rancher before you came out here, was you?"

"Nope."

"So if you could learn, why can't they?"

"Good question, and I'm sure if the government could figure that out, it might make some difference." Rand tossed the last of his coffee grounds out the door. "Chaps, you take first watch. I'll do second. Joe, you take the last tonight. Beans, you watch what we already brought in during the day, and tomorrow keep 'em from heading out again."

"Sure, Boss."

Joe stood and stretched. "Guess I'll get me some shut-eye." He ambled out the door toward the bunkhouse.

Chaps followed him to go saddle his horse, and Rand leaned against the doorframe. The cry of nighthawks hunting bugs in the starlit sky, the lowing of cattle as they settled down for the night, and the whisper of wind in the pine tree by the front porch sang of evening, a song that called to his very soul. Other than sunrise, this was his favorite time of the day. Work was done and the world was settling down for rest. The clatter of tin dishes as Beans washed them up blended with all the other night sounds.

Shame he didn't have someone special to share all of this with. The thought brought on another. Would he ever?

CHAPTER EIGHTEEN

They had set out again at first light, ranging farther in all directions, and after finding another fifty head of cows, Rand headed home to add them to the herd in the valley.

He'd just unsaddled Buck when a riderless horse galloped up to the other side of the river and splashed through.

"Hey, that's the horse Chaps was riding today!" Beans yelled from the porch.

"Saddle up." Rand swung his saddle off Buck and headed for the corral to catch another horse. When Chaps's horse came to a halt at the corral gate, Rand caught him and stripped off the saddle before sending him out in the corral.

Within a few minutes he and Beans, saddled up and leading a spare horse, headed back across the river. As they reached the western bank they met Joe and his cattle coming down the draw.

"You seen Chaps?" Rand yelled to be heard over the cattle.

"Nope, not since this morning. Why?"

"His horse came back without him."

"You want me to help look for him?"

"No. Stay with the herd."

As soon as they topped the butte, Rand stopped. "One shot means he's okay, two we need help."

"Okay." They kicked their horses into a gallop and spread out.

Every so often Rand stopped to holler for Chaps, listened,

then picked up the pace again, watching for any sign that Chaps had been this way today. He saw a pile of horse manure from the day before, cow pies crusted over, all signs of the herd from yesterday.

"Chaps! Can you hear me?"

Dusk blurred the landscape. He rode on.

Hoping for a miracle, fearing a tragedy, he stopped to call again.

"Here." The voice was faint.

"Where?" Joy leaped as did the horse at the prod of spurs. Rand scanned the terrain, called again, and waited for an answer. The voice had been faint. He rode forward a hundred yards and, hand cupping his mouth, called again, "Keep hollering."

"Here."

While the voice was louder now, no matter how slowly he scanned the terrain, he couldn't see Chaps anywhere.

The next time he called, the voice came from slightly behind him. "Where in — ?"

"The tree!"

One cottonwood tree stood higher than those around, but even as he drew closer, Rand saw no sign of his hand. "Chaps?"

"Over here. I'm tied behind the tree."

Now Rand could see the rope that banded the tree. He rode on up and dismounted, shaking his head as he stepped on the ground. "What happened to you?"

"How'd you know to come lookin' for me?"

"Your horse came home without you."

"I knew I liked that horse. Some sidewinder said he was hurt and asked if I would help, but when I dismounted, he conked me one, and I woke up tied to this tree. He and my horse were gone."

Rand took out a knife, but Chaps shook his head. "No, don't cut the rope. It's my lariat. You can untie it, can't you?"

"If I hadn't come along, you woulda been buzzard bait." Rand used the point of his knife to dig the knot loose.

"You ain't tellin' me something I don't know. How I let myself get into a fix like this . . . If'n I ever see that varmint again, I'll make sure he can't walk for a long time, if ever." With the upper rope loosened he shook his arms free and helped Rand finish the job.

"Thank God, I found you."

"Been doin' that ever since I heard your voice. Something like this tends to make a believer outa even as tough a cowpoke as me."

Rand pulled his rifle from the scabbard and shot once in the air. He handed Chaps his canteen for a long drink, and the two of them mounted up to head on home.

"You ever seen the man before?"

"No, but he looked like he hadn't seen civilization for some time. Squinty-eyed, he was, on the left side, and had a cough that didn't sound too good."

"Did he say why he was on foot?"

"Thought he had a broken leg, but he sure turned spry real quick as soon as I got off my horse. Thanks, Boss."

"Yeah, well, couldn't afford to lose a good man, not right before branding."

Chaps barked a laugh.

"How many cows did you have?"

"Had eighteen, twenty head. They all scattered. I'll set out in the morning and bring 'em in."

— ⚜ —

Ruby watched as Frank Vine and his brother finished loading the three pack horses.

"I told you to bring only what you needed, you . . ." His words that followed turned Ruby's cheeks red. It seemed Frank couldn't say three words without swearing, no matter who was around.

"I only brought one bag," the taller of the three easterners said, handing a tooled-leather valise to Frank's brother to tie on.

"I meant the size of a saddlebag." Frank stamped around as if he were doing the world a favor by taking these men out. But Ruby knew they were paying handsomely for the privilege.

She handed Frank the last packet of food, including the rolls that the men had pleaded for.

"Should just tie it on their backs. Never seen so much useless gear. Had to teach 'em to ride first. Most likely will have to tie up the buffalo so they can hit it."

At his last muttered comment, Ruby had covered her mouth behind her hand to keep from snickering. If what she'd heard about the riding lessons was true, she had done better in the saddle than the short paunchy one who had told her he knew of Mr. Brandon. And *she* wasn't heading out across the prairie in search of buffalo.

"You might say an extra prayer for us, Miss Torvald," the taller of the three said. "Frank says we have to watch for rattle-snakes too. Life is certainly different out here than in New York City, but I expect you know that far better than we do."

Ruby nodded, his request sending a pang of guilt right through her. How long had it been since she or Opal had read their Bible verses or prayed or written to the Brandons? Since she was young, because Bestemor had insisted, she'd read her Bible daily, and prayer had become as natural as breathing. But out here . . . She sighed and shook her head. How could time get away so fast and the work be so continuous that such important things went by the wayside? What did she intend to do about it? And what could she give Opal for her birthday?

CHAPTER NINETEEN

They had the fire burning hot in the morning when four men rode in from the Ox and the Triple Seven ranches and laid their branding irons in the fire along with the two from the Double H.

Soon as everyone had downed a cup of coffee from the pot steaming off to the side of the fire, the men mounted up and rode easy into the herd to rope a calf and bring it, bawling and fighting, to the fire. One of the hands would reach over the calf's back, grab a flank and front shoulder, throw the calf to the ground, and pin it with one knee to the neck while another hand shoved the white-hot brand against the calf's haunch. The stench of burning hair and flesh filled the air, and the calf was allowed up again. Once the rope was removed from its neck, it was released so it could run back to its frantic mother.

The team settled into a rhythm of roping, dragging, flanking, slapping on the brand, then letting the cow and calf head on out to pasture again as soon as they were finished.

Rand roped a calf and started him back to the fire, but this time its mother followed right along. "Hey, chase that old lady away," he yelled at one of the other riders.

"Sure enough." The rider came in and swung his rope to haze the cow off, but she dodged around him and headed for the branding pit.

One of the men from another ranch had just flanked the calf when the cow made a beeline for him. Seeing the cow charge, he leaped to his feet, the calf scrambled to escape, and Rand swung the brander up behind him on the horse.

Another rancher chased the cow off, and they started all over again. The brander tipped the calf on its side, the calf bawled, and the cow came after him again.

"You fools, quit laughing and get in here to help me." The brander ran for a horse again as the cow, shaking her rack of horns as if she would skewer him, dodged around the horse and came for her calf that was, of course, back on his feet and running toward her.

"She been at this too long!" someone shouted.

"Will one of you rope her so we can get this calf branded?" The man slid back off the horse, picked up the branding iron he'd dropped in the dirt, and stomped over to ram it back in the fire. "If you fools think it's so funny, you come work this end, and I'll ride the horse."

"Shame letting that old cow get the better of you." Beans looked up from adding wood to the fire, keeping the coals hot enough to heat the brands.

"Keep it up and I'll—"

"That's the trouble with you Ox hands, no sense of humor."

"Ready to try again?" Rand crossed his arms on the saddle horn, the calf still on the end of his rope but standing next to his mother, who hadn't quit alternating between sniffing her calf and raising her head to eye the riders. She shook her horns as if daring them to try again.

"I mean it, Rand, you get someone to rope her or . . ." The brander shook his head.

"You got to give her credit for protecting her baby."

"Credit or no, she hooks me with those horns, and I swear . . ."

"Good enough." Rand waved at two of the riders. "You two each put a rope on her and hold her back. Rod here is tired of our laughing at his expense. Can't understand why."

They finally got that calf branded, and Rod ended up the butt of the jokes for a good part of the day, much to his disgruntlement, but when Chaps rode in with his cattle, the men turned to ribbing him about being hoodwinked and tied to a tree.

At the end of the second day, when they let the last calf go, Rand and the others totaled up the tally. Double H had 234 head, Triple Seven had fifty, and the Ox Ranch, twenty.

"How many cows you had last year?" a rancher from the Ox asked.

"Two hundred, so I'm pretty close. When you want to start at your place? I can send Chaps and Joe on to help you round up."

They settled on the days, and Rand watched the men ride out. He might be the smallest rancher in the area, but since better than half his calves were heifers, one hundred sixty to be exact, in two more years he'd have a pretty good herd. That Hereford bull would be a help there. Soon as branding was done, he'd head east to pick him up.

"God willing and the creek don't rise."

"What's that you say?" Beans asked.

"Nothing, just asking for help keeping things on even keel here."

"Hope someone's listenin'."

"Me too."

— ❧ —

"Hey, Rand, you playing tonight?" Captain McHenry called as Rand rode into the cantonment.

"Yep. That's why I came in." Rand remained in the saddle. "Can I bunk here after?"

"You bet. So you're not planning to stay at Dove House?"

"It just don't feel right. Know what I mean?"

"I think I do. Come on in. The coffee's hot."

Rand dismounted and dropped Buck's reins, ground-tying him as he'd been trained. He followed the officer into a large room, complete with stove where a gray graniteware coffeepot held residence during all but the hottest months of the summer. The room really didn't need the extra heat in May.

McHenry poured two cups of prop-up-a-spoon coffee and handed one to Rand. "It's cooler out back."

Once he sat in a chair overlooking the northern buttes, Rand propped his boots on the tabletop like the captain, and both rocked their chairs on the back two legs.

"Why'd she have to go mess with things?"

"Come on, Harrison, how could a genteel young lady like Miss Torvald tolerate what was going on there? According to Belle, she had no idea what was what. Belle near to busted her corset laughing when she explained the facts of life in Little Misery to her. At least life as it was at Dove House."

"You mean Per never told her anything?"

"Nope, just asked her to come west for her inheritance—and to bring her little sister, the daughter Per had never seen since the day of her birth."

"What kind of man would do such a thing to his daughters?" Rand took a sip from his coffee, "And here I always thought he was a pretty good man, even though he ran a brothel. I mean, it seems like the girls chose to live there."

"Unless, of course, they had nowhere else to go. Or they owed him money."

"I thought Belle owned part of it."

"She thought so too, or at least she believed, if something happened to him, the place would be hers. Quite a shock when the Misses Torvald showed up one snow-spittin' night."

"I saw them on the train, you know."

"Really?"

"The little one got in trouble with some fella, and while I think Miss Torvald was winning, I stepped in and made sure. She's got a tongue on her that could fry eggs, but she's so genteel they wouldn't know they were cooked."

"So what else has been going on?" Captain McHenry drank from his cup.

"Done branding but for Ox Ranch. Goin' up there tomorrow. The boys already riding range for them. They got ten times more cows than I do."

"You read that the Apache left the reservation again down in Arizona Territory?"

"Haven't read a newspaper in months. What are they going to do?"

"Send the army after them. More bloodshed. Can't have the Indians burning and pillaging white ranchers and farmers."

"I know, even if the government has taken over Apache land.

Sure glad our Indians are under control."

"They won't be if the U.S. Government doesn't live up to its word to send supplies. Can't let the poor souls starve to death. You and I'd go to war to feed our families too."

"You heading down there?"

"I go where they send me, but right now I'd just as soon stay here." *And take the Misses Torvald riding and fishing again.* He sipped his now tepid coffee and stared up at the buttes. Talk about a charmer, that Opal, and someone worth getting to know, Miss Ruby Torvald. First woman he'd been around in a long time that could possibly be considered as marriageable for a man in his position. At times he'd even thought of going back home to Ohio to see if he could find someone. He didn't want to end up like some of his old-timers, talking about the war, reliving former glory, and never having a wife and children.

The latest letter from his sister had reminded him, not for the first time, that as the only son, he needed to get himself a family, or the McHenry name would fade away.

Interesting how he and Harrison had resolved their views on the war with a silent agreement to disagree or else skirt around the issue, as they did the Indian question. They both loved this awesome land, all the flora and fauna, a good horse, and giving each other a bad time.

"You had supper yet?"

"No, just rode into town."

"Good, let's go on over to Dove House to eat and then join Belle in the cardroom. I'm feeling right lucky for a change." Captain McHenry tossed the dregs of his coffee out onto the dirt. "Give you a gander at all Miss Torvald's done. Good food, that's for sure."

Rand followed suit and led his horse over to the livery on the way to Dove House.

Before he reached the front steps, he could tell that someone had been at work on Dove House. Windows sparkled, the porch was clean, and an old bucket had been given new life as a pot for some pink flowers. The brass doorknob shone.

He glanced toward the captain, who nodded. "See. I told you."

A bell over the door announced their entrance, and Miss

Torvald came through the swinging door, a smile of welcome lighting her face.

Jeremiah McHenry felt the now familiar kick in the gut. It happened every time he saw her.

"Good evening, Captain." The sound of her voice upped the ante. When could he take her riding again? What else could they do? He was sure she didn't play cards.

Rand removed his hat. "Good evening, Miss Torvald."

She nodded a bit abruptly and shifted her gaze back to the captain. "Where would you like to sit?"

"Anywhere is fine." All ten tables sported gleaming white cloths and napkins, as if it were a fine establishment in any major city. But here it was in Little Missouri, a place with a decided lack of appreciation for anything of quality. *Ah, Miss Torvald, I fear you have embarked on an enterprise of certain failure.* The two men set their hats on two chairs and sat down on the others.

"Tonight we are serving venison roast with potatoes and gravy, green beans, fresh rolls—"

"It's worth coming here just for the rolls." The captain smiled up at Ruby, but his comment was for Rand.

"Thank you, sir. Can I bring you coffee to start?"

"Fine."

When she left, McHenry leaned forward, his elbows on the table, fingers steepled. "When you goin' east for your bull?"

"Soon as branding is done. We had an old cow the other day that did her best to keep us from branding her calf." He told the captain the story, and it set them both laughing. "You ought to come on out, get your hands dirty for a change."

Jeremiah held out his hand, palm up, then rolled it over.

"Pushing a pencil doesn't give one too many calluses, that's for sure. You should have invited me when I was by your ranch."

"Didn't think of it. Coulda used another hand, though. I found Chaps tied to a tree after his horse came home without him. Some varmint knocked him out and stole his horse. But the horse didn't take kindly to his new rider, so it dumped him and headed back to the ranch, stirrups flapping. Thought sure I'd lost a man, but we found him, madder than a shot-up grizzly." Rand glanced around the dining room. "Sure fire different in here now. Too quiet."

"You want noise and a fight or two, stop off at Williams' saloon. That's where the excitement is these days."

"If you don't mind gettin' poisoned."

"Here's your supper, Captain, Mr. Harrison." Daisy set their plates in front of them. "Can I get you anything else?"

"No, thanks." McHenry glanced to Rand, who shook his head.

When she left, Rand leaned forward. "Where did she come from? She looks familiar."

"I asked Belle. She said that's Jasmine."

"Jasmine! You've got to be kidding. Jasmine as a shy waitress?" Rand let out a snort. "If that's Jasmine, where's Cimarron?"

"No idea, but then I've not been invited back to the kitchen."

"Cimarron would be pretty hard to hide. You think she left town?"

"Ask Belle."

So Rand did later in the cardroom where Belle was dealing. A couple of the other officers from the cantonment had joined them, along with Johnny Nelson, the Swede and owner of the town store.

Belle leaned close to Rand and McHenry. "Cimarron is still here but stays in the back so folks can forget what she was. Can you picture Cimarron as a seamstress? You ask me, a leopard can't change his spots, and the same goes for a dove."

"I wouldn't count on that if I were you. Looks to me like there are a lot of changes here."

"Ain't goin' to last. You saw how many came to the dining room for supper." She shook her head and blew cigar smoke out of the side of her mouth. "Little Misery ain't ready for the likes of this. Let her run out of money, and someone else will buy her out."

"You got an idea who that someone might be?" The captain studied his cards.

"I'll never tell." Belle gave him a long slow smile.

Two hours later and two dollars lighter, Rand pushed back his chair. "You were right, McHenry, Lady Luck was shining on you tonight."

"Surely you're not quitting already?"

"Sometimes quitting is the wisest move. I haven't had a decent hand all night. Belle, what you got against me?"

"You ain't played for so long, you lost your touch, that's all." She glanced around the table. "Another round, boys?"

"Naw, you and the captain cleaned us all out. You two in cahoots or something?"

"Just poor losers, eh, Belle?" Jeremiah McHenry pushed back his chair and paused halfway standing. "That gunfire I hear?"

"Most likely at the saloon." Belle gathered her cards back into her hand. "Happens near to every night, you know."

CHAPTER TWENTY

"I got me an idea."

Ruby stopped in the doorway to the kitchen. "What is it now, Charlie?"

"I think it's time you got out to meet the neighbors."

Ruby shuddered. "I met some of them, remember? That night we came to town, they slammed their doors in our faces. And I've watched you throw some of the men right out into the street." *All that* really *makes me want to get to know the folks around here personally. Yet if I don't, I'll never get their business. And if there is a conspiracy, how better to overcome it than to try to make some friends?*

So go bearing gifts. She felt like clapping both hands to her head to retain her sanity.

"Why do I get the feeling that you have something all planned and you are just now getting around to informing me about it?"

If innocence had a face, it was Charlie's.

"I thought to make up some cakes or perhaps some sweet rolls and we could put them in a basket or two and go calling."

"Isn't that what people who already live here are supposed to do to welcome new arrivals?"

He cleared his throat. "You got to admit circumstances here aren't what one would call normal or polite society."

"Charlie, don't try to sweet-talk me, just lay it all out there."

"I did. Simple as this—go calling on the townsfolk."

"What about some of the surrounding ranches?" Her mind seemed to be more agreeable to this plan than her heart.

"We could do that too, now that you can ride some. Although we could take a wagon out to the Double H and the Robertsons'."

"The Double H? That's Mr. Harrison's place."

"Rand Harrison, yes. He don't like to be called mister."

That's not all he doesn't like.

"Ruby, guess what?" As usual Opal blew in through the back door as if she rode a big wind.

"What?"

"I found that mean old hen. She hid away underneath the nest boxes. Milly said not to disturb her now because she's been sitting on those eggs for a while. We're going to have baby chickens."

"You call 'em chicks." Milly closed the door carefully behind her. She set her basket of eggs down on the counter. "I thought maybe something got her, but there she was, proud as you please and meaner'n ever." She held out a hand with spotted dots of blood.

"And here I thought I might get her in the stewpot any day now."

"Charlie!"

He raised his hands, palms out. "So that's what happens to chickens that don't lay eggs. You can't feed 'em forever."

"It's bad enough we have to eat wild animals that have been shot, but ones we know?" Ruby could feel her stomach churn.

Cimarron and Milly both rolled their eyes. "Welcome to the West." Cimarron stuck her needle into a pincushion and stood to stretch. "If you'd loan me a gun, Charlie, I could go out tonight and get us some grouse. A man said he was shooting them right out of the trees. Said if you shoot 'em in the head so they fall instead of fly, the rest just stay right there, waiting to be picked off. He's been shipping them on the train to eastern restaurants."

"You can shoot that well?" Ruby knew staring wasn't polite, but this was a shock.

"Might take a bit of practice, but I can get enough to feed us."

"Can I go along? I'd go pick them up for you." Opal looked

from Cimarron to Ruby and then checked with Charlie. Ruby shook her head, Charlie nodded, and Cimarron clapped a hand on Opal's shoulder. "You sure can. We'll make a right good team."

"How come you know how to shoot?" Opal's face radiated hero worship.

"My brothers taught me. When you live on the frontier, you learn to do all kinds of things city folk don't need. You just do what you have to do to stay alive."

"Can you teach me?"

"Sometime, maybe." She looked over Opal's head to Ruby, looking for permission. When Ruby only frowned, Cimarron continued. "Well, maybe we'll wait till you're a bit older."

— ⁂ —

Later that morning, not long after the eastbound train left town, two men walked in the front door and stopped at the counter.

"May I help you?" Ruby came through the door from the kitchen in response to the bell.

"I'd like a drink."

"I'm sorry, but we no longer serve liquor here. We have rooms and meals. Dinner will be in another two hours. We serve promptly at noon."

"Where's Belle and the girls?" asked the other.

"As I said, we have rooms to rent and meals. Would you like to register? Belle deals in the cardroom after supper." *How many times do I have to repeat myself before you understand?*

"And who might you be? Where's Per?"

"I am his daughter. He died and deeded Dove House to me and my sister."

"Now, ain't that a joke." One man slapped the other on the shoulder. He turned back to Ruby. "So what about the other places in town? Any of them offer . . . ah . . . you know . . ."

"No, I don't know."

One of the men leered at her, leaning slightly closer. The now familiar heat bloomed in her face. She bit back the words she really wanted to say and kept her voice even. She knew she could call Charlie, but if she was indeed the proprietress of Dove

House, she needed to learn how to handle all kinds of customers, even cantankerous ones. "If you want rotgut whiskey, you go to Williams' saloon. Mrs. McGeeney serves meals. Good day, gentlemen." She made as if to leave, wishing she'd not bothered to call them gentlemen, for they certainly weren't. However, her mother had not allowed such names as would fit them more precisely to be spoken in her home. And Ruby did her best to follow her example.

"Now, missy, don't be in such a hurry. We'll stay here tonight. How much is it?"

Missy. "That will be two dollars per room." She was glad she'd taken down the sign that listed prices. She'd decided it looked less than genteel. If they were going to have these men as guests, and she used the term loosely, they'd pay extra. "Please sign here and include your home address. Room charges must be paid in advance."

They did as she instructed, paid their money, and lifted their carpetbags.

"I'll show you to your rooms." She led the way up the stairway, feeling their lascivious thoughts with every movement of her hips. *You could still call for Charlie. No, you can't. Charlie's busy, and I have to learn to handle situations like this. We are still reaping what my father sowed.* The thought was no more pleasing than the two men behind her. She opened two doors, one on each side of the hall, and handed them their keys.

"Will you be here for dinner?"

"You can bet we will, Miss Torvald. Do you ring a bell or something?"

"No, but someone will call you if you'd like." She left them and headed back to the kitchen, jingling their money in her apron pocket. While she needed to put it in the till, right now the extra change felt mighty good. She refused to feel guilty for charging them more than normal. As proprietor, that was her privilege.

When the men came down for dinner, Cimarron peeked through the door. "I know those two. They stop here every so often, and always . . . ah . . . Charlie's had to reason with them a time or two after they'd had a few too many. The one with the muttonchop whiskers likes to cheat at cards, but Belle will take care of them."

Ruby told the others what she had charged, and they all burst out laughing.

Charlie dished up the plates and took them out to the men. Ruby knew he was taking no chances with the girls being recognized. They could hear him joking and laughing with the drummers.

"Put extra water on," he said on his way back out with more bread. "They want baths too."

"Knowing that one guy, he wants someone to scrub his back." Cimarron glared toward the dining room. "Heard tell he beat up a girl one time. That's the only one I heard about, but—"

"You make sure you stay out of sight, both of you." Ruby waited until both girls nodded. "I promise you will never have to go back to that life again." *Help me, God, to keep my promise.* She clenched her fists at her sides. Even this small glimpse into their earlier lives made her want to take a gun out in the dining room and . . .

Ruby Signe Torvald, what has come over you? And what is all this doing to Opal? Crude men, learning to fish, going hunting?

Belle came down for dinner and heard the men in the dining room. "Sounds like we have some new customers. Do we know them?" At Daisy's nod, she looked to Cimarron. "Ah, I thought I recognized the voice. They must have been surprised at the changes here."

"To say the least. And I'd thank you not to discuss the prices of things here with them. I have adjusted our rates to allow for . . . for . . . certain situations." Ruby clamped her teeth together. Belle and her father had knowingly put the others in danger with men like those out there. Of course, they considered it business, but what kind of business makes its profit at the expense of others less fortunate?

Most businesses, she had to admit. "They are not to know that Cimarron and Daisy work here. Is that clear?"

"Well, well, Miss Hoity-Toity. Got a dose of the real world, did you? Don't get your drawers in a tangle. I won't say a thing." Belle crossed the room and patted Ruby's cheek. "You done right good, sweetheart. Don't you take no sass."

Ruby tried to answer, but words wouldn't pass a throat tied up in shock.

"We're playin' blackjack tonight. Ought to be good for the house. Charlie's dealing too. Just a shame we can't get them drunk. They always lose more when they're near to under the table." She turned to Ruby, who'd been about to jump in, holding a hand up to stop her. "Just a comment, just a comment. I been followin' the rules. Ask anyone. That's why we don't have more'n four or so a night. Not like the old days."

Ruby started to say something but cut off the words when Belle winked at her.

"I know. I know. I'm just a dealer here and got no say in the runnin' anymore, but keep in mind if you really want to pay the bills, liquor is the cheapest and quickest way to do it."

Be that as it may, I won't go back to that. The card playing is bad enough. I will not go back. Ruby wasn't sure who she was making the vow to, but she meant it with all of her heart. She eyed the woman so peacefully drinking her coffee. Belle was acting too friendly. How much was it going to cost her this time? Here, she'd just about gotten enough nerve to confront Belle about ransacking her room and keeping the townsfolk away, and now the woman was being nice.

Charlie spent a good part of his afternoon lugging hot water up the stairs and carrying used water back down. He poured the used water in a barrel by the back door so they could water the garden with it later.

Ruby picked up her sewing after supper while Milly and Opal washed up, then took out the book she'd started reading to everyone in the evening. She'd brought *Pilgrim's Progress* with her on the train, but she expected a box of books and other school things to be coming soon from Mrs. Brandon. When the box arrived she planned to start teaching Milly along with Opal, although Opal already had her friend familiar with reading and writing the alphabet and her numbers.

Belle dropped in on her way to the cardroom. "You thought about making any popcorn tonight?"

"Popcorn?" Ruby wondered when she would stop sounding like an echo.

"I'll make it." Cimarron stood and headed for the storeroom.

"Good. See you later, children."

Milly rolled her eyes.

"Since when do we have popcorn?" Ruby kept her place in the book with one finger.

"We always had popcorn, good and salty. It made the men drink more because they were thirsty."

"I know, and if they drink more, they lose more money gambling. But we aren't serving liquor. Why did I keep the cardroom open? Even without liquor."

Cimarron turned from dropping a dollop of lard in the pan on the stove. "Because you were wise and listened to Belle and Charlie. Couple of nights ago the house took in forty dollars. Now that's not bad."

"But that's because we had those men from New York here." She had to admit they had been good for the till. If things kept on as they were, she would have some money to pay on the accounts after all. But was it worth the price of allowing gambling under her roof?

While the popping kernels ricocheted off all the sides of the kettle, she thought back to a conversation she'd had with Charlie. He wanted her to meet with the banker in Dickinson just in case she ever needed to borrow money to keep the doors open.

But she'd told him she was not going unless she had money to pay on the account.

The men were settled into their evening's entertainment when she took the buttered and well-salted popcorn in and set the bowls on the table off to the side.

"Can I get you anything else?" she asked Charlie.

One of the drummers leered at her. "Honey, you could get me anything you want."

He's been drinking, she thought but reminded herself they could have been drinking down at Williams' place before they came here. She nodded good-night and, leaving a lamp lit in the kitchen for Charlie or Belle to get more coffee, herded the other girls up the stairs.

"I sure would like a real bed again," Opal said as she kissed Ruby good-night.

"Me too." Ruby finished braiding her hair for the night, blew out the lamp, and slid under the covers. According to Milly, when summer came they could cut and dry grass for filling the pallets. Now, the thought of sleeping on dried grass didn't get her real excited, but a thicker mattress would feel wonderfully good.

She thought of the growing list of supplies they needed, including more sheeting for bed linens and pillowcases. If only she had some of that goose down from those geese that flew northward. How wonderful a feather bed would be. Even the lowliest of the help at the Brandon house had not been forced to sleep on the floor like this.

But at least for tonight, half of the rooms downstairs housed paying guests.

Her thoughts traveled to the Bible now in her trunk. She'd not read in it for far longer than she wanted to admit. And when had she ceased praying? And why? *I'll think about that in the morning when my mind is fresh,* she promised herself.

Sometime after she'd fallen asleep, a crash accompanied by men shouting, jerked her straight up. Outside? No, it came from downstairs. Was someone hurt? She grabbed her wrapper and headed for the stairs.

"No, you can't go down there." Cimarron stopped her with a hand on her arm.

"Why not? What if. . . ?" Ruby kept her voice to a whisper, surprised the others hadn't come out already. Good thing Opal could sleep through about anything.

"Charlie will take care of it."

"But what if he's the one hurt?"

"Then Belle will take over."

"Belle? Why? How?"

"She has a gun, and she knows how to handle it—and men who get out of hand."

"But I paid for a bed here!" The shout from below could most likely be heard clear up into the hills.

"You can come back in when you're sober enough to not break things."

"See. I told you Charlie can handle them."

"Did Belle serve liquor down there?" The thought made Ruby sick to her stomach.

"No, she wouldn't. Belle keeps her word."

"Then how?"

"A flask. Lots of the men carry them."

"Oh." Ruby crossed her arms and contemplated what she would like to say or do to the man she was sure was now picking himself up out of the dirt of the street. And after his nice bath too. Well, he could pay for another one in the morning and haul his own water besides.

She and Cimarron stood listening until they heard Belle go into her room.

"You think the men are in their rooms?"

"One is." Cimarron started down the stairs.

"Where are you going?"

"To see how bad the damage is."

Ruby closed her eyes. *Damage? Please, I have no money to repair damages.* Glancing down at her wrapper to make sure she was sufficiently covered, she followed Cimarron down the front stairs. *If Mrs. Brandon could see me now* ... The thought was too distressing to tolerate. Ladies did not run around in public in their wrappers. No matter that this was her business, her home. She could hear someone moving around in the cardroom. Hopefully it was Charlie. Did the man never go to bed?

"I hope you hurt him when you threw him out." Cimarron stopped in the doorway, hands on her hips.

Ruby hesitated on the last stair, wishing she could go back upstairs without knowing how bad things were. Had this happened before and no one told her?

"He might feel inclined to find somewhere else to sleep."

"I'm not returning his money." Ruby joined Cimarron in the doorway. Charlie set the last table back in place.

"Going to have to reglue some legs, I'm thinking perhaps I should go into the furniture business." He turned a chair upside down and studied the three remaining legs. "We should order a lathe. It would make fixing these go faster."

"What's a lathe, and where would we get it if we had the money to purchase one?" Ruby stared at the coffee stains on the rug. "That's it. No more rugs in here. If these men want to be animals, they deserve to be treated that way."

"Now, it ain't everyone." Charlie set another chair upright and rocked it a bit to see how tight the joints still were. "A lathe is used for turning square-shaped wood into round pieces."

"Oh. The man who did this—had he been drinking?"

"Musta been."

"Was he at your table?"

"Nope."

"Did Belle know he was drinking?"

"You'll have to ask her."

Ruby sucked in a deep breath. "I see." Would this help Belle realize what happens when drink enters the picture? Perhaps Belle should have to help pay for the repairs.

"I'll charge him for this. We got his kit and case up in the room. He wants it back, he'll have to pay."

They heard a knocking on the front door.

"That's most likely him. You two go on up, and I'll take care of this. Sorry to wake you."

"Good night, then. You go on to bed after you talk to him. The furniture can't be fixed until morning."

"Oh, don't you go worrying about me, Miss Ruby. I know how to take care of things."

"I know you do. Thanks, Charlie." Ruby turned to leave. Now she'd have to confront Belle after all. Might as well see if Belle had asked people to stay away from Dove House. Did Belle still think of the place as hers? That wasn't what she'd said earlier. Biting her lip, Ruby recognized the white-hot feelings as pure rage. Rage at the men who flaunted the rules; rage at liquor and how it affected men; rage at her father for leaving her in all this mess. She motioned Cimarron ahead of her.

"You got to remember, Ruby, some men are pretty sneaky. And some can hold their liquor, so's you got no idea that they're even drinkin'."

"You're saying Belle might not have realized it?" Ruby kept her voice even, the effort causing her jaw to cramp.

"Sometimes it's hard to tell, then all of a sudden the guy blows. That big one—he's like that. A mean drunk." Cimarron stopped at the top of the second flight of stairs. "I—uh—thank you I wasn't down there." The words came in a rush.

"You are most welcome." Ruby gripped the stair railing as if she could squeeze her feelings into the wood. "Thank you for all your sewing and cooking, and I know you don't like cleaning, but you do your share." *Not like someone else we know.* "I appreciate it all."

Cimarron sniffed and knuckled away a tear. "No one ever talked nice to me like you do. Without wanting *something,* you know."

Not really, and I'd just as soon not know. "Thank you, Cimarron. I'll see you in the morning." She knew her words were stiff, but it was the best she could do.

"You goin' callin' with Charlie in the mornin'?"

"Oh, mercy, I forgot all about that." *No, I'm not going. Calling on the people of Little Missouri won't do any good at all!* They'd slammed their doors the night she and Opal arrived. Why would it be any different now? *You have to go. You told Charlie you would, and he's set the dough for sweet rolls. If only I could find the box.* Surely there was money in it to make things better, or why would Far have struggled to mention it when he was so weak? But she had looked everywhere she could think of. Limp as a water weed now that the anger had drained away, Ruby collapsed on her pallet.

CHAPTER TWENTY-ONE

Charlie stood in the doorway with his arms folded across his chest. "You can't go looking like that!"

Ruby glanced down at her red traveling dress. "What's wrong with this?" She'd brushed it carefully; she knew all the stains on the hem were gone. And the hat was set just right. The mirror never lied. She knew she looked nice. Mrs. Brandon had said so.

"No one dresses that fancy in Little Missouri. People will think you're a . . ." He looked like he was going to swallow his Adam's apple.

"What he means is that the men will be so busy looking at how pretty you are, they won't pay attention to what you are sayin'." Milly turned slightly so that Ruby couldn't see the look she sent Charlie.

He tipped his bowler farther back on his head. "Yep, that's what I meant all right."

"But you said—"

"Just wear your better dark skirt and that nice blue print waist you have. You'll fit in better that way." Daisy looked up from measuring flour into the pancake mixture. "I'll have breakfast ready in a few minutes. We haven't seen hide nor tail of our guests yet."

The front bell tinkled.

Ruby started to go to the dining room, but Opal stepped in

front of her. "I'll go. It's my turn."

"Oh, and Ruby, I'll have the sweet rolls ready for you. They should be coming out of the oven pretty soon," Daisy said.

"If I had a particle of sense, I'd . . ." Ruby paused. She had to admit that real sense meant listening to Charlie. *He knows the people of Little Missouri far better than I do!* she thought as she climbed the stairs. And besides, those two houses they'd stopped at might remember her hat, at least, although it had been too dark at the one house. But at the other, she and Opal had been welcomed—at first.

She carefully laid her hat back in the hatbox and set it on the shelf. Her gloves she smoothed flat and laid them in the trunk, and the dress she hung on a hanger and then over a hook. How she would love to have that armoire back again. *How I would love to have that room on the floor below back again.* While it had seemed barren at first, compared to the space she and Opal now shared, the room had been palatial. She left her hair pinned up and donned the skirt and waist. She looked more everyday now. Once again stroking a hand down the dress on the hanger, she grabbed an apron off one of the pegs on the wall and tied it on while descending the stairs.

"Ah, that smells heavenly." The wonderful aroma of rolls fresh out of the oven met her halfway down. And they were all to be given away. Perhaps they should use the wheelbarrow that Charlie made for the garden.

The bell rang again as she entered the kitchen. She could hear voices coming from the dining room. Had they more than one customer for a change?

She pushed open the swinging door into the dining room and stopped. People were sitting at three tables. However would they handle such a crowd?

The two salesmen glanced up from their pancakes, one of them sporting a swollen jaw. When he caught her eye, he nodded toward Charlie. "He sure does pack a punch." He rubbed his jaw. "And I was winning too."

"You weren't winning." The more slender man took another bite of pancake.

Ruby glanced toward the man who stood just inside the door. Rand Harrison. What was he doing here? Was he planning to give her another piece of his mind?

Out of the corner of her eye, she watched him take a table as she stopped to talk to the drummers. "How are things this morning—besides the jaw?"

"Good. Sure some different around here than it used to be." The second one nodded in agreement with his friend. "The food is good too."

Ruby counted to six before making sure her lips were smiling and her eyes weren't. She kept her voice sweet and gentle. "I'm glad you like it here, and I do hope you come back and that you tell others of the good service you received here." She lowered her voice a trifle. "And if you are caught drinking again, you will sleep with the hens in the chicken house. There will be no whiskey at Dove House." She smiled as though she'd just shared a delightful secret with them.

"Miss Torvald, you are a chip off the old block, only a lot prettier."

"Do I have your agreement?"

"You'd turn down business?"

"Yes. I would." She straightened her shoulders. "You've already spoken with Charlie about the repairs to the cardroom?"

"Oh yes. Paid him up, though his prices were a mite steep."

She nodded. "Thank you." She wasn't sure what all she was thanking him for, other than for courtesy's sake, but he didn't seem a bad sort when he was sober.

Ruby glanced up, hoping Charlie would go speak with Mr. Harrison, but instead she saw his back as he returned to the kitchen. Back to smiling, she crossed to the rancher's table.

"Good morning, Mr. Harrison, what would you like this morning?"

"Coffee and some breakfast."

"How many eggs with your pancakes?"

"Two, three."

"Very good." Ruby turned his cup upright and returned to the kitchen. She gave Daisy the order, grabbed the coffeepot, and headed back out.

"I hear you had a bit of trouble here last night," Rand said as she filled his coffee cup.

"How did. . . ?"

"Small town, things get around fast. You're livin' in a dream world, you know."

"Pardon me?"

He gestured around the room. "All these changes. Might do in Dickinson but not here in Little Misery."

She'd heard Little Missouri called by that name before and liked it even less now. So was this the man behind the conspiracy? He sure did act like it could be true.

"Mr. Harrison." She clipped off each sound as if she'd just finished a lesson with an elocution teacher. "I don't tell you how to run your ranch, and I'd appreciate the same courtesy from you."

"But you're a woman. What do you know about running a business?"

"I may not know a lot, but I'm learning, and it is *my* business." *If I can keep the doors open.* She clamped her teeth, smiled in spite of the tight jaw, and took her coffeepot over to the other table. She'd rather serve the two louts than serve him.

"I swear I'm going to learn to shoot, and he'll be my first target," she muttered back in the kitchen as she plunked the coffeepot back on the stove.

"Who?" Opal looked up from buttering the tops of the rolls lined up on the table.

"*Mister* Harrison."

"Ah, is Rand here?" Cimarron started toward the door, then stopped herself.

"Here's his plate." Daisy set the plate on a tray that already had a syrup pitcher and a dish of jam.

Ruby picked it up and backed through the swinging door. She turned to see Charlie talking with Harrison and made her way to the table after dropping off extra pancakes for the drummers.

"Mornin' again, Miss Ruby," Charlie said, "that will work much better." His emphasis on "that" made her sure he meant the change of clothing rather than the serving of food.

"I'm glad to hear that." Ruby didn't quite manage to keep the resentment from her voice. She set the food in front of the man at the table.

Rand looked from one to the other. "Thank you, Miss Torvald," he said with a slight emphasis on her last name.

"You are welcome." She paused, "Will there be anything else?"

"I'll take care of him." Charlie set his cup down on the table and his rear in a chair. "So you're on your way for a bull, eh?"

Ruby turned away but not before hearing the man's response. Where would he have to go for a bull? She glanced back to see his carpetbag by the door. Obviously he was taking the train. She shook her head. What she knew about ranching would fit in a teaspoon.

— ⁂ —

The dining room had emptied, and they'd cleaned up again with Milly and Opal setting up the tables for dinner when Charlie asked if she was ready to go.

"We've packed the rolls in three baskets. That should give you plenty." Daisy tucked a cloth over the tops of the bread.

"Has anyone seen Belle yet?"

They all shook their heads.

"You want to use my straw hat?" Cimarron asked. "That sun is heating up."

"Thank you." Ruby accepted the broad-brimmed straw with green ribbon around the crown and trailing down the back. Good thing she had fashioned her bun down lower. She used the hatpin to best advantage and took a basket over her arm.

Is this what Daniel felt like when stepping into the lion's den?

"I'm going to introduce you as Ruby Torvald, owner of the newly redone Dove House." Charlie picked up the other two baskets.

"And I'll invite them to come for a meal in the new dining room to see the many changes I have made. And that there will be no charge."

"Good."

"And I will offer them our special rolls that have become so popular with the travelers on the train."

"Right." They walked up to the first house, the one that Ruby was sure had been her first to visit that dreary night.

Charlie rapped on the open door.

"Come in."

Charlie motioned for Ruby to go first. They stood for a moment before the woman came from the rear of the house.

"Good morning, Mrs. Fitzgerald, I brought Miss Ruby Torvald to meet you."

"Aye." Doubt blossomed on the woman's worn face. "Pleased."

"I brought you a sample of the sweet rolls we are baking. Folks on the train are really enjoying them, and I hope you like them too." Ruby held out the napkin-wrapped parcel. "And I want to invite you and your husband to come for dinner, at no charge, and see all the changes we've made. Dove House is a real family place now."

"Dining room, you say?"

"We redid the saloon. No more liquor served."

"What about the . . ."

"No more."

"Humph. Well, I'll be."

"I hope you'll be my guest very soon. My sister, Opal, and I are looking forward to meeting all the people of Little Missouri."

Holding the rolls in both hands in front of her like a shield, Mrs. Fitzgerald looked from Charlie to Ruby. "You sure don't look like one of them fancy ladies."

Ruby reminded herself to thank Charlie for his advice on changing clothes. While her traveling dress was appropriate for calling, it *was* far too fancy for this home. The large room was combination kitchen, parlor, and most likely bedroom, if the stack of pallets in the corner was any indication. The upstairs was most likely all one room too. Only difference, the large porch on the back of the first floor.

"Thank you for the rolls."

"You are welcome. I hope to see you soon." Ruby turned to leave, grateful they hadn't been asked to sit down for coffee.

Once they were out the door, she sucked in a huge breath of clean, fresh air.

"Friendly, isn't she?" Ruby allowed the bite of sarcasm to say what she really meant.

"She didn't throw us out."

"True. Thank God for small favors."

The man in the next house was glad for the rolls but disgusted that he could no longer drink while playing cards at Dove House.

"That swill over at Williams' nearly killed me." He glared at Ruby as if she had forced him to pour the drinks down his gullet.

Ruby didn't bother to invite him for a free meal.

Her basket lighter, they walked up to Mrs. McGeeney's boardinghouse.

"Since she serves meals, do you think she'll take affront with a gift of sweet rolls?"

"No, she's smarter than that. She likes good bread as well as anyone. Her biscuits are real good, but sometimes her bread better not be dropped on anyone's foot."

"That bad?" Ruby chuckled, glancing at him from under the brim of her hat just in time to catch his wink. "Charlie, I do believe you have a talent for storytelling."

"Whatever gave you that idea?"

The smell of the next place attacked them before they took the first step on the three treads to the porch.

"What is that horrible odor?"

"Oh, Bill must be mixing up his red-eye brand whiskey."

"With rotten eggs? No wonder people get sick." She blinked against the eye-burning stench.

"You get used to it after a while."

Ruby took a handkerchief from her reticule and held it to her nose. "Do we have to go here?"

"Can't leave anyone out. Come on around back. That's where he mixes it."

They walked around the corner of the slab-wood sided building to find the proprietor pouring ingredients in a large washtub. He stirred, tasted, grimaced, and added another bottle of cheap whiskey.

"Brought someone who wants to meet you," Charlie called as they stood a ways back from the concocting.

Williams let his wooden stirring stick bang against the side of the tub and came around to greet them.

After Charlie's introduction, Ruby held out the wrapped rolls and went into her invitation.

"Why thankee, miss. I been wantin' to come by and thank

you for sending so much business my way. Full every night now."

"Miracle half of Little Muddy ain't in the graveyard if they drink that stuff regular-like." Charlie motioned to the tub.

"When I get that bottled up, I'm set for a time again." Bill Williams nodded toward the mess. "Have to fix up a batch every week. I serve that good stuff only when someone's willing to pay extra."

"I heard tell you been accused of highway robbery."

Ruby held her ground with a smile, all the while wishing she were anywhere else.

"They don't have to drink it." He set the rolls on the porch, then cussed at the dog who came over to sniff. "You got any more of that hooch you brought by before? I can afford some more now."

"I'll bring it over. You want one case or two?"

"Or three, four, whatever you got."

"It's cash, Mr. Williams." Ruby interrupted firmly.

"I know that. Hear you had a bit a ruckus last night. *Hee hee*. That drummer . . . told him he'd never get by with that flask. Man can't hold his liquor nohow."

At Charlie's look of insistence, Ruby reiterated her invitation to come to Dove House for a meal, and after enduring a minute or so of small talk, they left.

Back on what could be called a street only through a flight of imagination, Ruby took a deep breath of clean air and stared out at the sparkles on the river. *All I'd like to do right now is go take a bath, a long bath.* She shook out her skirt and looked longingly back at Dove House. "I sure hope this is all worth it."

"Me too."

Mrs. Paddock at the livery promised to come for supper that night. Two houses, if one could call them that, were empty, so they left a package on each table after Charlie assured her that someone did indeed live there.

"What are those shacks over there?"

"Ah, you don't want to go there."

"They're vacant?"

"No. Trust me, Miss Ruby, you don't want to go over there.

We're tryin' to get you a good reputation in town, and goin' there won't do that."

"Charlie."

"Those are the cribs, and that's all I'll say on the matter. Let's get back on to Dove House."

What are cribs? But at the look on Charlie's face she decided not to ask.

"There are six of us females at Dove House and four women in town. Are there any women out on the ranches?"

"Mrs. Robertson and her girls. You'll like her, and then there's one north of here, I think. Don't believe I know her name."

"That's all?"

"Well, Little Missouri weren't here at all until the railroad went through."

"Oh. And the cantonment?"

"Built to protect the railroad."

"Oh." They needed more women here to civilize this place. Though it might have a name, it seemed impossible to call it a town.

They got back in time to help with dinner, at which they served two guests and Mr. and Mrs. Paddock from the livery.

"Best meal I've had in a long time," Mr. Paddock said, patting his middle and earning a glare from his wife.

"I always wondered what it looked like in here." She glanced around the room.

"Some different than it used to."

His wife glared at him once again. "Well, you should know." She pushed her chair back. "Thank you, Miss Torvald. I hope you can make a go of it here." She started for the door, and her husband followed suit.

"Please come again." Ruby watched them go. Obviously the wives in town had not appreciated Dove House.

When the train whistle blew east of town, Milly and Opal took their baskets of sandwiches and cookies over to sell to the passengers while the fireman filled the engine boiler with water.

When they came back, Opal handed Ruby the money along with a letter from the bank in Dickinson. "We could have sold more food. And they want coffee. What if we set up a table instead of bringing baskets? A lady said at most stops they get off to buy food. But since there's no platform here . . ."

"But they would get off. And they do want coffee or even fresh water," Milly added.

"We *could* set up a table. That is a very good idea." Ruby nodded and smiled back at the two excited girls.

"I'll build us one," Charlie said. "A bench or two might be a good idea too." He glanced out at the pile of lumber left over from building Dove House. "Going to run out of wood pretty soon."

"I hope not. I was thinking about flower boxes for along the front. Lots of places in New York have them."

"This ain't New York, Miss Ruby. We'd do better gettin' a milk cow."

"Really?" Opal spun around from sneaking a bite of dough from the molasses cookies Daisy was making. "A cow of our own?"

"We could sell milk." Cimarron took a pan of cookies from the oven. "And we'd need a churn."

Opal cocked her head. "For what?"

"Churning cream into butter. We could serve sour cream on pancakes or bread, along with chokecherry jelly or syrup. Bet we can find us some chokecherries come August."

Ruby listened to the plans and thought again how much things had changed. Now if she could only get Belle to cooperate. About the time she thought they were getting somewhere, a situation like last night happened. Trouble was, Belle really didn't see anything wrong with the drinking, so turning a blind eye was not difficult.

"I'm going to talk with Belle." *And explain to her that any breakage from now on would come out of her pay. Now that ought to get her attention.*

Ruby headed up the stairs to confront Belle before she lost her nerve. When she rapped on the door, she could smell cigarillo smoke. Of course, while the rest of them were working themselves to dead tired, Belle could sit in her room and smoke. She knew the feeling was unjust; after all, Belle did pay for her room and board, so Ruby clamped her jaw. Be polite. Be gentle. A soft answer . . . "Uff da," she muttered to herself, wishing she dared say something stronger.

Belle opened the door enough to let a wave of smoke out. "What?"

"I would like to speak with you, if you have a moment." *And if you don't, I'll speak anyway.*

"Sure, why not?" Still in her wrapper, Belle opened the door and stepped back with an entering motion with her other hand, the lighted cigarillo trailing smoke as she fanned the air.

Ruby cleared her throat. If only she could open a window. "I want to talk with you about the damage in the cardroom last night."

"Sorry, but that varmint caught me by surprise."

"You had no idea he'd been drinking?"

"No." Belle slitted her eyes. "Poured it in his coffee. Why? You think I let him?"

Ruby pictured the cardroom. They kept the coffee hot over a low candle on another table. It would be easy enough for a man to sneak liquor into his coffee cup. The sigh escaped before she could stop it. Now how could she demand Belle pay for damages?

"Me and Charlie are just going to have to watch 'em closer. Locals know Charlie will toss them out, so they get theirs before they come here. Drink enough coffee, play enough cards, and they are pretty sober before they leave." Belle waved to a chair. "Have a seat."

Do I ask her about the conspiracy? No, that might get Cimarron in trouble. Ruby rubbed her forehead. Things were so complicated.

She sucked in a huge breath of courage. "I would appreciate it if you were more careful. We . . . I cannot afford to make continual repairs to tables and chairs. Therefore, if—"

"What a minute, honey." The word did not sound like an endearment. "If you think to blame the breakage on me—"

Ruby took a cue from the other woman and interrupted her, something that went against all her precepts of good manners. "I am telling you that if there is more breakage, I will charge it to your account."

"My account! Now listen here—"

"No, Belle, you listen." She gentled her voice. "We offer the room for card playing, and since you run the room, it is up to you to convince our guests to leave their liquor at the door if they want a clean place to play cards where no one cheats them. The coffee and desserts are on the house." She had refused to stop at Belle's snort and plowed right through to the end.

Belle glared at her through the smoke haze, her eyes narrowed, her jaw tight.

"Is that all?"

"No, the night my father died, he mentioned a buksbom, which is Norwegian for box. I wondered if you had any idea what box he might have been referring to."

"And if I know, you think you can just waltz in here, threaten to charge me for the broken furniture, and then ask for my help?" She blew smoke directly toward Ruby. "Little girl, you just ain't got no sense a'tall."

Ruby ignored the voice that counseled quiet and leaned forward. "And I suppose you are not only planning on my failing, but doing all you can to make sure it happens. Ripping out signs, warning people to stay away." Ruby inhaled and almost choked on the smoke. "We will make a success of Dove House, and you have the choice to join us or take yourself elsewhere." She rose to her feet and gave her skirt a twitch. "You let me know what you decide."

"Oh, I will, little girl, you can bet your corset I will." The enmity glittering from Belle's eyes made a shiver run up Ruby's back as she stalked to the door.

Little girl, eh? She shut the door carefully behind her, even though slamming it would have felt wonderfully refreshing. There was no way she would return to the kitchen in this frame of mind, so instead she made her way upstairs so she could stand in the open window and get some clean air.

In front of the window she opened the letter from the bank and read it once, then again. Another demand for payment. And she'd promised Charlie they'd go to Dickinson tomorrow. Was there anywhere else her father owed money? Some inheritance this was. Would tearing up floorboards reveal the buksbom? The nerve of Belle. The rage that had burned so hotly previously flared again. She didn't like it before, and she didn't like it now.

CHAPTER TWENTY-TWO

This place was driving her crazy. Belle had to go.

"Ruby, can I help?" Opal pleaded with her sister. "I know Belle didn't mean it." She leaned against her sister's arm. "She won't have no"—Opal flinched and corrected her bad grammar—"any place to go, least not here in Little Missouri."

"Did she send you up to plead her case?"

"No. I just know you will be sad and worried about her and then Daisy gets worried about you and I get worried about Daisy and Charlie worries about all of us."

And Belle just blithely goes about whatever she wants without paying much attention to anyone else. Unless, of course, they get in her way. Yet Far was concerned about someone taking care of the girls. Did that include Belle, or did he realize she'd take care of herself, while the others couldn't? One thing for sure, Belle didn't want to do any of the work around Dove House. Unless one wanted to call dealing cards for hours every evening work. And while she was thinking about it, did she trust Belle to turn over the house portion of the evening's hands? She thought about that for a moment. Did she have any real basis for her doubt, or was it because she wanted Belle gone on general principles?

"What are you going to do?" Opal turned back from the window.

Ruby sighed. While she'd never considered herself a sighing person, lately she caught herself doing so more and more. "Opal,

I wish I knew." She headed for the stairs. "What I do know is that Charlie and I are catching the train for Dickinson, and I better be ready. That train waits for no one."

"Not even the president of the United States?"

"Well, maybe, but since he isn't here . . ."

"I wish I could go with you."

"Perhaps next time."

Opal followed her down the stairs. "Do you think Captain McHenry will come back from patrol one of these days? I sure would like to go riding again."

"Me too." At least when she was riding, she hadn't been thinking about Dove House. She'd been too busy trying not to fall off the horse. Besides, she wanted him back for Opal's birthday in two days. Keeping the party a secret was getting harder by the day.

"Good morning." Cimarron came in through the back door. "You all need to go outside and see the sun setting the dewdrops to blazing. Some house sparrows are building a nest on the back porch, and Cat thinks they are going to provide her dinner. I explained to her that mice are her food, not birds."

"And she understood you?" Milly asked.

"Most certainly. I promised her milk if she would come inside and leave the birds alone." She glanced down, and sure enough, Cat sat at her feet, the tip of her tail twitching as if counting the seconds until the promise was fulfilled.

Opal returned from the pantry with a saucer of milk, which she set on the floor at the back of the stove, out of the way of human feet. Cat did not like her tail stepped on. The last one to make that mistake wore claw marks on her ankle.

The bell announcing a customer sent Milly out the door to the dining room, coffeepot in hand.

Cimarron turned the bacon in a skillet on the stove. "Hard to believe, but I'm getting homesick for greeting the folks out there."

"But—"

"I know, Daisy. One of the men will recognize me, so I'll stay in back for a while longer, but still . . ."

"Breakfast is nearly ready." Daisy slid a platter into the oven.

"What are we having?" Ruby asked.

"Fried cornmeal mush is in the oven, bacon about done, eggs if anyone wants them, and warmed canned peaches." Cimarron flipped bacon onto a platter.

Milly hurried through the door. "Two orders including eggs." She set two plates on a tray and, using a folded towel, took the platter from the oven and dished up several slices before setting the platter in the middle of the table. "There's plenty more to be fried if we need it." As soon as the eggs were flipped and then dished onto the plates, she backed out the door carrying the tray.

Ruby watched as each of them took part in the meal preparation and serving, talking back and forth, laughing and doing whatever had to be done without anyone prompting them.

What a difference from the early days. She filled her plate and sat down, mentally running through all she had to do before boarding the train. And that included packing an overnight bag.

"With Charlie and me both gone, someone needs to make sure that any new guests are checked in properly."

"I will," Daisy volunteered.

"Milly and I'll clean rooms today." Opal took the chair next to her sister. "After we go fishing. We'll serve fried fish for supper."

"You'll stay away from the deep pools."

"Ruby." Opal rolled her eyes. "You say that every time."

"If you're going to be on the river, you have to learn to swim."

"Still too cold for that—give the river time to warm up some first." Cimarron shivered for emphasis.

"You can swim?"

"Of course. My brothers—"

"I know. Your brothers taught you." Opal finished the sentence.

"Actually they just threw me in the water, and I kinda taught myself. One of them yelled 'Kick,' and I did, and when I got out of that water, I went over and kicked him a good one."

"Then what happened?" Opal's eyes were round as her plate.

"They all laughed so hard one of them fell in the river backward. Nearly drowned."

"What did your mother say?"

"Didn't have no ma by then. She died birthing another baby."

"Oh." Opal glanced at Ruby. "Same thing happened to my mor, but it was me who killed her."

"Opal Marie Torvald, you did not kill our mor."

"Then God did?"

"No, not that either. Sometimes those things just happen. It's part of life."

Ruby dropped her dirty dishes in the dishpan on the stove. When Milly came back through the door, Ruby motioned toward the table. "You eat, and I'll go take care of our guests."

"Table two wants more coffee, and table one asked for another helping of fried mush."

Ruby filled the orders, greeted their three guests, and then headed back upstairs to pack. She changed into her red traveling costume, set her hat in place with a jeweled hatpin, and took her satchel back downstairs with her. She rubbed her midsection where it felt like bubbling mush. The thought of meeting with Mr. Davis, the manager at the bank in Dickinson, made her want to run farther down the river and hide behind the rocks so no one could find her. Just because her father had dealt with this man didn't mean he would be helpful to her. She'd thought to include the letters from her father to prove who she was and a list of the changes she had made in Dove House.

"Train coming," Charlie announced.

"I'll be right there." Ruby hugged Opal as if it might be the last time she saw her. "You behave now, you hear?"

"Ruby." Hurt looked back from Opal's eyes.

"I'm sorry, I know you work hard like everyone else here."

"You could take me along."

"I'll keep her out of trouble. Opal, perhaps this afternoon we can start on your piano lessons." Cimarron stirred the pot of beans cooking on the stove.

Ruby hugged Opal one last time. "All right, you two ready with your baskets?"

Milly and Opal nodded, took up the food prepared to sell on the train, and followed her out the door.

— ✄ —

Once they were seated and the train was heading east, in

order to ignore the knotting in her middle, Ruby turned to Charlie. "I have a question."

"Yes?"

"How did you and my father get to Little Missouri?"

"After we joined up on the gold strike, we stuck together ever since—Belle too. Per had a streak of good luck at the tables and decided to invest his money, and here we are."

"Didn't you ever have a family?"

Charlie looked out the window as if the waving prairie grass was the most intriguing sight he'd ever seen. He sighed and nodded. "Yeah, I had me a wife and a little boy."

"What happened to them?"

"Don't know."

"You don't know?"

"Guess you would call Per and me wanderers at heart. I always thought I'd go back, but then . . ." He shrugged and shook his head. "Just better not to. She prob'ly got a different life and . . ."

Ruby waited. What came over men to not go back? Per and Charlie and most likely many others. Bestemor had called it wanderlust.

"Perhaps sometime you could write and see."

"Maybe." He half shrugged. "Only Belle knows all this."

"I never share a confidence, Charlie."

"Thank you."

How can men just walk away from a family? Ruby shook her head slowly, the tip of her tongue worrying the back of her teeth.

Myriads of other questions droned like pesky mosquitoes, but she kept them to herself and turned her thoughts back to the hotel. Now she wished she'd never asked him.

"Do you think Belle has set the town against me and Dove House?"

Charlie sucked at the gap between his front teeth, then shook his head. "Belle looks out for Belle, and I know she wanted Dove House for herself, thought it her right. But she's not the sneaky kind. Leastways I don't think . . ." He twitched his mustache, then smoothed it with one finger.

Don't think what? Patience had never been Ruby's strength.

"Dickinson." The conductor swayed past. "Dickinson coming up."

Ruby wove her fingers together, then smoothed her gloves, sure the bank manager would throw her petitions right out the door and say that the funds they had worked so hard to collect would not be sufficient payment. She stepped off the train fighting to keep a smile on her mouth instead of a trembling frown. How had the money disappeared so quickly? But she knew where every dime had gone—into the refurbishing of the hotel.

Charlie unloaded the remaining cases of whiskey and commandeered a dolly to deliver the cases back to the store. They had decided they would get a better price returning the liquor rather than selling it to Williams.

"Do you want me to go with you, Ruby?"

"Do you think that would be better?"

"I believe so. I accompanied your father at times."

"Fine." Amazing how the load lifted somewhat from her shoulders. If only she could get the knot out of her middle.

Charlie held open the door of the Dickinson Bank to let her precede him. Together they approached a desk to the right of the doorway. A counter with two clerks behind green shades divided the bank down the middle.

"We're here to see Mr. Davis," Charlie explained to the young man behind the desk.

"Do you have an appointment?"

"Ah, no, but tell him Miss Torvald is here from Little Missouri."

The young man rose. "I'll be right back."

Trying to ignore her teeming midsection, Ruby glanced around the room. Several men stood in line at the two windows where the clerks waited on them. One woman stood at a window quietly conversing with the cashier. Two plate-glass windows fronted the street where horses and wagons either lined the hitching posts or traveled the rutted road.

"Mr. Davis will see you now."

Ruby smiled in response. At least she hoped it was a smile. The distance between a smile and a grimace was less than a dimple.

"Good day, Miss Torvald." A medium man stood behind a

shiny oak desk. Medium was the only word she could think of. Medium height, medium weight, medium brown hair, and a medium face; other than a gold tooth that flashed when he smiled. He even wore all medium brown clothing—but for a gold watch fob. He came around from behind the desk and bowed slightly. "Ah, Miss Torvald. I am glad to meet you. I enjoyed doing business with your father and was most distressed to hear of his demise."

"Th—thank you, Mr. Davis."

"Please be seated." He gestured to the chair in front of the desk and returned to his, clasping his hands on the desktop. "Now, how may I assist you?"

"Since you already know that my father died, I am sure you have heard also that I am now the owner of Dove House. The bill you sent, demanding payment. . . ?"

"Yes, it has been six months since I received a payment from your father."

"He was very ill."

"I see. Perhaps that is why . . ." He glanced at Charlie.

"Yes, sir. I called on you the last few times. Per—Mr. Torvald asked me not to mention his illness."

"I see."

Ruby glanced at the man sitting beside her. Had they been concealing her father's illness for a reason? And if so, why would they do that?

"So, Miss Torvald, how is it that I may help you?" Mr. Davis clasped his hands on the desk in front of him and waited.

Ruby thought of the money in her reticule. Would it be best to bring that out now to show her good faith? Had the temperature in the room really dropped enough degrees that she wanted to shiver? *Far, how could you go and leave me like this?*

She mentally squared her shoulders and leaned forward slightly, again hoping that the motions on her face indicated a smile. "Since I am now the owner of Dove House, I would like to know the arrangements my father had with you. I'm sure he had hoped to have time to explain things to me, but since his death prevented that, I hoped you could tell me what I need to know."

"Certainly." Mr. Davis proceeded to explain to her the dealings he had had with Per, from the initial deposit to the building transactions and on to the furnishing and operating expenses. "Your father had an open account that he paid quarterly and a savings account that now has a zero balance since we had to use that to pay for the last two quarters." He glanced to Charlie. "Since Mr. Torvald had always kept his account current, I am sorry I had to write such a firm letter, but the bank cannot carry an account in arrears for long. You understand that."

Both Charlie and Ruby nodded.

"So I am hoping you have sufficient funds to bring the note up to date."

At no point did a smile mar the man's medium face.

"I have some cash with me, but I would like to know the amount owed on the account."

Mr. Davis glanced down the page on the desk in front of him. "Six hundred two dollars and fifty-one cents."

Ruby closed her eyes and fought the nausea that threatened to choke her. Six hundred dollars. Where would she ever lay her hands on that kind of money? She met the gaze of the man behind the desk. "And how much of that is past due?"

"One hundred eight dollars and twenty-six cents."

Ruby's thoughts moved to her reticule, which held a grand total of eighty-five dollars, all her earthly wealth but for the ten-dollar gold piece she had sewn into the lining of her coat, as Mrs. Brandon had suggested. And if she paid it all to the bank it was unlikely that the general store would continue to sell them supplies. Was the money they needed in the illusive buksbom, the box she'd dreamed about in her few sleeping hours?

Had there been more money at Dove House, and if so, where had it gone?

"Mr. Davis, how long has it been since you have visited Dove House?"

His medium face adopted a tightening around the eyes and mouth. "I have never been to Dove House." The inference shouted from between the words: As if I ever would. You think that *I* would deign to enter such a place?

"Things have changed at Dove House. The saloon is now a dining establishment, and we have a cardroom open in the evenings or, if someone makes arrangements, in the afternoon."

"You are no longer serving liquor?"

"That is correct."

"But that was your most viable asset."

"Yes, well, I cannot have my little sister living in a saloon, nor myself."

"And, ah, the other?" One eyebrow slightly raised and a bit of color showed above his stiff collar. He looked to Charlie.

"As we said, things are different at Dove House. The. . . .the other is no longer."

All right, gentlemen. Ruby drew herself up a trifle straighter and planted her feet. "The girls, as you gentlemen"—she emphasized the word as if in doubt—"refer to the lovely young women, are now employed as maids and waitresses at my hotel. Because men with baser instincts, unlike yourself, of course, force innocent young women into that form of servitude, Dove House has acquired an unsavory reputation, which we must now put to rest." She ungritted her teeth and smiled with no semblance of warmth. She could hear Charlie shifting in the seat beside her and realized the red on the man's face in front of her had nothing to do with the red haze before her own eyes. "Pardon my frankness."

"Ah yes." Mr. Davis studied the papers in front of him.

Good, I've made you as uncomfortable as I am. She thought back to Mrs. Brandon. Would she have felt an urge to gloat? And was that the best way to handle this situation, or had she just fallen into the trap of speaking before thinking? *Oh me. What am I to do?* She waited, keeping the fidgets at bay only by relying on long years of training in deportment, thanks to first her mother, then Bestemor, and finally Mrs. Brandon, who had taught mostly by example. Ladies did not spout off and castigate gentlemen, and if they did, it was always done with grace and gentleness.

Thinking back, Ruby was fairly certain neither grace nor gentleness appeared in her diatribe. She trapped a sigh like she had the fidgets and sat perfectly prim and perfectly still, unless the pounding of her heart showed through her gown.

Mr. Davis finally raised his eyes to meet hers. "Be that as it may, Miss Torvald, I am sorry to be the bearer of bad news. Until this account is current, I cannot in good conscience offer you more credit."

"I suppose sixty dollars would not be sufficient."

"No. Is that all you have?"

"Yes." *For you.*

"I will apply that to the current payment. When do you believe you will have the remainder?"

"As soon as possible. I have never had debt of any kind, and I want out of this as quickly as I can make my way free."

"I see. You realize that if we are forced to foreclose to get our investment back . . ." His voice trailed off, as if he expected an answer.

Foreclose! Lose Dove House after all the work we've done? All that my father invested? You will not get your greedy paws on my inheritance! "How long can you give me to catch this up? The end of the year?" *Surely I can make this up by that time.*

"You realize there will be another payment due before then?"

"Of course." She tried to put some warmth and confidence into the smile. "Thank you for your time." She stood and gave a slight nod.

Charlie rose, hat in his hands.

"Good day, Mr. Davis. Please remember that the invitation to visit Dove House still stands." *In spite of your stiff-necked rectitude.*

"Good day, Miss Torvald, Charlie. Thank you for coming by. Oh, you can leave your payment with Mr. Struthers at the second window."

"I will." Ruby turned and, without waiting for Charlie, stalked through the swinging door in the low oak wall that divided the manager's desk from the rest of the room. She approached the second window and, with another of those empty smiles, laid her money on the counter. "Please apply this to the Per Torvald account. I am his daughter." *Next time I come, I will transfer the accounts to my name.*

"Glad to meet you, miss. I was sorry to hear of your father's death." Mr. Struthers took the money, counted it carefully, and completed the transaction, then passed the receipt he wrote back under the grillwork. "There you go, miss. I wish you every success."

"Thank you." At least there is one person in this bank with a heart. Ruby tucked the bit of paper in her reticule and allowed

Charlie to lead her out of the bank.

As they walked up the street to the mercantile with Charlie pushing the dolly, she debated how to ask her next question. There appeared to be no easy way.

"Charlie, from what Mr. Davis said, and from what I've read of the Dove House ledgers, there appears to be some money missing. In fact, at least an entire payment that was registered as paid. Do you know what has happened?"

"Can't say as I do. I know I did not take the last quarter's payment to the bank. Guess I thought it was still in the box at home."

"Box? You mean the till?"

"No, the box." He drew it with his hands. "'Bout this by this." He scratched his chin. "Come to think on it, I ain't seen it for some time."

"Is this the box Far referred to as the buksbom? He said something about treasures being in it."

"Not sure I know what you mean by buksbom, but this box just had money in it." Charlie shook his head. "So we might have two missing boxes."

"Guess so." Ruby pictured the box and in her mind surrounded it with a halo of hope.

"You think Belle has them?"

"Could be. Or . . ." He chewed on his lower lip.

"Or?"

"Or Per hid them."

"Hid them where?"

"Don't know." He took her elbow to assist her up the three stairs to the front of the mercantile.

"Why didn't you mention this money box before?"

"Guess I thought you already found it." He pushed open the door to the store. "The proprietor here is Boyd Rumsford. He was a friend of your father's."

"It sounds like my father had a lot of friends. I sure hope this one proves more helpful than that banker."

"Ah, bankers are always a stiff-necked lot. Get that way from trying to keep their ears above those collars they wear." He ushered her in the door ahead of him and motioned her toward the back where a counter ran half the length of the wall.

Ruby glanced around, trying to keep her amazement from showing. There wasn't a square foot of space—be it on the shelves, counters, walls, floor, and even hanging from the ceiling—that was not full of food, clothing, tools, household utensils, spirits in bottles, spices in cans, and pickles, flour, and sugar in barrels. A huge ham hung behind the counter, and a wheel of cheese lay under a glass dome. The proprietor closely resembled one of the barrels, only he wore an apron that had seen better days. His handlebar mustache appeared to make up for the lack of hair on his head and the two teeth missing in his smile.

"Hey, Charlie. Been a while."

"Miss Torvald, meet Boyd Rumsford." Charlie performed the introductions.

Ruby nodded. "I am pleased to meet you, and I have to admit to some amazement at your store."

Mr. Rumsford looked around. "Whatever for?"

"All the merchandise you have displayed here."

"Ah, that. And I can locate anything you need. What can I do for you today, Miss Torvald? Oh, and I offer my condolences on the loss of your father."

"Thank you. I have an order, but first we must discuss the financial arrangements you had made with my father."

"Being we're the nearest store of any size and carry a full line of spirits, he did most of his shopping here. We ran a chit, and sometimes he ordered by mail. He usually paid me when he came in again. Right sorry I had to send you that letter."

"I see. And how much is the balance on his account?"

Mr. Rumsford pulled a leather-bound ledger out from under his counter and flipped pages until he came to the right one. He ran his finger down the column and looked up to pronounce, "One hundred twenty-seven dollars and sixteen cents."

Ruby mentally flinched. "I have twenty-five dollars to pay you now."

He tipped his head to the side along with a tsking sound from between his teeth.

"Along with the return of three cases of whiskey. At two dollars a bottle, that is another seventy two dollars," Charlie put in.

"Was there something wrong with it?" Rumsford glanced to Charlie for an answer.

"Nope. We're just not serving drinks any longer."

"No drinks?" Horror looked normal on Mr. Rumsford's long face with its veined, slightly red nose.

"Dove House is now a family hotel with a good dining room."

"No whiskey? Sherry?"

"No, neither." She handed him her list. "You will fill this for us then?"

"Yes, of course. You want to look around while I get busy on this?"

"Yes, thank you. Where are your sheetings and dress goods?"

He indicated the stairs along the right wall. "Up there. You want I should send someone up to help you?"

"In a little while. I'd like to look around first."

"Good, good. You do that. Charlie, you want this all on tomorrow's train?"

"If we can."

Ruby ignored the slightly miffed feeling that his asking Charlie inspired and headed for the stairs.

Three hours later, after having supper at the Dickinson Hotel, Charlie and Ruby made their way to their rooms. Ruby spent part of the evening writing a letter to Mrs. Brandon, leaving out as much about their life in Little Missouri as she told. After all, she didn't want to horrify her benefactress. After that she made a list of changes and additions for her hotel based on things she saw in the one she was in. When she crawled into the bed, all she could do was luxuriate in the heavenly feeling of lying on a mattress again. Briefly she wondered what Charlie was up to before she floated off on a night of heavenly rest.

— ❧ —

The next morning they returned to the train station to await the soon-to-arrive westbound train. Once boarded, Ruby leaned back against the seat and closed her eyes. *How do we make enough money to pay the bank, keep our account current at the mercantile, and pay for things in Little Missouri?* Would it be cheaper to buy from suppliers in Fargo or Minneapolis? And if so, how would she pay them?

Where had the box of money Charlie had spoken of disappeared to? Was Belle the one behind the conspiracy to keep locals from coming to Dove House other than to play cards? Was there a conspiracy, or was it all in her head?

The questions rolled over and over in her mind like the train wheels rolling over the track. At least the train had a destination. "Charlie, where do you think the money box might be?"

"I would guess in Belle's room somewhere. If I could have a few hours in the room with Belle gone . . . or"—he looked directly at her—"you could ask Belle."

Ruby nodded, ignoring the clench of her stomach. A picture of the bank manager and his supercilious attitude made her narrow her eyes. "I'll ask her all right."

By the time the conductor announced Little Missouri, a headache hammered between her eyes.

When they stepped back on the ground, the baggage handler set down not only crates of their purchases, but also a box from the Brandons.

"How wonderful!" Ruby clasped her hands in joy. "Just in time for Opal's birthday."

"I'll hide it until tomorrow."

"Good. She's going to be so surprised."

Ruby turned to Charlie. "Do you hear what I hear?"

"Sounds like the piano."

"I know." Ruby gathered her packages, and Charlie took the rest. The nearer they drew to Dove House, the louder sounded the music.

"All right. Now kick, kick, and turn," floated out the open window.

What is going on? Ruby pulled open the door to see three females in short lace-flounced dresses turn and flip up their skirts, showing lacy drawers. Giggles and laughter accompanied the beat of the piano.

Ruby's jaw dropped.

"Opal, what on earth are you doing?"

CHAPTER TWENTY-THREE

The dancers froze. The music died midnote.

Belle turned the piano stool around as though she had all the time in the world. "Welcome home, honey. Come on and join us. We're just havin' some fun."

"Teaching my little sister to . . . to show off her legs and her . . . her . . ." Ruby could hardly get her breath. Good thing she'd given up tightly laced corsets, or she would have fainted right there on the floor.

"Now, Miss Ruby . . ." Charlie spoke gently from right behind her.

"But, Ruby, we weren't doing nothing wrong." Opal settled her skirt, her red taffeta skirt with black lace that trailed to the floor. Had it not been for the ribbon around her waist, the entire garment would have swished and fallen to the floor.

A red haze swam before Ruby's eyes. What would Mrs. Brandon do in a situation like this? She'd never be caught in a situation like this, that's what! She would stay in her lovely home and go to the park or out in a carriage. She would not be running a hotel in the middle of nowhere, a nowhere that didn't look to be becoming anywhere anytime soon.

"Take a deep breath and count to ten"—wise counsel from as far back as her mother and reinforced by Mrs. Brandon. So Ruby did as she told herself. She took in a deep breath and, with a hand on her middle, counted in measured beats. One, two,

three . . . and on up to ten. The red haze disappeared.

She caught a glimpse of movement off to the side and recognized Milly with a disapproving I-knew-this-was-wrong look on her face.

"Ruby, I just wanted to learn how to dance." Opal clamped her fists into her skirt and her lower jaw jutted out. "We didn't break nothing."

"Anything." *And I know you didn't break anything other than my heart.* Ruby turned to the three who should have known better. "You should know better."

"Like Belle said, we were just having some fun." Cimarron laid a hand on Opal's shoulder. "Hard as we all work around here, some fun sounded right nice. And dancing is fun, as you would know if you tried it." She gave Opal a gentle push in the direction of the kitchen. "You go change your clothes, darlin'. You did real fine."

"I thought those dresses—"

"Had been destroyed?" Belle shook her head. "Now why would anyone do that? If this place doesn't make it, we'll all be back doing what we know to survive. Dresses like these cost plenty. No one in her right mind would burn money like that."

Ruby pulled out a chair to use as a brace. She tightened her hands around the wood back and locked her elbows to hold herself up. First the disappointing—nay, heartbreaking—trip to Dickinson and now this. What was her world coming to?

"You sit down there, and I'll bring you a cup of tea." Daisy fled the room, leaving Cimarron and Belle to deal with Ruby.

"We'll all go on back to the kitchen, and I'll put the kettle on." Belle rose from the piano stool that rolled on glass casters with a seat that went up or down as she turned it. "You got to admit she was cute as a button."

Ruby closed her eyes and gritted her teeth. *One, two, three . . .* When she made it to ten and opened her eyes, she was all alone in the dining room, the door to the kitchen still swinging.

And worst of all, she couldn't even fire them.

She reached down for her satchel, only to find that Charlie had taken it with him. She stood alone. Alone amid tables wearing white cloths hemmed by Cimarron. The windows sparkled, thanks to Milly's polishing. The dark blue painted floor had not a trace of dirt because Daisy kept it swept and scrubbed.

That they all worked hard together was right. And there most certainly hadn't been any time for fun. Was she a hard task-mistress? A vase filled with wild plum blossoms reposed on the polished-to-glass counter, where drinks used to be served and now guests registered for the hotel.

The evidence of hard work and uncomplaining workers could not be ignored. And now she had next to nothing to pay them for their labors. Granted, she'd put enough money on the accounts in Dickinson to keep them from taking Dove House away, but unless they got more business in the door and did so on a regular basis, they were still in trouble.

She felt like laying her head down on the table and using the tablecloth for mopping tears that once started might never stop. To think that back in New York her biggest problem had been the broken Dresden shepherdess.

Now she was all alone with all this responsibility. The load on her shoulders threatened to push her down, right through the floor. She tried to take a deep breath, but it stopped halfway. *Father, Far, Papa!*

"Papas are supposed to take care of their daughters, not sad-dle them with a burden beyond endurance." Ruby shoved back her chair, the feet shrieking against the floor, and stormed out the door and down the street to the cemetery where her father was buried. The slam of her feet against the hardening ground could have slaughtered hundreds of unsuspecting insects — maybe even something larger, had such a creature found its way under her lace-up shoes. She halted at the foot of his grave, arms locked across her chest, a formidable frown furrowing her face, sparks flashing from her eyes.

"What kind of a father are you, Per Torvald? Why did you bring us out here when you knew you were dying? I know you said you wanted to give us an inheritance, but all I got was more hard work and more responsibility than *three* young women should have. And the influence on Opal! What in the world were you thinking of? While we had nothing of our own at the Bran-dons', at least we were respectable. Here, none of the women in town will even talk to me. All those years I waited to hear from you ... and look what you did to us!" Her raised voice was enough to invite an answering caw from the crow in the nearby cottonwood tree.

"And you keep your mouth shut too." She shook her finger at him, and the crow flapped his way off.

She paced three feet one way, spun around, and paced six back. "What am I supposed to do? You weren't even honest with me regarding the debts. You said there was enough money to cover things. Did you think I would be able to go on with the girls in the same line of work? Who do you think I am?" The beat of her feet punctuated her invectives. "Who were you to allow such behavior? You and Mor always took me to church— you even sang in the choir. Now I hear that you and Belle were quite the duet. What happened to you that you changed so much?" She dashed at the tears that had the audacity to seep by her fury. "Take care of the girls! Who's going to take care of *this* girl? And Opal? How can I be her mother and her father and her sister and her teacher and all that she needs?"

She wanted to throw herself down on the carpet of green that had grown over the grave, slam her hands into the ground, cry her eyes dry, but she still wore her lovely travel dress, and grass stains were hard to remove. She resorted to stamping her foot. Somehow it wasn't as satisfying, but during the weeks since her arrival, she had gained a far greater appreciation for the work that went into laundry and housekeeping and cooking. To say nothing of keeping the books, a job she could shove off on Charlie, but then how would she know exactly where she stood? The thoughts buzzed in her head like bees in a swarm, and surely the bees were more productive.

A horse snorted, and she glanced back toward the street at the sound. Rand Harrison sat on his buckskin, watching her.

If she'd thought her face red before, now it flamed like a roaring fire. She clapped her hands to her cheeks, wishing for a fan, a parasol, a tree, anything to hide behind.

Instead, she drew herself erect and marched across the ground to stop several feet in front of his horse's nose.

"And a good day to you too, Mr. Harrison." Her slitted eyes dared him to say anything, but before she could stroll on by him, a snort from a huge creature behind his horse drew her attention. A rope ran from the saddle horn to the animal's face, where a chain attached to the rope ran through a ring in the animal's nose and up to encircle the base of its horns.

"Ah . . . your cow there doesn't look real friendly."

"He's a bull, ma'am." Harrison touched the brim of his hat. "I went east to purchase him. We unloaded at the cattle chute."

All she could see was the bull standing between her and the hotel. All she could think was that Rand Harrison had heard her ranting at her father at his grave. Rand Harrison, who had berated her for closing down the saloon and its accompanying services—all because his cowhands would miss the company.

The bull eyed her and pawed the earth with one massive white front hoof. The chain jangled and Harrison tightened his grip on the rope. The beast's curly red hide glinted in the sun. Now she knew what they meant by white-faced cattle.

"We'd best be on our way." He touched his hat brim again.

Ruby could swear he was laughing at her, but his actions were perfectly gentlemanly.

"I do hope your day improves." He reined his horse to the left and headed for the ford through the river.

The bull's long tongue licked his nose, and he shook his head against the pressure before following. She hoped to never have such a close acquaintanceship with a bull again.

Carefully stepping around the flat mound and spatters of greenish brown manure, she held her handkerchief to her nose until she reached the street.

Horses were tied to the hitching rail in front of Williams' Saloon. A buckboard and team were tied up at Mrs. McGeeney's. But nothing, no one, was outside Dove House. Unless someone walked in, it looked as if dinner today would be family only. If those who worked at Dove House could indeed be called family.

If she didn't kill or maim some of those family members when she got back inside.

Instead of feeling better for her tirade at the gravesite, she felt more a failure than ever. And to think someone had overheard her. What a joke this would be for him to share with his cowboys. The entire town would soon be laughing. Not that there were that many people in the town to be laughing, but the thought made her stumble on the top step and grab on to the post for support.

She opened the front door, wishing for a way to stop the bell from jangling. When Milly peeked out the swinging door to see who was there, she waved her off and climbed the front stairs to the second floor, then up the back stairs to the attic, and entered her room, praying that Opal would be downstairs with the others and not waiting up here.

Removing her long hatpin with the pearl beads, she lifted her hat off and stuck the pin back in the crown. She carefully wound the veil draping it around the brim to keep it safe and set the hat back in the hatbox. She hung her dress on the padded hanger, wishing for an armoire instead of the pegs along the wall, then draped the sheeting back over her good dresses and eyed the pallet on the floor.

At the Brandons' she'd had a comfortable bed with a feather bed for the winter, a chest of drawers, a dressing table, a washstand with a pitcher of water, and a three-panel screen to change behind. And a necessary down the hall—no outhouse or chamber pot. There had been gaslights and running water, an icebox in the kitchen, a lovely flower garden, and a grassy lawn with big old trees to enjoy.

Here she slept on a hard wooden floor on a bag filled with dried grass in an attic that was heating up in spite of the open windows. If it was this warm in May, what would August be like?

More importantly, would the hotel still be in business come August?

And if it failed, what could she do? She had used all the money from Mrs. Brandon to pay on the accounts. There was no money for return tickets to New York.

Fighting the desire to lie down and pull the covers over her head, she dressed in a dark calico skirt and cream waist, donned an apron, and made her way down the backstairs. She paused before entering the kitchen, reminded herself that yelling at them would do no good, and entered to find Milly fixing a tray, Cimarron dishing up food, and Daisy exiting to the dining room, coffeepot in hand.

"We have diners?"

"Four, and the easterners went upstairs to wash up before eating, so that is three more." Cimarron wiped her brow with the back of her hand. "My, but this stove does put out the heat."

"But I didn't see any horses or conveyances outside."

"Nope. The easterners left their mounts at the livery. The other folks are from town."

"What are we serving today?"

"Baked grouse, baked beans, canned peas, dandelion greens—thanks to Milly and Opal—and gingerbread with applesauce."

"Smells wonderful. Where's Charlie?"

"Out in the garden. He brought back some more corn seed and wanted to get it planted right away."

"Were any rooms rented last night?"

"One besides the easterners. They're leaving on the train tomorrow. Said they had the time of their lives but no buffalo." Cimarron stopped talking and turned to look at Ruby. "About the dancing in there, we really didn't mean any harm by it. You know we wouldn't hurt Opal for anything."

"I know." Ruby went to stand by the window, looking out to see Charlie with a hoe in his hands and a sack of seeds hung over one shoulder. "It's just that dancing like that is part of a life I don't want her exposed to."

"It needn't be. There's all kinds of dancing, you know. I learned to waltz and two-step and danced the reels and polkas. Square dancing is right fun—circle dances too."

"Yes, but that was not what you were teaching her."

"I asked them to teach me." Opal, who had come in on the last line, planted herself in front of Ruby with clamped hands on her hips. Her chin jutted out and her eyes flashed. "So don't go getting mad at all of them."

"Opal, you and I will discuss this later." Ruby kept her voice even. She reached out and tucked a strand of hair back over Opal's ear. "I missed you last night."

Opal's chin quivered, and the starch melted out of her. She leaned into her sister and wrapped her arms around Ruby's waist. "I missed you too. I haven't been by myself like that ever. I was thankful for Cat. She stayed with me, and she caught another mouse in the storage room and brought in a garter snake from outside."

"How did you know it was a garter snake?" Ruby laid her hands along Opal's chin and looked into her eyes. "You know there are rattlesnakes here."

"Cimarron knows the difference. Besides, it was just a little snake. Cat is really a good hunter."

Ruby shuddered. "First mice, now snakes. Rand Harrison's bull and—"

"Rand is back?" Cimarron turned from the stove.

"Yes." She wasn't about to explain where she had seen him. Her neck grew warm just at the thought.

"Shame he didn't stop for dinner."

The thought of that unfriendly beast tied up at their hitching post made Ruby close her eyes. She didn't think much could stand in that bull's way if he decided to go someplace. And to think Rand was leading him around like he was a dog on a leash, not that dogs wore a chain through a ring in their nose.

When they'd finished serving dinner and eaten their own, Ruby gave in to their pleading and told them what she'd learned in Dickinson.

"I knew I shoulda gone along." Belle gazed at the ceiling along with a harrumph of frustration.

"What good would that have done?" Ruby was still amazed. Belle was acting as if their discussion never took place.

"They know me. I went with Per plenty of times. Sometimes you got to"—she rolled her eyes—"you know."

"No, I have no idea what you are talking about."

"Well, sweet talk, you know. That Mr. Davis at the bank is a sucker for . . ." Belle batted her eyelashes and puffed out her chest, pretending she had a fan to flutter.

"Belle, I never . . ."

"That's what I was afraid of. But you looked so lovely in that dress and so innocent; I hoped that would be enough."

"I was asking for operating expenses, nothing more."

"Did you invite him to come and see the changes around here?"

"Yes, I did that. And I talked with a man from a newspaper during supper. He said he would do a story on the growth here in Little Missouri and include Dove House and the changes we've made. He seemed to think there was a story here."

"Oh, there's a story here all right," Belle muttered into her coffee cup.

Ruby chose to ignore her comment. Any publicity would be helpful.

Well, not any. If someone had come in when she and Charlie did, they would have thought things were the same as ever, except for the white tablecloths and the clean floor and the lack of bottles behind the counter. *And Belle? What do I do about Belle? She was as nice as pie when I planned to question her about the missing money and boxes.* Ruby shook off the thoughts. "I'm going out to sweep the porch," she said and went to get the broom.

— ❦ —

"I know there isn't a lot of fun for you here, with no other children to play with," Ruby said that night as she brushed Opal's hair.

"We could go riding again. That would be fun. And when the river warms up, we can go swimming. I like fishing too."

Ruby dropped a kiss on her sister's head. Yes, they needed to have more fun. When you came right down to it, there wasn't much going on in the whole town, other than the men drinking and gambling. Maybe there was something Dove House could do after all—provide genteel entertainment. She could feel an idea stirring. *Have more fun, eh?*

— ❦ —

"Ruby." The whisper was accompanied by a slight shake on the shoulder.

Ruby tried to remain in her dreamworld where they were back at the Brandons' and a young man had come calling. A man who looked remarkably like Rand Harrison. That alone jolted her into full alert.

"What?" Her heart leaped into double time. "What's wrong?"

"Nothing."

Ruby opened her eyes to see Opal, fully dressed, sitting on the floor cross-legged beside the pallet.

"Today's my birthday."

Ruby covered a smile by letting her eyelids fall closed again and turning on her side. "Are you sure?"

"Did you forget?"

Ruby tried to feign sleep, but the plaintive voice made her smile instead. She reached under her pallet and drew out the packet of red-and-white peppermint sticks she'd purchased the day before just for such a situation as this.

"I'm sorry I couldn't afford more right now, but . . ." She daren't look at Opal in case the deception could be read in her eyes. Lying had never been easy or even possible for her.

"Oh, goody. Thank you." Opal gave her sister a poke on the shoulder. "You didn't forget."

Ruby sat up and opened her arms to give her sister a way to burrow close.

"I dreamed I got a horse for my birthday."

"Oh, Opal dear, how I wish I could give you a horse. Perhaps by next year we'll be able to think of such a thing." *If we make it until next year.*

"Daisy said she was going to make something special for breakfast for my birthday. Just think . . . I am ten years old."

Ruby tweaked her sister's nose. "Pretty amazing." *And I'm nearly twenty-one.* Ruby kicked that thought aside as she threw back the covers and went to wash and dress. She'd just dipped the cloth in the cool water when she heard the rooster crow for the first time that morning. No, she hadn't overslept. Opal just beat the rooster crow. Ruby yawned and buried her face in the dripping cloth.

A bit later after brushing and braiding their hair, they entered the kitchen to find Daisy slipping something into the oven.

"What's that?" Opal asked.

"What's what?" Daisy turned with a blank look.

"What's that you put in the oven."

"Ah." She shrugged. "What oven?"

"Daisy."

Ruby stood behind Opal and wrapped both arms around her for a hug. "Little girls shouldn't ask questions on their birthdays."

"Oh." Opal turned and looked up to her sister. "Can I share my peppermint sticks now?"

"Why don't you wait until after breakfast?"

"All right." She put the packet back in her apron pocket. "I'll go check the dining room."

A short time later Daisy called her back just in time to see her pull a skillet from the oven that for just a moment had a poof of browned dough that collapsed when the air hit it.

"Oh, how pretty."

Daisy set the pan on a wood board on the table. "It's a German pancake." She sprinkled powdered sugar over the top and slid it out onto a plate. "Happy birthday, Opal." She set it at Opal's place, and they all clapped.

"All for me?"

"Yes. All for you. The rest of us get ordinary pancakes."

Opal cut into her pancake and found sliced peaches with cinnamon and sugar in the center. "I never had a pancake like this." Her eyes turned blissful at the first bite. "Yum."

Ruby looked at Daisy. "Where did you learn that?"

"My mother. She was from Germany and loved to cook. I'd almost forgotten about them until I said I'd make something special for Opal."

"Special is right."

— ✤ —

After dinner was served to their one guest, Ruby stopped Opal. "Why don't you and Milly go fishing? You deserve some time off since this is your birthday. But don't be gone too long. I'll need Milly's help later."

Opal threw her arms around Ruby's waist. "Thank you, thank you. What a perfect birthday I am having." She grabbed their corks with the hook and string and sinker and dashed out the door before anyone could change their mind.

As soon as the girls left, everyone else, Belle included, prepared for the party. Cimarron set to frosting the cake Daisy had baked. Daisy made a drink out of ginger, vinegar, and sugar boiled together and mixed with cold water. And Charlie headed on over to the cantonment to make sure the captain had returned from patrol. The two men strolled back to Dove House behind the other buildings just in case the fishing girls should return early.

Once the presents were arranged on a table, Belle kept watch and let the others know as soon as she saw the girls returning home, each carrying a string of fish.

Knowing they would come to the back door, the others gathered in the dining room and waited.

"Ruby? We're home." When no one answered, Opal called again. "Charlie, Daisy, where are you?" Another pause.

Ruby didn't dare look at any of the others for fear she would burst out laughing. She bit her lower lip.

"Where do you suppose they all are, Milly?"

"I don't know," Milly answered. "Maybe you better check the dining room. I'll go upstairs."

As soon as the door swung open, those waiting shouted, "Surprise! Happy Birthday!"

Opal dropped her string of fish. She clapped both hands across her mouth, then lowered them bit by bit. "But I already had . . . I mean, Daisy made . . . oh, look, a cake!"

"I think we surprised her." Captain McHenry nudged Charlie, who laughed along with him.

"Come and open your presents so we can have our cake." Daisy beckoned Opal to the table.

"I never had so many presents." Opal stared at the stack, then turned her gaze on Ruby. "You knew?"

Ruby nodded. "One of the hardest secrets I ever kept. Daisy baked the cake and Cimarron frosted it."

"And I got you out of here." Milly hefted both strings of fish. "I'll go put these in water."

"Hurry." Opal sat down at the table, and the others dragged up chairs. She unwrapped the first box and discovered a braided bridle from the captain.

"I know you don't have a horse yet, but this is to remind you to keep dreaming for one."

"Thank you." She stroked the leather with a gentle finger.

The next gift was a beaded leather vest. "Had that in the trunk," Belle said. "Since it's too small for me, someone oughta use it."

By the time Opal had opened the other gifts, she had a new divided skirt of corduroy from Cimarron, a new shirt from Daisy, a tooled-leather belt made by Milly and Charlie, and lace-up boots from Ruby, along with three books from the Brandons.

After she'd opened the final package, Opal looked at each face around the circle, "Thank you all so much. How did you keep such a good secret?"

"It was hard." Daisy shook her head.

"You almost caught me a couple of times." Cimarron shrugged. "We did most of our work up in Belle's room since you never go in there."

Milly giggled. "Charlie helped me. You came in one time, and I thought for sure you saw it."

"How about cutting that cake I've been eying? You know what we eat out on patrol?" Captain McHenry made a face that made Opal giggle.

After the cake was passed around and everyone had complimented Daisy and Cimarron on their creation, they all rose and headed for the back porch to enjoy the cool breeze.

Opal went upstairs, put on all her new things, and came back down to show them off. "I look like a real cowboy now."

"Cowgirl."

"Ah, Captain, you knew what I meant."

"How about we go riding tomorrow so you can make sure all that stuff works?"

"Yes, please. Ruby too?"

"Oh, most certainly, if she can get away."

Ruby shrugged. "Why not?" *I have so much to do I'll never catch up anyway, so I might as well go riding. Tonight I am going to search for that box again. The bukshom. I know that was what Far said. And the money box too. Wish I dared search Belle's room while she's dealing cards.*

CHAPTER TWENTY-FOUR

Late June

Summer in Little Missouri left a lot to be desired. The heat, or something, had gotten to them all. Ruby hid out on the porch with the peas to get away from the bickering.

"I sure miss the Brandons." Opal leaned against a back-porch post.

"You can help me shell the peas."

"I picked 'em."

"And you'll help eat them too, so sit down here in the shade and put your fingers to work." Ruby knew she'd said something unpleasant about the time it passed her lips, but too late to remedy.

"Do we have to work *all* the time?"

Ruby breathed a sigh, similar to those her sister issued repeatedly.

"I know, why don't you go get the book and help Milly with her reading? That way you both can sit out here in the shade and keep me company."

"All right." Opal jumped off the porch and ran out to the garden where Milly, wearing a wide-brimmed straw hat, knelt to pull the weeds from along the carrot rows. She'd stormed out there when Cimarron said something that hurt her feelings. Charlie turned from hoeing the potatoes to say something that made Opal laugh. Making Opal laugh was never hard. While Ruby couldn't hear his comment, she smiled at her sister's lilting laughter that sprinkled smiles wherever it went. If only she'd hear laughter again from the others. And if Belle didn't stop snipping, she was going to get snipped herself.

Opal came leaping back. "She's going to finish the row while I get the book and glasses of sweet tea. You want some?"

"Of course. Thank you." Ruby split open another fat pea pod and, using her thumb, popped the line of peas into her bowl. The next pod, she thumbed the peas into her palm and then into her mouth. Fresh peas, straight from the garden, sweet and crunchy, were better than cooked peas any time. Unless, of course, they could have creamed peas, new potatoes, and ham over biscuits. She'd have to ask Charlie if there were any tiny new potatoes under the vines he'd been hoeing.

She thought back to the letter received the day before from Mrs. Brandon. Like Opal said, she missed them dreadfully. And they were sorely missed as well. According to Mrs. Brandon, no one could manage the children as well as Ruby had—they'd been through two more tutors, and now Mr. Brandon was threatening to send Jason off to boarding school and the others to a private school for girls.

A private note from Alicia said how much she abhorred that idea.

"Look, if you don't like the way I iron the tablecloths, you can get up here and do them yourself." Cimarron's voice carried clearly through the screen door.

"I was just givin' you a suggestion." Belle's *suggestions* had a queer way of always sounding like orders.

After deciding that she was in no way going to get involved with the conflict inside and with the song of peas pinging the pan, Ruby let her mind drift over the preparations for the Fourth of July celebration, the first one for the town of Little Missouri. There would be horse racing and calf roping in the morning. The cowboys from the local ranches and the soldiers from the cantonment would all be competing. Mr. Williams had set that up, since Ruby had no idea what that entailed.

Captain McHenry had encouraged his men to send for their families to join in the festivities. Perhaps there would be someone for Opal to become friends with.

So far the hotel was fully booked, and the evening's entertainment would be dancing in the street with the musicians play-ing from the Dove House porch. Invitations had gone out to all the local ranches, not that there were that many of them. To her surprise, Rand Harrison had offered a steer to roast over a pit, which according to Cimarron was a western specialty called bar-beque.

"Okay, Ruby, you ready to listen?"

She hadn't even heard the girls settle on the porch. "Of course. And thank you for the drink." She took a long slow sip, savoring the coolness.

Opal read first, and Ruby could hear improvement in her reading. She believed what some folks said: the best way to learn something was to teach it to someone else.

"Okay, now your turn." Opal handed the book to Milly and pointed to the place. "Start right there." Opal certainly enjoyed telling someone else what to do. She had adopted a schoolmarm attitude she'd learned from some of the former governesses at the Brandons'.

"John ran through the bush . . . es. His dog, Blacky, ran in front of him. John t . . . r . . . i . . . pp . . . ed, tripped"—her smile beamed at sounding out the word—"over the dog. He hit the g . . . r . . . ound with a smack. Ouch! Blacky barked at John, wa . . . gg . . . ing his tail, his t . . . o . . . n . . . g . . . u . . ."

"Tongue." Opal supplied the difficult correction.

"Tongue? How can that be?"

Opal looked at Ruby. Ruby shrugged.

"Just the way it is. You'll find lots of words that just don't make sense sounding them out."

"Then how am I supposed to figure them out?"

"That's what teachers are for." Ruby smiled at Opal. "Gives them plenty to do."

Milly turned up her nose. "Well, I sure wouldn't be a teacher. You got to know too much."

"Keep reading." Opal pointed back to the place.

While the words were slow in coming, Milly was persistent. When she finished the page and turned to the next, she traced the new line with her finger, the better to keep her place.

"Someday I am going to read the Bible. My ma used to read

to us from the Good Book. She said that was the whole reason to learn to read."

"It's a good reason, all right, but there are a lot of other books out there too, and magazines and newspapers. Just think, you'll be able to read Charlie's newspaper."

Milly laughed. "Now won't that just set his tail on fire."

Ruby looked up from the bucket where she'd just emptied the last of the pods into her apron lap. "Why?"

"Well, Charlie don't like no one messing with his paper, leastways until he's read it."

"Guess I hadn't noticed. I'm just grateful he shares what he's read with the rest of us, or I would have no idea what is going on in this country, let alone the rest of the world. Like the amazing invention in France that makes moving pictures, and Thomas Edison building an electricity plant in Wisconsin. Even though I don't understand how electricity works and can't begin to picture lights by a wire and no flame, I still enjoy learning about them."

"I like the one you are reading to us. Do you think Pilgrim will ever get to the Celestial City?"

"What do you think?"

"I sure want him to be happy. He's had a hard go of life."

With a laugh Opal joined in the conversation. "I like *Uncle Tom's Cabin*. Ruby read that to us back at the Brandons. It was written before the Civil War."

"Rand Harrison's father fought in the Civil War."

"How do you know that?" Ruby asked.

"I heard him telling some men one night. His family lived in the South. That's why him and the captain didn't get along too good at first."

"Well." Ruby automatically corrected.

"Well what?" Milly watched and waited.

"You need to use the word well in place of good in a sentence like that."

"Like what?"

"Mr. Harrison and the captain don't get along well." Ruby emphasized the last word. She started to give the proper reason for the word usage but just smiled instead. No sense overwhelming her pupil.

Milly returned to her reading, and Ruby dug a handful of

peas from the bowl and ate them one at a time, savoring the sweet ones and spitting out ones that had grown old and bitter. While she heard horse's hooves on the street, she paid no attention, leaning her head back against the post and enjoying the western breeze.

"Look who's coming." Opal leaped to her feet as she called, "Hey, Captain!"

Captain McHenry dismounted and tied the two horses he'd been leading to the hitching rail, along with his own. "I wondered if possibly you might be able to exercise these two horses for me." He tipped his hat to Ruby. "If you can find time, that is."

Opal was halfway to the horses before she remembered her manners enough to stop and look to Ruby. "We can go riding, can't we?"

Ruby thought through the myriad of things she had to do and the building tension inside Dove House, but she took in the look of pleading on her sister's face and capitulated without a fight. "I imagine we can work it in, as a favor to Captain McHenry, of course." She smiled up at him as he stopped in front of her with a slight bow. "Have some fresh peas, Captain?" She held out the bowl.

"Can't turn down an offer like that. My mother used to wonder why there were so few pea pods on the vines."

"You think she ever figured out that her children, rather than the rabbits, were eating them?"

"Well, even the most intelligent rabbits might have a hard time picking the pods off vines trailing on a six-foot fence." His sneaky smile made her laugh outright.

"I'll go change and be right back." Amazing how the thought of an outing lent spring to her step as she set the bowl of shelled peas on the table. Cimarron and Daisy were trading barbed silences now.

Ruby headed up the stairs without comment, and within minutes she had arranged her hair into a club so the broadbrimmed hat rode her head more securely, donned her soft deerskin shirt and divided skirt, and taken her boots to sit on the stairs and lace. With her gloves tucked into the back of her waistband, she returned to the kitchen where Daisy was rolling out pie dough.

"What kind of pie are you making?"

"One canned peach and the other canned cherry. Sure would be good if we could can our own."

"But we don't have peach and cherry trees."

"I know, but we could."

"In Dakota territory?"

"You'd be surprised what all will grow here in the valley if given half a chance." She flipped the dough over to give it another pass.

"If peaches grew, I'd really be surprised. Back in New York we'd get some off the train from Georgia. Folks aren't kidding when they talk about sweet Georgia peaches. Where's Cimarron?"

"Cleaning out the cardroom." Her rolled-eye look said "Good thing."

"Opal and I are going riding with the captain. Do you need us to help with supper?"

Daisy shrugged. "Not unless we get a houseful, and you know the odds on that happening." She wiped the perspiration off her forehead with the back of her hand.

"Would that we had such a difficulty." Ruby snagged another handful of peas as she passed the table. "You better put these away, or there won't be any left for supper."

McHenry had Ruby's horse standing beside the mounting block when she went back outside. Opal was already mounted and walking her horse in a circle out by the garden. "Ah, this is so much easier." Ruby settled in her saddle and wiggled her legs so her skirt left off bunching and hung straight. Even so more of her leg showed than was proper, but at least not much above her boot tops was exposed.

When they trotted down the street, she waved to Mrs. McGeeney, who was scrubbing her front porch.

"She still hasn't forgiven you for taking over Dove House, has she?"

"No, and I doubt she will. The ladies of Little Missouri seem to hold an exaggerated view of their propriety."

"Perhaps the Fourth of July celebration will help remedy that."

"I hope so. Before I came here, I never imagined how few women there were in these parts."

"That's going to change real soon. On patrol we talked with two families on their way here from Minnesota. They're coming in covered wagons. They should be in Dickinson about now. They hope to homestead on the Little Missouri or one of the tributaries. The ranchers most likely won't be real happy about that."

"Why not?"

"Cuts into their cattle range."

"These new folks won't want to run cattle?"

"Who knows."

"Surely there's enough room for everyone." Ruby thought of the land that went on forever.

"Takes a lot of land to feed cattle. But more people will come. You can count on it."

If I can only hold on till then. She watched Opal trotting ahead of them, following the river northward this time. She turned in her saddle and beckoned them on.

"That girl rides like she was born in a saddle."

"Well, having been nearby at the time, I know for a fact she wasn't. She'd never been on a horse until the first time you put her up. I can never thank you enough for this. As you've noticed, there aren't many children in this part of the prairie."

"As I said, that's going to change. Most likely you'll need a school here soon."

"Who will teach it?"

"Oh, the state would advertise for a teacher. That's what they've done in other places."

"But where would they meet?"

"Have to build a schoolhouse. Might have to build for a cattle company too."

"A cattle company in Little Missouri?"

"Sure. They'd have their headquarters here and range the cows wherever they want. That's the value of free range."

"How does anyone know whose cattle is whose?"

"They round them up and brand the new calves every summer."

"Brand them?"

"Heat up an iron brand to red-hot in a fire, then slap it on the calf's rump. Smells something awful."

"How terrible for the calf. Why, a burn hurts worse than anything."

"Don't bother them none. They jump up and run back to their mothers. Spring roundup is a real busy time for the ranchers. In the fall they round up the steers, and those that are big enough are shipped back east for butchering."

"On the railroad?"

"There used to be cattle drives. Some still come up from Texas that way, but east and west they use the railroad."

"I see."

When the trail widened, Opal dropped back to ride with them.

"You will understand things better once you've been through a year here." He stopped his horse and pointed ahead. "See that snag up there?" At the look of confusion on her face, he explained. "See that dead tree along the river? That bed of sticks in the upper branches is an eagle's nest. Been there for three years that I know of. Eagle chicks ought to be learning to fly pretty soon. Sometimes their mothers have to push them out of the nest to make them fly."

Opal glanced over at him after watching the nest. "Do you think the mother is there now?"

"Doesn't look like it, but I could tell better if I had my telescope."

"Have you seen eagle chicks?" Her voice took on awe.

"Yes. I got above a nest one time, on a cliff. There were three of them. The mother tried to chase me away."

"And did you leave?"

"You bet I did. She flew right at me, talons foremost. I vamoosed before she could rake me or beat me with her wings. She looked vicious as all get out."

Opal returned to watching the nest. "What do eagles eat?"

"Sometimes you see them catch fish when the streams are low, and rabbits. I heard tell of eagles taking a small dog and even a lamb. Usually they take small critters. They're raptors, like hawks, only much bigger."

"There sure are lots of kinds of birds out here."

"True," Ruby said. "I think we better be heading back." She nodded at the long shadows cast by the buttes. "I am always amazed at the colors of the rock formations, and when the sun rises or sets, the colors are even more wonderful." She pointed to one rock face that blazed in the light from ochre to rust to red, with a horizontal line of black and one of gray.

"I never get tired of this land." Captain McHenry turned his horse back toward town. "Every day you see something new, or at least you see it in a different way. I've heard people say this land haunts you, and I've begun to believe it."

"Well, it must be a pretty well-kept secret, when you think how few people live here."

"Look over there. What's that?" Just as Opal asked, they heard a whistle.

"Prairie dogs, small ground-dwelling mammals. They live in colonies—people call them prairie-dog towns. That whistle was the lookout telling the others that danger is near and to hide back in their burrows. If we had time to sit here and not move, they'd pop out of their holes again. They eat grasses and seeds, so they make their area pretty barren. You try running a horse through a prairie-dog town and, sure enough, he'll step in a hole and break a leg. You got to be careful about things like that."

"I hope I can come back here sometime," Opal said, all the while gazing at the place the prairie dog had disappeared from.

Ruby could hear Opal's unspoken wish for *soon*. If only horses weren't so expensive to both buy and feed. If Opal had a horse, she would have a friend indeed.

If—the biggest small word in the language.

— ❧ —

At least a tenuous peace had returned by the time Ruby re-entered the kitchen. Perhaps having two customers to serve helped with that. It sure encouraged her.

Later that night Ruby listened to Opal's prayers. "And dear God, thank you for the chance to ride again, and thank you for the captain who is so nice to us. Lord, if you please, I would surely love to have a horse. I'd take good care of it, and a horse would make it easier to go fishing, so I could help make sure there is enough food for our guests to eat. Thank you. Amen."

Ruby captured her sigh before Opal heard it. How long had it been since she'd been able to pray like that? So simply, with a certainty that God heard. And cared. And might really answer. Life surely had changed and not necessarily for the better. At least for a change they had a celebration to look forward to. If nothing went wrong, of course.

CHAPTER TWENTY-FIVE

A rifleshot announced the Fourth of July dawn at the same time as the rooster crowed. The bugle at the cantonment answered, letting everyone know that the cavalry was in attendance. A platoon of soldiers had ridden in the day before, while some of their families had arrived by train. Many of them were staying at Dove House. Tents had sprung up like weeds, and a chuck wagon from one of the ranches had set up cooking by the corrals.

"Don't you leave the hotel," Ruby cautioned from her pallet as Opal tried to sneak out of their room.

"I just wanted to go down to see the cows and calves again."

"No." Ruby shuddered at the memory of the span of horns on the cattle in the corral. While someone had said the horns made an easy target for roping, all she could think of was the damage they could do to an inquisitive little girl.

"We have too many guests to take care of. We'll need every hand to help cook and serve." Ruby crawled out of her sheets and straightened her bedding. "I promised you we would watch the competitions . . ." As she spoke, she went behind the three-paneled screen to wash and dress. "And we will."

"Calf roping." Opal's lip stuck out far enough to give a bird a good roost.

"Yes, calf roping." Ruby threw her nightdress over the panel. "And horse racing."

"Yep, but you have to use the right words, or they will think we are dumb."

"Or . . ."

"Or dumb people from the east. Greenhorns, they call them, or dudes."

"Oh. If you have already washed, you may start brushing your hair."

"I can tie it back."

"No. You don't want the people staying here at Dove House to think you are not proper, do you?" The snort she heard adequately described Opal's opinion of other people's opinion. "Well, I care, so you better have a clean dress on under your apron."

"But that's what aprons are for . . . to cover up."

"No, they are to keep your clothes clean." Ruby buttoned her skirt and came out from behind the screen. Taking the brush from Opal's limp hand, she began brushing her own hair and twisted it into a rope to make a bun. No matter how she dampened it, fine wisps managed to curl around her face as soon as it dried. She turned to Opal's hair with the brush. "You have to brush the underside too."

"Ouch. I know, but do you have to be so rough?"

"Where were you yesterday that you have bits of leaves and sticks in your hair?"

"I can do this my own self." Opal flinched away.

"Then why didn't you?" Ruby started at the bottom and worked her way up. "What a mess, and I should already be downstairs."

"Ouch!"

"Sorry. Whatever happened to brushing your hair every night before bed?" *Probably the same thing that happened to us reading the Bible every night together. We get so tired, and we forget.*

Ruby parted the hair down the middle and picked up three strands from one side, starting the French braid just back of the brow hairline.

"You're making it so tight I get a headache."

"Sorry, but if you'd stand still, I wouldn't have that problem." Was this going to be one of those days when sorry had to be said far too often? As Mrs. Brandon would say, *"If you think before you act or speak, you won't have to say I'm sorry so often."* Sometimes

Ruby wanted to plug her ears and mind so that Mrs. Brandon's admonishments didn't intrude so often.

"There now. All done." She patted Opal's shoulder and laid the brush back on the shelf. "You are most welcome."

"Thank you. I guess."

Ruby heard the last two words but made no comment. Since she'd been up late baking an extra batch of bread, she was in no mood to argue. Never had they cooked so much food for so many people for so long. And besides the meals at the hotel, they had promised to make pots of baked beans to go along with the barbequed beef.

"People are still coming in," Opal announced when she returned to the kitchen from resetting a table. "Last night we had a lot, but nothing like this."

Ruby turned from flipping pancakes. "Your order is ready, Daisy." She started stacking the pancakes on the three plates on the tray. When she finished, she handed each plate to Cimarron who added two strips of bacon and two fried eggs and set the full plate back on the tray.

"Opal, another table to clear." Milly backed into the kitchen with the coffeepot in one hand and the milk pitcher in the other. "Is there more coffee ready?"

Opal turned from filling the syrup pitchers. "I'll be right there."

"You better hurry. We need the table."

Ruby poured more batter on the griddle. "Watch these while I mix more, will you, Cimarron?"

"Sure."

"Don't fill that tray so full you can't carry it."

Opal gave her sister a disgusted look. "I don't make the same mistake twice."

No, you don't. Sorry. But Ruby didn't say the words because Opal was out the door again.

Daisy returned to the kitchen with four more orders. "Some of these people are taking you up on your offer of a free meal from when you went calling."

"What a day for that," Ruby groaned. But when she thought about it again, she changed her mind. This way they would see how busy they were today and perhaps think it was like that all the time. And tell their friends.

Belle strolled in midway through the serving and sat down at the table after pouring herself a cup of coffee.

"My, my. You all sure are busy." Belle twitched her skirt out of the way of Cat who rubbed against her leg.

"She wants to be picked up." Milly took up the now refilled coffeepot and headed back out the door.

"I don't hold cats when I am dressed up."

Ruby and Cimarron exchanged looks that clearly stated what they thought of that. No one had ever seen Belle pick up Cat, dressed up or no.

If you think any of us are waiting on you today, you've got another think coming. Ruby gave her batter one more beat and began ladling it out on the griddle.

"Can I have some of those?" Belle asked.

"I guess so. You know where the plates are."

Cimarron looked over her shoulder. "And if there aren't any clean ones, check the back porch where Charlie is washing dishes."

"Oh, well . . ." Belle was wise enough to keep the rest of her comments to herself, even though two words had already taken the place of twenty. She dished up her plate and returned to the end of the table to eat. Other than snitching a slice of bacon or grabbing a pancake, none of the rest of them had taken time to eat.

"More dishes." Charlie carried a tray of clean supplies in and set them on the counter, then picked up a tray of dirty ones. "We got any more hot water?"

When Ruby glanced at the table again, she saw that Belle had left, leaving her plate and cup right where she had sat.

That woman. She could see how busy we are and still didn't pick up after herself. I'm going to have another talk with her and this one will not be to her liking. Ruby tried to think back if Belle was paid up with her room but someone called for more pancakes, and she forgot.

Sometime later Daisy pushed through the door and set a tray down. "That's the last of them." She wiped her sweating face with the bottom of her apron. "I know we've been wanting business to pick up, but if we serve like this very often, we'd need more help."

"Set up a couple of tables in case someone comes late, then let's all eat. The washing up can wait a few minutes." Ruby set a platter of pancakes in the center of the table. "Help yourselves."

"Any idea how many we served?" Cimarron asked after they'd all slowed the eating.

"Close to fifty, I think." Daisy closed her eyes to try to remember. "Four of them were free."

"We can count the till, that'll tell us."

"But the children were only two bits."

"That's right."

"We'll still know close enough. I know how much was in the drawer to start with."

"One of the army wives said we did real good and that she was so happy to see the changes in Dove House." Milly dug in her pocket. "Here's my tip money. I think we should divide up what we got between everybody. Cimarron never gets tips."

Ruby stretched her neck from side to side. "That's up to you, but don't include Opal and me."

"Opal worked as hard as the rest of us."

"I know, but—"

"If it's our money, we can do what we want, right?"

Ruby rolled her eyes and shook her head. What did Opal need money for anyway?

"The calf roping starts at ten," Opal reminded them.

They all fell to the remaining chores, and within an hour everything was put away again, the dining tables reset, and two cakes were baking in the oven for later.

"Come on, Ruby, or we're going to miss everything." Opal shifted from one foot to the other as Ruby changed her mind and settled her western hat in place instead of the small straw one that had no brim to protect her face.

"You should wear a hat too."

"No. I don't need a hat. Now come on." Opal was halfway down the stairs before Ruby could respond.

When Ruby entered the kitchen, Cimarron was just taking the cakes out of the oven. "Are you coming?"

"Think I'll just stay here and frost these. I've seen calves roped before. Helped out with branding too. It's hot and dirty work."

"Ruby!" The cry came from the porch.

"You go on and have a good time," Cimarron said.

"You're sure?"

"As I'll ever be. Be right peaceful here with everyone gone. Besides, I want some time to get ready for the dancing. And I'll come on over for the barbeque. Wouldn't miss that."

"I'll be back to help get things over there."

"R-u-b-y."

"You go on before she faints from excitement."

CHAPTER TWENTY-SIX

"You entering the roping?" one of the cowboys from the Triple Seven called to Rand from atop his horse.

"Soon as we get this settled." Rand looked up from rearranging the coals under the sizzling steer half. He wiped the sweat from his face with the back of his hand. The day was hot enough on its own, but working the fire pit made the air almost unbearable.

"I can take care of this," Beans reminded him. "You go on and keep the Double H in glory."

"They're not quite ready to start." Rand glanced up to see a small crowd heading for the makeshift corral and the three-tiered stands that the army had built for the spectators. A few minutes later, with the meat sizzling again, Rand waved good-bye to Beans and headed for the long line where he had tied Buck.

"You racing that old nag?" one of the Ox Ranch cowboys called.

"Maybe so, maybe no." Rand laid the saddle blanket in place and threw the saddle over Buck's withers.

"Hey, Mr. Harrison."

"Hey yourself, Opal. You come to watch the calf roping?"

The girl nodded, her braids flapping. "Captain McHenry taught me to ride."

"Good for you. I bet you want a horse too." He reached

under the belly for the cinch and slid the strap through the brass ring.

"Always wanted a horse."

He recognized the plea in her voice. His little sister had been the same way.

"I hoped when we came west I would get a horse."

"They're pretty necessary out here." He finished looping the cinch strap through the two brass rings and secured it in place. "Anyone teach you how to saddle a horse yet?"

"Nope. What's your horse's name?"

"Buck."

" 'Cause he's a buckskin?"

"That's right."

"You going to enter the calf roping?"

"Yep."

"I hope you win."

"Me too." Rand caught a movement out of the corner of his eye. Oh-oh. Big sister's come to the rescue.

"You shouldn't be bothering Mr. Harrison." Ruby laid her hands on Opal's shoulders.

"But I'm not." Opal looked up and over her shoulder.

Lady, you've got to give that girl some freedom. "We're just being neighborly." Was that a slight snort of derision he heard? He turned from settling Buck's headstall to catch a fleeting glimpse of an emotion that belied the polite smile on Ruby's face. Her hat shaded her eyes, so he couldn't tell if the smile made it to them or not.

"Come, Opal, let's get a seat."

"Good luck, Mr. Harrison."

"Thanks. Enjoy the show." He watched them walk off, wishing he had offered Opal a ride over. *Girl that age sure should have a horse.* He mounted, checked his rope, looped and tied it right under the pommel of his saddle. He'd looped the pigging string around his saddle horn.

Captain McHenry, mounted on his big bay, motioned to the bugler to blow a few notes to get everyone's attention.

"Welcome folks to the first Fourth of July celebration here in Little Missouri. We're asking all you children to take seats up in the stands where you'll be safe in case some of our animals get away from us."

Rand glanced over to see Ruby nudge her little sister. He'd have bet Buck that Opal had been begging to get closer to the action.

"All right, you cowboys," McHenry continued, "if you will choose what pair goes first, we can begin."

"Better explain what's happenin'!" one of the riders yelled. "Got lots of greenhorns here."

A chuckle rippled through those on the three-tiered stand.

"Rand, how about you do that?"

Rand nodded and nudged Buck forward so people could hear more easily.

"This is the way we catch calves for branding, which we just finished in June. The calf will come out of that chute there, and two riders will come after it from the sides of the chute, one to haze or keep it running straight and the other to rope and dog it, which means leap from your horse, flip the calf on its side, and tie the legs together with a piggin' string. When the cowboy throws his hands in the air, he is finished. This is a timed event, and the pair with the fastest time wins the pot."

"Our first pair will be from Triple Seven Ranch." The captain nodded to the man on the chute gate.

"Ready?" he called, looked to both riders for nods, and swung open the gate. A red-and-white calf burst out of the chute with the two horses racing after him, one rider swinging a loop around his head. The loop dropped over the calf's head, and the horse sat back on his haunches, skidding to a stop with the rider already on the ground and running toward the calf fighting at the end of the rope. The man reached over the calf's back, grabbed the flank, and tipped the calf on the dirt. Knees planted on the calf, he whipped the pigging string around the legs and raised his hands in the air. They waited for a couple of seconds to make sure the string held, and the man on the stop watch announced the time.

The crowd applauded as the horse stepped forward to loosen the rope so the rider could retrieve his pigging string and loose the calf.

The calf leaped to its feet and was hazed into another corral by two other riders.

"Not bad," Rand said to his partner, Joe.

"They let the calf get too far ahead of them. We can beat them."

Rand glanced over in the stands to see Ruby and Opal discussing something. Their smiles said they were having a good time as they settled back down for the next pair.

Everyone groaned when the second calf broke free of the ties before the time allotted and ran out of the arena, bawling like it had been near killed. The two cowboys shook their heads, the roper mounted again, and they rode to the sidelines where the others gave them a bad time.

"You ready?" Rand asked.

"As I'll ever be." Joe nudged his horse forward. "I'll rope if you'd rather not."

"No, this is fine."

They took their places on both sides of the chute. Rand clamped his pigging string between his teeth, loosened his rope, and waited. Waiting for the signal was always the hardest part. If they jumped too soon, they'd be disqualified, too late and they'd lose for sure.

Buck settled on his haunches and leaped forward at the same moment as the calf hit the ring. Rand swung his loop twice, and it sailed over the calf's head like it had a mind of its own.

Rand hit the ground running, hand on the taut rope, grabbed ahold of the calf, flanking it to the ground. As Buck kept the rope tight, Rand flipped the loop of the piggin' string around the upper front foot and scooped up both back feet with his left arm, binding them together with two wraps and a hooey, as the cowboys called the ties. Still sitting on the animal, he threw his arms in the air.

"Not bad for an old codger like you," someone yelled from the sidelines.

Rand waited for the sign, and when Buck stepped forward, he loosened the rope from the calf's neck and jerked on the loose end of the piggin' string to free the calf. The calf scrambled to his feet and ran bawling back to where his mother was frantically pacing the corral.

As if he had no will of his own, Rand gazed across to the risers to see Ruby clapping and Opal dancing and cheering, her arms above her head as she clapped her hands. Ignoring the smile he could feel stretching his cheeks, Rand slapped his hat against his thigh to get rid of the dust, looped his rope in his hand, and remounted Buck with a firm pat on the horse's shoulder.

"Well done," Captain McHenry called as Rand and Joe returned to the sidelines, ready to watch the next release.

"Mighty smooth." Joe crossed his arms on the saddle horn. "Puts us in the lead."

"For now. You want to switch places and run again?"

"No, I ain't got the speed. Might haze for Chaps if he decides to put the money up."

Rand watched as the next calf broke loose and the riders leaped after it. His gaze strayed back to the stands again. Ruby and her western hat stood out from the straw hats and sunbonnets. Daisy sat beside her, and he wondered again at the difference. Hard to believe Daisy was Jasmine and she hadn't left after all.

Amazing what a difference a fancy dress and face paint made.

The calf struggled to its feet before the timer, disqualifying the pair.

Two soldiers lined up for the next entry, but they hadn't near the experience of the cowboys and came in two minutes over Rand's time.

"You better teach your men to rope and tie," one of the hecklers called to the captain.

"Ah, the pay's better in the army," Captain McHenry answered.

"The food ain't." General laughter answered the comment, even though the cantonment was known for having good and plentiful food.

The next pair from the Ox Ranch turned in a near perfect performance.

"I think they beat us." Joe spat off to the side.

When the time was announced, Rand nodded. "Less than a second faster—not bad."

Rand and Joe ended up with second place, since no one else entered.

"Decided to save my money," Chaps said when he rode up. "You near to saved our reputation."

"Near to don't bring home the pot." Joe turned his horse and rode off to the starting line to watch the races. The quarter mile would run first.

"You entering Buck?" Chaps asked.

"I don't think so. You want to ride him?"

"He runs best for you. Why not ride him? You have as good a chance as any."

"Not with that half-Thoroughbred McHenry rides. That horse goes like the wind."

"Buck gets off faster. You could take him on the quarter." Chaps spoke around the chewing tobacco that puffed out his lower lip.

"Too much weight."

"Take the saddle off." A glob of tobacco juice splatted in the dust.

"That's a thought. Those military saddles weigh hardly anything." Rand sucked air through his teeth, a sure sign that he was thinking.

"I'll put the money up."

"No. If I race, I'll do that. How many are entered?"

"Five in the first race and six in the second."

"I need to go on over and check the meat."

"No, you don't. Beans knows what he's doin'. He got a young private to spell him on turning the crank."

"He might be running low on wood."

"He knows how to split more. The stack is right there." Chaps gave him a look painted gray with doubt. "You really don't want to run, you don't have to, you know." He tipped his head slightly. "But then we on the Double H won't be able to hold our heads up without winning something."

Rand leaned over and punched Chaps on the shoulder. "Yeah, I saw how you did your best to hold our name up."

"So you going to run?"

"Why do you care?"

"I plan to make good money on the bet."

"You better keep your money in your pocket where it's safe. I can't guarantee a win." Rand rode on over to see how Beans was doing, but the cook waved him off before he could open his mouth. He leaned forward and smoothed Buck's mane to the side. "You want to run, old boy?"

Buck's black-fringed ears swiveled back to listen better. He blew out a snort, as if daring the other horses to challenge him, and pawed one front hoof.

Rand glanced over at the crowd where the captain was already mounted and sat like he'd already attained a general's stars. Opal and Ruby stood by the horse chatting with McHenry. From where he sat, Rand figured they looked to be fast friends. He'd seen them riding one day up the river.

Nudging Buck, he rode on over to the crowd, drawing another dollar out of his shirt pocket on the way.

"You in, Harrison?"

"Guess so." He handed his money to Johnny Nelson, owner of the only store in town.

"Anyone breaks over the line before the pistol shot is disqualified."

"I get it."

"The captain wanted to take a run at it, but I told him no. Start from a standstill is the only way out here." Johnny scratched his cheek. "You bettin'?"

"Nope. Not a bettin' man."

"Winner takes all."

"I know." Rand tipped his hat at one of the military wives and rode on over to the sidelines, where he dismounted.

"So you're going to try to beat Kentucky here, after all?" Captain McHenry stopped his horse beside Buck.

"Looks that way." Rand unbuckled the rear cinch and started loosening the front.

"What are you doing?"

"Lightening up my horse. What does it look like?"

"Won't help."

"We'll see." Rand sent McHenry one of his slow smiles, daring him just a bit.

"Opal, stay back from the horses." Ruby's voice made Rand break off the stare down.

"But I—"

"No buts. You heard me."

Rand set his saddle on the ground with the horn down and flipped the rope over the cantle so it would be out of the way. He tossed the heavy woven wool blanket on top and brushed a gloved hand along Buck's spine.

"How come you took the saddle off?" Opal had edged closer in spite of her sister's warning.

"So Buck has less to carry." At her questioning look, he added. "Then he can run faster."

"Oh. Is he real fast?"

"On short distances." He nodded toward her sister, who was picking her way past a pile of horse manure. "You better get back before you get in real trouble."

"Yeah, I know. Thanks." She flashed him a grin, saluted the captain, and meandered on over to the side before Ruby caught up with her.

Rand kept his smile to himself. She surely did remind him of his little sister. Same sass, same determination to get what she wanted.

"Mount up." Johnny shouted to be heard over the boisterous crowd.

Rand swung aboard and signaled Buck forward. He stopped to the right of Captain McHenry, whose horse was already shifting his front feet and tossing his head.

"Bit high-strung, eh?"

"Ready to run, is all."

Buck stood quietly, although Rand could feel the horse's muscles bunching. He glanced ahead to where another group of spectators stood at both sides of the finish line.

The pistol fired, and within three strides Buck was a length ahead of the other horses. As one body with his horse, Rand melted into the mane and withers. While he could hear the others behind him yelling at their mounts and flailing their hides with whips, he only murmured, "Come on, Buck, old boy. You can do this."

Halfway to the finish line, he could hear a horse coming up on the left side and one still farther back on the right. Buck drove for the finish line, his ears flat against his head, nose reaching for the prize.

With each stride the captain's horse drew nearer. At the flank, then the girth.

Rand glanced to the side to see the Thoroughbred's nose even with Buck's shoulder. The horse was coming up faster than the finish line.

Nose to neck.

"Come on, Buck." Rand whispered in his horse's ear.

The buckskin gave his last surge, and they were over. Rand had no idea who won. He eased himself straight up and back on the reins as gently as if they were riding on the ranch. Down to a lope, a jog, and a walk before he turned around to the cheering crowd.

"You did it, Rand!"

"Harrison, you ever want to sell that buckskin, I'll take him."

"Yeehaw, what a race."

The men surged around him, patting Buck and slapping Rand on the knees, his hands. Rand glanced up to see McHenry shaking his head.

"Three more paces, and I'd have had you."

"I know. That was too close for comfort."

"You want to go in the half mile?"

"Nope. Buck only does the quarter. You going to run again?"

"Of course. Kentucky just got warmed up. Give him a few minutes' rest, and he'll run 'em all into the ground."

While Rand and McHenry were talking, the others were laying out the turn. Since there wasn't a convenient half mile of straight flatland to run on, they compensated with an easy turn and back to the starting line.

Johnny handed Rand the jingling leather bag. "Here you go. You won it fair and square."

"Thanks." Rand looked down to see Opal, eyes shining and with a grin from here to there, standing between Buck and the captain's horse, one hand on each sweating shoulder.

"You were both so . . . so . . ." She made a funny face. "I can't think of a word big enough and good enough." Buck turned and whuffled her hair, making her giggle.

"Thank you, Miss Torvald." Captain McHenry reached down

and patted her hand. "Someday you'll ride like that."

"I think not." Ruby stopped five feet in front of the horses.

But Rand could tell she'd enjoyed the race as much as her little sister. Excitement pinked her cheeks and widened her eyes. If he wasn't mistaken, she had a slight case of the heaving bosoms too. *Harrison, keep your eyes on her face where they belong.*

"Hey, Rand," Belle called, waving some bills in the air. "Thanks."

"You're welcome."

"I never thought he'd do it," muttered someone in the crowd. "Thought sure that big bay had it in the bag."

"Thankee, boss man." Beans waved as he headed back to tend the barbeque.

"Don't drink it all in one place."

"Never fear."

"Are you going to race again?" Opal paced along beside him as he led Buck back to the long line to tie him up.

"Nope. Buck doesn't do long races."

"Why?"

"He's bred for short spurts. That's what makes him a great cow horse. He's quick on the start, hits top speed, and can stop just as fast."

"Like he did roping the calf?"

"Yep. That's what cow horses need." Rand flipped the reins around Buck's neck and removed the bridle. He knotted a thick soft rope around the horse's neck, gave him a pat, and headed over to check on the meat.

"They're getting ready to run again." Opal looked over to where the crowd had gathered again.

"You'd best get on back, or your sister will get after you."

"I know. Thanks." She waved and trotted back toward the stands.

Rand watched her go. *If your life had been different, you could have had a daughter her age. Or a son.* He shook his head and hung his bridle on the horn of his saddle that most likely Beans had brought back to the chuck wagon. *You can't change the past, so let it go.* Sometimes the saying was easier than the doing. McHenry's winning was a foregone conclusion.

CHAPTER TWENTY-SEVEN

"I'm here to help, miss." A young soldier saluted smartly from the bottom of the steps. "Captain said you could use a hand."

"Why thank you and thank the captain. You are . . .?"

"Private First Class Adam Stone, ma'am."

"I'm glad to meet you. You don't by any chance have a team and wagon that we could use to haul all this food over to the tables, do you?"

"I will go get one." He saluted again and spun on his heel to mount the horse he'd ridden down.

"Oh, he's so cute." Milly stared after him.

"Perhaps you can dance with him this evening." Ruby caught the wink that Cimarron sent her way.

"I'd like that." Milly looked to have spent the last hour in the noon sun without a hat.

"Huh. I'd rather watch the garden grow." Opal gave Milly a sad glance.

Ruby tucked her smile back inside. One of these days Opal might decide young men were cute too, but she hoped that was a long time coming.

Rand Harrison and two of his men were lifting the roasted half of beef off the spit when they arrived. Long trestle tables already held food others had brought. Coffeepots lined the edge of the long fire pit, and from the raucous laughter, it would be needed fairly soon, hot and strong, to counteract the effects of

Williams' brew among some of the men.

As Rand and his men began slicing slabs of meat off the carcass, the bugler called them all to eat with the army notes to charge.

And that they did. Soldiers, ranchers, townsfolk, hunters, women, and children all fell into lines on either side of the table and dished up their plates.

"Would you mind if I sat with you?" Captain McHenry asked softly.

"I thought I should carry the coffeepot around." Ruby looked up from under the brim of her hat.

"I've set one of my men to doing that."

"Oh, why then, I guess not."

"You don't have to be the hostess here, you know."

"I feel like I do." Ruby glanced over to see that Opal had joined up with several of the children of the military. Belle and the girls were surrounded by men both in uniform and in chaps and shirts. Since things seemed peaceful enough there, Ruby looked around. The military women, who'd come from Bismark and Dickinson, had gathered in a circle, and other women from the area were off by themselves.

"We don't have much mingling going on here." She shook her head. "I thought something like this would break down the barriers, you know?"

"The music and the dancing will help do that. The only other social events this town has known were put on by the army, and there weren't enough people here then to make up a party."

"I keep forgetting this town is so young."

"If you want to call it a town. It's more like a settlement, I'd say. There's some room on those benches over there." He nodded toward the shed-roofed barracks of the cantonment. With bleached vertical siding, the long low building looked like a series of shacks strung together to hold each other up.

"Not too impressive, I know. We never even got them painted."

"And you've been stationed here for better than three years?"

"Our job was to keep the railroad safe, not to pretty up our housing. Besides, the army doesn't spend much money on housing for the posts out on the frontier. This was never meant to be a fort."

Ruby took a bite of her meat and closed her eyes to better savor the flavor. "This is marvelous."

"I'm sure Rand will appreciate hearing that from you."

"I doubt it." Rand Harrison might know how to cook a cow, but as a gentleman he failed to make the grade. She glanced up to catch a question in the captain's eyes, but he returned to eating without asking.

She watched Rand stroll over to the group that was laughing at something Belle had said. Insufferable would be a good word to describe him, far as she was concerned.

"May I sit with you?" Holding her full plate, Milly stopped in front of Ruby.

"Of course." Ruby tucked her skirt closer beside her.

"I see Cimarron is still here," McHenry commented.

"Yes, of course. Dove House is her home."

"I wondered since I hadn't seen her."

"She's the one responsible for all the hemmed tablecloths and napkins. Also for new clothes for all of us." She caught herself before referring to them as "girls." But the Cimarron of today looked far different than the one she'd first met. With her flaming red hair severely rolled around a long rat instead of piled high with curls, no face paint, and a high-necked demure waist, Cimarron looked the picture of elegance rather than flamboyance. Her wide-brimmed straw hat shadowed her flashing green eyes.

With her new name and modest demeanor, Daisy could have fit right in with the military wives or daughters, so only Belle spun a parasol that matched her emerald green silk dress complete with bustle, overskirt, and low-cut bodice.

Ruby savored every bit of the beef, having never eaten anything quite like it.

"Yep, that Rand sure knows how to spit beef." Captain McHenry wiped sauce off his chin.

"Spit beef?" All Ruby could think of was the filthy spittoons that all of them hated scrubbing.

"You roast an entire half over the coals. The spit is what

holds it up and what they turn it with. Didn't you ever cook over an open fire or in a fireplace?"

"No." She didn't bother to tell him that she never really had much experience cooking. First her mother did it, then her grandmother, and the Brandons had a full-time cook. She'd done more cooking since arriving at Dove House than in all the previous years of her life combined.

"I see."

"I think I better go around and invite everyone to join the dancing later."

"Just get the music going, and that'll be call enough. I'll have a couple of my men do the cleanup. Most likely the leftovers will become a late supper."

"Thank you for all your help."

"You are most welcome. As soon as the sun sinks behind the hills, the flag will come down and our bugler will blow taps. That should be a good way to end a patriotic celebration like this one."

"In the park at home there would have been bands, political speeches, fireworks, and ice cream with strawberries. New York does know how to celebrate."

"Some different from here, all right."

"Where is home to you?" She turned slightly to watch his face.

"I was born in Ohio, but we moved enough times that home is wherever I hang my hat. The army is my home, I guess, and wherever they send me, I'll be content there."

"And what about a family?"

"I figure somewhere, sometime, God has a woman for me." His level gaze made her glance at the plate in her lap.

"Forgive me for getting so personal."

"Ruby!" Opal skidded to a stop in front of them. "Mr. Harrison said I could ride one of his horses. Is that all right with you?"

"Who'll be with you?"

"Mr. Harrison. We'll just be right around the corrals and such. I won't go out of sight."

"Rand wouldn't put her up on a horse she can't manage." McHenry leaned back against the wall.

Rand, as you call him, might do anything to aggravate me. In fact,

264

everything he does irritates as bad as the pesky black flies. "You be careful."

The sigh and rolling eyes said it all. "I will."

Ruby watched Opal run back across the parade field and follow Rand Harrison out to the long rope between fence posts where horses were tied.

The laughter of small children rang like music on the skittish breeze. Several of the young soldiers were playing mumblety-peg with a pocket knife, their expert tosses sticking the knife blade in the grassy bank. Several of the young boys were down wading in the shallows for crawdads. If she didn't know better, Ruby might have believed this was a real community.

A young drummer beat the cadence as six soldiers marched onto the parade grounds, squaring off the corners as they marched half the perimeter and then straight into the circle around the flag pole, where the Stars and Stripes fluttered in the evening breeze. At a barked command one man unwrapped the lanyard and lowered the flag in cadence to the bugler blowing the haunting notes of Taps. Another soldier caught the flag, keeping it from touching the ground, and once it was unsnapped, two men folded the flag in half the long way and in half again, then starting at one corner, folding the triangles over, back and forth until the final end was tucked into the packet. Following more orders, they traversed the same pattern out of the parade grounds and took the flag inside the office.

"Dismissed," barked the officer of the day, and the crowd relaxed again, a pleasant buzz echoing around the grounds as children darted and laughed and adults visited while they gathered up their belongings.

When the last notes of the bugle had drifted off, Ruby cleared her throat and blinked, hoping the tears that threatened would stay put. "My, that was beautiful."

"It always chokes me up too, and I see it every day." The captain settled his hat back in place and offered her his arm. "We'll start the folks back up that way, and as soon as they hear Belle on the piano, they'll know the dancing is about to begin."

"Belle already left?" How strange it felt to have one's hand imprisoned between a man's elbow and chest. She glanced up from under the brim of her hat and saw him studying her, a slight smile on his smoothly shaven face. Hopefully her hat hid the beat warming her neck. Had her heart skipped a beat also?

The other officers gathered their families and followed suit. They passed Williams' Saloon, which seemed to be doing a brisk business, if the laughter and shouting were any indication.

Ruby hoped that anyone too drunk to behave properly would not bother to come to the dancing but stay inside that vile place and drink to their heart's content.

"A fiddle." Ruby glanced up at her escort. "Did you know about that?"

He nodded. "It's one of my men. Rand plays a guitar, so I imposed on him to join the musicians."

Opal caught up with them. "Sure is pretty."

"You didn't ride long," Ruby smiled back.

"I didn't want to miss out on anything. Hasn't this been about the best day ever?"

"You said it just right."

"Come on, folks . . . find your partners and Virginia reel." Charlie stood on the porch step, his voice carrying above the music, his bowler hat pushed back on his head.

"Shall we?" The captain bowed slightly and motioned toward the couples lining up, men on one side, women in a line about eight feet in front of them. Feet tapping, they waited for the signal for the first couple to sashay out and do-si-do. The captain's smile when she met him again to promenade made her heart skip a beat.

With so few women present, the men lined up to dance with them. Ruby had never danced like this in her entire life. She waltzed and reeled, two-stepped and polkaed. She learned some names and forgot others. Even Mrs. McGeeney danced to near collapse. When Belle struck a couple of resounding chords, the music stopped, and everyone collapsed on benches, railings, porch steps, and chairs brought out from the dining room. More food and a huge bowl of punch waited on a table.

"Charlie, is that your doing?" Ruby nodded toward the table.

He just grinned at her and shrugged as if he didn't know what she might be referring to. "Help yourself folks," he invited, as if he were the host and all those in attendance his personal friends. *No wonder people frequented Dove House,* Ruby thought. *I never realized how charming he can be. He and my father must have been quite a pair.*

Little children were carted off to bed before the music began again, and whether her feet thought it a good idea or not, Ruby danced with the rest of them. The moon rose, changing from orange to silver, shedding enough light for the dancing to continue.

"Did you order this all up?" Captain McHenry asked when he got a turn to dance with her again.

"Of course, I waved my magic wand, and presto, we had light."

He swung her around, and her feet hardly touched the ground.

"No, I said it, and I meant it!"

Ruby stopped in midskip. Cimarron's voice. McHenry turned at the same time, searching for the culprit.

Ezekiel Damish, one of the faithful customers at Williams' Saloon, had Cimarron by the arm. She jerked back, her jaw clamped, enough fire flashing from her eyes to light up the area without the moon.

At the captain's nod, two of his men grabbed the offender by the arms and hauled him off behind Dove House. Someone else stepped into his place, and the music picked up again as if nothing had happened.

As the final chord drifted away, swaying skirts settled back primly about weary ankles, and people thanked the musicians for playing, Rand for the meat, and Charlie and Ruby for all they'd done. Within a few minutes the street was empty but for the military detail cleaning things up and putting the chairs back where they belonged.

"That was some to-do." Belle let them carry her stool back inside. "Best thing that happened to this town since it came into being."

Ruby followed her inside. Late as it was, they would still have to have breakfast ready for their guests by seven. And all those dishes to wash. They trailed back to the kitchen to find everything cleaned up and put away.

Ruby stared at Charlie.

He shrugged. "They must have taken turns. I thought every

soldier from the cantonment danced tonight."

Milly smoothed her hair back from a brow still damp from all the dancing. "I never . . ."

Cimarron draped an arm over her shoulders. "Me neither." At Ruby's questioning look, Cimarron shrugged one shoulder and tipped her head slightly to the side. "It was bound to happen. Several gave me a hard time, but one of 'em just got too insistent. I was about to deck him myself, but the men in blue saved his hide and his pride." She raised an eyebrow and rolled her bottom lip to be smoothed by her upper teeth. "I do know how to protect myself. Never fear."

While her words sounded brave, Ruby felt sure she saw a hint of fear in Cimarron's eyes, or was it rage?

"Hey, Milly," Cimarron called, "did you dance with that young private? The cute one?"

Milly turned fourteen shades of red, and the others laughed and teased her as they made their way up the steep stairs.

Opal was sound asleep, toppled over on the top of her pallet wearing all but her shoes, when Ruby entered their room.

Ruby drew the sheet over her sister and undressed in the moonlight silvering a square on the floor. She pulled her sheet up and listened to the others settle down. All in all the day went better than she had hoped, not that she'd really had any idea what to expect. And as Daisy had commented, the captain surely had been attentive. There was something to be said for an attentive man who treated one like a lady.

CHAPTER TWENTY-EIGHT

"We got the last section cut." Joe leaned against the door-frame.

"Good. That first cut is ready to turn." Rand pulled his leather gloves back on. Haying at the Double H could have used a couple more hands, but other than the riffraff that hung around town, he knew of no one to ask. So they'd been trading off on using scythes to cut the field and wooden rakes to turn the drying grass. Up to now Rand had pastured the horses near the cabin during the winter, but putting up hay would keep them in better shape in case of deep snow. The cattle ranged all winter, using the draws and small meadows as protection when the wind and storms grew too fierce. He planned to build a shed and corral for the bull, so he'd need hay too.

If he wasn't careful, he might turn into a farmer like his family back in Missouri. Ranching appealed to him far more, but cattle needed to be fed.

He followed Joe on out to the corral where Beans was working on a new bed for the wagon, one with a tall frame in front for hauling hay. "Lookin' good there, old man."

"Now don't you go old mannin' me." Beans drove another nail home before looking up. "Goin' to get this done just in time, you'll see. If'n the rain holds off, that is."

Rand glanced up to see only cerulean blue above them. "Sun addling your brains? There's no rain in sight."

"You just get that hay dry fast as you can. My right knee ain't never wrong. Says it's gonna rain, so you better dig out your slicker."

Rand settled his hat lower to shade his eyes and shook his head. "Contrary old man."

"But, Boss, he's always right." Joe kept his voice low so that Beans couldn't hear, not that he'd hear anything above the pounding of the hammer.

"I know, but he'll be on us from now till the first snow if we give him a chance."

The two men laughed as they headed back to the field where Chaps was swigging from his canteen. "Better put your shirt back on, we're turnin' that first cut." Joe took a sneak peek at the sky, arching his back like he wasn't checking for rain clouds.

Rand chuckled to himself. Those two hated to admit an old guy like Beans might know more than they did. "Best we get at it."

—————

The bats were out on their nightly insect foray by the time the men turned the last fork. The hay lay in rows, snaking across the field like long strings of giant proportions. "Two days and we can haul it in. I marked out the new corral and shed for the bull. We'll stack it right to the north, give him some extra protection."

"And close so we don't have to pitch it so far." Chaps was always one for saving on labor, but he'd ride a horse dawn to dark with nary a complaint.

"Thought I was gonna have to come lookin' fer ya," Beans muttered when they slumped through the door after washing up. He took the lid off the pot on the back of the stove, and the aroma of stewed grouse perked up all three of the men.

"Fresh bread too?" Joe took a chair and propped his elbows on the table. "I used muscles I didn't even know I had, and now every one of them is yellin' at me."

"You young pups don't hardly know a real day's work. You oughta try settin' train rails. Now, poundin' spikes, that'll wear you out some."

"How's the wagon bed coming?" Rand dished up a plateful from the kettle Beans set in the middle of the slab table. Like most of the other furniture in the cabin, Rand had fashioned it from cottonwood logs he felled during the winter and whipsawed into planks. He'd laid them for flooring and the interior wall that separated the living quarters from his bedroom. The hands bunked in the other cabin he'd built. Shelves of cottonwood held books, baskets he'd learned to make from an old Indian woman, and extra clothing. He'd built the cupboards on the wall near the stove this last winter. A wolf pelt in winter prime lay thrown across the chair he'd fashioned and put in front of the fireplace, his only heat source and place for cooking until he had brought home the cast-iron stove with an oven.

By local standards, he had a fine home and was known as a man who did things well.

Conversation not only lagged but was nonexistent while the men ate, shoveling the food in quickly so they could sleep long enough to repair their bodies for the next day. After the others left, Rand banked the stove and, taking the kerosene lamp with him, headed for bed, hoping to read for a bit. If he could keep his eyes open.

— ❦ —

The rain held off until they had the first section stacked where Rand had indicated and the final section windrowed.

"Now we're gonna have to turn that section again." The four of them sat on the cabin porch and listened to the rain drumming on the shake roof. Water running off the eaves sang its own tune as it bounced on the gravel below.

"Quit yer grousin', Chaps, and go find us a deer. I got a hankerin' for liver tonight." Beans took up his carving knife and the piece of dry wood he was turning into a spoon or fork. One couldn't tell since he was still working on the handle.

"I'll do just that." Chaps rose and stretched, then reached inside the door for the rifle and deerskin bag that held the bullets, both hung on pegs over the doorframe. As he headed for the horses, Rand nudged Joe.

"Come on, we can sink some of those corral posts, holes are easier to dig with the ground soaked."

"And here I thought I might go on into town." Joe yawned and, arms over his head, pushed against the slanted porch beams.

"Guess you thought wrong." Beans held his carving up to the gray light. As usual, an intricate design was taking shape under the sharp point of his knife.

"We'll all be goin' into town once the hay is up."

— ❦ —

Five days later Beans drove the wagon to haul back supplies, and the other three rode alongside.

Rand nudged Buck into an easy jog. "You guys playing cards tonight?"

"Well, we sure as fire ain't goin' home before dark." Chaps patted his pocket where he'd stuck his monthly pay. "I'm feelin' real lucky. Belle better be lookin' out."

"Anyone hear of a dog for sale? I'm thinkin' on getting one."

"Cow dog would be good," Beans said.

"Yeah, take Joe's place." Chaps slapped his thigh and hooted as if he'd just made the funniest joke of all time.

"I wasn't the one tied to a tree." Joe eased over and shoved Chaps' shoulder, nearly knocking him off his horse.

The two galloped off, their laughter floating back on the breeze.

"Them two ever grow up, be an outright miracle."

Rand chuckled and nodded. "But you got to admit they're entertaining."

Rand was still smiling when he flipped the reins over the hitching rail on the east side of Dove House.

"Hey, Mr. Harrison."

"Hey, yourself, Miss Torvald."

Opal scrunched up her face. "That's my sister, not me."

"All right, then, Opal. But you're growin' up mighty fast. Why I heard tell that you can ride right well now, and so I thought maybe you'd like to try out Buck."

Opal leaped down the steps. "You really mean it?"

"Cross my heart."

"I'll be right back." The girl dashed out toward the garden.

Rand shook his head. "She never walks when a run will do."

"That's our Opal, all right." Daisy leaned on the porch railing. "How ya doin', Mr. Harrison?"

Opal leaped over the rows of beans, waving two carrots. "Does Buck like carrots?"

"Buck likes anything that smells like food. He's even been known to eat leftovers." Rand glanced back at Daisy. "I'm doin' good, Miss Daisy. Things sure look different around here." He tipped his hat back. "By the way, I'm sure you have a last name."

"Daisy Whitaker."

"Fine, Miss Whitaker."

Daisy ducked her head, and he was sure he saw a tear amble down her cheek. *Now what did I do?*

Daisy sniffed and looked back at him, the tears making her eyes glitter like sapphires in the sun. "Thank you, Mr. Harrison. No one ever called me that before."

Opal skidded to a walk before getting close to Buck.

"You are most welcome. Good girl, Opal. You didn't spook him at all." *You'd think she'd been around horses all her life, when I know for a fact that she hasn't, and if her sister has her way, most likely won't.*

Opal broke off the carrot tops and palmed the orange treat for Buck, who whiskered her palm as he lipped the carrot. She giggled and scratched her palm before offering him the other.

"He'll take the tops too. He's not choosy." The green feathery tops disappeared as fast as the bottoms, and Buck sniffed Opal's hair, down her arm, and her hands again.

"He wants more."

"Buck always wants more. Here, I'll give you a boost up." He cupped his hands and nodded for her to put her foot in them.

With a question on her face, she paused. "My foot's awful dirty."

"So are my hands. Come on."

Opal reached up for the latigos that hung from the leather conches on the saddle, put her left foot in Rand's cupped hands, and giggled as she slapped into the saddle. "You almost threw me right on over."

"Shortening my stirrups would take too long. You're all right without them?"

Opal shrugged. "Guess so."

"You'll have to squeeze your legs harder to be felt through the leathers."

"I will. Can I go now?"

"Yep. Rein him around and ride on down to the ford and back."

Rand and Daisy watched as Opal did exactly as he told her.

"What's Opal doing on—" Ruby came through the door in a rush, stopping when she saw Rand. "Oh. It's *your* horse."

"Yup. Buck's been mine for nigh on to four years." *Why was teasing her so much fun?* He smiled as he watched her dither between good manners and telling him off. He hadn't found her good side yet, that was for certain. And the way other folks talked about her, she was all good. Not prickly at all.

"Oh." Ruby nibbled her bottom lip. "I don't suppose you'd like a drink of ginger fizz."

"Why that sounds right good. Thank you, ma'am." He touched the brim of his hat.

"I'll get it." Daisy brushed past Ruby, the screen door slamming behind her.

Rand checked to see how Opal was doing before returning his attention to Ruby.

She was still fidgeting. "I haven't thanked you yet for playing your guitar at the Fourth of July celebration."

"Everyone had a fine time—that they did. I heard tell the whole thing was your idea."

"Yes, well, Captain McHenry got things in motion."

"Here, I'll set the tray on this bench, and we can sit in the shade." Daisy kept the door from slamming this time with her hip, earning an approving smile from Ruby.

Now why can she smile so easily at everyone but me? Rand pondered the thought as he took the step indicated. "You've done a lot of work around here."

"In spite of your bad advice?" An eyebrow arched, the tone tinged with frost.

"My bad advice?" Rand shook his head. "I never gave you . . ." *Oh yes, when I told her off for changing Dove House. I'm afraid I did not make a good impression. Fact, if I remember right, I read her the riot act. My mama would have had conniptions six times from Sunday.*

He caught Ruby watching him over the top of her glass. He was about to make a comment he would probably regret when

Opal came thundering to a stop in front of them.

"Hey, Mr. Harrison, you want I should tie Buck to the hitching post?"

"Unless you want to ride more."

"I think that is quite enough. Mr. Harrison no doubt has business elsewhere." Ruby's right eyebrow arched again.

I'd say I've been dismissed. Whatever happened to forgive and forget? He thought of staying just to get her dander up again but instead rose and handed the glass back to Daisy. "Thank you, Miss Whitaker, that was most delicious. I'll be back in time for supper."

— ❧ —

By the time he headed home that night, several dollars lighter, he'd not seen Ruby again. And he was sure he'd caught Belle skimming the take. *Should I tell Miss Torvald or not?* The question nagged him all the way back to the ranch.

CHAPTER TWENTY-NINE

July sweltered into August. The garden grew, the weeds were hoed out, fish were caught, rabbits were chased out of the garden, trapped, and eaten, and August eased into September.

"Wait until you see who is coming down the street." Opal stormed through the back door like she'd been riding the wind.

"Who?" Ruby turned from checking the meat pies baking for dinner. She wiped the perspiration from her face with her apron.

"Someone from France. He and his entourage"—Opal decorated the word with fluttering hands and rolling eyes—"asked the conductor where they should stay and he said Dove House. There are four of them, and they weren't too happy that no one was there to take their trunks, so I told them to leave them there and someone would bring a wagon." She paused long enough to suck in a deep breath. The bell over the front door announced visitors. "And here they are."

"Anyone here speak French?" Charlie set a basket of fresh carrots down on the table.

"I do." Ruby whipped off her apron, wiped her face again, and smoothed back her drooping hair. She headed out the swinging door.

"*Bienvenue á Dove House. Merci beaucoup pour venir. Pardonnez-moi, s'il vous plaît. Je parle seulement un peu français.*"

— ❧ —

"That woman never ceases to amaze me." Cimarron used the back of her hand to wipe her forehead.

"I was just making a joke." Charlie stared after Ruby. "I had me no idea . . ."

"She speaks Norwegian too," Opal added from her place on the floor dragging a bit of deer hide on a string for Cat to play with. "But she'd tell you her French isn't very good. In fact, if I know my sister, right now she is apologizing for her poorly spoken French. She reads and understands pretty good . . . er . . . well, though." She flashed a look at Daisy, who grinned at her. They'd both been corrected more than once on the uses of well and good.

When Ruby returned to the kitchen, she'd shown their French guests to their rooms and promised to have water sent up for washing.

"How did you know all the right words?" Daisy asked.

"I didn't. They had a man along who also spoke English, although his French accent on English was about as bad as my American one on French. They want to go hunting, so I said you would be up with water and help them make arrangements."

Charlie nodded. "They didn't want the hip bath?"

Ruby shook her head.

"Good thing—carrying up enough water for four would be awful in this heat."

"Ah, Charlie, you gettin' soft or something?" Cimarron looked up from the tablecloth she was mending. Some oaf had set his burning cigar down on the cloth instead of in the ash trays they provided. Daisy had doused the smoking cigar with a glass of water and accidentally splashed some on the man. He'd called her names until Charlie strolled up.

"You know, sometimes I wonder if we shouldn't say no smoking or spitting in the dining room. We already trained 'em that they can't drink here." Cimarron held the patch up to the light. "Or else we should quit putting tablecloths on—white ones, anyway. I once saw an eating place that used red-and-white-checked oilcloth. That looked real nice too. Kind of homey."

"That's a thought." *Right now I can't afford to buy anything but food—and hardly that.* Ruby hated to admit she was squeezing every nickel and dime to screaming. While business had been pretty steady, since the army went on extended patrol in August, they'd served far fewer meals.

Everyone said that things would pick up in the fall with more easterners coming west for hunting. If their French guests were any indication, Ruby figured that now there was room for hope. Adequate income was especially needed now since another quarterly payment was due at the bank. No matter how hard she searched, she still hadn't found the buksbom or the money box. At night she dreamed about finding them, but she always woke up before seeing where they were hidden.

"Someone want to come help me twist these sheets?" Daisy poked her head in the door. They'd taken to doing the wash over a fire in the backyard rather than in the kitchen, where there was never room for the boiler on the stove. Another stove was on Ruby's dream list.

"I will." Opal tied the string over the back of a chair, left Cat to bat at her toy, and headed out the door.

After serving dinner, Cimarron came back through the swinging door. "That creepy fellow is out there again. He watches me like Cat watches at a mousehole."

"When his meal is ready, someone else can serve him." Ruby turned to see how Cimarron really was. "In fact, I will."

"Or we could ask Charlie to tell him not to come back," Daisy suggested.

"No, he's not really done nothin'. I got to get over this or else remain here in the kitchen. But since the dance everyone knows I'm still here, so I'd rather take my turn serving. I kinda missed the—" she cocked her head with a slight shrug—"you know, the back and forth talk."

"Just be careful who you smile at," Daisy cautioned. "Your smile could make a man rise up and follow like that Pied Piper fellow Opal read us about."

Cimarron whipped around, hands on hips. "I did not flirt with him."

"I know that." Daisy rolled her eyes, shaking her head all the while. "It's just . . . just . . ."

"Say what you're thinkin'."

"I'm tryin' to. Cimarron, you just don't know how beautiful

you are. Why, I see men panting when you give 'em one of your smiles—like a gift they are."

A slow smile brightened Cimarron's face. "Why, Daisy, you are a poet. Such a beautiful thing to say."

"Well, it's true." Daisy turned back to her bread kneading.

"Thank you."

"Welcome."

Ruby watched the exchange, pleasure and concern pushing and shoving for the same space. She too had noticed the way Ezekiel Damish watched Cimarron. He'd apologized after strong-arming her at the dance, saying he was drunk, but she had a feeling the captain had applied pressure in that arena. Apologizing didn't seem to go along with the mean look of the man. Of course, if he cleaned up, he might look more friendly. But some people seemed born mean or else life taught them to be that way.

She'd already realized that bathing didn't seem important or even necessary to some of the hunters and drifters who passed through Little Misery, as the locals often referred to the town. Little Missouri, Little Muddy, Little Misery, all interchangeable names—the most accurate being little.

A knock moved her gaze to the back door. Private Adam Stone stood at attention.

Ruby opened the screen door. "Won't you come in?"

"A message from the captain, Miss Torvald." He handed her a folded piece of paper.

"Thank you. When did you all get back?"

"About an hour ago."

"I see. Would you like some refreshment?"

"No, thank you, not right now. I need to get back with an answer." He indicated the paper. "But I could do with some refreshment later, after supper at the mess."

"Perhaps Milly would like to go for a walk then." Ruby loved to watch the young man's neck get red and his Adam's apple bob up and down. "You might ask her on your way out."

"Thank you." He kept his eyes straight forward as if she were his commanding officer. She was tempted to say, "At ease, soldier," but refrained from embarrassing him even more. She quickly read the note and nodded. "Tell the captain that will be fine."

When he exited, closing the door gently so it didn't slam, Cimarron chuckled. "It's hard to resist the urge to tease him, isn't it?"

"You're saying I didn't? Resist the urge, that is?" Ruby tried to look innocent, but the others laughed anyway. "He is so young."

"It's that baby face. And he blushes so charmingly." Cimarron put away the last of the dinner dishes, then paused as they heard the men coming down the stairs and then going out the front door.

Ruby wished she had time for a cooling bath, but a quick wash after supper would have to do. At least she had a clean dress to put on.

Later that evening she and Captain McHenry strolled down toward the now meandering river. They'd discussed the uneventful patrol, the few things happening in town, and the French visitors, but Ruby could tell something was bothering him. They stopped under a cottonwood where the river chatted with the rustling leaves—not big secrets but friendly banter. The breeze lifted the tendrils of hair from her face and caressed her skin.

"Ah, this feels so wonderful. Thank you for the invitation."

"I . . . I have something to ask you."

"Yes?"

He turned from studying the river. "Is there any chance that someday you could think of me as more than a friend?" He picked at the corrugated bark of the tree as if afraid to look at her.

"What are you asking me?"

"I have my orders. I am being transferred to Fort Bowie in Arizona Territory."

"When?"

"Immediately. Lieutenant Wilson will be in charge here."

Oh, I shall miss you. "I . . . I don't know. I've never had a friend. I mean a man friend like you before."

"If I write, will you answer?"

"Of course." *That's Indian territory down there.* The thought sent shivers up her back. She'd heard the Apache were fierce warriors.

"Have you ever thought of living elsewhere?"

Yes, back home in New York, but I promised my father. "I have commitments here."

"I know. But that could change."

"Yes." She glanced up, catching the full intensity of his gaze. *What are you asking me?*

"And you will write?"

"Yes. And you must promise to keep safe."

"I'll do my best." He offered her his arm. "I cannot tell you how much I shall miss you."

"And I you." When he closed his other hand over hers, she remembered the pleasure of dancing with him. What was that she saw in his eyes? Hard to tell in the dusk but close to him felt like a good place to be.

"You mean that?"

"Of course."

"Good, then there is hope."

She cleared her throat. "Won't you stop for a glass of tea?"

"No, I need to get my papers in order and talk with my men. Thank you."

"God bless."

He gently squeezed her hand, touched the brim of his hat, and marched off down the street toward the cantonment.

"Good-bye," she whispered as his broad back shimmered in the twilight. She dashed away the offending moisture and made her way around the building on the porch. *Why couldn't I have said yes, that there could be more? Why does my life seem all of a muddle?* And now one of her few pleasures was being taken away.

Few pleasures? Think again, my girl. The inner voice sounded amazingly like Bestemor's. Bestemor, who always saw the bright side of life, who always spoke of the things she was thankful for, who not only said and believed but lived her gratitude. Every day she looked for something new to thank God for. And insisted Ruby do the same.

But how can I be thankful when one more thing is being taken away?

Ruby sank into the rocker that gave her a view of the rocks and buttes north of town. Dusk had grayed the colors that flamed in the setting sun. But though dark now, the color was there, waiting for the light again.

I can be thankful for the light that returns. I can be thankful he has become my friend. I can be thankful I can write and read and that letters can come from far places. She let her head rest against the back of the rocker. *Lord, forgive me for my lack of gratitude.* Mosquitoes whined about her ears. After slapping one on her arm, she rose and went inside.

"What did he want?" Cimarron sat in the lamplight, her mending on her lap.

"He's been transferred to Fort Bowie where the Indians are uprising again."

"I'm sorry."

"Me too. And so will Opal be, because this means no more riding." Ruby sat down at the table. "Every night she prays for a horse of her own, but there is no way I can buy her a horse."

"No, but then you are not God. She's not asking you for a horse."

"True."

"When I was her age, I rode all over the country."

"Did you have a horse of your own?"

"Not really. I took care of all the horses. Pa had a team, and we had two riding horses. The four of us rode to school on them until the winters got bad, then Pa took us in the sleigh."

"How did you end up out here?"

"My man run off and left me when he thought I was dying."

"How could he?"

"Same as he could smack me around without a lick of remorse. He was a real charmer, who turned meaner 'n a cornered badger when he'd had too much to drink. Belle found me, nursed me back to health, and I been with her ever since."

"I see."

"No, you don't. You wonder how I could do what I did. You got to understand that, when you're hungry enough, you'll do anything to eat. And after a while you grow a real thick scab over your heart and mind and dream of something else while . . ." Cimarron closed her eyes and swallowed. "Like some wonderful man is going to come in on a white horse and carry you away. Only in my case it wasn't a handsome man on a white horse but a young innocent woman with blond hair and a little sister who looks up to me and makes me feel ten feet tall." Her voice dropped to a whisper. "Like I'm worth something after all."

"Thank you, Cimarron, oh thank you." *It has all been worth it. There really is a reason for all this.* Ruby thought awhile before asking, "Would you go back?"

"Not on your life. I know now that I've got some other choices." Cimarron held up her needle. "I can sew about anything, and while the pay isn't as good, at least it would be money made through honest work. Belle thinks we'd go back, but she ain't never asked us, just figured she knows best. Like she always has. But she ain't earned her living on her back in a long time."

Ruby flinched at the plain language, but she'd asked. "Do you want to get married?"

"Yes, I do. But finding a good man isn't the easiest, even with all the men around here. Think about it. There's your captain, and he's leaving."

"He's not *my* captain."

"He would be if you gave him any encouragement. And then there's Rand Harrison."

"You call him a good man?"

"Most certainly. And some of the guys over in the barracks are all right, but they'd just as soon pay for their pleasure as marry us soiled doves. That's why Daisy and me, most likely we got to get out of here and start over someplace else—where no one knows our past."

"You are welcome to stay here."

"I know. We'll just have to see what happens."

Opal and Milly came through the door from the dining room. "I'm hungry. Can I—" Opal stopped, made a face, and sighed as if she was the most put upon girl in the West. "I know—*may* we have a couple of cookies? Milly is reading better and better. You want to hear her?"

"Of course. Why don't you put cookies on the plate for all of us? Milly, sit by the lamp so you can see better."

Opal passed around the cookie plate. "Do any of you want a glass of milk?"

The others shook their heads, so Opal poured one for herself and sat down at the table. "Go ahead, Milly, read some of that chapter in Matthew."

Milly found her place. "'Come unto me, all ye that labour and are heavy laden, and I will give you rest. Take my yoke upon you, and learn of me.'"

Opal dunked her cookie in her milk. "What's a yoke?"

"A yoke is carved out of real solid wood and laid across the necks of oxen so they pull together. You hook the wagon tongue to the yoke between them." Cimarron drew a picture of a yoke in the air with her hands.

"So why would God say, 'take my yoke'?"

"Perhaps He is saying that when we yoke with Him, He will pull harder so we don't have to work so hard." Cimarron looked toward Ruby. "You think?"

"Could be. I could use some of His rest right now. Thank you all. I'm going to bed. Are you coming, Opal?"

"Soon as I finish this." Opal took another cookie.

Each step seemed three feet higher than the one below, or was it just the heavy yoke she carried all by herself? As she folded back the sheets, she thought of the verse again. "'Come unto me . . .'" *Lord, I'm just too tired to even look for my Bible. Tomorrow, tomorrow, I'll look.*

— ⸘ —

After the send-off for the captain at the train, where everyone gathered to tell him good-bye, Ruby felt on the verge of tears for the rest of the day. To overcome the voices arguing in her head, she threw herself into a frenzy of cleaning and polishing in the dining room. Cleaning the windows, she thought of their conversation down by the river, replaying it word by word. While washing, then waxing the counter, she wondered what he'd really meant.

Was it friendship you wanted or more? And what does more mean? Were you asking me if I'd be amenable to courting?

She emptied the cigars out of the ornate box that sat on the counter and wiped it down, inside and out. *What does love really feel like?* Smearing beeswax on her cloth she rubbed it into the box, making sure that every tiny corner and nick got a wax feeding.

How is love different than the enjoyment I felt in just being with you? Taking a clean cloth, she buffed the beautiful box until it shone. She put the cigars back, set the box on the now burnished counter, and stood back. It needed flowers.

Captain McHenry had brought her wild daisies once. The tears brimmed again. Could all this be the beginning of love? At least there would be letters.

CHAPTER THIRTY

"No! No! Get away from there!"

"Ruby, stop. It's all right. You are dreaming."

Ruby forced her eyes open, trying to still her pounding heart. "What?" She reached through the fog to panic. "What's wrong?"

"Nothing. You were dreaming, yelling at something." Daisy stroked damp tendrils of hair from Ruby's face. "You go on back to sleep. Everything is all right." She rose and glanced over at the other pallet where Opal slept on, sprawled across the pallet like she'd collapsed there and not moved again.

"Thank you." Ruby rubbed her eyes. The dream had been so real, no wonder she'd been shouting. A hawk dove down through the lattice Charlie had built across the chicken pen and stolen one of the half-grown chicks. She'd tried to grab it but the hawk beat her with his powerful wings, never dropping the chick. The bird's talons had dripped red blood.

Ruby shuddered and, after turning her pillow to the cooler side, pulled her sheet back up over her shoulders. She took in a deep breath, held it, and let it out again slowly. On the second repeat, she could feel her body soften, her breathing slow, and warmth start in her feet and work its way up—not the warmth of too much heat but of peace and comfort.

She still remembered the dream when she woke at the rooster's crow.

"You all right?" Daisy asked when Ruby entered the kitchen some time later.

"Just such a crazy dream." Ruby described the hawk and the chicken. "How that bird flew right through the lattice, I'll never know."

"Dreams don't have to make sense, you know. There's an old song, 'We Are Climbing Jacob's Ladder,' that's based on Jacob's dream in the Bible. He saw angels going up and down on a ladder." Daisy sang a couple of lines. "I heard some Negroes singing that once. My, could they sing."

"I don't think I ever remembered a dream in such detail."

"I had to call you a couple of times to wake you up," Daisy said. "Some dreams seem to go on forever."

"That one did." Ruby shivered as she tied her apron in place. "You want to make the biscuits this morning or shall I?"

— ❧ —

The Frenchmen were getting ready to leave for hunting right after an early breakfast. It took three packhorses to carry all their baggage, much to the dismay of their guide, Frank Vine.

"Never saw anyone with so much gear," he muttered as he adjusted one heavily laden pack saddle. They were finally mounted, and the three Frenchmen waved a jaunty good-bye.

"You'd think they were going to be gone a month or more." Daisy stood beside Ruby on the porch watching them ride to the river ford where they would head south.

"Well, give Mr. Vine enough to drink, and he'll get over his ill humor. You about ready for a cup of coffee?" Together they returned to the dining room and began to clear off the tables on their way back to the kitchen.

By the time Ruby had told her dream to each of the others, it no longer held such terror, but that didn't keep her from wandering out to the chicken pen and checking to make sure all the lattice was in place.

"Dreams can be like that," Charlie said with a smile.

"You caught me in the act." Ruby pulled a carrot and, after wiping off all the dirt, took a bite. "You sure have had a good garden out here."

"I know. We got just enough rain this year. I'll dig all the chicken manure in this fall, and by spring this ground will be so rich we won't even have to plant the seeds."

"Oh sure. They'll just volunteer. About like Opal does at the dishpan."

Charlie went down the row, pulling the smaller beets and laying them in a basket. "We can cook the tops in one pot and boil the beets in another. The rest will be ready for pickling and canning anytime."

Ruby took the basket. "Thanks for working so hard out here. I've heard people comment on the variety of food we offer, and that's all thanks to you."

"Working in the garden is just about as good as going to church, not that I've done that in many a year. When you think that's where God met man during the cool of the evening, walking in the garden, I guess He loves gardens too. I 'spect that garden was some bigger than ours, with trees and rivers and all manner of beautiful growing and blooming things."

"Why, Charlie, how beautifully said. You keep coming up with things to surprise me."

Guilt stabbed Ruby like little pins. Perhaps in the winter she would have more time for reading her Bible again. As Milly had read, "'Come unto me all ye that labour and are heavy laden...'" That certainly did apply to her. So why was it so hard to do that?

She looked up from studying the lay of the beets in her basket. "Charlie, do you mind if I ask you another question? About my father, I mean."

He leaned on the handle of his hoe. "Ask away."

"I ... I remember my father as a good Christian man. He took Mor and me to church on Sundays, and I remember him reading the Bible. He read so beautifully, his voice so deep— sometimes I thought it was God himself talking." She worried her bottom lip. "So how could he have a ... a saloon with ... with the girls?" Her voice dropped on the final words.

"I'm not sure I can give an answer that will help you."

"Please try."

He nodded. "Per didn't start out with ... with ..."

"Soiled doves?"

Another nod while he leaned down and smashed a potato

"He won big at the tables for a whole week in a row and

thought he was rich. All he could talk about was going someplace small and building a real nice hotel. By then he had hooked up with Belle, and he asked her to come along. She said she would, under one condition—that the girls came too. She told him they might end up in the cribs if she didn't take care of them. Well, Per couldn't let that happen, so we all came up here and built Dove House. At first the girls were just singing and dancing, but one thing led to another and . . ."

"But he took money from them."

"Well, out here on the frontier, a man does what he has to do to survive."

"I see." *What a thing to say. No, I don't see at all.*

"If they'd ever wanted to go, he woulda let them. It weren't like they were slaves, like some other places. And he gave them the best life he could."

Ruby watched a gold-and-black butterfly taste a bean blossom. *He did the best he could.* But what if his best wasn't good enough?

"He talked about you and Opal often. And he hoped to provide for you with Dove House."

"Right. And if I don't pay the bills, we will lose it. And then everyone will be out in the cold." She raised her gaze to his. "I've got to find that money box and the buksbom."

"Do you have enough to pay the bank?"

"If I don't pay Mr. Rumsford. The money we bring in goes out so fast, like water running through my fingers." She glared at her hands as if they were indeed the culprits. "No matter how hard I try to be frugal, feeding people takes a lot of money."

"It will get better soon."

Ruby sighed, started to leave, and turned back. "Do you think Belle is keeping out more than her share of the evening's take?"

Charlie shrugged.

Ruby waited for him to say something, but when he returned to his hoeing, she nodded once and took her basket of vegetables back to the hotel.

— ⚬ —

The next afternoon, Opal burst into the kitchen. "Mr.

Harrison is here, and he asked if I would like to go riding. I can, can't I?"

Ruby shook her head. "You have lessons and—"

"Oh, for goodness' sakes." Cimarron gave a snort. "Let her go. Rand Harrison is trying to do somethin' nice, so let him. He'll take good care of her."

"It's not that. I—"

"You and he can't be in the same room without gettin' in a tangle, but you know Opal wants to ride more than anything, and with the captain gone, she—"

"All right." Ruby raised her hands in front of her as if to stem the torrent of words. "You may go."

"Oh, thank you, Ruby. Thank you, Cimarron. I'll do extra chores later."

"Just get on up those stairs to change before he changes his mind," Cimarron said. "I'll take him a cool drink. We got any of that plum swizzle left?"

They could hear Opal thundering up the stairs.

Ruby turned to Milly who was working sums on the slate. "Please go remind her to wear her boots."

The speed with which Milly put down the slate let Ruby know that Milly would rather be doing about anything else too.

— ❧ —

After supper that evening, Ruby glanced around at everyone gathered to listen to another chapter of *Oliver Twist*, the book she was reading. "Where's Cimarron?" To the best of her ability she ignored Rand, who'd stayed at Opal's invitation.

"I don't know," Daisy answered. "Guess I haven't seen her since shortly after supper."

"Last I saw her, she was sitting out on the back porch. Said she had a bit of a headache." Milly looked up from her paper where Opal had set her to copying a paragraph out of the Bible. She could sign her name now and had learned to print the alphabet.

"Opal, please go upstairs and see if she is lying down. It's not like her to disappear like this."

Opal came racing down the steps minutes later. "She's not up "

"Did you check Belle's room?"

Back up the stairs and down. "No, and Belle says she hasn't seen her."

"I'll go out and look." Charlie laid down the ax he was sharpening with a file.

Rand stood and reached for his hat.

"Me too." Milly set her work aside.

"I think we'll all go, but in pairs," Ruby said.

"Maybe she went down by the river and tripped or something." Opal followed Milly out the door.

"You two go up the street, Rand and I'll check over toward the buttes." Charlie wore a frown that made Ruby wonder if he suspected something he wasn't telling. As she and Daisy went up the street, they could hear the girls calling down by the river.

"Cimarron!" Ruby and Daisy called together.

"Has she said anything about wanting to leave?" Ruby asked just before they reached the cantonment.

Daisy shook her head. "Cimarron wouldn't just take off without telling anyone. You know her better than that."

"I thought so."

"Is there a problem, Miss Torvald?" The soldier on guard met them at the corner of the parade grounds.

"Miss Cimarron is missing."

"Since when?"

"We're not sure. Perhaps since right after supper."

"Maybe she just went for a walk? Or . . ."

"Or? Just what are you implying?"

"Well, perhaps she . . . ah . . . went back to her former line of work." His words trailed off at the end as Ruby nailed him with a look that would have shriveled the most hardened of campaigners.

"Thank you for your assistance."

"But I never . . ."

"No, I know you never. And you never will!" She took Daisy by the arm and hustled her away so fast her feet hardly touched the ground. "The nerve of him, why I could—"

"Ruby, that's just the way it is out here. Once a whore, always a whore, far as most of these men figure."

"Well, he better not hope to eat at Dove House again." She

kicked a clump of dirt in the road, and it shattered into pieces. Just the way she wished she could have kicked that man with the hopes of the same ending.

"The soldiers could ride out and see if she really got lost out walking."

"If we don't find her, I'll go back and talk with Lieutenant Wilson."

Opal came running up the street. "Charlie found her! She's hurt bad."

Ruby and Daisy picked up their skirts and ran toward Dove House.

"They put her in Belle's bed." Opal followed them inside and up the stairs.

Ruby pushed open the door. Belle sat on the edge of the bed, sponging dirt and blood from Cimarron's face, murmuring words of comfort.

"What happened?"

Charlie shook his head and motioned her back out of the room. "Opal, you go on down and help Milly."

"But I want—"

"Do as Charlie says." Ruby waved her sister away. As soon as Opal went down the steps, she turned back to Charlie. "Where did you find her?"

"Out behind those ramshackle sheds to the north. They tied her up and"—he gritted his teeth—"and raped her."

Ruby felt her knees go weak and leaned against the wall. *God above, how can this be?*

"Took two of 'em to do it. I find 'em, and I'll kill 'em myself." He flexed his hands, hands with the power to throw men out of Dove House. "Rand is saddling the horses."

Ruby had no doubt he meant it. "Do you know who did it?" She swallowed against the urge to vomit.

"She told me."

"How bad is she hurt?"

"Beat up mostly. Unless she has broken ribs. She said one of 'em kicked her."

"What kind of monsters are they?" Tears burned as rage burst into flame.

"Just men who thought she oughta do what they wanted, and when she wouldn't—"

"They near to killed her." *How I wish that Captain McHenry was here. He'd find them and mete out the punishment they deserve.* "How can I help her?"

"Don't leave her alone. Get her wounds dressed. Belle has some laudanum, and that will make her sleep. Right now a good shot of whiskey would help."

"Do we have any?"

"Nope. Got rid of it all. Laudanum will do the same. You go on in and help Belle. Before I leave, I'll bring up more water and the hip bath."

Ruby nodded and stepped back into the room.

"I . . . I thought I could ch-change, Belle. I'd even started to believe it."

The broken words tore at Ruby's heart. She crossed the room and knelt by the bedside. She stroked Cimarron's forehead, fighting the nausea at what she saw. One eye was already swollen shut, a split in her bottom lip swelled her mouth, and another cut on an eyebrow did the same. One side of her face was scraped as though she'd been dragged through gravel.

Though Belle had covered the young woman, Ruby could see the front of Cimarron's dress had been ripped from the shoulders and one sleeve was missing. "Oh, Cimarron, I am so sorry."

"Not . . . your . . . fault." The swollen lips made talking difficult.

"Charlie is bringing up the hip bath. We thought a good soak would help."

"It will." Belle spoke gently, but her jaw said she was thinking otherwise.

"Do you think any bones are broken?" Ruby took Cimarron's hand.

Cimarron moved her head only slightly from side to side.

"Here." Daisy handed Belle a spoon and the brown medicine bottle. "I got water here for her to drink with it."

"Here, dearie, you take this now, and we'll give you more after a good wash."

Cimarron winced at the little she could open her mouth but swallowed the laudanum.

"You think her jaw is broken?"

Belle shook her head. "Just terribly bruised. Those dirty . . ." A string of names followed that made Ruby's ears burn, but right now they almost seemed appropriate.

She and Belle worked together to remove Cimarron's tattered garments.

"Take them out and burn them," Belle instructed Daisy. "She won't never want to wear them again."

Charlie poured the final bucket into the tub. "We'll be going now. Back when we can."

Belle nodded. She and Ruby helped Cimarron into the tub, steadying her when she listed to one side.

Cimarron winced as the water covered her scrapes and bruises but sighed when she was finally settled in. Tears trickled down over her puffy cheeks, leaking from beneath the lid of the swollen closed eye. "Someday I'll find them, and I'll kill them, real slowlike, maybe use my knife to carve a little." The words hissed, forced from between swollen lips.

Ruby wanted to clap her hands over her ears, run out the door, and keep on running. *It's all my fault. I promised to take care of the girls, and I let them down.*

Later, when all the others in Dove House had found their beds, Ruby sat beside Cimarron, watching her sleep, grateful that she could sleep. So far, there had been no word from the men.

God, how could you let something like this happen? You say you take care of your children, but you don't do any better than my pa did. He ran off and left us, and now you must have done that too. Who needs fathers when they do like that? Trust me, you say. Why? Why would I want to? Why would I tell these poor souls to trust you?

Who else is there?

The question came from deep inside her. *I don't know. I failed her. I know Charlie is feeling the same way, but he's doing something at least. And Cimarron always said she could handle anything that came her way. Her brothers made her tough and strong. But look at her.*

A tap on her shoulder made her jump. "I'll take a turn now," Daisy said.

"She's been asleep ever since we put her back to bed."

"Good." She handed Ruby a cup of water. "Drink this. You've cried buckets."

Ruby drained the cup and, after setting it down, rose and stretched. She laid the back of her hand against Cimarron's cheek. "No fever."

Daisy took the chair. "You go on and get some rest."

Ruby staggered up the steep stairs and collapsed on her bed.

Come unto me, all ye that labour and are heavy laden, and I will give you rest. The words seemed to float in on the breeze that lifted the light curtains and caressed Ruby's skin.

I can't do this.

But I can.

But you didn't.

She's still alive.

On the outside, but what about her heart?

CHAPTER THIRTY-ONE

"I've hunted for that money box everywhere. There is nowhere else to look." Ruby looked up from going over the ledgers. She'd been searching for any mistakes but was also trying to keep from thinking of the men who had attacked Cimarron, the men whom Charlie and Mr. Harrison had failed to locate in spite of two days' searching. Disappearing into the badlands was an easy thing to do.

Charlie smoothed his mustache with the tip of his finger. "No, there must be another place."

Ruby shook her head. "I can't go into Belle's room again, not without asking her first." *Belle.* Why does everything come back to Belle? Even the thought of her set the fire inside to simmering. Perhaps this was the time to confront her.

"Unless she has found it and didn't tell anyone," Charlie said. "She's as interested in it as you are."

Ruby closed her eyes. The lion's den. What an apt picture. God closed the mouths of the lions for Daniel. *Would He do the same for me? Why would He? When He didn't even keep Cimarron safe, why would He bother with me?* Besides, if she remembered her Bible correctly, Daniel had been talking to God, praising Him every day. Even when praying to God was against the law of the land. Not like here, where there was no law to speak of. She looked up from studying the calluses on her fingers and her cracked nails. Belle's hands always looked nice, but then dealing cards wasn't exactly strenuous labor. "Is she home?"

"I saw her go up a while ago."

Since the others were in the kitchen fixing supper, this would be as good a time as any to talk to her.

Ruby started up the stairs with Charlie close behind. Her heart thumped harder with each riser. *What am I going to say? How can I be gracious? Even Mrs. Brandon would have no idea what to do in this situation. Bestemor, Mother, if only you were here to help me.*

I am here.

Ruby stopped so fast Charlie had to take a step backward or bump into her. The voice in her mind was certainly not her mother's.

"What's wrong?"

"Ah, nothing." She started down the hall. *Lord, is that really you?*

I am that I am.

She remembered the words spoken so many years before. *"I am that I am."* Spoken by God to Moses. She paused at the door to Belle's room, took in a deep breath, and knocked. *Help me, please, Lord.*

"Come in."

"Belle, Charlie and I need to talk with you." Ruby blinked at the cigarillo smoke in the room. Why couldn't Belle at least open the windows?

Belle came from behind the screen, tying her wrapper. She motioned to the two chairs. "Have a seat." She pulled out the velvet padded stool in front of the dressing table and seated herself. "This looks mighty serious."

"It is." *Just get this over with.* Ruby took in a deep breath and leaned slightly forward. "Belle, I know you've been as mystified by the disappearance of the money box as we have. We've searched everywhere—"

"Except here in your room, unless you've already found it and just didn't happen to mention it." Charlie leaned back and crossed one ankle over the other knee.

"You sayin' I stole it?" Belle's eyes narrowed.

"No, just that we need to find it, and your room is the only place we haven't looked."

"I've looked."

"Did you tip furniture over, tap the walls, the floorboards?"

"Well, no. But I didn't take it—you got that straight?"

Might as well get it all over at once. "There's another matter also." Ruby kept her voice low and gentle. "The ledger shows a payment made to the bank, and yet the bank has no record of it. Do you—?"

"You accusin' me of stealin' that too? You can look for the box here, but . . . but. . . ." Belle glanced off to the side instead of looking head on, one hand clenching and unclenching the skirt of her wrapper.

She looks like Jason when he tried lying to me. She's lying. Now what do I do? Ruby thought a moment about the difference between Belle's first answer and this one.

"Charlie, why don't you start searching for the box?"

"All right." He heaved himself to his feet. "Where all you looked, Belle?"

"In all the . . ." She waved her hand around the room.

Ruby moved closer to Belle. "And in my room too, when we lived on this floor?"

"I didn't take nothin', just looked. That was my money too, ya know. I worked hard as Per, and those last months when he was so sick, I did it all."

Charlie looked up from tipping a small chest of drawers forward and cleared his throat.

"Well, Charlie and I did the work . . . and the girls."

"About that last payment? Who went to Dickinson with it? Perhaps there was an error at the bank."

"Not me." Charlie leaned his shoulder into pushing out the armoire.

Ruby stared at Belle. *Do I mention the skimming now or wait?* "Far didn't go?"

She shook her head. "He could hardly get out of bed."

"Would he have sent anyone else?"

Belle slammed her palm on the dressing table, sending up a cloud of face powder. "All right. I took it. He owed it to me, and after he made me send that letter, I . . ." She dropped her gaze, then glared at Ruby. "I worked hard for that money."

"Belle, I know you worked hard, but if the bank forecloses on this place, we will all lose all the time and hard work we've put in here. Unless you were planning on buying it yourself?"

"With what?"

"With money from your pals down at Williams' Saloon."

"They don't have no money."

"But you asked them to make sure no one came here, didn't you?"

"No, I never done that." She stopped, her eyes narrowed like she was looking back. "I mighta mentioned that would be a good idea. But if they took it from there, it weren't my fault. I was just thinkin' out loud."

Charlie took out his knife and began tapping the walls with the handle.

"Where's the money?"

"I lost it at the tables."

Ruby sighed, closed her eyes, and gave a slight shake of her head. *So much for that avenue.* In the blink of an eye, all she wanted to do was leave. Leave the room. Leave the hotel. Leave . . . She straightened her backbone. No, she wasn't a quitter.

"Then I expect you will want to return the money from your earnings in the cardroom. Along with the extra you've been raking off the top."

Belle half stood. "I never . . ." She glanced over at Charlie who stared at her without a trace of a smile, his face as washed of expression as a statue. "You got a lot of nerve comin' in here like this and accusing me of all kinds of things."

"Yes, I do, but my job is to keep a roof over all of our heads, and if you want—"

Belle held up a hand. She dug in a drawer of the dresser and pulled out a leather drawstring bag. She tossed the clanking bag into Ruby's lap. "There's fifty dollars in there—and your father's watch. That's all I got for now." She gnawed her upper lip. "And there'll be no more skimmin'." The last words were muttered into her bosom, but Ruby heard them.

On his hands and knees, Charlie started tapping on the floorboards.

So how do I trust her after all this?

"Do you know of a box that my father referred to as the buksbom?"

Belle shook her head. "He didn't use any of that Norwegian with me. Knew I didn't understand a word. Toward the end, he slipped back into it at times."

"I see." Weariness washed over her like a huge wave and threatened to pull her out in the undertow. *You should ask her to leave, to move out.*

I can't do that. Sometimes she tired so of the arguments going on in her head that she wished she could pull the covers over her face and sleep for a week. That she'd been up twice during the night to check on Cimarron didn't help.

Charlie pushed the bed over and kept on tapping. He stopped and tapped one place again. Sure enough, even the women could hear the difference in tone. He tapped around the area, then dug the tip of his knife into a corner of the floorboard. Working his way around the section, he pried it up with a screech. Lifting out the box, he stood and brought it to Ruby.

"Here you go. It's the money box."

Ruby slid open the lid of the cigar box, her heart pounding, mouth dry. *Will there be enough here to pay the bills?* The pile of cash looked large until she realized it was mostly one-dollar bills, thirty of them, one ten and two fives. Fifty dollars. Disappointment warred with relief. Together with what she had, what Belle had given her, and this, they could at least pay the next payment.

"Huh. That old fox." Belle rose and crossed to the stand beside the bed and, pulling open a drawer, removed a matching box. This one was full of her cigarillos. She took one from the box, bit off the end, and held it between two fingers. "If that don't beat all. Guess I better go see how Cimarron is feeling."

Ruby stood, the box in one hand, the pouch in the other. They'd made it through the confrontation. Perhaps they could go forward now and forget the things of the past, another verse from the Bible that had trickled through her mind lately. Perhaps.

CHAPTER THIRTY-TWO

"Is Cimarron any better?" Opal stood up from the table, where she had been helping Milly with her schoolwork, and traced a design in the flour on the counter with her fingertip.

"Some." *Her body is better.* Ruby gave the pie dough another pass. *But the dead look in her eyes is still there.* Ever since her vow to get those who attacked her, Cimarron had not said a word. As soon as she was able, she had crawled up to her pallet in the attic, and if they hadn't brought her food, she would not have eaten. Even then the plates came back more full than empty.

It's all my fault. The words had been beating on Ruby ever since they had brought Cimarron home. If she had paid more attention, those reprehensible men would have been chased away.

If she hadn't set up the party in front of the hotel, this would not have happened. Had they not had the celebration, Ezekiel Damish would not have known Cimarron was still in the vicinity. Like the others, he'd have thought she moved on.

And now she wasn't moving at all, at least very little.

Ruby pushed so hard on the rolling pin that it ripped a hole in the pie crust. Even "uff da" was no longer sufficient for relieving her ire. Nay, not ire. Ruby fought against fury and rage, the likes of which she had never known. Even though the money problem had temporarily eased, the men had not been caught and Cimarron lay suffering.

"You want me to finish the pie?" Opal spoke softly, as if tiptoeing around her sister might make things easier for her.

"No!" Ruby clamped her eyes shut. "I must not take my frustrations out on you. Forgive me, Opal. "

"I do." Opal came around the table and wrapped her arms around her sister's waist.

Ruby no longer needed to bend over to rest her chin on Opal's head. She sighed and, when that wasn't enough, sighed again. She kissed the part in Opal's hair and released the hug. "Thank you. I have no idea what I would do without you."

"Do you miss Captain McHenry?" Opal looked up and wiped some flour off Ruby's cheek. "I sure do."

"Yes, more than I thought I would." That was another thing that ate at her. They had yet to hear from him. He'd said he would write, but she had no idea how long it would take for a letter to come from Indian country in Arizona to her in Dakota Territory. And until she received one, she had no idea where to send a letter.

"Think I'll go up and sit with Cimarron. She seems to like it when I read to her."

"Opal, honey, if everyone treated each other as kindly as you do, we'd have far fewer fights." That was another thing that added to her boiling temperament: the renewed bickering between Milly and Daisy, with a dose of Belle thrown in at times. Even Opal had been involved.

"I miss our old Cimarron. Do you think she'll ever come back?"

"Yes, I do."

"I sure hope so. Well, I'll see if she wants company. Call me if you need help."

Ruby watched Opal leave. *God, I know I don't have any right to pray because of the way I've been ignoring you, but this is for someone else, not me. Please help Cimarron.* Ruby had found herself in this state a lot lately. But while she still doubted at times that God listened to her prayers, she knew He heard Opal's.

She usually was too mad to pray anyway.

"You want I should peel more apples?" Milly looked up from her schoolwork.

"No, we have enough. You just keep doing what Opal told you."

Milly sighed and returned to doing simple sums on the slate Charlie had fashioned for their schoolroom.

Ruby laid the patched pie crust in the pan, and after patting the remaining dough into a circle, she started rolling it out.

Daisy returned from cleaning the cardroom and took her bucket of water out to dump on the rose bush Charlie had planted by the back steps. On her return she glared at the seated girl. "Milly, can't you help around here? We got two more rooms to clean, and without Cimarron—"

"But I . . ." Milly slammed her slate down. "Ruby tells me to study, and you tell me to clean. I been working all day just like you and—"

"Enough!" Ruby raised both hands in the air. "No more! Daisy, you've been at everyone lately. That's enough!"

Daisy slammed out the door muttering something unintelligible.

The bell jangled over the door in the dining room. "Would you please go see who that is?"

Milly leaped to her feet. "Yes, ma'am." She returned a moment later. "It's Mr. Harrison, and he asked if he could speak with you."

"Oh, land." Ruby glanced down at her hands, covered with flour and pie dough. "Tell him to take a seat, and I'll be there as soon as I can."

"Should I take him some ginger swizzle?"

"That would be fine." Ruby held the pie plate in one hand and, taking a knife, trimmed off the extra pie dough around the rim. She cut three slashes in the top of the crust, pulled open the oven door, and set it on the rack to join the other two.

She washed her hands and face, smoothed her hair back, and removed her dirty apron. The gingham dress she wore looked clean enough, thanks to the apron.

"I poured you a glass too," Milly said. "I'll start peeling potatoes now, if you want."

"No, you better go help with the cleaning first. Opal can peel the potatoes."

Milly rolled her eyes, and Ruby didn't even bother to try and figure what that meant. What on earth could Rand Harrison want with her? Of course they'd been more cordial lately with all that had gone on, but she surely wouldn't term that as friendship.

"Good afternoon, Mr. Harrison." She hoped there was some semblance of welcome in her tone.

"Thank you for the fine drink." He lifted his glass as he stood to greet her. "I hope I didn't come at a bad time."

What does that mean? Ruby sat and motioned for him to do the same. "Now, how can I help you, Mr. Harrison?" She could hear Bestemor tsking at the abruptness of her tone.

"How's Cimarron doing? Was anything broken?"

"No, but . . ." Ruby shook her head. "She's not doing well."

"Tell her if there is anything I can do . . ." he paused.

"Yes, I'll tell her that. She—we all—appreciated you and Charlie trying to find those fiends."

"Just sorry we didn't catch the—"

She realized he cut off the words he would normally say and right now she knew exactly what he was thinking. But thinking the words only made her more angry, for then she was mad at herself also. Ladies didn't think that way, no matter what the provocation. She took a sip of her drink and concentrated on the coolness flowing down her throat.

Rand shifted in his chair and drank half his glass. He smoothed the tablecloth with the edge of his hand. When she glanced his way, he was studying the glass as if it might come alive any moment.

"Mr. Harrison?"

He nodded and took in a deep breath as if he couldn't get enough air. "I've been thinking a lot lately about how I'm not getting any younger and if I don't get married and start a family pretty soon it might be too late and so I'm asking if you would be my wife."

"You are what?"

"I thought we could get married and—"

Ruby shoved her chair back, hardly believing her ears. She stood and braced her hands on the table. "You are asking me to marry you?"

"Yes." The look on his face made her want to shake him.

"You walk in here and toss this idea out like you're wondering if I want to play five-card draw."

"I didn't know you knew how."

"That is not the point. Marriage is a serious business, and if you think I want to undertake such a momentous thing with you . . ." She could hear her voice raising higher so she sucked in a breath of air, forcibly lowered the pitch, and leaned slightly forward. Her whisper left no room for him to claim misunderstanding. "You are addled." She closed her eyes and shook her head as if it were too heavy to hold up any longer. "Good day, Mr. Harrison."

She left the room without looking back, straight-arming the door to the kitchen so that it slammed against the wall.

Charlie came in through the back door as she blew through the front. One look at her face, and he took a step backward.

"Whoa, what happened now?"

Ruby rounded on him, shaking her finger at him as fast as she talked. "You men, what in the world is the matter with you? Thinking all women are just panting to . . . to . . . and just taking what you want without even asking. You ought to be tarred and feathered." She clamped her hands at her sides, fighting the scream that threatened to deafen them all.

"Wait, now!" He held out his hands in a placating motion.

But Ruby ignored him. "No matter how hard we try to turn you into civilized creatures, you persist in . . . in . . ." She grabbed the sides of her hair with both hands. "I could just scream!" She huffed out a breath and stared at the ceiling, fighting the tears that shrieked for release. *I will not cry! I will not scream! I am a lady! I will behave like a lady!*

Charlie wisely kept his mouth shut and, deducing that whatever set her off was beyond that swinging door, went on into the dining room only to see Rand stomping out the front door, setting the bell to jangling so hard it looked to fall off its hook. Returning to the kitchen, he found Ruby scrubbing potatoes so hard the red skins disintegrated before they hit the water.

"Where is everyone?"

"Milly and Daisy are cleaning rooms. Opal is reading to Cimarron, and Belle . . . well, who knows what she is cooking up now." Her glare accused him of something over which he had no idea or control.

"I see." He sniffed. "I take it we are having apple pie for supper. Can I help you with something?"

"The old hen you butchered this morning will soon be ready for dumplings."

"And the potatoes?"

"These will be mashed. The carrots are about done and . . ." Ruby felt an attack of the vapors or a deep tiredness roll over her so that she could scarcely breathe. She closed her eyes and let her head fall forward.

Charlie's hand on her shoulder and his gentle, "Are you all right?" cracked the staunchly fortressed dam. One tear meandered down her check, then another. She sniffed and swallowed hard. "I will be."

"Why don't you take a glass of tea out on the back porch and enjoy the sun setting over the rocks. Let me finish up in here."

She nodded and did as he suggested. But the thoughts continued to batter her, *Who, why, what?* Fiends of Satan himself attacked, regrouped, and attacked again.

Guilt headed the troops.

By the time she caved in to all the "you ought to's" and "you should have's," she wished only that she could go to sleep and not listen to them any longer. Instead, she dragged herself back into the kitchen and went about her duties for supper, not daring to look Charlie in the face for fear of mortification swamping her. What all had she said to him?

With only two guests, supper was a silent affair, the rest of them taking their cues from her. While the others cleaned up, Ruby took the ledgers into the dining room, lit a lamp on one of the tables, and set to work.

Sometime later Charlie placed a cup of tea on the table beside her, along with the piece of the pie she had turned down at supper.

"Thank you." *Why are you being so good to me when I ranted and raved at you, and it wasn't even your fault?*

"Mind if I join you?"

"No, take a chair."

He took a bite of his pie. "You know, you've gotten to be

pretty good in the cooking department."

"Thank you." *Why don't you just yell at me so I'd feel better?*

"How bad are things?" He indicated the ledgers.

"Thanks to our treasure hunt the other day, we can make the loan payment at the bank and catch up at the mercantile."

"That's good."

"I suppose so. I just want to pay off the debts, and so far there is no way to do that. If only I could find Far's buksbom."

"We've looked everywhere I can think of. Unless he took it out and buried it. We've been to the bottom of every barrel and crate, tapped on every loose floorboard. I just don't know where it can be."

"If only we could get more people staying here."

"We've had more this last month than before. And the hunters will start coming now with the cooler weather. Sometimes it freezes here before the end of September. Then we have some beautiful weather before winter sets in."

"How are we going to get enough wood for winter? We can't buy coal unless we don't pay the bank and mercantile the full amounts due." Here she'd thought things would be easier with the extra money. Talk about only temporarily plugging the hole in the dam.

"Milly and Opal can help me get wood. I might ask that young private to help too. He'll see it as a chance to be with Milly. The two of them are so tongue-tied, they don't talk without having something to occupy their hands."

Ruby smiled in spite of herself. "Charlie, you never miss a thing, do you?"

"I try to pay attention. Sometimes it keeps you alive out here." He leaned forward. "I know things are tough right now, but you got to hang in there. The banker said you have until the end of the year to catch up, remember?"

If it were just the finances, I would not be in such a dither, but Cimarron . . . She shook her head. The latter was so much more important than the former that they shouldn't even be mentioned in the same breath.

Later when she lay awake in the darkness of her room, all the arrows of the enemy came flying back. No matter which way she turned, she felt the stings. When she woke after a far too brief sleep, she checked her dried-grass-filled pallet to see if she'd bled all night. Tired as she was, it seemed that the enemy's arrows might well have caused her to bleed to death.

At the moment that seemed like a fair idea.

She sent Charlie off on the train to pay their bills and bring back supplies, even begrudging the cost of the train ticket. He took along a bedroll so he wouldn't spend money at the hotel, assuring her that someone would loan him some floor space.

That afternoon she climbed the stairs to check on Cimarron. "I brought you some tea."

"Thanks." The woman on the pallet didn't even roll over but kept staring at the wall.

"I'm going to sit here until you drink it with me."

Cimarron pushed herself into a sitting position. She ignored the lanks of hair that fell forward and covered her face.

Even so, Ruby could tell the bruises had turned to yellow and Cimarron was breathing more easily. She hadn't winced at the movement. Ruby handed Cimarron the steaming cup and sat cross-legged on the floor in front of her. "Amazing how a cup of tea makes one feel better." *Oh, Cimarron, come out of this.*

Though Cimarron sipped her tea, she didn't answer.

Ruby cast around for something else to say, but nothing came to mind. Good manners or no, what do you say in this intolerable situation?

"Has Cat been up to visit you?"

Cimarron nodded. "With Opal."

"She does follow Opal around. She's never had a pet before. What kinds of pets did you have?"

Cimarron gave a slight shake of the head.

"We miss you downstairs."

The shrug would have been easy to miss if Ruby hadn't been watching so carefully.

"I think it time you come down for supper." Ruby ignored the fright that emanated in waves from the woman on the pallet. "Cimarron, I won't take no for an answer. You can come after the guests have left—so far we only have two or three—and then we will have supper together. Do you need help getting down the stairs?"

Another quick shake of the head.

"If you would like a bath, I know Charlie would gladly haul the water up here, but it would be easier on everyone if you took it in the pantry."

"No bath."

Ruby stood and reached for the cup, laying her hand on Cimarron's head. She closed her eyes when Cimarron flinched slightly. Those men should be . . . Instead of finishing the thought, she took the empty cup from the woman's limp hands. "I'll see you tonight." She watched a moment, hoping for some sign of the former woman, but when none came, she left the room, heaving a sigh as she started down the stairs. *What can I do? What can any of us do?*

When they were all ready to eat and they'd heard nothing from Cimarron, Ruby sighed again. "You go remind her to come down," she told Opal.

But when Opal returned shaking her head, Ruby just nodded. They'd keep working every day until Cimarron would come down.

"Let's eat."

" 'Bout time she gets on down here." Belle slathered butter on her bread, studiously ignoring the look Ruby sent her.

CHAPTER THIRTY-THREE

"You did what?" Beans stared at Rand as if he'd sprouted buffalo horns.

"I asked her to marry me, and she blew up like a howitzer." Rand waved his arms in the air. "You can close your mouth now before a whole flock of mosquitoes flies down your throat."

"You been with the cows too long. Even I know that women want to be courted." Beans slammed the frying pan down on the stove. "You being from the South and all, I didn't figure I'd have to give you instructions."

"St. Louis is not the true South." *Fool old man. Wouldn'ta told you had I thought you'd get all het up like this.* Who'd she think she was anyway? Most likely sweet on McHenry. He stepped back outside so he wouldn't have to listen to Beans muttering and leaned against the porch post.

Guess I better look elsewhere. Maybe I should write to my sister. She could most likely find me a woman back there.

He wandered down to the corral where the horses were settling down for the night. Gazing out across the river, he could just see the outline of the buttes in the dusk. Overhead, the sky ranged from cobalt dotted with stars in the east, to the brilliant azure of just-past sunset. The evening star hung halfway to darkness. Frogs croaked from the cattails in the little marsh where the creek took up with the river. The lonesome notes of a mouth organ said that Chaps was killing time before supper.

Buck ambled over and nudged his arm.

Rand rubbed his dark furred ears. "She turned me down, Buck. But then you got an earful on the way home. Sad thing is ... well maybe not sad ... but you should have seen her. Pretty don't begin to cover it. She was magnificent. Daddy always said find a woman with spirit and your life will never be boring. I do indeed think I found me one."

— ❧ —

After another night of fragmented sleep, Ruby was beginning to wonder if she would ever sleep well again. She did her best to be civil to everyone, but they failed to offer her the same consideration. Milly snapped at Opal, Daisy snapped at Milly, and Ruby wished they would all take a long walk in the rain that was coming down in sheets. But most of all, she wished Cimarron would make her way down those stairs.

When Charlie walked in from his trip to Dickinson, she sent him off to get into dry clothes before he could report on his trip. He shook his head and returned with his bowler brushed off and his short wool coat on a wooden hanger so he could hang it behind the stove to dry properly.

"What all has gone on here since I left?"

All four shook their heads.

Charlie dug in his vest pocket and pulled out a packet he handed to Opal. "This should sweeten things up around here."

Opal thanked him and handed around lemon drops before setting the remainder in a dish on the table.

"I'll take Cimarron one when I take up her tea." Ruby smiled at Charlie. "So you had a good trip?"

"Davis at the bank said yes to your arrangements, and Rumsford said not to worry, things will turn around soon, but that you could help that by serving liquor again."

Ruby huffed a sigh. "I'm taking the tea up, but perhaps Cimarron will come down tonight." As she climbed the stairs, she could hear a raised voice—Belle's voice—the words becoming clearer the higher she climbed.

"Why in thunder did you resist? You been selling it for years. What was one more time? You've given free ones before too. Look at you. It's all your own fault. You know the rules. Whores get hurt. It happens all the time, and no one gives no nevermind. You're just lucky they didn't kill you."

Ruby stopped only long enough to see through her rage and stormed into the room. She grabbed a startled Belle by the arm and marched her out the door. "And don't come back." She added an extra shove, wishing she could send Belle head over heels down the stairs. What kind of female viper had she kept under her roof?

Picking up the cups of tea she'd had the control to set beside the doorway instead of throwing, she returned to the room to find Cimarron sobbing into her blankets.

"Hush now, honey, you'll be all right."

"She's right, you know."

"No, she's not." Ruby gathered Cimarron into her arms and rocked her as she would a child. "You did nothing to provoke that attack."

"But if I hadn't fought them I . . . I was so stupid. I was just beginning to think I really could have a different life, that I could have something more than one man after another. But it'll never be any different."

"Cimarron, oh, dear Cimarron . . ." Ruby stroked the stringy hair back from the woman's eyes and face, gently rocking all the while. "You are wrong there. You will heal. You already are, and you have a home here for as long as you want. You are beautiful and—"

"I wish I was ugly as sin."

"It's not you. It's men who can't control themselves." *Belle, how could you do such a thing? I thought Cimarron was your friend. Lord, I cannot handle all this.*

"Here." Ruby picked up the cup of tea from where she'd set it on the floor. "Drink this and you will feel better." *A cup of tea is all I have to offer her? I should have some answers.*

Cimarron rubbed her eyes with the sheet and took the tea, clasping both hands around the cup. "I'm so c-cold."

Ruby reached over and pulled the blanket free to wrap it around her shoulders. "Come down by the stove, and let us all take care of you."

"I can't."

"I'll help you."

Cimarron shook her head and kept on shaking it. "Not today."

"All right, then, tomorrow. If you don't come down of your own accord, we will come up and get you. We love you, Cimarron, and we miss you dreadfully."

Cimarron's look of disbelief stayed with Ruby as she descended the stairs. She stopped on the second floor and turned down the hall to Belle's room.

Pushing open the door without knocking, she caught Belle lighting a new cigarillo. "Out!" Ruby pointed at the door. "Get out now!"

"You can't throw me out. I paid my rent."

"I'll give it back. Anyone who would treat a friend like you did Cimarron is not fit to be around the rest of us." Ruby grabbed the fancy garments tossed across the door of the open armoire and threw them out in the hall.

Belle's scream made Ruby's ears ring. "You'll ruin my clothes. Stop that! You think you know everything. No, give that back. You . . ." The string of vile names rolled off Ruby as if she were waxed.

"What is going on?" Charlie burst through the door, tripping over a froth of petticoats that clogged the entrance. He caught himself with a hand on the wall. "Miss Ruby, what's got into you?"

Ruby stopped scooping up another armload of clothes and let those in her hands drift to the floor.

"She's gone crazy!" Belle snatched back her garments.

"What did you do?" Charlie turned on Belle.

"She . . . she was cruel, mean, and vicious to Cimarron. No one should ever treat a friend like that."

"Huh." Belle looked to Charlie. "She just don't understand. I did it for her own good." She took a drag on her cigarillo. "Cimarron's got to get back on her feet."

"Her own good?" Ruby took two steps forward, her hands coming up like claws.

Charlie stepped between them. "You don't want to do that, Miss Ruby." His voice sneaked gently past Ruby's haze of red.

She spun on her heel and strode out of the room. *Where can I go? Upstairs is Cimarron. Downstairs, all the others. Where can I go?*

She felt like shrieking the last. *God, where can I go?*

Dry-eyed, she turned left instead of right and slipped into the empty room at the end of the hall where she and Opal had stayed when they first came to Dove House. Hot, as if she had a stove burning within her, she crossed to the window and threw up the sash. Wind and rain blew in, and she fell on her knees at the windowsill.

Within minutes the rain had soaked her fire out, and she shivered in her wet clothing. Rising, she shut the window and began pacing, her arms wrapped around her for warmth.

"I cannot stay, but I cannot leave. What kind of mess am I in?" *Not one of my own choosing, that's for sure. Why? Why did Far do this to us? Did he hate us? He said he loved us. What kind of love is it that saddles your daughter with something like this?* The window darkened and still she paced, her clothes now dry from the heat of her body. *How could I? Why did you?* The questions with no answers swirled, kicked up by the winds of rage as the falling leaves whirled from the trees, driven by wind they could not see but could not withstand.

When she finally ceased her ranting, she could hear again. *Come unto me, all ye that labour and are heavy laden, and I will give you rest.*

"But I need more than rest."

I will shelter you under my wings. Come. I will hold you in the palm of my hand. Come.

A knock came at the door. "Ruby, are you in there?"

"Yes."

"Can I come in?"

"No." *Opal, I cannot deal with even you right now.*

"Ruby, please."

"Oh." Ruby growled to herself, started to say no again and instead went to the door. "Opal, I just need to be alone for a while. You needn't worry about me, all right?"

"Can I bring you some supper?"

"No."

"Cimarron came down for supper."

"Oh. Good. I'll be down later."

"Promise?"

"Opal, I said I would." Ruby resumed her pacing, listening

for the voice again. All she heard was the rain against the windows. "I don't deserve to come to you. I've managed to wound nearly everyone here. And the way I flew at Mr. Harrison. He'd done nothing wrong."

I love you.

"I don't deserve it."

You are mine. I have redeemed you.

A knock at the door sometime later brought her up short. She'd promised Opal she'd go down, and even without a clock, she knew a long time had passed.

"Yes."

"It's Daisy and Milly. Can we come sit with you? We promise not to say anything."

Ruby rubbed her eyes that had leaked and dried so often they felt like grit from a sandstorm had taken up residence. Along with a raging thirst.

"You may come in." They filed in and sat down on the floor by the wall.

"Where's Opal?"

"Gone to bed." Milly waited before answering, looking to Ruby until she received a nod.

"Already?" *I broke a promise to Opal. Can't I do anything right?*

"Yes, she was sad," Daisy answered.

"And crying," Milly added, just in time to receive a poke in the ribs from Daisy.

"I am so thirsty." Ruby could hardly clear her throat.

"I'll be right back." Milly rose and scampered out the door, leaving Daisy to sit quietly.

"What are you doing?" Ruby stopped from her pacing.

"Praying."

"Praying? For what?"

"For you and for Cimarron and Belle."

"Oh. Thank you." The young woman sat so quietly that Ruby grew uncomfortable pacing and perched on the edge of the bed.

"I'm not sure I believe in praying anymore." The words scratched her throat. The thoughts did the same for her mind. *And yet you spoke to me. I know it was you. So you are there. Why do I doubt so? I used to believe.*

"You said I should read the Bible because it is God's word letting us know how much He loves us." Daisy moved slightly so she could look Ruby in the face. "You said that, and I believed you."

Ruby thought all her tears had dried up, but she was mistaken. They surged again at Daisy's simple words of faith.

Milly came through the door carrying a glass of water and handed it to Ruby. "Charlie said you should sleep in here."

"I can't do that to Opal."

"I'll go get her." Milly started out the door but stopped. "And your nightdress."

— ❧ —

Sleeping in a real bed with Opal lightly breathing beside her calmed Ruby, but still she woke often, plagued by nightmares and a thirst that wouldn't be quenched. *I give up, Lord.* That thought burst into her mind even before she opened her eyes. *I just give up. I don't care what happens next. I give up.*

— ❧ —

The next afternoon Cimarron came down after dinner and took up her sewing in the window as if she'd never been gone. Except that she neither smiled nor talked. Ruby and Daisy were chopping, cooking, and bottling the last of the garden vegetables for relish when Daisy asked a question.

"Ruby, why have you stayed here?"

Ruby paused in stirring. The starting reason of the inheritance or . . . She forced herself to say the real reason. "Because my father made me promise to take care of the girls. And Opal wouldn't let me go back on a promise."

"Even when your father died?"

"Yes."

"Why did you let us stay? Most women turn the other way."

"It started as the promise, but later it was because Dove House is my home and you became like my sisters. I never had sisters my own age. We were sisters all along, I just never realized it." Ruby looked over at Cimarron. "But I failed in my promise to take care of you."

Cimarron looked up from her stitching. "You think this was

your fault? What kind of crazy thinking is that? You don't . . . you can't rule the world no matter what kind of promises you make."

Ruby watched the relish bubble in the kettle. The scents of vinegar, mustard, celery seeds, and other spices floated around them, weaving them all together in spite of what had happened.

"Milly is going to read now," Opal announced. "She's been practicing."

"Good," Daisy said as she set the pan with clean jars ready for the relish on the stove.

"Jesus is talking. 'The blind receive their sight, and the lame walk, the lepers are cleansed, and the deaf hear . . .' You think He still does all that?"

Ruby nodded. *I was the blind one. Lord, you have indeed opened my eyes. I'm sorry, I'm so sorry.*

Cimarron snorted. "Well, if we're looking for someone who was lame, I guess that's me."

"But you don't even limp anymore." Opal glanced over her shoulder from where she was sitting, following the words over Milly's shoulder.

"See, what did I tell you."

"Cleansing the lepers is you and me both, Cimarron." Daisy nodded. "We are free. Thanks to Ruby."

"I memorized another verse." Milly kept her finger on the place she'd just read. She screwed up her face in the effort of remembering. "'For God so loved the world, that he gave his only begotten son, that whosoever believeth in him should not perish, but have everlasting life.' I asked Opal what perish meant."

"Perish is to die," Opal added with a complimentary nod to her pupil.

"I won't be free until those two brutes perish," Cimarron muttered.

Ah, but you are down here with us and you are talking. You're on the way. Ruby dipped relish out of the kettle and poured it into the jars. Daisy wiped off the rims, placed the rubber rings that had been softened in hot water in place, then the glass lids, and set the wire bales over the top.

"So that means God loves us all that much, right?" Daisy

refused to let the subject go. "That's pretty wonderful, you got to admit." She looked around, waiting until everyone nodded. "So that means we are all going to heaven if we believe in Jesus." She stopped for a moment. "I believe in Him, what about the rest of you?" She looked each one in the eyes until they nodded, then Daisy smiled. Frustration wrinkled her brow. "But what about Belle?"

Ruby shrugged both inside and out. *God, how come you make this so simple? Definitely not easy, but simple.*

"We're going to eat better this winter than we ever have." Daisy stood back to admire the jars of relish. "And think how much we have down in the cellar."

"Thanks to Charlie's garden."

If only we can keep this place. We're doing better, but I know the gambling must go. Lord, please help us find a way. Ruby slid the coffeepot closer to the heat, ignoring the question of Belle. "When we're done here, we need to do some polishing in that dining room. Dust sure comes in this place."

They'd just passed out the cookies, and Opal had her coffee fixed with the perfect balance of milk and sugar, when Charlie came in the door.

"Leave it to a man to arrive in time for a meal." Daisy stood to pour another cup.

"I just followed the aroma right on in." Charlie reached for a cookie. "Anyone seen Belle?"

"She don't come in when Ruby's here." Opal dunked her cookie in her coffee. "She's in her room."

Ruby stopped like she'd hit a vertical sheet of ice. *I have to tell Belle I'm sorry. Oh, Lord, no. I cannot do that. You ask too much.*

Take care of my girls. She wasn't sure which father was speaking. Per or her heavenly Father, not that it mattered much. She'd still made a promise. Only it wasn't *the* girls now, but *my* girls. Definitely heavenly Father.

She met Belle coming down the stairs into the dining room. Belle looked the other way until Ruby touched her arm.

"I'm sorry, Belle." Ruby choked out the words. "P-please forgive m-me?"

Belle nodded. "We all was crazed there for a bit. But we're better now." She patted Ruby's arm as she swished on by.

Ruby stopped as a feeling of lightness almost made her float away. Was it dizzy she felt? No. Something far greater. "I'm free," she whispered. *To think I doubted when God heard and answered so clearly.* A mighty crash turned her so fast that she teetered, nearly tumbling down the stairway before she clamped her hand on the stair rail and righted herself.

"I'm sorry. I didn't mean to." Opal's cry ripped through her sister. How often she'd heard that cry—the very same words—but not for a long time, a lifetime perhaps.

Cigars, some broken leaving bits of tobacco leaves scattered about, littered the floor along with pieces of the shiny box that always sat on the bar.

Opal's whisper filled the room. "There's money."

Ruby stopped at the edge of the circle of open-mouthed people and surveyed the wreckage of the box. The box that had been sitting right on the bar all along. The box she polished so carefully because it was a beautiful work of art. She focused on a stack of bills tied together with string. A note tucked under the string caught her eye when she picked up the packet. She pulled the paper out and unfolded it. The silence in the room held everyone still.

Ruby read. "'For my treasures. Far.'" She laid the bills on the surface and counted them, flipping the corners with one finger. "Five hundred dollars." *I can pay off the bank, or nearly. We are saved. Dove House is indeed ours.*

"That money's no good." Charlie checked the stack more closely and slowly shook his head.

"What's no good?"

"The money. It's Confederate. Not worth the paper it's printed on. Sorry to be the bearer of bad tidings."

I should have known. In one hand, out the other. Ruby sighed. "Oh well."

"Look here." Opal held a small package in her hand. "This was in there too." She unfolded the corners and folds of cloth that Ruby recognized as one of their mother's cutwork lawn handkerchiefs with a fine picot edging. Her mother always kept one tucked in her sleeve.

"Aren't they pretty?" Opal held out the nest of two stones, a deep red one and the other creamy with glimmers of many colors.

"That's a ruby," Charlie said. "Per won that years ago. I thought he lost it gambling, but I guess not. The cream is an opal, and those others are gold nuggets. Didn't know he still had them. I cashed all mine in."

Opal held out her hand and Ruby took the bird's nest of treasures. She touched each with a reverent finger. Gems for his treasures.

"Per kept them all these years, even all the times when he needed money so desperately. And that flat little box must have been wedged right inside that big one." Charlie shook his head real slow. "Who'd a thought it."

"The buksbom." Ruby held out her hand so the others could see.

"Guess Papá . . . er, Far loved us after all, huh, Ruby?"

Ruby nodded. "I guess so."

Charlie leaned over and started picking up wood pieces. "I might be able to put this back together, not as good as it was, but usable."

Kind of like all of us, Ruby thought. *Put back together and all usable. The Father's treasures, all of us.*